Nina's Book

Nina's Book

BY EUGENE BURDICK

HOUGHTON MIFFLIN COMPANY BOSTON
THE RIVERSIDE PRESS CAMBRIDGE

FOR CAROL

Contents

Introduction:
The Slime of Excellence

THERE is a small, hard-bitten and prosperous hillside village in southwest France which produces a peculiar product. It is called "the small wine." It is sold in dark green, unlabeled liter bottles. None of it is ever shipped outside the village. The entire product, some four or five thousand bottles, is consumed in the village.

The wine is made by pressing ordinary grapes a second time, several days after the first press. During those few days the whole purplish mass of stems and skins has fermented slightly. At the second pressing, tiny bits and flicks of seed and skin, loosened by the fermentation, flow from the bottom of the press. By some curious process, each of these tiny bits of debris becomes the core of a bubble. What happens is that each droplet of matter becomes the rotten core around which a bubble forms. This bubble nourishes itself from the droplet, then drops the bitter used-up piece of matter to the bottom of the bottle. When the wine is uncorked it fizzes for a few seconds and looks exactly like champagne. But the bottom of the bottle is slimed over with the thin coating of spoiled matter from which the goodness has been sucked.

It is this flaw, this thin black residue of slime, which makes the wine seductive. When a glass of the wine is poured the upper portion of the wine is golden colored and has a good taste. Not a superior taste, but clearly above average. But the slime is unbelievably bitter. Not merely bitter, but repulsive beyond description. If even the tiniest fleck of the slime passes into a person's mouth, the tongue, the throat, even the lips recoil and try to throw it up. The taste is the perfectly unmistakable taste of rottenness, effluvia, discarded spoilage. It makes the eyes bulge and the whole body ache to vomit. The taste is no joke.

By some odd chemistry, which no one understands fully, the wine becomes sweeter and richer the deeper one drinks. But if one goes a shade too far and drinks the black slime it is a disaster.

The residents of the village have made a game out of the drinking of the wine. On Sunday mornings the men gather in the three cafés which face onto the circular *place,* order a bottle of "the small wine," and begin drinking. Their wives, black-shrouded, plump, and serious, circle the *place,* with battleship solidity. The children, shrill and intense and flea-like in their hard, crusty, woolen suits, dart across the *place,* through the thin trees in the center of the circle, and into the side streets. By midafternoon, however, the wives and the children have slowed their pace for the game of the small wine begins to reach a climax.

At first, in the morning when everyone is sober, it is easy to play the game. Even amateurs can play it with such success that above the layer of slime is only the thinnest layer of golden wine. The thinness of that layer, of course, is the measure of success.

But in the afternoon as beginners become slightly drunk

and the eye and hand are not so precise, the experts begin to emerge. They are older men, the quiet ones, the ones made cautious by time and experience.

The younger men begin to show the signs of having drunk the bitter slime: a quick bulging of the eyes, a working of throat, a convulsive, irrepressible jerk. No one can drink the slime, not even the smallest fleck of it, without the telltale signs. No one cheats at this game. The surge of the body to throw out the slime is unmistakable and certain. Few men drink again during the day when they have tasted the slime of excellence. It ruins the palate for hours.

The older men drink on steadily. In front of each of the experts will be a collection of glasses which are the symbol of his skill. The women and the children begin to flow quietly past the various tables, checking a layer of golden wine on each glass. Although the difference is infinitesimally small, everyone in the village is expert at judging. Every Sunday, regardless of who is participating, there is a shrewd and intuitive judgment on who is winning. Quietly, in a collective and animal-like unanimity, the wives and children will group themselves around the table of the probable winner. This excites the older men who fear they are losing. They begin to take greater chances. More and more frequently one of them catches a fleck of the rotten slime, his face flushes and puckers, and he stands up in defeat. Others, possessed of more conservative judgment, simply acknowledge that this is not their day and push away from the table.

Every Sunday, regardless of the weather or the time of year, there is a fierce competition in drinking the small wine. Every Sunday there is also a clear victor.

The afternoon ends with a quiet crowd gathered about the seat of the victor. All of the other seats are empty. Everyone looks at the glasses of the victor, the victor compares his glasses with previous victors, and there is a muted expert discussion. Oddly enough, no one compliments the victor. There is a reason for this: no one knows precisely what the victory means.

Book I

1. A Hum in the Warm Sky

RODNEY CARTWRIGHT opened his eyes and looked straight up. The sky was blue and empty. He was not sure where he was, but he was comfortable. Across his back was a slight pressure as if he were in a hammock. His body was eased, as if he had strained hard and was now resting. He rolled his eyes to the right and saw that the sun was low in the sky, almost to a black and strange horizon that was seen only as a straight and simple line. There was not a thing that broke or eased that simple line. He knew that if he swung his head that simple line would be a complete circle about him. He did not swing his head, but he was sure he was right.

Having opened his eyes so suddenly, seeing nothing but the sky and the horizon, Rodney's mind was empty. For a long moment nothing suggested anything else, no tiny mesh of association began, no questions intruded. No words went across the flat surface of his mind, he felt only an ease, a sense of rest. He did not, for the moment, even know his name. He felt no sense of wrongness or alarm. He was utterly neutral. His mind was completely open to one thing: the blueness of the sky. He sensed that it was not blue close at hand. But at

some point, at some middle distance from his eye, the sky
began to harden and turn a soft blue. And as the distance
grew, although none of this was put in words, he knew that
the blueness grew. At some point the blue would become perfect: hard and pure blue.

For a moment he was aware of a sharp tiny cut of regret. It
was as precise and telling as a small nail driven sharply into
the trunk of a large tree. He longed to be at the point where
the sky became perfectly blue and perfectly hard. His eyeballs bulged slightly as he tried to focus on that distant point.
But just the effort of straining caused the tiny shard of despair
to disappear. It was as if the nail had been jerked out. For a
moment he thought it left a bright drop of blood somewhere
or a minute speck of hardened resin. Then he forgot it.

He forgot it for there was a sound. The sound came suddenly and without preparation. It came like black on white,
like the first gush of water on eternally dry sand, like pain
over pleasure . . . original, solitary, compelling. It was a
hum. It gave no clues to recognition. It was merely a hum.
For the first time since his eyes opened his mind functioned
in the old orderly way. His mind arched back through the
years and with an incredible precision isolated out memories
of hums and tested them against the reality of this hum. With
speed, alertness, certitude he shot back over the memories
and each one came to him perfectly without a blemish or
imperfection . . .

There was a hum once . . . it came from an exhausted
phonograph which had finished a record and now hummed.

His father was standing beside the phonograph, looking
at Rodney.

"That was the voice of President Franklin Delano Roosevelt at his Inaugural Speech," his father said. "Did you hear it
plainly?"

Rodney looked up and nodded. The room, each detail of
it, was exquisitely clear. On the desk next to the phonograph

was a tray holding a bottle of Old Grand-Dad and a bottle of Haig and Haig and two sparkling crystal glasses and a crystal pitcher of water. Behind his father were the bookshelves with their neat rows of leather-bound books, not one of them printed in the twentieth century for all modern books were shelved in the living room and not in this room, not in his father's study.

In one corner there was a world globe held in place by two beautiful ribs of polished oak and swinging easily on polished brass gimbals. Across the globe, in neat red lines and tiny copper-plate writing, were the routes of great explorers his father had inked in. Cook, Bougainville, Tasman, Magellan, and de Gama all had their distinctive tracks marked on the globe. In beautiful stylized handwriting, which his father had learned for that purpose, his father had lettered the names of each of the great men.

On the desk was an open humidor of tobacco which smelled of burley, Virginia, Turkish, and the harsh tart odor of Sobranie. On the desk there was also an inkwell, a glue pot, a pewter jug of pencils . . . and each of these had its own smell. The tobacco, the ink, the glue and even the pencils had been custom-made for Rodney's father. Mr. Cartwright valued uniqueness and antiquity very much. There were two red leather chairs in the study which were hundreds of years old. Each year the leather was oiled, reworked, softened by an expert who had been trained in England. Rodney was aware that the chairs must be very comfortable, but he always sat forward in them, never really enjoying their comfort.

All of this was caught in the sharp warm sunlight of Los Angeles that came in through the open windows.

"Your nod means you heard it plainly?" his father asked.

"Yes," he said softly.

"That was the voice of a man who might have been great, but has, instead, become a tyrant, a cheap demagogue, a

clown for the masses," his father said without emotion, but
with very complete conviction. "He had a chance to be great.
He came from a wealthy and aristocratic family. He knew
what greatness called for, what statesmanship required.
And he gave it all away just to be sure that he got a large vote
at the polls. He got that, but it was only vanity. Just vanity,
pure and simple. He could have been as great as Caesar or
Alexander or Napoleon." His father paused, put his hand out
so that it was caught in the slanting beam of sunlight. A
strong, tough, selfish, well-muscled, short-fingered hand. A
hand which would never grasp the wheel of a ship discover-
ing a new island or rounding up into a tough reach . . .
even though the hand had the capacity. He closed the hand.
"He had history in his hand, could have molded it, shaped
everything. But vanity was there first and everything was
wasted."

Rodney waited without even the slightest thought of talking. The phonograph hummed on. His father backed up a
step. Without looking, his hand found the globe, gently
whirled it. Rodney was bemused by the odd irregular chunks
of Africa, Australia and South America slowly turning in
front of his eyes.

"Men of breeding, blood and brains have an obligation,
Rodney," his father said. "The three great B's. I have told
you before. If you possess them you must lead or must suck
meaning out of the chaos or must influence thought. Burke
was a leader, the Huxleys were organizers of chaos, and
Santayana is one who influences thought. But remember
that they did not *ask* the people or the chaos or ideas which
should be done . . . they imposed meaning upon them.
That is the thing, Rodney. One must impose meaning upon
things and events and people. They have no meaning on
their own. God did not mean things to be orderly. He
gives us chaos and we must make order of it. Do you understand now what Roosevelt has done? He has asked for per-

mission of the brutes when he should have given them an order."

His father paused, inclined his head toward Rodney. Rodney knew that now he must speak.

His father spoke first.

"The brutes can only brutalize anything they touch," he said. He was pleased with the idea. He began to stuff tobacco into his pipe.

"In school they tell us . . ." Rodney began, and then hesitated.

"In school they tell us what?" his father asked. He leaned forward and although he was a heavy man, at that moment he looked birdlike, delicate with curiosity and intensity.

"They tell us that in a democracy the people must consent," Rodney said firmly.

"Consent?" and in his father's mouth the word was hard. "Consent to what? To what the great man says? That is correct. In that sense they must consent. That is democracy. But they cannot originate, they cannot begin, they cannot know." He paused, struck by a new idea. He jammed one hand into his heavy tweed coat and with the forefinger of the other hand scratched in a pocket of his weskit.

Rodney had always been embarrassed at introducing his friends to his father because he dressed in heavy woolen clothes the whole year. Even when it was very hot in Los Angeles.

"Knowing. That is what is necessary," his father went on. "You must know, know, know. Behind everything there is an order. You must know others and yourself and events and fact. Claw it out of them." He summed up. "Life is knowing. Never forget that."

His father became aware of the hum from the phonograph. He reached over and snapped it off.

The moment the phonograph hum was off, Rodney knew it was not the hum he was trying to identify. His head swung

sideways with a suspended ease. He gazed at the hard line
of the horizon. He felt vaguely restless about the hum. It was
wrong to leave it nameless, floating in nonrecognition . . .
but there was another hum . . . an earlier hum . . .

The hum was the summed sound of several thousand
voices murmuring their disgust.

They were playing off the Los Angeles City High School
Football Championship against Fremont High, and if they
won they would play Los Angeles High and probably be
champions. It was early in the game and Rodney had faded
back to pass and he stood easily on the turf, watching his
ends run zigzag down the field, watching his right half
run flat and glance over his shoulder. He listened to the
thud of feet, the strange creaking symphony of leather
equipment under sweated jersey. He waited with utter confidence.

Then abruptly, as savagely as a whip, his feet were
knocked out from under him and in some mysterious way he
was smashed flat on the grass. He looked down his body and
saw the grinning face of the Fremont right end who had
broken through and with one slash of his body had done the
damage. At the same time the whole complex movement
of the two teams stopped. The creaking of leather ceased,
faces were disappointed or exultant. The players paused
and then started back for their positions.

In that moment Rodney heard the hum. It came from
the thousands of people in the stands. They were utter
strangers to him, but their disgust was directed at him. He
stared up at them, at the rows of knobby heads, at the
faces brown in the sun. Their disgust, their humming anger,
their disappointment was tangible in the warm air. Rodney
was astonished at the intensity of their mood, the depth of
their resentment, the undercurrent of violence that flowed
off the stands and focused sharply on him. His shoulders

contracted as if he were flinching and he held the ball pressed in hard against his stomach.

He was frightened of them and he knew nothing about them. He had never noticed them before, had been oblivious of them. And suddenly he was blindly and completely frightened of them. He got up slowly and was terribly aware of the mob in the stands. He wondered, fully, what he might do to appease them, to ease their formless rage at him.

He played very well the rest of the day. In fact he played better than he had ever played before, and two sports writers nominated him for All City. But he knew he did it only to keep the hum out of his ears or to make sure it was directed at someone else. And, afterwards he never quite overcame his fear of a crowd.

This was not the right hum. The hum was somehow a warning. It had an undertone of menace in it, a very slight trace of danger . . . but there was another hum . . . an earlier hum.

It was the hum of a bee flying several inches over his head and above the grass in which he and Hilda Hough were lying.

He and Hilda had left the junior high school when the playground closed. Usually he left with whatever boys were still around and went in the opposite direction toward Van Ness Avenue. But today, for some reason, he left with Hilda and they walked through the big open fields toward the Baldwin Hills. Across the huge prairie of grass they could see the streetcars lumbering down Santa Barbara Avenue like elephants at the edge of an African veld. The grass was mottled over with yellow mustard and from somewhere there came the smell of greenness and from over the hills the faint wet smell of the ocean. Rodney knew it was the smell, the odd mingled odors, that had led them in the direction of the hills. Only a few days each spring were so perfect. Later the grass would turn brown, smell dusty and resist the invasion of the sea smells. But that day, that single day, it was perfect.

As they walked Hilda talked to him of her family and her violin lessons. Her father was an immigrant Pole who ran a delicatessen on Jefferson Avenue. Rodney had seen it several times. Her father was a lean unhappy man who stood behind the glass cases which held pink Polish hams, trays of pastrami, pickles, yellow potato salad, stuffed eggs each topped with a tiny anchovy, huge dismembered turkeys and the neat browned bodies of chickens with their legs crossed and tied together.

Rodney remembered that whenever there was a slack moment in the delicatessen Hilda's father opened the cash register and counted change. He did it in an elaborate, intricate, ritualistic manner . . . stacks of pennies maneuvered between stacks of dimes and nickels and then the whole chess-like pattern changed. He obviously derived great pleasure from the handling of change.

Hilda said that her father was determined to make her a child prodigy on the violin. He assured her that this was the only way to claw up out of the working class. His father, he told her, had worked completely with his hands . . . shoveling night soil into wheelbarrows, taking it to the edge of the Polish town and dumping it into open pits. He worked partly with his hands and partly with money . . . cutting ham and counting money. She would go a step further and work with her hands and brain . . . playing the violin. Her children, he said with fervor, would make the last step, the ultimate release from bondage and work with their brains only . . . as lawyers or professors. It was a vision he had and he worked for it as systematically and faithfully as if there were no chance of it misfiring. The vision was so beautiful, so balanced, so just, that Hilda felt guilty whenever she even questioned it.

Her father made the vision become real, but the solid fragments of it Hilda did not like. She did not like the endless hours of practicing, the finger exercises, the harsh voice of her teacher. Nor did she like the three recitals she had given with the Los Angeles Symphony. Nor did she like the fact that the kids at school called her Hilda the Hog . . . not because she was ugly, but because of her odd skill with the violin.

As they walked Rodney looked over at her dark crisp hair, her very red lips, her large frightened eyes. Her eyes were always frightened, as if the next thing she must do was the final and last test of something important. Rodney looked away and down at his feet which were cutting through the strands of grass and breaking them by the thousands. The toes of his polished brown oxfords cut into the thin green strands with a hiss that reached to his ears as a small mowing sound. As the stalks fell they shattered the mustard into tiny clouds of yellow pollen.

Rodney paused and looked behind. The white glittering cement of the school looked diminished, bleached, far away. And marking their trail through the grass was a long thin cloud of yellow pollen. The millions of motes hung in the still air, catching the sun as they spiraled and whirled above the trail of broken grass.

Normally Rodney did not respond to the conversation of other people. He listened, but he did not react. But today, as if released by the crazy irresponsibility of the motes of pollen, he responded to Hilda. He knew she was confused and so he became fearless.

"Who cares about the violin or what your father says?" he shouted. He grinned at Hilda. "Do what you want. Make them like it. Be Hilda. Be you."

He jabbed his finger at Hilda's arm, grinned broadly. He
hopped through the grass, slashing with his feet, ecstat-
ically happy at the terrible destruction his feet were wreak-
ing. He had an image of adults as great figures of vulnerability . . . capable of being punctured by tiny strokes, of
being maimed by the shrewd blows of infants. Adults, all of
them, were wordy, grotesque and defenseless. The adults, all
of them, were like a soft clot of a stupid army. He was armed
with pubic hair, muscles beginning to harden, the secret
of masturbation, the ability to lie, a really huge rage. Without knowing the precise words he was sure he could communicate this to Hilda, could tell her how to protect herself.

"Be me?" Hilda asked hesitantly. "Me?" Disgust played
vaguely over her lips. Then she was angry. "That's easy for
you to say. Your family's big and rich and you bring those
fancy little lunches to school. And on rainy days a driver
picks you up. You go home and its all . . ." She paused,
sought for the word. "It's all . . . roomy. Very roomy. I go
home and Daddy says, 'Practice, Hilda. Practice makes perfect.' And my sisters and brothers are all over the place. And
Momma is putting sauerkraut in crocks and making pumpernickel and the place stinks. No room. No place in that
house is there room."

She was at the edge of tears, her eyes glistening.

Rodney roared with laughter. He reached out and took
her hand and began to run, Hilda protesting at first, but then
her hand tightened up and she ran with the same eager-
ness as he. Words tumbled out of Rodney's mouth; big words,
ferocious words, sure words. They went through a swale
where the grass thickened and the hiss of their shoes became
a slow-paced whir of destruction. They came out of
the swale, stood panting and suddenly Rodney dropped in
the grass, pulling Hilda after him.

They were at the bottom of a saucer-shaped hole. The
grass rose above them, ended, and the sky began. The pol-

len went by in clouds, densely yellow and obviously screen-
ing them. They watched as the filaments of pollen went
weaving past and then, as the stir of their passage ceased,
became steady yellow bands that were utterly motionless.
In the sudden stillness they heard the hum of a single bee.
The bee came over their burrow, flew in tight circles and was
very black against the sky. He moved out of sight, but they
could still hear his diminished hum.

"I wish we could stay here for a long time. In this burrow.
Bring in food and live here. Not go to school," Rodney said
speaking very rapidly. "Potato chips, pop, salami, Tootsie
rolls, milk. Bring 'em in and live right here."

"You?" Hilda asked. "Oh, no. You couldn't. Me maybe,
but not you." She paused. "My mother has got a kind of mustache on her upper lip . . . fine black hair. I could live
here forever."

"There wouldn't be enough food," Rodney said.

"We could smuggle it in. Like you said."

"We'd need money to buy it. All I've got is thirty cents."

The bee went by, a black line of energy that scarred the
hot evenness of the air. Far away, a distant tiny sound,
came the wail of a siren.

"We could catch rabbits with thongs; eat honey; grind
acorns into meal; catch fish," Hilda said, and her voice
was fine with urgency.

"I don't know how to do that," Rodney said.

"We could learn. We could eat grass. Cows live on it."

She reached out, grasped some of the green stalks and bit
into them. Green foam rose from her teeth, smeared her lips.
She swallowed and her eyes smiled slightly. She turned
away and coughed.

In some way the green froth and the impulsiveness of her
chewing made Hilda seem wanton. Rodney sensed that beneath her surface order she sensed his rage. Also there was
something more. Under the neat cheap dress, smeared by

chalk dust, there was a body and Rodney was suddenly very curious what Hilda, if she were naked, would look like.

He narrowed his eyes, squinting into the moted yellow light, and the shape of Hilda's nakedness became a kind of reality. The detail was vague . . . only the concept of her breasts was clear. Everything else was hazed and obscured, lost in a golden aura of gossip and hot erotic images. For the first time in his life Rodney felt a concupiscence which was directed at a given person. He opened his eyes full. Hilda, he sensed, was aware of what he was thinking. He stared at her. Then he rolled over on his back.

For a few more minutes they lay on their backs, not daring to look at one another.

"I'd stay if you would," Hilda said finally.

Rodney did not reply. He could think of nothing to say.

Maybe they dozed or perhaps time just went quickly. But it was dark and a chill started to flow through the grass. It was no longer hot.

"Rodney, have you ever . . ." She paused and Rodney knew what she was trying to say. "Do you know about girls? Have you ever done it?"

He turned quickly and looked at her, but it was getting dark and he could not see her plainly. Her face, in the dimness, was pretty.

"Sure," he lied boldly. "I've done it."

"Look, Rodney, do it to me," she said. "If you do it to me I'll be able to stand all the rest of it. The practicing and the pumpernickel and everything. Please."

"I couldn't. Not to you. You're not that sort of a girl."

"I won't cry. I'll help," she said and her voice rose with pleading. "You won't hurt me. I'll never tell anybody."

"I can't. Not to you."

He moved closer to see her face and it was contorted. He read the meaning. She thought he did not find her attractive;

it showed in the wide eyes, the glitter of tears, the resigned mouth.

"You'd love me, Rodney," she said. Her voice went heavy with lasciviousness, with a wanton excess, with a rich promise. "I'd be really good. Better than any of those other girls. Better than anything you'd ever had." She paused and moved her head forward and he saw a quick expression cross her face.

"Look, I've heard the men say it at Dad's shop . . . a virgin is the best. I'm a virgin. I'd be good."

She tore at her blouse and a button gave way and suddenly she had it open. A strap and white flesh showed. Her small breasts, catching the light that remained in the burrow, glowed. She put her hands under them, pushed up to make them larger.

"Kiss one, Rodney," she said breathlessly. "Go ahead. Then you won't be able to stop. Go ahead."

He bent forward obediently. He put his lips over her breast and kissed it. Her hands pressed the back of his head and she sobbed with relief. His lips spread and he mouthed the breast, ran his tongue over the nipple.

He waited, but nothing happened. His heart grew in his chest, moved to his lungs and pulsed in his breath and he was turgid with excitement. But nothing happened. He made some gestures, calling on his memory of what he had heard at school, but deep in his mind he was frightened.

He ran his hands over Hilda's hips and they were soft and surprisingly abundant. Her legs slid apart. She was ready; everything waited for him. There was no obstacle except him. He waited. He kissed the other breast and at some point Hilda's breathing became choppy and irregular and her hips began to contract and ease, backward and forward. He could not wait much longer. Then the shame started to spread in him; like a stain starting very small and nourishing itself and growing. He could not stand that.

"I can't do it to you," he said and pushed her away. "It wouldn't be fair. I'd hate myself."

He hated himself anyway. The lie made it no better. He was split in two. He wanted desperately to do what she wanted and a kind of wild urge rose in him, a savage excitement. But he knew he could not and the shame of that stained the excitement, degraded it, took off its fine edge.

"But you've done it before," Hilda said, and in her eyes he could see the sharper, newer fear of rejection raising through the other, more basic need. "Why not with me? I'd never say anything about it. Even if I had a baby I'd never say anything."

She reached out with a small strong fist and although a knotted fist should be a threat there was a plea in the clenched fingers. She touched the hand to his chest.

He shook his head and she pounded softly and frantically on his chest.

"You're too good, Hilda," Rodney said, his lips very stiff, his mind searching for relevant words. "You're not that sort of a girl."

Her face formed again, curiosity gave it form, just as despair had made it anonymous. Her very red, unlipsticked lips firmed up.

"What kind of a girl am I, Rodney?" she asked. "You tell me."

Rodney shook his head. Her hips had stopped the motion, the strange instinctive undulations. He was relieved. In the fading light he could still see the whiteness of her breasts; the small breasts that he could cover easily with his mouth. He felt a desire to pull her blouse shut, but he quickly put it down.

"You're a good girl, Hilda," he finally said. The bee

passed over their burrow again, but now the same sound seemed threatening, ominous, busy. "You play with the Symphony. You're a genius."

The curiosity crumbled slowly from her face and the despair returned. She saw that he had never intended to say something serious; had not really intended to help her.

Rodney saw the look in her face and knew that she felt deserted. Sharply, with a kind of hard lucidity, he knew why she felt this. He could sense the hard driving momentum of her father and his endless energy at making everyone in Hilda's family perform according to the requirements of his personal illusion. He could sense Hilda's confusion and resentment and anger for he also felt this toward his own father. He felt a bitter resentment at the mystery which his father was always forcing upon him, urging him to penetrate to the heart, to understand.

He knew clearly that every adult had some sort of nagging, big awful, persistent vision. Relentlessly they pushed the image on others, on children, and tried to make them see it, to understand its meaning, to share the mystery with them. Rodney ached to know what his father's vision was and why he had never succeeded. He knew that Hilda caught the sense of her own father's vision, but did not share in it. He wanted to tell her this, but he could not. There were no words for it.

The desire for something burned in her face, made her eyes black, her cheeks pink.

"Look, Rodney, please, please, please do it," Hilda said. "Don't argue just do it. Like you did to the other girls."

She put her face up toward his and kissed him on the mouth. She took his hand and moved it back to her breast. Her body began to move again rhythmically.

He kissed her very coolly, his lips stiff. Finally she pulled her head back and looked at him curiously. Across the field, shattered by the millions of blades of grass, thinned by the night air, came the sound of the Santa Barbara Avenue streetcar. They heard even the crackle of electricity as the trolley passed over junctions. The sound of the bee had gone.

"I can't do it to you, Hilda," Rodney said savagely. "You're too good."

Hilda buttoned her blouse and they stood up. Slowly they walked back through the grass, which now was a black and colorless substance through which they swished. They came to the school and went past it and then they came to the first of the houses and finally to Third Avenue. Hilda walked quietly.

Under a streetlight they stopped and she started to say something, but Rodney could not wait to hear. He turned and walked away quickly, and then began to trot and finally was running.

He never went back to the school. The next week he transferred to Black Fox Military Academy. He never knew what Hilda the Hog told her parents. He never saw her again . . .

. . . He sighed and the memory was ended. It ended as completely as a black-and-white photograph turned over. His mind was empty again. The whole recollection had come to him instantly, consumed almost no time. Was known completely and was then gone completely.

The humming sound was still in his ears; however, he knew very surely that it was not the memory of the bee's hum. He felt the restlessness again, the tiniest gnaw of fear. He moved his head slightly and at the very edge of his vision he saw a black, fast-moving airplane wing. The whole plane came into view. It was a B–24 and coming fast behind it was a Focke-Wulf, the leading edge of its wing glowing red and the tracers arching out and into the B–24.

The Focke-Wulf swept under and beyond the B–24 and then the B–24 softly whooshed into a huge fireball. Black pieces of debris fell out of the red cloud; a motor, a man, a single 50-cal. machine gun.

Then everything came back to Rodney. He jerked his head quickly and across the sky, far to his right, he could see the great drawn-out formation of B–24's and around them, humming and buzzing, were the Focke-Wulfs. The battle swirled forward, covering the sky for miles, but at such a distance that he could hear only the faint hum and see the faint burn of tracers.

The other things had been memories, but with a cold stab Rodney knew that this was *now*. This was now and he was scared.

He jerked over suddenly as he thought of something. Below him the world was stretched out in patchwork; tilled squares, forests, the stitching of a railway, the black ribbon of a highway. With an expert eye he guessed he was 20,000 feet above the world. He was free-falling toward the earth.

Quickly, but with no fear, he jerked his hands up. He saw that they were burnt and blistered, but intact. He fumbled across his chest for the metal D-ring of the ripcord and pulled. Something snapped open with a pop, there was a fierce rustling and then with a jerk the parachute was full and he swung back and forth.

Rodney Cartwright, Captain, USAF, pilot of a B–24 operating out of Norfolk, England, and headed for a target in Southern France which he could not remember, floated quietly to earth in France. He landed in a plowed field, collapsed his chute, stepped out of the harness. He walked toward a copse of trees and tried to hide chute and flying clothes where the leaves were thickest. A truck was whining down the nearby road and he knew it would be German troops out to pick him up. He walked down the middle of the copse and when he heard the motor of the truck running he worked toward the road. He looked out on the road.

A weapons carrier was parked at the edge of the road. A German sergeant was standing beside a mounted machine gun and a line of soldiers was just disappearing into the copse on the dead run making for his parachute.

Rodney looked at his hands again. The right one was the most badly burned, but the palm was intact. He could hold his .45. He slid it out of its holster, pulled back the slide to put a bullet in the chamber.

He walked out of the copse toward the weapons carrier holding the .45 high in his right hand. The sergeant saw him at once, half stood up, his face confused. He shouted something in German, but Rodney only smiled and continued to walk toward him. The sergeant reached down, pressed a lever, cocked the machine gun and trained on Rodney.

Rodney smiled, shook his head in disapproval and the sergeant blushed. He shuffled his feet and was confused, but he was still restless about the gun. Rodney walked to the carrier, stepped under the gun and held his arm up toward the sergeant. He felt like a marvelous actor; every gesture he had made indicated he wanted to surrender to the German, to give up his gun. The sergeant reached for the .45 and when his fingers were a few inches away from Rodney's hand Rodney fired. The bullet went directly into the sergeant's stomach. It gave off a large knicking sound as it penetrated his bright brass belt insignia. The bullet tore the sergeant completely out of the weapons carrier and he lit on his back in the middle of the road. Rodney walked around the carrier. The sergeant was getting up, but very slowly and the center of his jacket was stained. He was trying to breathe, but there was a faint whistling sound like air escaping from a balloon. The sergeant got to his feet, then slowly sat down again, deflated to the ground. His eyes misted and he rolled over backwards and was dead.

Rodney jumped up on the weapons carrier and quickly checked the machine gun. He found the trigger, made sure there was a full belt in the gun and then waited. In a little over a minute the German platoon came bursting out of the copse. They came in a nervous and excited bunch as Rodney had hoped they would. They were a mixed group. As they rushed, pell-mell and in a kind of joyous disarray, Rodney could see that some of them were young boys, others in their sixties and skinny around the neck, a few had the solid rotund body of the satisfied clerk. They were, Rodney thought, very green, very new. They were out of the copse and only thirty yards from the truck when they noticed that it was not the sergeant who was behind the gun. They stopped, embarrassment on their faces. There was a quick glancing at their young lieutenant and he turned red. He said something and then, very reluctantly, started to reach for his pistol. Rodney pulled the trigger and the gun began to jump. The first few shots kicked up dust in front of the tight group of men, but at once Rodney lifted the sights and the bullets began to beat tiny puffs of dust out of German uniforms and the men screamed.

Most of them fell or sprawled, but two started to run in opposite directions. Rodney swiveled the gun, ran the dust puffs after the man on the right and hit him a half-dozen times. He turned quickly in the other direction and caught the other man just as he reached the copse. The burst caught the man in the back and picked him off his feet and slammed him into the green foliage and he disappeared.

Rodney emptied the belt into the mass of the platoon. Then he turned, climbed into the driver's seat and started the carrier. He drove off down the highway.

2. The French Girl

FOR the first few minutes Rodney had trouble with the gear shift of the weapons carrier. Then he saw a shift diagram on the dash and soon had the carrier moving at 40 kilometers an hour down the highway, away from the direction in which it had first appeared.

He looked curiously at the landscape. The road was lined with horse chestnut trees, backed by thick hedgerows, and beyond those were peat meadows. Some cows grazed over the low hills. On a hilltop in the middle distance he saw something move. It was a tractor. It was a sharp black figure; a tiny ancient machine. Smoke actually came from a thin stack in the front of the tractor, drifted back in a black fan. Rodney felt elated by the sight . . . the tractor looked like a small antic ship that had been equipped with wheels.

He jammed his foot down on the brakes. He stopped. He saw a white marker along the road which said 380 K. He was in France. This was the first time he had ever been on the European continent, but he knew the kilometer markers from history books. They were, he thought, emplaced by Napoleon. Secondly, he heard the hum in the sky again. It swelled in volume as the engine of the weapons carrier grew silent. He looked up. The sound came from a vast stream of bombers which moved across the sky. Fighters swirled about them in twos and threes, cutting into the stream in sharp arcs, their leading edges suddenly flashing red. One of the bombers was trailing smoke from two engines and the fighters grew dense around it.

Suddenly Rodney was shaking. It was an utterly new sensation. It started with a quivering in the stomach which spread out to his extremities. It was unmanageable, beyond his control. He sat jittering in the seat, unable to believe the thing that was happening to him. He looked at his fingers. They wobbled with a life of their own, at war with his palms which seemed steady. Now that he saw other bombers in trouble he realized how close he had come to dying. A few more seconds and he would have thudded into the earth like a rock. He had a very precise sensation of how his bones would have snapped, his body would have burst open.

He sensed he must be going through a form of shock.

Do something, he said to himself. Do just one thing yourself. Then you will regain control.

"Is the smoking Fortress flying to its target or back to England?" he said in a voice which was a thin whisper, dry and mumbled at first, but which grew in strength. He tried again. "I hope it's going back. It may make it to England."

Speaking helped. The quivering eased. He rubbed his tongue against the back of his teeth. His tongue seemed hard as bone and his teeth were suddenly soft as nerve pulp.

"I am alone in France," he said loudly. "I was flying a B–24 and talking to Chuck Whitaker and we both saw the fighters coming in high at two o'clock. I remember it was hot and white for a little while. And then I was floating on my back." He paused, forced himself to go on. "The plane must have exploded. I must have been blown clear. In the clearing back there I just killed a lot of Germans."

It was unbelievable. How could he have been blown through the explosion of Plexiglas and aluminum and rivets and bombs and humans and not have been torn to pieces? For a moment he felt a stab of hope. Maybe others had survived. Timidly he raised his eyes and looked for parachutes. There was nothing between him and the stream of bombers except blue air. He felt a terrible self-pity and then raw guilt because the others might all have been killed.

"I should have thought of them first," he said aloud. His trembling had almost disappeared, but he felt more isolated, more alien, more exposed than he could remember.

"No one else from your plane survived," a voice said quietly. The voice had an accent. It was a feminine voice and it came from behind him.

Now again he felt encased in something not of his own doing, a strange reality, but not his reality. Since jerking the ripcord everything had been like watching a motion picture. A very bad one. He tensed, reached for his .45 and even as he swung around with it in his hand he was aware of how silly he looked. He knew from watching Westerns that the person behind him could easily shoot him down.

A girl was standing beside the kilometer marker. Her thinness was accentuated because she was wearing heavy hiking boots and thick stockings. Her boots were covered with mud. She was carrying a steel-tipped pole in her hand and she wore a small pack on her back.

"How do you know no one else survived?" Rodney asked.

"Because I saw your plane explode," the girl said. "One body came out of the ball of fire and that must have been you. I watched for a long time until all the explosion had disappeared and there was just a cloud of black particles in the sky. None of them were as big as a man. Just you. You took a long time to open your chute. It frightened me. I thought you must be dead."

"I was knocked out, I think," Rodney said. "For a long time I did not know where I was. When I realized I pulled the ripcord."

"You were flying very high," the girl said. Rodney realized

that her accent was French. It was pleasant. "When the sound of the explosion reached me it sounded like something very small. You must have been around 6500 meters high."

"It was around 20,000 feet," Rodney said. "I guess that's around 6500 meters."

"I'm sorry," the girl said quickly. "I should have expressed it in feet. There are about three feet in a meter, yes? That's 19,500 feet approximately."

Rodney's trembling had stopped as he talked to the girl. His voice had regained its timbre. Now, however, he felt a surge of anxiety come back. The girl's estimate of their height was better than most fliers would make. It seemed unnatural for a girl to be so accurate. He was reminded that he was in alien land. Also he remembered the dead Germans back in the clearing.

"You were only off by 500 feet," Rodney said slowly. "How did you guess so close?"

"You are suspicious. Actually it was not a guess. I knew," the girl said with surprise in her voice. Then she smiled. When she spoke her voice was decisive. "Look, we are wasting time here. This is a dangerous situation. I heard some firing a few minutes ago so I assume that you fought with the Germans sent out to capture you. I was sent out also."

"Who sent you out?" Rodney asked. He put the gun back in the holster, but it was not a gesture of confidence. He was merely certain that he could overpower the girl if he had to.

"The Underground," she said simply. "Don't bother now with what part of the Underground. But we are warned when a big strike might occur and are assigned districts to patrol where it is likely that Allied bombers might be shot down. Our instructions are to rescue the survivors and to blow up the bombsight if it lands intact."

"What do you use to blow the bombsight?" Rodney asked. If the girl were really with the Underground she would be able to produce the explosive. If she could not produce the explosive Rodney decided he would shoot her. Again he felt himself drifting into the strange dreamlike motion picture role. It seemed impossible to him that he could have been terrified only a few minutes before.

The girl moved toward him, slipping the pack from her back. She undid the straps and took out a small object that looked like a small loaf of bread. With her other hand she took out three pencils.

"The pencils are really fuzes. You can determine the time of detonation by the length of the pencil," she said. "These are dropped to us by the Allies. They are very clever. The lead in the pencil actually writes. If German soldiers search us the bread and the pencils do not arouse suspicion." She was thoughtful for a moment. "Our group leader in this district says that eventually the Germans will discover the trick, but then we will make up a new one."

Rodney felt a great sense of relief, but it was not complete. The girl, like the entire day, seemed unbelievable. "What do we do now?" he asked her. "I mean you must have worked out some sort of procedure once you find a survivor."

The girl climbed up into the front seat of the weapons carrier. She had very dark straight hair which was caught in a bun at the back of her neck. Her skin was white, although her cheeks were tinged pink by the cold. The flesh beneath her eyes was blue, as if she had not slept recently. She was young and one day she would be beautiful. Although she was dressed in hiking clothes she had a style which was quite unconscious.

"As long as the planes are overhead we are safe," the girl said. "The Germans are either manning anti-aircraft guns or rearming the fighters at the fighter field back there." She gestured down the road in the direction from which Rodney had come. "The civilians in town must go to air-raid shelters."

"I saw a man running a tractor back there," Rodney said,

and his voice was stubborn — about what, he did not quite know.

The girl laughed. It was the first sound she had made of real pleasure.

"Those peasants," she said and shook her head. "Nothing can stop them except a direct hit. They don't even raise their heads to see the planes. Plow, plow, till, till, plant, plant. They think of nothing else. In a way it is rather wonderful."

"What happens when the planes disappear?" Rodney asked.

"Then the Germans will make a routine patrol down the main roads," she said. "This is one they will patrol. They will also have time to wonder about the fact that the search platoon has not returned. Are any of them in shape to walk back to the fighter field?"

"I am not certain," Rodney said. "Some of them were running when they disappeared into the forest. I think we should assume that at least one of them could walk back to his headquarters."

He recalled the puffs of dust that came from their uniforms, the slow-growing wetness of blood on the uniforms.

The girl eyed him carefully. She closed her eyes for a moment. Almost at once she opened her eyes.

"The first thing to do is to get as close as we can to Montauban in this weapons carrier," she said. "As soon as the planes have disappeared or we see another vehicle we will have to abandon the carrier and walk the rest of the way. Let's start. I am tired from walking."

"Which way is Montauban?" Rodney asked.

Again the girl laughed.

"Of course, there is no reason for you to know," she said. "It is straight ahead. About fifteen kilometers. Drive fast."

Rodney put the carrier into gear and shot it through the gears. In a minute he was going 80 kilometers an hour. The road was completely empty. Occasionally they passed a house, but it was always closed and shuttered. He saw a few more farmers working in the fields, but none of them looked at the road.

The girl looked over her shoulder at the bomber stream. "Are they flying toward the target or back toward England?" Rodney asked.

"Toward England," the girl said. She sounded surprised.

"I lost direction," Rodney said flatly. He was relieved.

"What way were you flying when you were hit?" the girl asked.

"Toward the target," Rodney said. He took his eyes from the road a moment, looked at the girl. "I can't remember the target exactly. In fact I can't even remember the date."

"It is March 3, 1944," the girl said. "I don't know what the target was either. All we get on the radio from England are code words indicating when a flight might pass over our territory. In a few days we'll hear rumors. They usually are accurate."

For a few minutes they were silent. They could not hear the hum of the bomber stream above the sound of the carrier motor. The indicator on the speedometer indicated 90. The dial indicated 100 as the highest speed, but Rodney could not get beyond 90. Even so he had the impression of remarkable speed. The trees whirred by, the rectangles of fields were clear in the distance, but dissolved as the carrier rushed by them.

They came to an inn. It had small tables and chairs on a veranda and looked cheerful. A poodle lying in the sun looked up at them. The inn was shuttered tight, except for one window. Rodney thought he saw a face in the window . . . the face of a woman, well rounded, an abundance of hair. The girl leaned forward and stared at the inn as they went past.

"We've got to stop," she said when they had passed the inn. "The woman in that inn is, we think, a collaborator. This is a good time to find out. If a German patrol comes out from Montauban it will mean that she has called in and reported us. The inn is the only place we have passed with a telephone. In any case it only makes our walk a few kilometers farther. We're almost to the outskirts of Montauban."

Rodney stopped the weapons carrier directly in the middle of the road. The girl looked at him and throwing back her head laughed. A real hard solid laugh, surprising in a person so small. Instantly Rodney lost his last doubt about her.

"It is crazy what war allows us to do," she said and shook her head. She had already put her pack on her back, but was holding the explosive loaf in her hand. The moment they stopped she was out of the carrier, had opened the hood and had placed the explosive against the carburetor. She did something to the eraser end of the pencil and then stuck it in the loaf of bread.

She trotted back and jumped onto the bed of the weapons carrier. She quickly shuffled through the assortment of clothes, food cartons, munition cans. She lifted her hands once and three fingers were tipped with blood. She glanced at Rodney, but said nothing. She threw him a German greatcoat, two small boxes of ammunition, a box of rations, and held up a bottle of cognac. Rodney nodded and she threw it down to him.

"Let's go," she said and jumped down from the truck bed. "If Madame Bovet called it will take them about eight or ten minutes to get out here. That leaves us about five more minutes."

She led him to the edge of the road. Beside the road was a ditch about five feet wide and filled with muddy water. She stood back and then jumped the ditch. Rodney threw her the things he was carrying. Suddenly he turned and looked at the weapons carrier.

"You forgot to light the fuze," he said.

"It doesn't need lighting. When you pull the eraser off the

fuze, it ignites a powder train that runs down the center of the fuze. It will take ten minutes to go off."

She held up a tiny bit of rubber. It was the eraser.

Rodney smiled at her.

"Look, can your people use the machine gun?" Rodney asked. "I can dismount it and throw it in the ditch here. If you get it out in a few days it can be cleaned up and used again."

She nodded.

"But make it quick," she said.

Rodney ran back to the carrier, jumped up on the bed and looked at the gun mounting. Instantly he recognized the lock which held the gun to the mount. He unlatched it and slid the gun free. It was heavy and his knees buckled slightly. He walked to the edge of the truck bed and carefully climbed down. He reached back into the carrier and picked up a can of machine-gun ammunition. He walked quickly across the road. He pitched the gun into the ditch, reached over and carefully dropped the ammunition box beside it. Both objects disappeared into the brown water.

He jumped across the ditch. The girl handed him half of the material they had taken from the weapons carrier. He noticed that she had placed a few rocks on the ground at the point where he had dumped the gun and the ammunition.

They ran across a field, heading for a copse of trees that trailed off, like an inverted comma with its tail touching the trees that ran along the low hills. When they reached the trees it was dark in the shadow. Rodney was aware of how much warmth there had been in the thin sunlight. He looked at the girl. She glanced at her watch.

"It's been twelve minutes since we passed Madame Bovet's," she said. "If the Germans don't arrive in a few more minutes she will be clear."

She unslung her pack, opened it and passed Rodney a sandwich. It was dark bread filled with liver pâté. She started to eat a sandwich. Rodney uncorked the cognac bottle and offered it to the girl. She was stamping her feet to keep warm and she shook her head. Rodney took a long drag of the cognac. He had never drunk cognac before and was surprised at its heavy rich aromatic flavor. He shook his head, whistling. The girl smiled.

Then they both heard the whine of an engine coming from Montauban. The girl looked up, glanced at her watch.

"It's been thirteen and a half minutes," she said. Her jaw hung slightly open as they stared down the road. She held the sandwich at her waist. Her body bent forward, a strangely innocent and childlike posture.

The whine grew louder and a weapons carrier, exactly like the one they had abandoned, tore into the curve. It was going at high speed and as it came out of the curve the driver saw the abandoned carrier and hit his brakes. The carrier screeched, went into a long slide on the slippery road, the soldiers in the rear were rolled into a chaos of green khaki, rifle butts and helmets. The carrier came to a halt a few yards from the abandoned carrier.

"The cognac please," the girl said to Rodney. The blue under her eyes was now very deep. She drank without looking away from the two carriers. She said something to herself, it reached Rodney like an echo, thin as an exhalation, "Merci, non. Merci, non."

Two Germans were walking cautiously toward the abandoned carrier. The rest of the soldiers spread out behind them fanlike, keeping distance between themselves and the other two men. One of the two started searching the body of the truck, running his hands expertly under fenders, under the seats. The other lifted the hood.

Rodney and the girl heard his voice clearly in the cold still air. He was holding the explosive loaf in his hand, staring at the fuze.

"Throw it, you idiot," the girl said. "The fuze doesn't give off smoke so he doesn't know it is burning. Throw it, please."

Rodney looked at her. She swung the bottle to her lips, her eyes glanced fixedly down the length of the bottle, as if it were a strange telescope. Tears came to her eyes as she gulped.

The explosive went off. The German holding it disappeared in a ball of yellowish-white smoke. The second German close to the carrier spun sideways reflexively, but before he could drop below the carrier the debris of the windshield hit him and his body was shredded from the chest up by glass and bits of metal.

The rest of the platoon staggered backward. Two helmets sailed off into the air. Only one man fell and he quickly clambered back to his feet. They were looking at where the first German had been standing. They were also beating their hands against their heads, as if they were trying to pound themselves into wakefulness. Where the first German had stood there was nothing except a slight darkened spot from which a few tendrils of smoke rose.

One of the Germans looked at his companion, reached out a tentative finger and plucked something from the other's uniform. He looked at it and then, with a high piercing scream, he tried to shake the object loose. "Fleisch, fleisch," he yelled. In some way the others understood, although they could not hear his words. They all began to beat at small gobbets that clung to their uniforms. They screamed "Fleisch, fleisch" over and over. They crawled inside their uniforms, writhed to pull back from the contamination. They danced frantically on the road. One man tore off his jacket and threw it away. As if by instruction the others did the same.

They still danced and they still flailed, their winter underwear very white against the black of the road. Those men that had thrown off their jackets and pants now returned to beating their heads.

"It must have broken their eardrums," Rodney said.

The girl was not watching the road. She was on her knees packing the rucksack. She stood up. She was crying silently.

"Put on the greatcoat," she said, her voice unbroken by her tears. "It will help going into Montauban. Stuff your hat in a pocket."

She waited while Rodney put on the coat. She picked up her share of the material and started up the trail.

Rodney looked at her slim, almost skinny back. "How old are you?" he asked.

"Seventeen years," she said, "last September."

"What is your name?"

"Nina."

"I am twenty-one years old," Rodney said. He did not give a birth month. "My name is Rodney."

They did not talk again for a half hour. The girl walked quickly through the dimness of the forest. Occasionally she got too far ahead of Rodney and he trotted to overtake her. He felt a stitch in his side, but he said nothing.

They came out of the forest and were on a low hill overlooking a town.

"Can you speak French?" Nina asked.

"Yes, very well," he said. "I studied it in school," he said in French.

His father had insisted on fluency in French. He had hired a French maid so that Rodney could speak French with a native. He had hated the French maid; a girl with a small tight mouth, hair on her legs and a passion for long fast walks through the hills.

They stood on the hill for a moment, talking in French. Nina pointed out the checkpoints in the town.

"Don't speak French unless you have to," Nina said. Her voice was hesitant, gentle. "You speak very well, but your accent is so very American."

She turned and they walked down into the misty coldness

of the dusk. The town was smeared by a mixture of darkness and of smoke. It looked very ominous.

Rodney stayed very close to Nina. He walked by her side. She took his arm as they came to the streets of the town.

3. A Day
with Nina

ONCE he was in the town Rodney had, again, the feeling that everything was contrived, the heavy stone buildings were really made of thin plaster, the people wearing berets had put them on only a few moments ago for effect. It was a marvelous act, a huge set, an entertainment of some kind. He felt certain that he had not killed the German platoon that afternoon . . . all of this he felt with relief.

But when, he thought, does it end? The *ending?* It was a black solid falling rock of a question. It smashed his euphoria.

The town was stranger than anything he had ever seen. It was Europe, he told himself. The first town he had seen in Europe. He had known Los Angeles; the training camp in Texas which shimmered in the heat, and black Angus cattle fenced off from the long dreaded strip of asphalt where they practiced landings; and then New York. Of England he had seen only their airfield and its buildings. Occasionally he had heard a strange accent which seemed a mangled kind of

English and realized it was the English accent. He had not been in England long enough to take a leave in London.

Montauban's streets were made of cold stones. They gave off a cloud of mist, only a few inches deep but as thick as snow, so that the Frenchmen walked through it footless. The faces of the buildings had only a few windows cut into the stone and these were barred and shuttered. At the first intersection there was a shop which said "Charcuterie" in old gold and red letters. A line of women in shawls were standing in front of the closed entrance.

"*Charcuterie?* It means pork shop, doesn't it?" he whispered to Nina. He spoke in English, "Doesn't it?"

"Yes," she said, speaking in French, her eyes glancing down the row of women. "Speak French now. And do not whisper or bend toward me. Those are the little signs of the conspirator. Walk as if you belong here. With the German greatcoat they might think you are a German. But you are not wearing a German cap and your shoes are brown . . . not black boots. Be careful."

One of his feet, in midair and reckless, came down and hit the pavement with the fear of a man who would like to start running. Nina's words transformed the whole thing. No boy guerrilla he, no quick-draw artist. He had shot up a platoon of the enemy and someone would be chewing ass at some headquarters and some Frenchwoman had seen him and knew he had blown up another chunk of Germans. No more Mickey Mouse, good buddy. His teeth chittered against one another and then he brought them together, gnashed . . . and then quickly smiled in case anyone was looking for a tense person.

He glanced at the women in the line. All somehow like nuns in a bitter lay order; their white faces peering out from their shawls. They gave off a thin acrid odor, oddly familiar. It was the odor of the gymnasium. These women did not bathe much. They were not talking among themselves. Their heads swung softly and followed Nina and Rodney.

This was not how he had expected France to be. Not heavy and cold and menacing.

"If, for any reason, you come down in France," the Intelligence captain had said at the first briefing two weeks ago, and then waited while they laughed and the wiseacres yelled out what they would do to the French girls — "If that happens, you will find that some French will dislike you because of our bombing program in France. Others are collaborators. They are only a tiny fraction." The fragment of recollection came back to Rodney.

"We'll sweet-talk 'em into a little quick action," a handsome Nebraska boy who had a famous reputation with the women said. "I talked a Boston girl into the sack and she thought I had a Hugo . . . Jugo . . . oh, shit, Jewish or something accent and it was cute." He put his hands out, manipulated a shape, made it into a woman, stood up for a few quick grinds and slumped back, eyes rolling and mouth moaning like a man just after coming. "Let me at them copulators and I'll collaborate them into the next county. And get out of the shooting part of this for a few weeks."

"Sure you will," the captain said. "No one else can con them, but you can. She'll really arch her back for you. You're so nice and you're American and suffering for your country." The captain grinned, chuckled for a moment, made a decision. "The smartest agent we had in Europe got to sweet-talking a peasant woman whose husband was off fighting for us. *Us* . . . remember that. Not a beauty, remember. Just a stout horny-handed girl of the soil. He massaged, oiled, blew smoke, back-gainered with a double twist, ran a four-minute mile, blew sweet breath in her ear, bullshitted a mountain, rubbed her toes, said modestly he was Henry Rockefeller Ford, drew a design for a skyscraper he was going to build her, endured her garlic breath, ran his fingers down her arm like it was velvet, nibbled her earlobe and other things and gave her food . . . more than she had seen in two years. And all this in good French."

A hand went up.

"Where else'd his finger get?" a navigator asked.

Again the captain waited.

"It got there and so did the big carrot," the captain said. "The smart boy got over his hots and he felt so good." He paused and went on, his voice was still joking. "Then he woke up in the middle of the night and she had sliced off his balls with her husband's straight razor and was running away and he was sitting in a little pool of blood and feeling no pain. She did it because he spoke English in his sleep and she was suspicious." He paused again, grinned. "He got his balls back. In a Bull Durham bag which she sent him through the Underground, with a letter of apology. She was sorry. Now he's in Los Angeles with a funny voice and breasts which keep him off the beach and talking five hours a week to a service psychiatrist."

The captain paused, finished a few more minutes of the briefing. Then his voice went flat and without force, a statement so underplayed that they knew it had emphasis.

"Just give 'em name, number, and rank, men," he said. "That's all. If you land in enemy territory pray for one thing: instant stupidity. If you aren't that way naturally, learn it quick."

No one laughed.

The quiet, misty, chill of the town seeped through the greatcoat. Under his shirt he felt the skin begin to set up small trembling waves. He felt as if hunching forward would ease the new strange sensation. He fought the urge to hump over and walked straight beside the girl.

"At this corner we come to a *place*," Nina said. "The soldiers from the *caserne*, French soldiers, come here to drink and . . ." she paused and then went on in English, "to meet girls."

There were three cafés in the *place*, three looms of light just starting to pierce the gloom of sunset. Some figures moved behind frosted glass. Nina led Rodney directly across the *place*, avoiding the three cafés. They crossed the *place* and started down a dim street. Three soldiers, French soldiers, walked out of the street. They looked casually at Nina and, more curiously, at Rodney. One of them half stopped, peering through the thickening mist. Rodney could not see his face, but his posture was questioning, his head to one side, curious.

The other two soldiers stopped. One of them yelled impatiently. The curious soldier hesitated, yelled an expression which Rodney could barely understand, then turned around and caught up with the other two.

"What do they mean 'pigeon of the Germans'?" Rodney asked.

They were alone in the street. The girl stopped and turned to Rodney. She was trembling and he knew she was frightened. She was blushing slightly, a faint flush, around her cheeks. It made her look even younger.

"That is a phrase they use for French girls who go out with the Germans," she said, speaking in English. She tossed her head, trying to dismiss the idea. "It means . . . I do not know the English."

Nina stopped beside a doorway in a thick gray stone wall. High above the door, and like two rectangular eye sockets, were two narrow windows. Nina turned to Rodney.

"Only my father will be inside," she said. Her head was cocked to one side as if she were puzzled. "He understands about the Underground, but at the same time he doesn't."

"What the hell does that mean?" Rodney asked.

Nina hesitated a moment.

"Father is a scholar," she said with quick guarded pride.

"All he knows is the classical political theorists. He is barely aware that this war is on. Try not to upset him."

She turned, took a large iron key from a pocket in her jacket, and opened the door.

They walked through a cold entrance hall and opened another door. The room was bright, so bright that for a few seconds it blinded Rodney. But the room was also very warm. He stepped into the room. He was aware only of the warmth. The heat relaxed him instantly and made him aware of an enormous fatigue. He realized with a mild shock that his head was bent forward; he was staring at the floor. A strange voice spoke and he lifted his head in a protective gesture. The fatigue was forgotten. But he still felt an estrangement between his mind and his senses.

The room was lined on three sides with books. The fourth side was broken by a small fireplace in which a combination of logs and coal were burning. To one side of the fireplace a tiny man was sitting behind a very big desk. The man was too small. Rodney moved his head to reestablish perspective. He stared again at the man. The man remained the same size.

"This is my father," Nina said. "Mr. Faures."

"I am very pleased to meet you, sir," Rodney said in English.

"Ah, you are an American," Nina's father said. His English was not as good as Nina's, but it had a curiously precise quality to it. "I have never talked to an American, but you do not have an English accent. Therefore you must be American."

He stood up and walked around the desk. He was a full head shorter than Nina. He shook hands with Rodney. His grip was firm, but the hand was diminutive. He was wearing a black alpaca coat, heavy woolen trousers, a white shirt with a tie at the neck and slippers. In a way that Rodney could not quite identify, the man looked disheveled. The only thing

about his person that seemed to be done with care was a small
full beard.

"If you would like we could try to speak in French," Rodney said. "I do not speak French well, however."

"It is merely that you are tired, Lieutenant," Nina said
quickly. She was speaking in French. "I think you should
speak in French at all times. It is part of the discipline. In a
few hours your French will improve greatly and you will
speak only French. If the wrong ears hear you speak a single
word of English there will be trouble."

"My daughter talks tough like a sergeant in the Foreign
Legion," Faures said. He shook his head in amusement.

He waved Rodney to a seat in front of the desk. It was not
a comfortable chair, but it was better than standing. It was
probably the chair in which Nina's father placed his students,
Rodney thought.

"Do I call you Professor?" Rodney asked, looking at the
little man.

"Oh, no. In France we do not have the system where every
instructor in the university is called a professor," the little
man said with a pleasant little laugh. "The title 'Professor' is
reserved only for the head of a department. I will never be a
professor. I do not possess the administrative skills, nor the
desire. You may call me Mr. Faures."

Rodney looked at Faures' desk. Nina was leaving the room.
She said something about getting food. Rodney did not turn
his head, he continued to look at the desk. There was a book
open on the center of the desk. To the left of the book was a
jar of very sharp pencils. To the right of the book was a large
pad of cheap paper covered with notations in red and blue
ink. The handwriting was as precise as the type turned out
on a typewriter. Beside the pad of paper there were two
heavy old-fashioned fountain pens. One was red-tipped, the
other blue.

Rodney lifted his head. Faures was leaning back in his

chair, but his eyes were glancing over the book. He raised
his eyes once, saw that Rodney was looking at him and
smiled.

"It is Machiavelli's counsel to the Prince," Faures said.
"Have you ever read it?"

"Yes, when I was in college," Rodney said. "It was a little
paperback book. Much smaller than that."

"Probably so, probably so," Faures said. He jumped to
his feet and picking the book up carefully turned it around
so that Rodney could see it. "This is a Latin original with
commentaries and footnotes by an Italian. The Italian claims
to have seen Machiavelli's original manuscript and argues
that Machiavelli was really a believer in popular democracy.
He wrote during the Risorgimento." Faures shrugged his
shoulders. "The man is, I think, a patriotic fool. You know
how the Italians started to twist history, especially their own
history, toward the end of the nineteenth century?"

"No, I do not know," Rodney said.

"It is a fascinating subject," Faures said. His voice rose
slightly with excitement. "Patriotism seems to unsettle the
intellect of man. Is that true also in America?"

Rodney felt his interest rising. Even through the fatigue
there was something appealing about Faures.

"I'm not a scholar, so I really don't know," Rodney said.
"But a lot of our politicians say ridiculous things in the name
of patriotism."

Faures stood up and began to pace back and forth behind
his desk. His face was very animated.

"That is precisely the point," he said. "A thousand years
from today scholars will look over the patriotic speeches
which our statesmen make and believe that they are the reality. It is so foolish. What political people say publicly should
never be trusted."

"What can be trusted?" Rodney asked.

"What they write, even if for public consumption, is a bit

more trustworthy," Faures said. "But the best of all, the thing
which is most likely to be true, is what the political person
writes with the intention that it be viewed only by himself.
The diaries of a politician are the best. There a man tells the
truth . . . sometimes. Love letters are also good. It is odd
but in their passion over a woman vain men often reveal
much of themselves. They want their lover to know precisely
why they are great. So they sometimes tell their lovers the
truth. Strange, is it not?"

Nina came back into the room. She was carrying a tray
which she put on a small table opposite the desk. The tray
contained a large piece of cheese, a long thin loaf of dark
bread, a mound of butter, and two bottles.

"That bottle has Calvados, the other is wine," Nina said.
She paused for a moment and then looked at Rodney. There
was a faint smile on her lips. "Where did you eat breakfast
this morning?"

"At the airfield someplace in Norfolk," Rodney said. He
recalled the meal perfectly. His mouth started to salivate.
He had eaten three fried eggs, six pieces of bacon, several
pieces of toast and three cups of coffee. Some of the crewmen
ate little or nothing for breakfast on the mornings that they
flew. Most of them said nothing about their loss of appetite.
A few said that they heard from a doctor that if you caught
shrapnel in the intestines with a full meal the chances of in-
fection were greater. Inbeles, a waist gunner, was the most
honest. He said that he had eaten a huge breakfast the first
morning he flew and had thrown it up the moment he saw
the gray coastline of Europe through the haze.

Faures poured Rodney a glass of Calvados. He poured
himself a small glass of wine. Rodney sipped the Calvados.
It had a sharp bite and fumes rolled through the back of his
nose. After he had swallowed it there was an odd fruity taste
in his mouth.

"What is it made of?" Rodney asked. The alcohol seemed

to be absorbed as it went down his throat. He felt slightly drunk even before he had put his glass back on the desk.

"It is made from apples," Faures said. "I do not like it particularly. It makes me lightheaded. I do not enjoy the sensation."

Rodney drank the rest of the glass of Calvados off in one gulp. Suddenly he was warm from the skin inward. He felt very relaxed. For no reason at all he smiled at Faures. He looked at Nina. She was cutting the bread and cheese into three equal parts.

Something about Nina's work troubled Rodney. Then he remembered that in Intelligence briefings they had been told that food was severely rationed on the Continent. In case they went down over the Continent they had been instructed, rather vaguely, to "live off the land."

"I have some food in my jacket," Rodney said.

He reached into his leather jacket and took out two D-rations. They were bars of very rich chocolate fortified with vitamins and cereals. Normally no one would eat them. They were rich enough to make a man throw up if they were eaten too quickly. But Rodney carried them as a kind of precaution. He explained the contents of the D-rations to Faures and Nina. He noticed that Nina was blushing.

"You are a guest in our house, Lieutenant," Nina said. "It is not necessary for you to bring us food."

She said it in an odd stilted way. In the manner of a little girl making a rehearsed speech.

Nina drew up a chair to the desk and they all began to eat. Rodney poured himself another glass of Calvados. The cheese was a rich creamy variety. The heat of the room caused it to gently flow over Rodney's plate. Spread over the chunks of bread it was delicious.

Rodney felt like grinning. He restrained the impulse. It is the alcohol, the food and the warmth of the room, he told himself. Now is the time to be steady.

"Please call me Rodney," he said suddenly. They both looked up at him and smiled. He went on quickly. "What do we do about getting back to England?"

Faures looked quickly at his daughter. He had very innocent eyes; they seemed somehow to reflect great intelligence but a kind of childish openness. Nina spoke first.

"I do not really know how it is done," she said. "Some other part of the organization is responsible for passing you along until you reach the coast of Spain or some kind of arrangement is made."

Her face was suddenly anxious. Faures took a sip of wine.

"How do we make contact with the responsible people?" Faures asked Nina.

"It has already been made," Nina said. "One of the women in the line in front of the pork butcher's is a member of the organization. She gave me a sign as we passed her."

"What kind of sign?" Faures asked with a sudden interest.

"Father, I have told you before I cannot tell you such things," Nina said gently.

Faures laughed delightedly. He laughed until the tears gathered in his eyes. He collected himself and stroked his short beard. He bent forward, gazed comically at Rodney.

"These children and their mysterious organization," he said. "Sometimes I think that if it were not for the food rationing and the shortage of petrol they would like the war to go on forever. For a young romantic it is very exciting."

Nina's cheeks grew red. Rodney realized that whenever she felt an emotion it made her look younger than she actually was.

"Father, it is no joke," Nina said sharply. "We have lost six of the twenty-five people in our group in Montauban. Also I have heard that no downed flyer has yet made it back to England."

She was trembling slightly. Faures looked at her and again his face showed a very intense interest.

"I did not know that your group had suffered any casualties," he said softly. "That really makes the game more interesting. When one's comrades are killed then the war can seem holy, take on a moral coloring, become a crusade. Early in every movement someone must be killed, a martyr must be produced . . . then even the most pure intellectual loses his mind, becomes a ravening animal."

"It does not take much for the Germans to shoot someone," Nina said. She looked sideways at Rodney and shook her head slightly. "If one is out past the curfew hour or is carrying a weapon or even has a copy of the Underground paper it is enough. Also, whenever a German is killed they make a roundup of suspects and pick five of them to be shot at random. One way or another they have gotten six of the twenty-five in our group."

"You have never told me that before," Faures said, with a shade of reproach in his voice.

Nina looked straight at Rodney.

"I did not want to bother you," Nina said. "The only reason I mention it tonight is that Rodney must know what the difficulties are. It is very unlikely he will be able to make it back to England. If he uses a German uniform while escaping and is caught he may be shot as a spy. In fact he will be technically a spy the moment he alters his American uniform in any way or takes it off."

"That is the dash, the excitement, the childish part which the intellectual must have," Faures said, speaking softly and so obviously to himself that neither Rodney nor Nina looked at him. "The costume, the chase, and the murder and he has a cause."

He made a neat note on a card, put it to one side and looked back at Rodney.

Rodney felt the mild euphoria of food and drink vanish. He sat up straight in the chair.

"I'll get through all right," he said to Faures. He said it

with utter confidence. He sensed that Nina was very protective of her father. Nina smiled at him. Rodney felt a slight
surge of anger. "I mean it. I will get out safely."

"Maybe it would be better to surrender and go to one of the
prisoner-of-war camps," Nina said. "They are said to be quite
good. There is adequate food and no one is bothered unless
he tries to escape."

Rodney leaned back in his chair and laughed.

"I don't want to spend time locked up in a camp," he said
flatly. "I'll take my chances on getting through."

For a long moment there was silence in the room. Then
Faures spoke.

"The young man is right, Nina," he said in his small precise
voice. "Any rational man should be able to overcome a larger
rational organization. The larger an organization the more
imperfect it becomes. In theory I see no reason why Rodney
should not be able to move through the meshes of the German organization."

Nina looked at the two men and she was puzzled. She
shook her head as if they were children. Then she smiled.

Rodney felt a first pang of doubt. The girl seemed so young
and inexperienced and at the same time she had the manner
of one who had a special knowledge.

There was a single knock that came from the rear of the
house. Nina looked up.

"It must be someone from the organization," she said.
"They must have come over the back wall."

She walked out of the room and Rodney heard the latch
lifted on a distant door. There was a quick exchange in
French. Nina returned, followed by two young men.

4. Rouge for Red

NINA came through the door first. She was followed by
a large, not fully grown boy. He had a coltish look about him,
the impression of something still unformed. His most prom-
inent feature — his eyes — were large, brown, innocent and
intelligent. He smiled at Rodney. Nina muttered a name.
Rodney thought it was "Blackie."

"It is Blackie?" he asked Nina in English.

"Yes. Everyone in the group has a nickname and they are
in English," she said. "Everyone except the section leader
has an English nickname. Our section leader is called Rouge.
Please, Rodney, do not speak again in English. Speak only
French. Also use the colors for names. It's just a device so that
if we have to yell at one another or shout a warning or identify ourselves in the dark most of the French and Germans
don't understand readily."

"It is a nice part of the romance of the thing," Faures muttered. "Everyone is called by a color. Conspiracy is another
element of the crusade. One must become a secret person,
seem to be lost in the grand movement."

Blackie heard the words and was embarrassed. When he
grew up, when the face filled in around the eyes, he would
be handsome. Now the largeness of the eyes gave him a feminine face, which seemed odd because of the big ungainly
stature of the boy.

Another man, a smaller man, stepped from the shadow of
the boy. He used this shadow economically, moving at its
very edge, avoiding the light, and when he turned to face
them it was a threat . . . he could see all of them; they could
see only the side of his face.

He was closest to the escape door. He was silent and this
made others silent. He was unrevealed while they were all
caught in the light. He was authority. He was poised while
they were either relaxed or uncertain.

Rodney's hands tightened on the chair in front of him.
His back prickled . . . it was, he realized with a low cunning
surprise, searching for a corner against which to brace.

The stranger brought pressure with him. And a kind of
power. He was leashed, bowed, held back, appraising . . .
and no one knew quite what he would do. The man was authority of a manic and coiled type. One's back itched for protection.

Rodney was relieved to see that Faures had come half out
of his chair, was looking at the stranger with absorption. Easy
now, Rodney, he told himself. Now is the time to be calm.
Pluck and daring come later.

"This is Rouge," Nina said, using the French word.

The illuminated side of Rouge's face split. It was his mouth.
Several very white teeth showed. It was not half of a smile
. . . it was no part of a smile. It was a response, unaccompa-
nied by any impression of pleasure. Above the split half of
the face, an untrimmed mustache showed, and above that an
eye which slowly, very slowly, worked at Rodney. It was no
common scrutiny, no look of pedestrian curiosity: the eye
worked. It was far beyond rudeness, for there was nothing of
malice in the scrutiny. The eyes studied Rodney's shoes, the
mud on his pants, the buttons on his shirt, his hands, the insignia on his collar. The eye stopped at the insignia and Rodney stiffened. Rouge spoke without turning his head.

It was quick colloquial French, spoken so fast that Rodney did not catch it. It was spoken to Blackie. Blackie looked at Rodney, walked toward him. Rodney's hand stiffened again on the chair. Stop, now stop, you are trying to work this chair into a club, he told himself. Just stop and roll with it.

"It is a precautionary thing," Blackie said. "We can trust no one."

The hands, so enormous that they seemed incapable of manipulating anything, went to Rodney's collar, took off his silver bars. Rodney marveled at the agility of the hands; was astounded that such hamlike things could manipulate the insignia.

Blackie took the insignia to Rouge. Rouge's left hand came up, took the silver bars, his eye dropped. He turned the bar over, held it very close to his eye. As if they were jewels he turned them over, examined the clasp, worked it back and forth.

"How long have you been a captain?" Rouge asked.

The words came out of his mouth without his eye or face turning toward Rodney.

"Three months," Rodney said. "We spent some time training . . ."

"This clasp has been used for months, well over a year," Rouge said, and he did not interrupt Rodney, but simply had not heard him. "It is surrounded by hundreds of little scratches. More than would accumulate in three months."

The eye went back to its scrutiny of Rodney. Rouge was interested in Rodney's hands and the eye studied them as if they were artifacts in a museum, public things to be examined by any qualified expert. Meanwhile the insignia was held in empty air, waiting for explanation.

Rouge had already burnt the mild euphoria of the Calvados out of Rodney. Rodney was trying to understand the rise in pressure, the tightening of muscles, the speeding of metabolic rates, the smell of tension which Rouge had brought to *everyone*. Faures was half bending forward, still

regarding Rouge. Why, Rodney thought, were they all trying
by little physical tricks to regain their balance?

He looked closely at Rouge. Rouge was lean, almost at the
edge of gauntness and he was very muscular. He wore work-
ingmen's clothes . . . blue pants, a darker blue jacket, a
beret, shoes that looked like a kind of crude sandal. Nothing. Not a thing to regard. But if Rodney passed him in a
crowd he knew that he would have been aware of a . . . a
what? A presence.

Rouge was the presence of suspicion, agony, dedication,
injury. Easy now, Rodney thought, slow it down. This has
been a big day. Go slow. But he went on naming the qualities.
Work, certainty, single-mindedness. He hesitated, a black
flicker at the edge of his mind sobered him. He went ahead.
Rouge was also the presence of murder. Rodney relaxed. That
was a big part of it.

"How many hundreds of scratches can you count?" Rodney asked.

The rest of the people in the room looked up sharply.
Faures sat down and automatically picked up a pen. Blackie
came to a kind of stiff rigidity, like a puppy suddenly shocked.
Nina watched Rodney, glanced sideways at Rouge.

"Maybe if you counted out the number of scratches I could
tell you how many times I have changed the insignia from
one shirt to another and we would both be happy," Rodney
said.

In his mind he knew that the bar would be a spidery-
scratched web where the pin was supposed to fit into the
clasp. In one sense Rouge was right: one could judge the
general age of a bar. But no one could count the number of
individual scratches.

Rouge had no sense of humor.

"There are so many scratches that it is impossible to count
them," he said tonelessly, his voice somehow mechanical.

"But in three months no one could have changed shirts often enough to have gotten this much wear."

"Do you know the habits of American fliers well?" Rodney asked.

The eye moved, flicked toward Rodney, caught his eyes, but made no effort to hold them. Rouge had no vanity.

"Yes," Rouge said.

"Then you must know where I got this bar," Rodney said. His voice was interrogative.

The others in the room moved, slight seismic movements, indicating their anxiety. They rolled back and forth as the exchange went on. But Rodney was making his points. They rolled with him. Rodney felt better.

"Yes," Rouge said. "I might know."

"Then you might write it down on a piece of paper and hand it to Nina and then I shall tell you how I did get it and we will both know where the other stands," Rodney said. He felt bold. "You see, there is no more reason for me to trust you than for you to trust me. The Underground is . . ." and he waited for the word, ". . . is rotten with counteragents."

"Of course," Rouge said.

Rodney felt disappointment. Rouge was not offended, was not combative. He felt Rodney's question was perfectly reasonable.

Rouge scribbled something on a piece of paper which Blackie produced. Blackie handed it to Nina.

"Before I tell you what is on the paper I should have a protection," Rodney said. "You probably have a gun. If our answers do not correspond and *you* are wrong then you could shoot me and run. Maybe you should give your gun to Blackie."

Rouge laughed. Rodney had heard that sort of laugh before. It was not genuine, but it had a meaning. It was the kind of laugh that "command officers" had in the Army Air

Force. The kind of officers who were marked to go far. Just because it was artificial and too sharp it got respect: any officer who laughed like that was a dedicated man.

"That is reasonable," Rouge said. "You are well trained. We will see how reliable you are."

Rouge took a small pistol from his back pocket and tossed it to Blackie. Blackie missed it; it clanked on the floor and there were a few moments of scrabbling on the floor. Blackie came up with it slowly. It looked tiny in his hand.

"I got the bars from a captain who was promoted to major the same day I was promoted," Rodney said. "It is a custom. Promotions generally come through on the same day."

Blackie had shifted quietly until he was behind Rouge, lost in the shadow. Nina was watching Rouge. Faures was writing. He hummed to himself.

"Open up the paper," Rouge said to Nina.

She opened it and read, "It is the custom of American officers to give insignia to other officers who have achieved inferior rank." She looked up. "There are two other things. Should I read them?"

"No," Rouge said.

Rouge was back in authority.

"We have to move fast to get the American moving out of this area," Rouge said. "Excuse us. We must talk." He motioned to Blackie and Nina to join him in a corner. They began to talk.

Rodney was just at the edge of audibility. Faures looked up from his books. He glanced at the three in the corner. He put down his pen, composed himself, became a host.

"Do you study Greek at your universities in America?" he asked.

Rodney heard the question, but he could not answer. He was too much aware of the other three people, trying to follow what they said. He nodded. Faures seemed gratified and surprised.

"All students?" he asked.

Rodney shook his head. He turned away and looked at Nina, Blackie, and Rouge. He knew without looking that Faures was relieved. He did not like to play host. He thought the whole thing was silly. Rodney heard the minute tiny shuffle of a page turned, the even slighter slash sound of a pencil underlining something. Faures was back at work.

Rodney gradually overheard the conversation and quite apart from that, as if it came from his bowels, he knew what disturbed him about Rouge: the man was a muscle of rage. He was in a convulsion which was years old, had been with him so long that it was now habitual, an accepted part of his personality. Everything about him was arced, tensed, drawn taut, deliberate, poised . . . and, most of all, rageful.

Alone in the center of the room, the Calvados making itself felt again, Rodney felt thoughts and impressions wisp by him. It was like being both fatigued and drunk simultaneously. He could make order out of nothing.

Then something firmed up: how much food does it take to nourish a human muscle like Rouge? A lot, came the ponderous answer. Rouge was like a fire which has become hotter than the combustion point of its fuel . . . food would fall into his gut like dry tinder into a steel furnace. Touch, glow, burn, instantly turn into carbon. Cheese, wine, bread, veal, roast beef, fruit . . . everything would fall into the glowing furnace, untasted and unnoticed . . . glow and crisp . . . pass away as flaky carbonized crap.

Sex? Not enough stuff left to fill those mysterious sacs and ducts. Whatever it was that went into sperm, the stuff that created the marvelous pressure, Rouge's body could not spare. Rodney's mind fuzzed a bit, could not make the simile clear. Forget it.

One thing that character did. For sure and for absolute and without fail: he raised the pressure in a room. Another thing: he was not for real. Someone took a chunk of flesh here, spread magic glue over it, stuck it to a leg, stuffed gray brains into an old whitened skull, jammed sausage guts into a viscera, got eyes from a panther or some kind of fast animal. All the parts were spread out and then more magic glue applied, allowed to get tacky, and then you whack the pieces together.

Rouge turned away from the group and spoke to Rodney.

For the first time Rodney saw both of Rouge's eyes. They were identical . . . the tiny crystal windows, no bigger than a fingertip, which allow a metallurgist to look into a white-hot crucible.

"We have a few questions," he said. Rodney was surprised by the gentleness of his voice. It had lost the flat quality. So someplace along the way they had glued on a device for a gentle voice. Also they had given him control: the glow in the eyes was masked and became more dull. "They are just formalities."

"It will not take long, Rodney," Nina said. "I know you are tired."

"I'll talk to him, Blush," Rouge said.

Rodney grinned. "Why do they call you Blush?" he asked. Nina shook her head.

"It was Pink at first, but I blush so they used that," Nina said. She did not put her face down. She stood there, reconciled to the blush. "It just changed into Blush as a nickname. One of those crazy things."

"It's a good name," Rodney said.

"How did you learn to speak French fluently?" Rouge asked.

Rodney stiffened, not because of the question, but because of the change in voice. Rouge's voice was now hard, tough, mechanical. The bits of sound were solid, came with velocity. They came like bullets and they were designed to come that way.

"In high school and the university," Rodney said.

"You do not have an English accent to your French," Rouge said. "By that I mean British."

"Of course not, I'm an American and our accent is different," Rodney said. Without changing position, he felt as if he were going into a crouch.

"If you are an American you are the first one I have ever met," Rouge said. "I have never heard an American accent."

"It is an American accent," Faures said suddenly, looking up from his book. "I've met many American scholars who came through France before the war. They all have the accent the Captain has."

Immediately he was back at work, the pen poised.

"Let me tell you at once the difficulty you present," Rouge said.

For a moment Rodney did not concentrate on the words. He was too stunned by Rouge's eyes. They *were* like transplanted eyes. They were not courteous; not like normal eyes. They went flatly from part to part of Rodney, occasionally looked directly at his face. But even when their eyes were level they did not *meet:* Rouge looked at something three inches behind the ridge of Rodney's nose.

"The Germans have been trying for months to penetrate our organization," Rouge went on. "It would be the easiest thing in the world for them to have a French-speaking German dressed in an Allied uniform parachute from the sky during an air raid. We would rescue him. Then the organization would be cracked."

"He doesn't have a German accent," Faures said again, his voice sharp and authoritative. He was impatient. "I guarantee he is not a German."

"Then maybe an American prisoner of war who has decided to work for the Germans," Rouge said simply, the voice suddenly soft again. He turned to Rodney and when

he spoke the voice shifted again to the gritty sound. The
words seemed formed by his teeth, to carry some of their
hard porcelainlike quality. "Quite possible, eh, Captain?"

"Quite," Rodney said.

He was puzzled. Rodney was not bothered by the questions
or even by Rouge's suspicions. They would be normal in any
Underground operation. But the man converted the room
into a chaos, his swaying tightened body seemed to shed a
deadly excess of energy. He controlled all of them and he
would control them if he were mute.

"Look, Rouge, it's all right to be cautious," Nina said softly.
"But would a real German agent kill German soldiers?"

Rouge swung around, glanced quickly at Nina. Nina told
him about the booby trap they had put on the German
weapons carrier. She also told him about the weapons they
had dumped into the ditch beside the carrier.

"Did you ask him to take the weapons or did he do it on his
own?" Rouge asked. His voice was very gentle.

"He did it on his own," Nina said uncertainly. "It was his
idea. I never thought of it."

"The Germans wouldn't hesitate a minute to sacrifice a
platoon of their men if they could crack the Underground,"
Rouge said. The other two looked at him and their response was affirmative. But it was not spoken. They wove
slightly, dropped their eyes, shrugged their shoulders.
"Maybe the weapons are a plant. We'll go and see. If they
have made an ambush we can conclude that the American is
lying. Right?"

Nina and the boy nodded agreement.

"Because no one, except me, saw him throw the guns and
ammunition in the ditch," Nina said.

"Right," Rouge said. He glanced again at Rodney and it
was a different look, appraising, calculating, no longer rageful. "We have to get him civilian clothes. Then we'll drop by

where the carrier was ambushed and if we recover the weapons without trouble we'll take him on to the next unit.
They'll pass him along toward the coast or wherever he is
supposed to go. I'll get the clothes."

When Rouge left the room Rodney was not the only one
who felt a sagging sense of decompression. Faures smiled at
him and shook his head, the way a man might shake his head
at mildly delinquent children out to perform pranks. Rodney,
absently returning Faures' smile, suddenly understood something about Rouge: those people he trusted were at ease with
him, felt peculiarly protected. Everyone else was an enemy.

"It is rather silly to call him Rouge," Blackie said, his big
intelligent eyes looking at Rodney. "We have all known him
for years. He is a Communist and that's why we call him
Rouge. He doesn't mind, but we all know his real name.
Funny, eh?" He put his finger alongside his nose and
laughed.

"Has Rouge been a Communist long?" Rodney asked.

He had never seen a Communist before. It seemed incredible to him. He had heard about them, but they always
existed as faraway unreal people. This might account for the
odd aura which Rouge gave off.

"Since he was born," Nina said and laughed. "His father
was a druggist, but it was only a sideline. He was really a
syndicalist."

"His father was insane," Faures said flatly, his voice piping
through the room. He was sitting very straight, a pencil in
his right hand, a blue one. "He took Sorel seriously and even
Sorel did not make that error."

"What is a syndicalist?" Rodney asked. Again he had the
tic of unreality which had gripped him periodically throughout the day; ever since he had turned over and seen the
earth below him. Breakfast in England, killing Germans in
the afternoon, now sitting in a cozy room half gone on a crazy

apple brandy and talking politics. It was a long, long day. He wished the tic would stop.

"They are the madmen of the Left," Faures said. "Their spiritual leader is a man named Sorel who wrote a book called *Reflections on Violence.* He argued that the proletariat should never make a reconciliation with the bourgeois class. Each should stay pure and refined and then they should do battle with one another. The proletariat could hold itself together only by continual acts of violence. That was its function."

"Rouge's father was always experimenting with bombs, grenades, and flares in the back of his shop," Nina said.

"He was a first-rate pharmacist," Faures said primly. "Well educated. Latin, Greek, firm understanding of physics and chemistry. But politically a madman."

"He finally developed a phosphorous flare which worked," Nina went on, ignoring her father. "It was nothing but a little lump of gray-colored material. It felt wet in the hands. The flares were carried in a neat metal box, about as big as a cigarette package. Each package would hold five of the phosphorous flares. Rouge's father was delighted. He went around town demonstrating how clever the flares were. They were perfectly safe as long as they were in the box and wet. Once taken out of the box they could be stuck against a house, placed under the seat in a railroad coach, tossed in a haystack, dropped in all the paper that gathers in a corner of the Paris Bourse after a busy day. Exactly one hour later the little lump would burst into flame. Water couldn't put it out. It just had to burn itself out."

"Very ingenious, but the instrument of a madman," Faures said.

"He dreamt of putting several of them in the Bourse and watching it go up in flames," Blackie said, his face wrinkled with laughter. "That was his ambition. He told it to everyone.

He was very simple. The police arrested him a week after he had perfected the phosphorous flare. They let him go very quickly; just making sure that he did not receive any more shipments of phosphorous."

For a moment the fire flared in the tiny grate and Rodney could see the expressions on the faces of the three people. Nina and the boy were smiling, remembering something antic. Faures seemed abstracted, shook his head. He stared at his pencil and back at the big open book. He started to work.

"What happened to his father?" Rodney asked.

Instantly Nina's face and that of the boy went smooth. Something like a tremor, as if they had tasted something unexpectedly bitter, broke the smoothness. The antic memory was gone.

"He was killed by the Communists," Nina said evenly. "He heard of some syndicalists in Catalonia during the Spanish Revolution. He got a supply of phosphorous, no one knows how, and announced he was going to fight with the Catalonian syndicalists. The Communists pulled him off the train at the first stop outside of Montauban. They tied his hands and legs together and then placed little balls of phosphorous under his armpits, inside his pants pockets and inside his shoes."

She stopped and no one spoke for a long moment.

"They must have ignited simultaneously," Blackie said, and he blurted the words out. "They burned so hot that the corpse weighed only fifty pounds when it was discovered. Flesh apparently catches fire if the temperature is high enough. I saw the corpse. It was like a black lump of tar." He hesitated, sought for the right word. "Shaped like a very little man."

Rodney was stone-sober. He felt very cold. The people in the room were, instantly, very strange and foreign. He only half believed what he was hearing, but he knew that it was

a whole truth. He licked his lips . . . and it was the first time
in his life he had made the gesture.

"And Rouge remained a Communist?" he asked.

"No. He *became* a Communist after that," Nina said. She
looked at him without deception, with no sense of shock.

Rodney glanced at Faures. He was busy with his book.

"He felt no anger at the Communists for killing his father?"
Rodney asked.

"He thought his father was a fool," Blackie said. "Too ideal-
istic. Not practical."

They stood without talking for a few minutes. It was, Rodney thought, like steers standing outside the stockyards in
Chicago. Dazed by the sun, thirsty, unaware of what awaited
them. Rodney made the first move. He sat down across from
Faures. Faures looked up and smiled his teacher's smile. He
went back to work. The pencil in his hand was red. He drew
firm straight lines in the book, dropped the pencil and picked
up a pen to make entries in his notebook.

Nina and Blackie sat down in the shadows across the room.
Rodney looked at his watch. It was 2100 hours. Back at the
airfield they would be coming out of the movie, going to the
snack bar. Some of the sack hounds would already be asleep.
He calculated quickly and figured that he was maybe 300
miles away, an hour and a half flight by B–24, from his bunk.
Deliberately, as if to fasten on something manageable, he
worked up a panic on what would happen to his personal
effects . . . Bronson, that efficient son-of-a-bitch, would
probably already have them bundled up and ready to be
sent back to the States. He should make some effort to stop
Bronson, prevent his parents from receiving the inevitable
telegram. He grinned, relaxed, leaned back in the chair and
dozed.

Later, he thought hazily, his consciousness clouded with
the slow unbelievable images that come before sleep. He

wanted fiercely to go to sleep. He drove himself to it. Later he would work out what had happened today. Sleep now.

The door opened with a soft scraping sound. Rodney's eyes snapped open. He knew it would be Rouge before the tamped-down glow of the eyes came around the door and swept the room.

5. *The Escape*

THEY left in ten minutes. Blackie had brought clothes for Rodney. Rodney took off his uniform, aware of only two things: gratitude that Nina looked aside, and remembering what the Intelligence had said about not taking off one's uniform. The pants were four inches too short for him, but the jacket was roomy. He was also handed a pair of rubber boots which came almost to his knees.

Faures looked at him with amusement.

"The children get ready for the drama, eh?" he asked. "Now the main actor is in uniform. The play commences."

With a clever antic gesture of his fingers he imitated little people sneaking and crawling, falling on one another, then all collapsing in laughter. He had a sense of humor, but it was wry and full of double meaning. No one in the room was really sure if Faures was mocking or merely easing their tension.

Rouge paid no attention to Faures. Nina shook her head at him. Blackie stared down at his big outsize hands. Rodney laughed. He walked over and shook hands with Faures.

"I will see you after the war is over," Rodney said.

"Said like a hero," Faures said. His face lighted, he stuck his hand in his shirt, stood up as if to make an oration. Nina cut in quickly.

"Not tonight, please, Papa," she said firmly. "We have a lot to do. Just remember. Say you have seen nothing."

"And that will be the simple truth, my dear," Faures said.

They turned to leave. Rouge held his hand out toward Rodney, the palm up, asking for the .45 in its holster and web belt.

"I will take that," Rouge said. It was not a request.

"Why?" Rodney asked.

"Because if you are caught with civilian clothes and a gun you will surely be killed," Rouge said patiently. "If you are caught only in civilian clothes you have a chance of survival. If I am caught, with or without a gun, I will be killed. Also," and his lips pulled back in the acquired grin, the sneer of civilization, "you are still not trustworthy. And further I am a better shot with a pistol than you. So . . . hand over."

Rodney handed him the gun and belt.

As they left Faures had already turned back to his manuscript, had the blue pen poised, his back hunched with excitement. There was no doubt it was excitement over the manuscript. He had really been bored by the whole evening.

In the yard back of the house Rouge paused. It was a very bright night, one night from full moon. There was a cold mist over the buildings. The moon was magnified by the mist, exaggerated into a huge cold blue loom which illuminated everything with a flat even light.

The shadows from the buildings were abrupt, distinct, black and sharp. The hard shadows gave a sense of unreality to the yard: everything was heavy and sharp.

The difference between sunlight and moonlight, Rodney thought, is that the moon does not show anything beneath shadows. Sunlight slips around, throws a bit of light into the shadows. It had never meant anything before. Now suddenly it seemed a remarkable difference. And important. He was not sure what was solid and what was fragile. Everything gave off an equal shadow.

"If we are separated, each person go to his home," Rouge said. "I will stay with the American. If we get the machine gun, Blackie will take it to Latourette's bicycle shop and put it in the big trough of used oil. Do not try to carry the ammunition. We will get that later."

"The gun is very heavy . . ." Rodney said, and Rouge cut in.

"Blackie is very strong," Rouge said. "No more comments unless they bear on the operation. If you cannot recognize a person, simply say 'hey, zig-zig' and the other will reply with the same expression. They sound the same in German or French. Anyone who does not reply with the phrase is an enemy."

They nodded in the strange blue light. Then Rouge leaped for the fence and the rest followed him. They moved quickly through the town and were at the edge of it in a few moments. The countryside was cut by countless hedges, small canals, ancient walls, little copses of trees. Rouge went at a fast walk, slipping easily through the obstacles, keeping to the high ground.

Once he paused. He was looking at the highway, glistening purple-black, a hundred yards away. Someone was riding a bicycle down the shiny surface, a perfect shadow, even to the whirring of the wheel spokes.

"It is the regular German patrol," Rouge said.

At once he was on the move again. In twenty minutes they
were in the trees above the highway where the weapons carrier had been exploded. The remains of the carrier were still
there, a black skeleton, canted to one side, a thing obviously
ruined . . . even if one were seeing it for the first time one
would know it was destroyed.

Rouge paused. He tensed, moved sideways for a different
angle. He came back sniffing and was more simple, more attuned to smells and dangers and the odd things which might
be threatening. It was reassuring.

"They should have hauled it away by now," Nina said to
Rouge. "They have the big tractors and repair trucks in the
caserne at Montauban. It is unlike them."

Rouge sniffed again, peered closely at the wreck. This was
the way an ape might sniff at a distant carcass, trying to see
if the original killer had left the scene.

"Not necessarily," Rouge said. "The heavy equipment was
moved today from the *caserne* to work on the train that
Group Zena blew up last night. We checked with one of the
civilian mechanics at the *caserne*."

"Wouldn't they leave a guard behind just to see that no
one makes off with the debris?" Blackie asked. "Batteries,
wiring, lead, clothes. Christ, Rouge, any of that stuff is worth
a fortune on the black market."

"Maybe," Rouge said. "Probably not. The bicycle patrol
goes by every so often. In any case we have to go look for the
machine gun. Otherwise there is no way to check out the
American."

He looked squarely at Rodney; that straight blank look that
Rodney had never seen before. In the moonlight, with Rouge
sniffing, with the air hardened in the weird light, Rodney felt
it was like two apes daring one another to make a dash across
some blue Pliocene landscape.

"Rouge, it is not fair," Nina said quickly. "He must make
an approach across an open field. If the Germans left a single

sentry behind he will surely fire on him. It will prove nothing about the American." She paused, noted that Rouge had not moved, was still taut. She looked at Rodney. "It is one of Rouge's eccentricities. He must test everything and everyone. It is what the Party taught him. But this time the test exceeds what is reasonable."

Rodney laughed. Rouge jerked around. His tension was so acute he seemed frangible. A touch and he would have either cracked into pieces or gone into some sort of logical and very dangerous action. Rodney felt control.

"I'll take Blackie down and find the gun for him," Rodney said, and he had to compress his lips to keep from laughing. "But you have to give me the gun in case they left a sentry. If they left an ambush through my cooperation, the .45 will not hold them back. They will kill me with or without the .45. It is the most inaccurate gun in the world. If it is only a sentry, then I need the .45."

Rouge took a single pace, halted, came to rest in his crouched stance. He listened to some distant experience, some faraway voice. Without a word he took off the belt and holster and gave them to Rodney.

He started to speak, but Rodney was already in motion. This moment was a part of the rest of the day. He did not understand it, but it was a play, an acting out of something, a doing of things which one had read about or seen on a film, but had not believed were real. He was back in the fine antic mood when he had shot down the platoon. Just a second, don't rush in and start believing that, Rodney said to himself. You didn't really shoot down any platoon. You *saw* yourself shoot at them, and they all jumped around and fell down like soldiers really die in the movies, but don't go believing you really did it.

By this time Rodney was fifty yards from Rouge and Nina. Blackie was running along behind him. He held the web belt loose in his hand, using it to balance himself as he ran

over the tilled field. He tried to hit each rubber boot
smartly on top of each tilled row, because he did not know
what was in the shadows between the rows. His strides were
gigantic and the boots sogged into the rows, wreaked their
damage, came out with a sucking noise which added to his
excitement, but which did nothing to slow him. He was racing; skimming the mud of France, rendered free of gravity
by the lunar light, weightless, and reminded of his body only
by the occasional soft grunts Blackie made when he pulled
out of the mud.

The skeleton of the wreck grew. Rodney was intoxicated by
the vision of the weapons carrier as a stricken and ant-ridden
dinosaur. The major joints of the beast were clearer . . .
the transmission and the black bone of the axle. The meat
was stripped off the beast. Now he could see finer detail.
There was the splinter of reflected light and it must be the
pieces of the brute's shattered eye. The moonlight caught a
battery and turned it into a black mass which shot out red
nerves that fluttered in the eerie light. Rodney did not
really really believe any of this.

He knew when he came upon the wreck it would have lost
its animal qualities, would not be skeletal, would be nothing
but the metallic carcass of a vehicle. But now, from
fifty yards, flying over rows and jumping puddles, it still
seemed like a downed brute, a huge and wounded animal
to be finally subdued.

The moon caught, in a quick slash of light, the oil from
the carrier. It looked like blood. Blood that was still fresh and
uncoagulated.

"The son-of-a-bitch is still breathing," Rodney yelled at
Blackie. "You ready for the coup de grâce?" He spoke in
English.

"Coup de grâce?" Blackie said, his voice gasping for air,
the only words he knew repeated like a fetish. He said it

repeatedly until they came to within twenty yards of the ditch alongside the road.

Then everything changed. A shadow stepped out from the carrier. It was black, human-shaped, medium height, and it swung a weapon which looked like a rifle toward them. The shadow yelled.

Everything fell into place. The motion picture was over. But Rodney heard uncertainty in the shadow's voice. He detected it so quickly that he did not even bother to slow his pace. They were no longer storming a wounded brute but the situation was not totally changed. The exaltation stayed in his voice. He roared something at the shadow . . . he did not know in what language or even what the words were. They were only words which were heavy with command, which ordered the shadow to stand still.

Rodney came to the edge of the ditch with a rush so strong that he almost went in. He hovered, arched over, then wavered back. He pointed an accusing finger at the shadow. He felt Blackie sprawl to a stop behind him.

"Where are the others?" Rodney screamed in a hard accusing voice, speaking French. "Everything must stop. Where is the officer?"

The rifle wavered, fanned between Rodney and Blackie and then drooped toward the ground. The shadow, still, undefined, and without features, was confused.

"They are where they are supposed to be," the shadow said in terrible French.

"Listen, one last chance for you, you miserable bastard," Rodney roared, speaking French as fast as he could. He knew his accent was not excellent, but the German shadow would have shot him already if his had been any better. Rodney roared again and his indignation was almost genuine. "Everything is changed. The Maquis are with us. If one of my men is touched you will be responsible for losing the loyalty of two hundred . . ." He paused and glanced at Blackie and directed the question at him. "Two or three hundred, eh?"

Before Blackie could answer, Rodney screamed again.

"Closer to four hundred Maquis who want to be with us are in the trees and the plan you have is off," Rodney said. "Canceled, over, done with. Understand? There is a new plan. Can you reach the officer?"

"No," the sentry said. "He is with the troops in the hills around us. If I fired my rifle he was to close in with the troops. That is the only order. I have no way to reach him. The first shot was to be the signal for action."

Rodney looked across the ditch at the shadow. He let the silence draw out. He stood motionless. The light, now that he was not running, started to yield detail. The sentry was a middle-aged man with a thick waist. Rodney waited.

"I am sorry," the sentry said sadly. "No one . . ."

Rodney leaped across the ditch. He walked to the sentry and took him up by the collar. The man was gelatin over an armature of bone. A lower lip trembled. The head lolled, asking to be shaken. The mouth uttered small words, so slight that they were inaudible, but Rodney caught their sense . . . they were all apologetic. It was like the whining of a distant figure in a nightmare.

Holding the man, Rodney knew that if he let go the man would collapse to the ground, the armature unable to bear the weight of the gelatin.

Rodney felt a quick pang of responsibility for the sentry. Also he must get him back into shape. Shape, he thought. Don't make jokes about shaping up now. He bent close to the man, as if to spare him from the humiliation of being overheard by Blackie.

He twisted the man until they were facing the moon. He took the rifle from the man's hand and tossed it across to Blackie who caught it neatly.

Rodney held up his free hand and brought his thumb and

forefinger together so that only a sliver of the moon showed between them.

"You have come that close to ruining the whole operation in this area," Rodney said quickly and very softly. "Maybe in all of France. You did not listen to what the officer said. You were frightened at being left alone and so you remembered only the signal . . . the rifle shot. Right?"

The man shuddered and the words stopped and then took form. His lips muttered "Yes."

"Were the choice mine, I would do this," Rodney said.

He snapped his thumb and forefinger closed. The moon vanished for the German. The man went rigid, his body jerked, his head spun on a loose neck toward Rodney and begged forgiveness.

"Straighten up. Be a German. I am trying to organize the Maquis to support us rather than slaughter us. The first German they see is you," Rodney said with contempt. He chuckled and hoped it was bitter. He let go of the sentry's collar. The man sagged, gathered himself, came weaving and uncertain to an erect position. His eyes glistened with tears of self-pity.

"I will do better," he said in a slow voice. Rodney knew the voice. It was the way a child replied to a teacher when the offense was beyond bluffing.

"First, get into the ditch and get the machine gun out which has been dumped there," Rodney said.

The man walked to the ditch, went precisely to the point where Rodney had dumped the gun. So, Rodney thought, they were as careful as Rouge thought. The man hesitated, looked down at his clothes, his spotless uniform.

"Oh shit, it is no use," Rodney said. "Some people never learn. Shoot him."

The man did not wait. He jumped obediently into the ditch. The water came to his waist. He hesitated a moment and saw that Blackie had swung the rifle toward him. He plunged under eagerly, like a child diving for shells, like someone going under a pleasant wave. He came up with the long mud-covered shape of the machine gun in his hands. Through the slime his lips were curved into a smile. He looked at Rodney, awaiting approval.

"Up and out," Rodney said. "Carry it up the hill."

The sentry struggled out of the ditch, water flowing from him in marvelous purple-white tendrils, his uniform glistening, transformed into a marshal's elegance by the moonlight and mud. He stood at the edge of the ditch, breathing heavily, but proud.

They walked slowly up the hillside, back to the copse where Nina and Rouge waited. Rodney knew that the German officer must be seeing what was happening, but would be as uncertain as the sentry. Through the officer's night glasses it would appear as blurred and ambiguous, lacking any real meaning. The officer would be waiting for the signal.

The sentry began to gasp halfway up the hill. Rodney uttered one word of reproach and the puffing stopped. The man breathed quick shallow and very quiet breaths.

Blackie walked beside Rodney. Once Rodney looked at him and saw a look of admiration. Blackie leaned toward Rodney and spoke in a whisper.

"The son-of-a-bitch is more scared than we," Blackie muttered. "He is even afraid to breathe hard."

Rodney laughed aloud. He glanced around the set. The primitive skeleton at the center, the stretch of flat highway, then the slowly rising hills, the evenly laid out fields, the trees at the tops of the hills. And behind the trees: Indians, bad guys. It was a bathed scene, drenched in unreal light, occupied by figures who were not people, threatened by guns which could not shoot, tilled and ordered by farmers who did not exist, run by an American who dropped from space. Nothing could possibly make this believable.

"Very droll," Rodney said to Blackie.

The sentry paused, his head cast back for orders. He took the time to gasp.

"We were not talking to you," Rodney said. "Continue."

They came to the copse and walked into it. Rodney ordered the sentry to put down the machine gun. He laid it down gently, stepped back and came to a snappy attention. Rodney waited. It was almost a minute before Rouge came out of the trees, Nina walking behind him.

"What happened?" he demanded.

Rodney knew he had to speak quickly, before the sentry understood the betrayal.

"The fools have laid an ambush around the valley," Rodney said. He was astonished at his skill. His language was ambiguous to the sentry, but meaningful to Rouge. "They left the sentry as a decoy, hoping to bring the Maquis out." He turned to the sentry. "How many men do you have in the hills around us?"

"Two companies," the sentry said. "The circle falls just beyond the first line of trees on each hill." He looked over his shoulder. "They are probably only a hundred yards behind us now."

Rodney could see Rouge tighten, respond to the signals, go protective.

"Why did they let you bring the gun up the hill?" Rouge asked. "Why didn't they shoot you?"

"He bluffed them, that's why," Blackie said and then hesitated. There was no way to go but ahead. He looked at the sentry and shifted his gun so it bore on the puffing and slightly dazed man. "They think that the American is leading a group of Maquis who want to surrender; to work with the Germans."

Rouge was caught. The information and the trees and the surrounding troops and the servile sentry and the unbelievable ease with which the American had taken the gun were too much. He smelled trouble in the air. He did not panic. This was what he had been trained for, what he wanted, what he steeled himself for. In the strange light Rouge grinned, bobbed his head, showed not the slightest sense of alarm. He was happy, Rodney guessed, in the way the bull-fighter is or the deep-sea diver or the fighter pilot . . . just before they must do what they wanted to do.

The sentry knew he had been bluffed. He groaned. On his tight clerk's face was a look of agony and of torment that stretched his face into a cartoon. The tears started again. But this time the armature and the gelatin firmed up simultaneously.

Looking straight ahead, his eyes wet marbles in his head, his lips quivering, the sentry started to run. He passed into a patch of pure unobscured moonlight and was no longer lustrous. The sheen on his uniform was dried mud.

"Shoot," Rouge said softly.

Blackie made the mistake. He obeyed Rouge.

In the noise of Rouge's voice Rodney was not heard. He yelled for Blackie not to shoot. But Blackie shot.

The rifle streaked out a small jet of flame. A pod of sound, hard as clay, hit their ears. The sentry bucked forward, seemed to be propelled by the shot. Dried mud sprayed off his back in a bizarre design which held for a few moments. He kept moving. The rifle blazed maybe three more times and the sentry slumped down the hill . . . took almost a hundred feet to collapse.

"All right, good buddy, you just tore it," Rodney said to Rouge. "A rifle shot was the signal for the ambush to move in. So now they are moving in. If you had waited a minute you might have learned something, but you had to go shoot from the hip."

Already from behind them was the rustling of bushes, the soft tread of feet, the sound of the circle closing. They all realized that they had been allowed to pass through the cir-

cle. Now they had to see how they would do against the closing ambush.

"We'll fight our way out," Rouge said.

Rodney marveled at his certitude.

"Follow me and don't shoot unless I do," Rouge said.

He turned, ready to go. Blackie fell in behind him. Nina
hesitated and looked at Rodney.

Rodney studied her skin, delicate and shy in the moonlight. Her face was shifting, altering as the thin clouds
passed over the moon.

"You don't have a gun so you can't shoot in any case,"
Rodney said.

He was pleading.

"I know," Nina said. In the incredible moonlight she licked
her lips, shivered, stared about her; images of death passed
across her face. "But Rouge is the leader. We took an oath.
A kind of allegiance."

The closing of the circle was more audible. The bushes
shook. Voices checked with one another. There was the quiet
oiled click of gun slides retracted; the unmistakable harshness of a noncom's voice giving an angry order. There was a
universal order, Rodney thought, some things everyone understood . . . guns cocked, noncom's roaring orders.

Rodney remembered the strange shadows, their solid
opaqueness.

"Just crouch in the shadow of a tree," he said in a low
urgent voice. "They won't be able to see you. Only if you're
moving can they see you."

Nina glanced at the shadow of one of the big trees. It was
convincing. She turned toward Rouge. He was moving
boldly in the open spaces, clearly visible.

"He wants to be caught or shot," Rodney said. "You don't."

"I have to go with him," Nina said. She turned and ran
after Rouge.

Rodney walked to the closest shadow, crouched against

the tree. When the search line got close he would put his head down. He would look like a rock or the stump of an old tree.

Rouge, with Nina and Blackie behind him, started to run down an aisle of trees. Their movements caught moonlight, gave them a black definition. They were figures running toward destruction. They knew it and their bodies twitched and jerked, fought against the slug which was meant for them. They seemed, abruptly, to be part of another world, to be far away and detached from Rodney. They shrank rapidly in size, were no larger than puppets.

A voice sang out, called to them to stop. Rouge hesitated, glanced in the direction of the voice. He raised a matchstick arm and flame shot from the end of it. Instantly a tree close to them ripped into a torrent of flashes. The sound of burp guns came to Rodney's ears. Blackie raised his captured rifle, but the bullets caught him before he could fire. They punched him backward, each slug making his distant and diminished body jerk. He dropped his rifle and Rodney sensed that he would like to fall, but was propped up by the unending impact of the bullets. Although leaning forward he was pushed farther backward and then slowly, by a fit of jerks, he lowered himself to the ground. The last few feet were so graceful and boneless, done so effortlessly, Rodney knew he was dead.

Silence flowed back over the forest like a physical presence. It pushed against the eardrums with a snap. Rouge and Nina had their hands in the air. Four soldiers walked toward them, burp guns at their hips.

Five minutes later they marched by the shadow in which Rodney was sitting. Four soldiers were carrying Blackie's big body. Another group of soldiers were talking behind Rouge and Nina. The Germans were laughing; delighted at finding a girl Maqui. They were no longer searching and Rodney did not bother to lower his face as they filed past.

Nina was looking straight ahead. Her face was flat with concentration. She had the look of a person remembering the past and curious about the future. Rouge was a new man. He walked like a man moving toward something he had known would happen eventually. There was almost a lilt in his walk.

Rodney waited in the shadow for an hour. Then he walked slowly back to Montauban and to the Faures house, retracing the route they had taken. The back door was locked and Rodney had to knock several minutes before there was a response.

Faures finally opened the door. He had the blue pen in his hand. He listened quietly as Rodney told him what had happened.

"The boy is really dead?" he asked when Rodney was through.

"He was dripping when they carried him past me," Rodney said.

Faures shook his head in disbelief.

"It was not all a child's game after all," he said finally. He undid the top of the old-fashioned pen, screwed it over the nib. He slipped the pen into the pocket of his alpaca jacket. When he spoke his voice was decisive.

"They will come here very soon," Faures said. "I know only one other member of their group. I will go to him. You had better wait in the yard in case they come while I am away. If the Germans do come, make for the copse where you went tonight. It will not occur to them to return there."

One hour later Faures returned and brought with him a young, rather stout man who was a schoolteacher. He took Rodney and at once started to walk south. Two days later Rodney had reached the coast. A month later he was in England. Before he flew again the war was over.

6. The Delicacy
of Charity

IN THE last weeks of 1944 three things happened to Rodney. First, he was returned to the States as a war hero. Secondly, he went back to Yale to finish his A.B. degree. Thirdly, he married Charity Britten.

Of these three things being a war hero was the most interesting. He was carefully escorted from factory to public square to high school auditorium by a chain of public information officers who all looked the same . . . bright-eyed, intelligence showing in their faces, a bit of fat around their waists, a way of glancing away from him as they talked.

"Always begin by saying that public speaking scares you more than flying your bomber over Nazi Europe," the first one said and so did all the others.

"It doesn't," Rodney said. "I've never spoken publicly, but I'm not afraid of it. It can't kill you. Flying over Europe can."

The officer looked pained.

"I know that, Captain," he said. "But if you don't say it they get to thinking maybe you're a slacker, that you enjoy the speaking tour more than the flying."

"They're right," Rodney replied. "Nothing I can think of scares me more than flying. I haven't tried everything, but of the things I *have* tried it's the worst. I should not say that in my talk, I guess."

The officer brightened. He reassured Rodney that he

would do all right. He asked him again to open with the statement about being frightened of public speaking.

Rodney did and he was astounded. The audience, whether they were factory workers or Red Cross workers or college students or Rotarians, always made a quiet lowing sound of appreciation as he said he was more frightened of them than of bombing runs. Rodney could not understand what their lowing meant. Could they really believe their blank identical faces, their smiling faces, were as dangerous as that mass of blinking lights along the valleys of Germany and France? Those blinking stuttering lights meant that AA batteries were firing at his plane. Did they think that their tinkling laughter was as scary as the chatter of the machine guns in the waist of the bomber?

Once he almost told them the truth. Someone raised a hand and asked what he felt when the German fighters started for his formation.

That they would pick the plane in front of or behind me, he almost said. But he didn't.

"I just thought about the importance of getting through to the target," he said. The audience burst into applause.

Occasionally he longed to be back on the tour. He knew he had learned something from the way the people responded, their slack-jawed attention as he spoke, their rigid attention as the National Anthem was played. He was not certain what he had learned, but he knew that these people were different from the three people he had met in Montauban. Those three, Rouge, Blackie, and Nina, were, each of them, someone. Here the crowds seemed to be a *somebody;* a somebody with many faces and voices which all responded in identical ways.

The time at Yale was pleasant, but not memorable. The Air Corps arranged for him to be assigned to a unit located in New Haven. While talking to a personnel officer he had indicated he would like to finish the year of college he had

not completed. The officer had been instantly sympathetic.
Being an old Yale man he had assured Rodney that Yale was
the proper place to go. Rodney had nodded.

He had married Charity largely because his family approved of her and because he had met her a few times before.
He knew very little about her. Nor did anyone else.

Charity's parents, from the day she was born, were astounded. They were a stout, ham-handed, puffing, shiny-
skinned pair who looked oddly like brother and sister. Their
blue china-doll eyes flickered out of the suetlike faces and
were innocent, shrewd, calculating. For years they had only
one interest in life and that was chocolate making. After
Charity was born they had another: the delicacy of their
child.

Charity's parents were German-Swiss and when they came
to Los Angeles from Lausanne her father changed his name
from Hans Herstenburg to Henry Britten. They much admired New England and its people although they had seen
neither. They took the name Britten because they thought it
was a good New England name. They very much wanted to
forget their Swiss background and although they could never
lose their heavy figures, their sausagelike fingers, their
shortness of breath, they could change their name.

Charity was born to the name. Her parents had hoped to
invoke New England angularity, sparseness, leanness by the
use of the name. And they succeeded with Charity. They
defeated the genetic theory. As a child Charity was tall,
rather lean with very beautiful blond hair, long calm hands
and deep-blue eyes. The Brittens were astounded by the
child. They did not dare touch her themselves. They hired a
very experienced English nanny who had raised "English
aristocrats," or so her papers said. The Brittens devoted themselves passionately to their chocolate business. When they
came home they had audiences with their incredible child.
Their business prospered.

The cheap candy business was brisk in Los Angeles in 1912 when the Brittens first arrived. The town was growing fast and most of the new citizens came from Iowa, Arkansas, Kansas and Oklahoma and they were used to heavy fudge, divinity, big tugs of saltwater taffy, Hershey bars and blocks of heavy-sweet chocolate.

The candymakers of Los Angeles responded by making a gross, sweet, bulky kind of candy and selling the product in brown manila bags for twenty cents a pound.

Everywhere, on the Long Beach boardwalks, the school-yards, the beaches, the cottages of Norwalk, the circus tents, the big bowl of the Coliseum, the promenades through the sunburnt undeveloped subdivisions, the state picnics, along Wilshire and Western and Century boulevards, in saloons, in waffle shops, under the orange trees and beneath the bright stars, everyone ate from the brown bags. Each bag was almost identical in its contents: to choose from one was to choose from all. The odor of candy was everywhere. Its presence was made known by sticky bags hanging improbably from telephone poles where glutted children had stuck them, and by the gluey quality of the straps in the streetcars.

The Brittens, however, were determined not to be in the cheap candy business. They had higher ambitions. No one had tried to make the kind of fragile, delicate, hand-dipped chocolates that were so famous in Lausanne. However, the same thing that led Henry Britten to change his name also gave him a special sensitivity to the moods of people. He sensed, with his short fat fingers or somewhere behind his blue round eyes, that the great sprawling mass of Los Angeles was almost ready for "society." He sensed that people would not long stay so indiscriminate and chaotic; that some few would be on top and the rest would have to be below.

Henry Britten figured, and correctly, that a town which lacked standards would soon seek for them. Shrewdly, with a sort of muted sure instinct, he knew that candy could be part of this. He concentrated wholly on elegant candies. He aimed at the few people who would be willing to pay eighty cents or a dollar a pound for candy which was unmistakably expensive, distinctive and aristocratic.

He rented a shop on West Adams, just at the edge of the big Victorian houses, hired two Negro helpers and with the help of his wife began business. First, he made a specialty of very thin mints. The ingredients were the same as those used in the cheapest mints at any corner shop. But these mints were rolled very, very thin. Then they were dipped in bitter chocolate and finished with a swirled B on the center of each mint. Laid out on the marble tables in his shop, the mints had the elegance of a very thin watch. The black chocolate had a velvet glossiness; a thinness that could only come from handwork. They looked truly expensive. When they had hardened each one was slipped into individual waxed paper slips which were stamped in gold lettering with the letter B. Twenty of these were then put in a small box and tied with a ribbon. They sold for sixty cents.

The marketing was, of course, most important. Henry Britten very carefully scrutinized the social columns of the papers, studied the backgrounds of people who were emerging into prominence, watched the lists of people who were admitted to various clubs. He knew it was important that the mints be used first by people who were really powerful and upper class; the true leaders of the new aristocracy. He put the mints in the homes of such people by a variety of means. In some cases he bribed the butlers; in one case he simply mailed a box of the mints to the wife of a lawyer with a very ambiguous note. It might have come from an admirer. A number of times he sent a trial box of mints with a personal note saying very frankly that this was a luxury product and he wanted to sell it only to a small number of people.

These boxes went only to the very new rich. With the brutal

sensitivity which comes only from long immersion in a class society, Henry Britten knew that such people were desperately uncertain as to what was proper. He undertook to tell them.

Later, yacht brokers and foreign car dealers would cater to more expensive and developed tastes. But in a society where sweetness was a passion, where gluttony was the order and where the most talked of organ of the body was the stomach, Henry Britten knew what had to be done.

In a very few years, indeed, Henry Britten knew more about society and the rise and fall of the toiling social aristocracy of Los Angeles than anyone else in the city. He knew, even before the person knew, when someone would be tapped for admission to the new aristocracy of Los Angeles. Sometimes he knew even before the people who did the tapping knew. Out of raw economic desire he had acquired an exquisite and overdeveloped social sense.

By the time Charity was born the Britten Candy Company was well established and prospering. The mints had been augmented by New Orleans pralines; a group of figures made of marzipan; boxes of exquisite small chocolates, each half the size of regular chocolates. Only a very small part of his expenses went for the ingredients of candy; much more was spent on expensive wrappings, a delivery system, gathering social intelligence and making sure that a few times a year (never more than four times) the society columns mentioned that "Miss Cynthia Brown, daughter of Cecil and Roberta Brown, last night passed tiny Britten chocolates at her house to announce her engagement to Mr. Lloyd Sharp of Pasadena."

These newspaper announcements, he often told his wife, were the trickiest part. If they appeared too often, or if the wrong names were mentioned, it could be fatal. The names must be perfect, the situation right, the reference to Britten

chocolates must not be blatant. And the society reporter must
be paid off in so subtle and careful a way that she hardly
knew she had been paid off.

The Britten enterprises were based on supplying elegance,
petiteness, delicacy to a place that hungered for it. When
their daughter turned out to have these qualities, candymaking and heredity seemed to the Brittens to be mystically
linked. Their child had inherited the qualities of their candy
and they felt close to revelation, to some secret insight. They
were at first only aware that Charity had none of the
chubby, gurgling, friendliness of Swiss babies; that she
seemed almost not to be flesh of their flesh. She was thin,
graceful, calm. There was a quality of quality about her. It
showed in the way her rich hair could be pressed into any sort
of wave; the way her eyelids were blue-veined and translu-
cent; the way her voice rose easily with assurance and a
rather unusual accent; the way she waited easily for things to
come to her so that other children were suddenly shamed by
their own greed and grasp.

When the time arrived for Charity to go to school it came
to the Brittens that they had a problem. The knowledge came
with a sort of cold ferocity. Charity deserved, and they
wanted her to have, the highest social status possible. She
was, clearly, one of nature's aristocrats. They sought status
for her not to glorify themselves, but because she deserved it.
One had only to look at her. How many times in Magnin's
and Robinson's had the salesladies turned to Charity, asking
her what she wanted, assuming that her mother was actually
a nanny? And her mother had been pleased by this.

Her parents did not want to elevate themselves. They
knew, however, that the savage law of social elevation
hinged largely on what the parents were considered to be.
They must lift themselves high before Charity could be
lifted high.

One thing made it impossible: a candymaker was not socially desirable. In fact he was quite impossible. No one knew this better than Henry Britten. He knew that real estate, oil and stocks were the correct ways in which to make money. Cattle, agriculture and the movies were next. A man could, lately, even become socially distinguished if he had made his money on contracting or in the stockyards behind Union Station. But he could not break through if he was a candymaker . . . there was no doubt of that.

Britten, who had read Goethe as a boy, knew exactly what had happened. The best knowledge one has, one's greatest advantage, is also his weakest point.

If he had not needed to learn of social distinctions and discriminations to advance his economic life he would not even have known that there was a "society" in Los Angeles. He would have remained in blissful ignorance of the clean-limbed boys and girls, the elegant homes, the parties, the beach houses and the complex rules of the game. But now he knew all of this. And the thing he knew most surely was that the daughter of a candymaker could not become "society." Although he and his wife had a secret contempt for the socialites and used to mutter, in German, beer hall jokes about them, they now wanted Charity elevated.

Charity sensed from the start what had happened; had glimpsed something of the situation. She went to St. Anne's School on Pico Boulevard and although she knew that it was the school for the children of the best families she knew that she was not one of the best. She sat in class, her long beautiful hands laid palm down on the desk, the nails on her fingers naturally pink, her hair naturally wavy and kept very very clean. She did not smile frequently. Smiling was social currency. One used it carefully. She played with the other girls, took Latin with them, learned to hem and stitch, went to dancing class . . . but she never made a mistake. She never imagined they were on equal footing. She knew she was below them somehow. When one of the other girls made a mistake and tried to invite Charity to visit for a weekend, Charity would smile gracefully, pause as if considering, and then shake her head.

The lumpish daughters of Iowa farmers who had sunk oil wells at Seal Beach stared at Charity the first day of school. The sunburned impish children of financiers who owned two hundred acres of boom land walked carefully around Charity for the first week of class. In a cool, detached, quite ineffable way she was the embodiment of what they hoped to be . . . the composite, fragile, impressionistic amalgam of what they thought life and New York fashion magazines and Paris were about.

The girls learned quickly about Charity. In a week they knew she was the daughter of a candymaker and had begun to snub her. In four weeks they were shyly, with longing, trying to make friends with her . . . attracted by the coolness, the poise. In eight weeks they hated her because the coolness could not be broken; she was utterly lacking in brittleness; was opaque and quite impenetrable. Then they would come drifting back, gazing at the cool image, the fine bones, the face that was beautiful in an adult way. Attracted and repulsed, they performed a vicious, filmy, adolescent dance around her.

Long before their parents accepted the adult Brittens as equals, Charity was adored by her classmates. They were willing to break the unwritten rules, but Charity would not permit it. She looked at them calmly, did her work with a disconcerting ease, never gossiped.

The nuns at St. Anne's were aware of what happened, but they did not interfere. They kept their apple-bright faces straight ahead, their habits hissed as they bustled down the corridors . . . they were concerned with souls and education. They were not concerned with social standing or economics. Besides they felt ambiguous toward Charity. When they discussed religion with her she managed to convey that they were very inadequate and unconvincing. She listened attentively, but without fear. She nodded her head at times and the sisters were not quite sure what that meant. She spoke very little. And she smiled less.

For five years events at St. Anne's unfolded quite normally. As Los Angeles real estate tracts pushed out La Brea and into the Baldwin Hills and down Firestone Boulevard and into the great dunes above Hermosa Beach, a number of daughters of realtors joined the student body. There was a period when Standard Oil and Shell Oil and Union Oil, the big corporate giants, went hard after oil leases to assure their supplies and quietly, with hardly a murmur, the daughters of several of the retired independent oil men were withdrawn and started to go to other private schools or to Hollywood High. Their fathers were still wealthy, but it was not productive wealth.

The kind of ordered, intricate and complex social hierarchy that took generations to hammer out in Boston and London and Paris was here evolved very easily in ten years. Henry Britten told his wife that in a generation inherited wealth would be fashionable. Right now it was almost wicked. Los Angeles immigrants came from the Bible Belt. They were moral. They believed in work.

The appearance at St. Anne's of the daughters of rich vice-presidents of large oil companies automatically and quite mysteriously lowered the position of the oil speculation men. Their daughters were not forced out nor did the parents openly discuss the matter . . . they simply withdrew their daughters from the school. Society arose and it had form and substance. Positions were assigned. A new car dealer was higher than a bank vice-president. A Hollywood star was very high as long as he glowed brilliantly, but at the first sign of tarnishing he fell more quickly than any meteorite. A Jew was nothing. A rich famous Jew was somebody, but he was not admitted to the country clubs and athletic clubs and

luncheon clubs that sprang up. A doctor who specialized in
diseases of the sigmoid colon or the thoracic cavity was well
regarded as a social object; general practitioners and obste-
tricians were common as dust. But in a town dominated by
ex-farmers land was the most dignified, responsible and
honorable way to high status.

Henry Britten began to invest his money in land. Not
"spec" land, but good solid orange groves, long sweeps of
empty desert where the smart ones knew towns would spring
up, land with the possibility of oil underneath it, land which
faced on the dazzling blue water of the Pacific.

Then at the end of the fifth year Henry Britten took his
books to an accountant. He had speculated carefully and
cautiously. His books were intricate, complex and very confused. He dumped them in the accountant's office and came
back in ten days. The accountant had drawn up a summary
that was reproduced on a single piece of paper. Britten picked
it up and ran his little bright eyes over it.

"You are sure that this is perfectly correct?" Britten asked.
His jaw quivered slightly, a gobbet of saliva worked in one
corner of his mouth. He licked strongly at it with his tongue.

"It is correct, sir," the accountant said. He stood straight,
almost at attention.

"This means that my main income is not now from candymaking but from the owning of land," Henry Britten said.
"And the total amount of my assets is one million and twenty
thousand dollars."

"Correct, sir," the accountant said.

"I am no longer a candymaker," Britten said. His jaw no
longer quivered. "I am a landowner who has an interest in
candymaking."

"Yes, sir," the accountant said ringingly.

Henry Britten's mind was working furiously, although his
face was calm. Old attitudes were revalued, discarded,
shaken up, dusted off, twisted into new shapes. His life,

broken now into manageable units, flashed through his mind as a tape runs through a computer. In a matter of minutes a decision was made. Henry Britten turned and left the accountant's office.

Henry had come to the accountant's office in a black alpaca coat which he usually wore to work. He also wore a derby hat and in his dotted tie there was a tiny diamond chip pin. He looked like a slightly vulgar shopkeeper . . . and in his mind, in his deepest coil of insight, he knew exactly how he looked. And he hated what he saw. He knew most painfully how vulgar the derby looked, how gross was the little diamond stickpin. But this was what a shopkeeper, a candymaker, wore. He literally could not have worn anything else . . . although he knew precisely what would be in the most impeccable taste.

When he left the accountant's office Henry walked to Oviatt and Company, Clothiers. He took off the alpaca coat and the thick tweed pants and the heavy brogue shoes. He asked for smooth gabardine suiting and sharkskin and exquisite worsted flannel. All in dark colors, all modestly tailored, all very expensive. He slipped into shirts made of broadcloth so fine that it sang when rubbed between his fingers.

His instinct for quality was impeccable. He looked sharply at the clerk.

"There is something better than this, surely," he said. His voice was not scolding; it was superior. "Maybe with more silk in it."

"Yes, sir, there is. It is very expensive," the clerk said.

Henry said nothing. He merely looked at the clerk; knowing full well that people who assured clerks they could afford expensive things were nouveaux. An hour before, Henry Britten would have coughed, said something in explanation, asked the price. Now he stared flatly. He had authority. He and the clerk were no longer in the same business.

Even more sure than his instinct for quality in cloth, shoes, suits, linens was Henry's incredible impulse for how an upper

class person should act. It was as if his eyes, always looking
up from below with intensity and shrewdness, had seen more
than the eyes of people who walked on the higher level. He
had learned, with the precocity of the desperate, what a gen-
tleman was. He knew, somehow, by some overdeveloped and
exquisite sense, how to stand in a crowd of people on a corner, merely raise his finger and stop a cab. The cabdriver
would savagely order other people away from the cab and
tip his hat when Henry stepped in.

Henry also knew how to deal with his peers. Almost at once
the oil drillers, the real estate men, the department store owners, the few old Mexican families that still had money, the
politicians knew that Henry's status had changed. In a few
months he was invited to join the Jonathan Club, the Petro-
leum Club and the University Club. But so sensitive was
Henry to social innuendos, so much a part of his nerves and
viscera and eyeballs had the social estimate become, that he
unhesitatingly refused membership in these clubs. And thus
he assured himself membership in the San Francisco Bohemian Club which was, without doubt, the socially dominant
club of the Pacific Coast. Had he joined the others the directors of the Bohemian Club, without even knowing why,
would have rejected Henry for membership. That he had
had the chance and rejected it at once made him a serious
contender for the Bohemian Club.

Charity's mother did not adapt as quickly to the changed
situation as did Henry. She had not known, as Henry had
known all along, that when one stumbled out onto the pla-
teau of great wealth certain things at once became more relaxed and fluid. She had thought, for example, that manners
would be high, formal and elegant. She found that manners
were more careless and that slight vulgarities were accepted
as the sign of good breeding and aristocratic background.
With astonishment she found that she could dress more simply than she had before . . . richer material, but more

simply cut. Indeed, Mrs. Britten realized with a shock that society was a sort of pyramid with a very narrow apex and a huge base . . . and the lower one was on the pyramid, the heavier the weight of social class above them, the more proper, formal, ritualistic and inhibited they must act. The people at the very bottom of the pyramid, the bums, drunkards, whores, wastrels, migrant laborers, Mexicans and Jews were the utterly unfree . . . because no one cared what they did, because their actions were valueless, they must act more and more rigorously. This, actually, was the greatest thing to happen to Mrs. Britten when she became wealthy. She became a social philosopher and discovered for the first time why the huge, chaotic, tumbling, roaring, vulgar society held together . . . because the people who had the least to lose were the most restrained and timid in action. The bourgeois shopkeeping part of her had always feared the masses, was fearful that they possessed a great capacity for violence and upheaval. Now, viewing from above, she saw how docile and manageable were the lower classes. It eased something inside her.

Mrs. Britten, once she understood, became a very successful society woman. She deepened her accent and told slightly risqué stories of European nobility. She scorned the health foods and the physical culture fads of Los Angeles. She ate rich French dishes and her dinner parties were fabled in a town which revered thick steak and stuffed potatoes. She was, in short, a character. A character dressed in Paris originals.

In Charity's pure white skin, behind her blue eyes, at the roots of the long blond strands of hair, in the crescents of her smooth fingernails . . . in all of these primitive surface places . . . Charity had extra sensitivities. She knew their social position had changed the very day it happened. She did not translate it into words, but she knew they were not only wealthy, but they were respectably wealthy. The Brittens now had prestige and wealth, but they also had the most valuable of social assets: position. Charity knew even more surely than her parents what that position was. It was very high.

Henry prepared for Charity's debut into the upper society of Los Angeles very carefully. His own peers he could handle easily; indeed almost too easily. He was superb. But Charity, he well knew, must be carefully engineered into the right social setting.

Children's parties among the very rich of Los Angeles tended to be very much of a pattern during this time. The wealthy fathers tried to get Shirley Temple or Freddie Bartholomew to attend the party; a Hollywood comedian or two was either paid or pressured into giving a performance; a professional magician was hired; elaborate molds of ice cream and enormous elegant cakes were served; presents were given to every child . . . stuffed animals, wristwatches, charm bracelets of pure gold. A number of hired Cadillacs were sent after the children and, after the party, delivered them home. It was, with the exception of alcohol and scatological jokes, a diminutive replica of adult parties.

Henry Britten broke the tradition most neatly and beautifully. Each of the girls at St. Anne's received a simple handwritten note from Mrs. Britten inviting her to the party at the new Britten mansion in Bel Air. Later, when the party was over, a number of the mothers picked up the invitation again and realized the paper was heavy and stiff, streaked through with tiny red veins of some dissolved metal. Quietly they realized that it was the most expensive paper they had ever handled. As they phoned back and forth they discovered that the paper could not be purchased in Los Angeles. It had been imported from Italy. At the bottom of the invitation was a single line "To meet a guest of Miss Britten." Before, all of the children's parties had been for birthdays.

The children were driven to the Britten home by their own

parents or chauffeurs. When they arrived they found a small, poised girl standing beside Charity at the door. The parents were nowhere to be seen. Charity soberly and calmly introduced each of the girls to her guest. It was only after the girls, suddenly impressed with the solemnity and shaking of hands, had taken a few steps past the door that they realized that the little plain dark girl had been introduced as "Lady Rose Penthorn of the Hebrides." They realized dumbly, with astonishment, with a bursting of magic bubbles in their blood, that the dark little girl was titled, a real aristocrat . . . a British aristocrat. The girls were paralyzed with respect and enchantment.

Somehow, through his innumerable connections, Henry Britten had arranged to have the youngest daughter of a visiting Scotsman who was titled, but impoverished, attend the party. Lady Rose's parents were staying at the Britten beach house at Malibu and were marvelously drunk on exquisite Rhine wines which they loved, but could not afford in Scotland.

The girls watched, standing in clots inside the huge ballroom, as Charity and Lady Rose walked away from the door. A butler who had been invisible until that moment quietly closed the door. Charity took her guest to the middle of the room. Lady Rose walked with a languid, unbrittle, perfect ease . . . as if she had never known strain or doubt. She smiled slightly.

"I thought you might like to hear Lady Rose read a few selections from her collection of A. A. Milne's original manuscripts," Charity said. "If you will be seated, she will give us a few selections."

The butler appeared again with a small table in one hand and a thick leather box in the other. He put the table in front of Lady Rose and opened the leather box. Lady Rose took out a red folder, undid some strings and picked up some pages covered with handwriting:

*In Which Christopher Robin Leads an Expedition to the
North Pole—
One fine day Pooh had stumped up to the top of the Forest
to see if his friend Christopher Robin was interested in Bears
at all. At breakfast that morning (a simple meal of marma-
lade spread lightly over a honeycomb or two) he had suddenly thought of a new song.*

She read the story easily and quickly and her strange Scots
accent, the first the St. Anne girls had ever heard, gave the
familiar story a subtle luster. Also the fact that the pages she
held in her hands were the originals of the stories seemed
to make them somehow more exciting, almost as if the author
were in the room. The St. Anne girls stared with eyes that
were, for once, unprotected, open, perfectly accessible. They
clapped politely when the reading was over.

Lady Rose handed the folder and box back to the butler.
He picked up the table and the children were again by themselves. Lady Rose curtsied to the girls and then stood beside
Charity with her hands folded together, quite completely
poised.

Charity talked for a few moments with Lady Rose and although the St. Anne girls usually talked hard and fast, that
afternoon they stood quietly, watching the two girls talk.
After perhaps ten minutes Charity turned and lifted her
voice. None of the girls were talking so they all heard easily
what she said.

"I thought it might be entertaining to see one of those duels
that German fraternities have," Charity said. "As you know
these are affairs of honor and the scars on a boy's face are
really a mark of his acceptance into a worthwhile fraternity.
It is a very old and precious tradition. Fortunately we have
had as guests for the last few days Baron von Bertlich and
Herr Erich Strutt. They are both members of one of the best
Heidelberg fraternities and consented to put on a practice
session which, they say, is very much like a real duel."

Charity motioned for the girls to take their chairs again. She walked to a door, opened it and ushered in two boys, both around twenty years old. Baron von Bertlich was the younger and the girls of St. Anne's gulped when they saw him. The Baron had a beautifully molded, angular and very set face . . . except for one thing. A dueling scar had cut away a tiny triangle of his upper lip and showed exactly one well-formed and very white tooth. It had very much the attraction that a beauty mark has on a woman. The tiny blemish, the shard of white tooth, the diminutive tragedy, seemed to emphasize the beauty of the rest of Baron von Bertlich's young face. Herr Strutt was a tall lean boy who had nothing of the confidence of the Baron, but he was very strong. One could tell by the way he carried sabers easily in his hand. The boys were wearing the traditional padded fencing uniforms and each carried a mask under his arm.

The Baron spoke very rapidly, explaining the ritual of the duel. His German accent was superb. The girls felt as if they were hearing a real and authentic and younger Erich von Stroheim. His voice was low and powerful; and he was not the least embarrassed by the accent. When he was finished he smiled, then the smile vanished from his face, the lips grew tight and the exposed tooth became almost invisible as the lips compressed. The two faced each other at a fixed distance, saluted with their sabers, then snapped the masks down over their heads. The two men acquired a bug-headed, insectlike look the moment the masks were down. One of the girls giggled.

"The arm is steady above the shoulder at all times," the Baron whispered from his mask. "The padding about the neck is to protect the jugular. The left foot must not move."

On guard, padded and masked, the men looked ominous now. The giggles stopped. In the middle of the parquet floor the two boys began to attack, the two sabers clashing against one another.

The St. Anne girls sat rigidly in their seats, their hands clutched together on their laps. By the time the two boys had slashed twice at one another and the sound of steel, ringing and dangerous, had clanged in the room, most of the girls had red spots on their cheeks.

"God, it's like the movies," one of the girls, the daughter of a corporate oil man, said in a whisper that came out too loud.

The Baron hesitated, his mask turned toward the girl, his posture frozen. Herr Strutt hesitated.

"Please," Charity said without looking at the girl. At that moment her social position in Los Angeles was secured.

The boys went on fighting, not only the menace but the weight of the blows palpable at every stroke. There was the rasp of steel across a mask and both of the boys stopped instantly. They flipped their masks up.

"If we were not wearing masks the blade would have left a scar on the right cheek of Herr Strutt. It was powerful enough to reach his cheekbone. It would have been a very fine scar," Baron von Bertlich said.

The girls clapped, tense with excitement. They stared at the Baron's cut lip, at the magnificent endearing scar. The boys put their weapons under their arms and walked over to Charity and Lady Rose.

Charity talked in a low voice to the Baron. No one heard all of the conversation, but later the St. Anne girls reconstructed the conversation; put it painstakingly together.

"That was very exciting, Baron," Charity said.

"Thank you, Miss Britten," he said. "We hope you enjoyed it. It was a pleasure."

"But with the masks on it must be rather boring," Charity said. "I mean it must be boring for you and Herr Strutt."

"Oh, no. It is good practice. Always exciting," he said. "Maybe it was boring for you though?"

He did not expect an answer. He said it unthinkingly or,

perhaps, because this was the conventional place for a compliment.

Charity looked over his face and then past him.

"Yes. It was, rather," Lady Rose said. "With the masks and the padding and all it seems rather like a . . ." She paused.

"Like a movie?" the Baron asked.

"Not like a movie," Charity said evenly. "Like a performance."

"But that is what we were doing, a performance," the Baron said. He was puzzled and irritated. "That is what we were supposed to do."

"It looked it," Charity said. She smiled. "Without the masks would it be different?"

"It would be serious."

"But it is never serious, is it?" Charity asked softly, but persistently. "I mean at the fraternities you really never are fighting because you hate the other person. You're fighting to carry on a tradition and pick up honorable scars . . . that sort of thing. That and the ritual."

Baron von Bertlich smiled, but there was the hint, the faint suspicion of tension in the smile. He had gone beyond irritation and was unsure of where he stood.

"But the ritual is the important thing," he said. "That must be taken seriously, done ceremoniously, among peers."

"That is very silly, Baron von Bertlich," Lady Rose said. She did not elaborate. The two Germans stood for a moment, waiting for one of the girls to tell them more. Both of the girls looked straight ahead.

The Baron's lips drew tight and the triangular scar shrank until it showed only a speck of white moist tooth. He turned and walked over to Herr Strutt. He spoke rapidly in German to him. Herr Strutt listened, made a reply, then looked around the room in confusion. The Baron kept talking very swiftly. Herr Strutt smiled, shook his head. The girls sat quietly, not sure what was happening, but feeling that the whole party was so jeweled, improbable and strangely adult that they should not interfere. Then Baron von Bertlich said something very sharp, guttural and cruel. They knew it was cruel because Herr Strutt turned pale and his eyes grew hard and bright in his schoolboy's face. The boys looked at one another like two cocks; tight, muscular, unpleasant. Then Herr Strutt turned and threw his mask in a corner.

The St. Anne girls realized that the boys were really going to duel, that soon Herr Strutt might have a scar. One of the girls sobbed. Another mentioned something about blood on the floor.

"Stop," Charity said abruptly. "The girls do not want it."

The two boys, still half angry with themselves and confused by Charity, looked at her. They were almost beyond recall; dogs let loose and just beyond whistle call. Charity stood up. She turned her back on the two boys and began to talk to Lady Rose.

Charity looked once around the room. She looked calmly at each of the girls and noticed that they were shivering in their beautiful I. Magnin chiffon dresses. Some of them were staring at the boys, but a few, the very tender girls, were staring down at their fingers twisted and blue in their laps. Charity waited. The tender girls finally looked up. A ripple of agreement, a barely perceptible nodding of heads, swept over them. Charity smiled.

"Go ahead if you wish," Charity said abruptly. "They do want it now."

The two boys began to duel. This was, instantly, different from the first fight. Steel eyeglasses hid their eyes, but now that the masks were gone, the girls could feel every flicker of concentration. The blades clashed against one another with a sharper ring. Each slightest pause was keyed to the next fierce stroke. And there was, as subtle and slight as the odor of grass or the smell of water, the attar of danger in the room.

It ended very quickly. Suddenly Herr Strutt feinted, leaned back, hesitated and struck. It was a skillful downward slash. His own body pulled away as his saber moved, but his feet were solid on the floor.

Strutt's saber lashed against the Baron's jaw. Before the blood came, the sound of the blade against bone had knicked out into the room.

Ceremonial took over. The two saluted. The Baron glanced at the blood which dripped down his body but did not raise his hand to the wound. He and Strutt turned and bowed to Charity and Lady Rose.

One of the girls, Sally Benson, was sitting rigidly in her chair, her feet straight out in front of her, her head lolling loosely. Saliva ran from her mouth. The other girls just stared, bound by some odd and new tension that resulted from the steadying pressure of Charity's calmness and the horror of seeing real violence and real blood.

The two boys bowed and left the room. Lady Rose left and came skipping back with a handful of Kleenex and wiped the blood from the floor.

Charity took the girls out into the garden where a buffet table was set up. The girls talked and moved about and some of them even laughed. The laughter was glasslike, clear and bubblelike. The gestures of the girls were abbreviated and jerky. Sally Benson vomited in the bushes and no one even noticed her, probably because she came back and ate enormously. The girls were abstracted and calm; their voices more detached and pure than when they were in school. They looked at one another and thought that their vision had never been more pellucid but were disturbed by the fogginess they saw in the eyes of everyone else.

The fact was that, with the exception of Charity and Lady Rose, all of the girls were quietly and very deeply hysterical. If Charity had not been there they would have gone off into fits.

Dimly, through their talk and their incredibly sharpened
senses and the bright Los Angeles air, the girls were aware
that they were eating small open sandwiches made of pâté de
foie gras with specks of truffle through it; tiny molds of lobster mousse with a perfect pink claw caught in each mold;
cold asparagus with pepper sauce over it; tiny ripened pineapples that had been drenched in crème de menthe; cookies
of a very rich texture and tasting heavily of almond. The
food was not displayed lavishly, it was not abundant, indeed
by Los Angeles standards it was almost Spartan in quantity.
But it was put together with an elegance, a craftsmanship,
an eye for color and balance that no girl missed. The buffet
was, for one moment, a beautiful setpiece of art . . . the yellow of the pineapples, the green stalks of the asparagus, the
miniature elegance of the lobster claw . . . all caught in a
simple perfection. And then the girls were allowed to ruin the
whole beautiful thing and eat it.

As the girls left the party, Charity handed each of them
a small box, wrapped in tissue paper. Their parents were
waiting and as the girls came down the steps they seemed
the same as ever. But they were not and neither were the parents. For although no girl ever told her parents of the duel,
and no one ever told Henry Britten and his wife, the parents
did hear of the food and Lady Rose Penthorn and the parents
saw the presents. The presents were all identical. Each was a
simple champagne glass. There was no design on the glass, no
etching, no figure. They were of extremely simple design.
But the glasses were made of very pure crystal that hummed
when it was moved through the air. The stems were as thin as
wire. Held up in sunlight the glass simply disappeared.
Turned a certain way and it was a mass of light too bright to
bear.

The parents knew that the food and Lady Rose Penthorn
and the single champagne glass were a message. In the way a
primitive will study a civilized language and sense, even

before he knows the words, that it will tell him things of unknown beauty and complexity, the parents knew they had received a message. Mr. Henry Britten was moved in a single afternoon to the top of Los Angeles Society.

Charity was also. Or, to put it more exactly, she was given the offer. She was invited to every party, to every dance, to every weenie bake. She was consulted, as the girls grew older, on every engagement. She was the first to share a confidence, although she never shared her own. None of the girls forgot that simple afternoon party of Charity's. And Charity was never deceived. She knew that behind their invitations, their yearning for love, was fear. Fear that Charity might decide to punish them; fear that she knew something they did not. In short, just simple black fear.

With all of this, however, Charity was a very simple and loving girl.

By the time Rodney returned from the war and as a hero, Charity had just turned twenty. She was tall for a girl, but inches shorter than Rodney. She had long legs, hands with fingers that were so remarkable that she often wore gloves just to escape compliments, small high breasts, and a beautiful face. Her parents had, abruptly at the start of the war, lost the last trace of their German-Swiss accents. Mr. Britten was the leader in several war-bond drives and gladly supplied famous actors and actresses for charities which were connected with the war effort.

Rodney's father was delighted when Rodney told him he was going to marry Charity Britten.

"He is a good man," Rodney's father said. He never told Rodney what he knew of the Britten family. "Made his own way. She is a lovely girl."

7. The Girl in the Flamenco Restaurant

THE house in the Tuileries mystified Rodney. He had merely mentioned that he and Charity were going to take a business trip to Paris and the house had been mentioned.

"You haven't been to France since the war," his father said. "You ought to stay in the Tuileries house. It would be a treat. Charity would love it."

"What Tuileries house?"

It was something his father had bought just after the war, he explained. It was part speculation, part convenience. He and some of his colleagues went to France frequently on business, and it was nice to have a comfortable place to stay and a good cook. It helped business and the overhead of a cook and a couple of maids and a butler were all deductible.

"It's only a bit more expensive, I figured out, than staying at one of the best Paris hotels and as a piece of property it has appreciated eleven times," his father said. He looked up at Rodney. "You ought to travel more, Rod. It doesn't really broaden a person, but there is something exciting about seeing strange places. Just for the sake of seeing them." He twirled the antique globe which had the first voyages of Magellan, Bougainville and Cook marked on it. "I've traveled further than all three of those men together. It's not just brute mileage, Rod, it's just that you only live once and seeing all this," the globe twirled, the faded colors and the cracked ancient paint blended into a slick whir of color, "happens to you just once."

Rodney knew that there were only a few things about him that his father fully approved. One was his leanness, which Rodney maintained merely by playing squash, tennis and not being much interested in food. Another was the fact that Rodney had made money on his own. Not great money, not the kind his father was used to, but enough money to have three servants in a Bel Air house and afford Charity's piano lessons and private schools and some travel to Hawaii and Tahiti. Soon after Rodney had married Charity her father and Mr. Cartwright had put Rodney into an oil venture. Rodney was not sure of the precise nature of the deal, but it involved several thousand dollars of his own money. The well had hit, as the two older men had told him it would, and in addition Rodney had an option on a few thousand acres surrounding the well. A year after the war was over, Rodney was very comfortably off and he was able to go into the thing he wanted; boat designing and boat racing. He had a small boat-yard and a designing office which employed three draftsmen. On little more than enthusiasm he had done very well and now, after some defeats and a few victories, he was making boat designing profitable. But his father, although pleased with the profit, was surprised at how meager it was. He also disliked Rodney's racing yachts to Tahiti and other places. He constantly tried to interest Rodney in other ventures and even to loan him the money to go into them, but Rodney had refused. He was well off and he liked what he was doing.

With a slight sense of shock and then a feeling of relief Rodney knew the house was used for love affairs. Not just his father's love affairs, he was certain, for his father would not be that lavish. But Rodney guessed that his father's business associates also used the house for the same purpose. The knowledge of the house ended a curiosity Rodney had felt about his father for years. Rodney's mother had disappeared

into a sanitarium of some sort with an undisclosed affliction
when Rodney was very young. By the time he was old enough
to ask, his father had told him bluntly that his mother had
been a drunk and she had died some years ago. Rodney often
wondered what his father did about women. Now he knew.

Now, standing at the entrance to the "house in the Tuileries," Rodney felt almost embarrassed. They had invited a
dozen people for dinner their second night there; people
they had met in Tahiti or had been given introductions to.
The butler had moved toward the door when the first guest
arrived and Rodney, quite suddenly, had ordered him away.
He would receive the guests.

He looked down the street. All the houses had the harsh
brown gritty wall which, since the French Revolution, the
bourgeois had learned masked their homes from the rage
of the masses. Inside the wall there was a garden surrounded
by an L-shaped house that was three stories high. It was
elegantly furnished, done entirely in period pieces, and it had
a solid almost British look about it.

Rodney had been surprised by the elegance of the place.
He knew, five minutes after he was in the place, that it was
not used for what his father had said. With a flick of memory
he remembered his father's way of becoming bull-like, hunching his shoulders, whenever a beautiful woman came into the
room.

In the coolness of the evening, waiting for guests, having
no duties, Rodney sensed that his father was probably a
powerful lover and had been for years . . . and that was
what the house in the Tuileries was all about.

Rodney met two more guests at the door. He smiled easily,
shook hands, made a few remarks about Los Angeles and
then led his guests down a long corridor.

The corridor was a curiosity. It had been designed at a time
when pride in France was not only possible but was possible

to build into a house. The corridor was broken at regular intervals by rounded cupolas and each of them contained a white marble bust of a hero of France . . . Voltaire, General Ney, Napoleon, Rousseau, Flaubert. At the very end of the hall was a bust of General de Gaulle and it was only when one saw this that one realized how yellowed and aged the other busts had become. De Gaulle's bust was sharp and white, the eyeballs opaque and outsized, the face surprisingly thin.

"It's my father's house," Rodney said. He shook his head in mock despair. "When he bought it only half of the niches were occupied by statues and the original owner obviously intended for history to fill them. But Dad couldn't wait. He rushed out and bought busts of anyone whose marble matched the ones in the corridor. De Gaulle had him licked. There was no way to make it look old, but he felt it brought the corridor up to date. If he had it antiqued it would be offensive to de Gaulle, if de Gaulle ever comes to the house . . . which my father would like very much. In fact the good man would probably fly over here for the occasion."

Rodney opened a door and led the guests into a room which held about eight people. They were talking and hardly noticed the new arrivals. Charity, sitting in the middle of a group, raised her eyebrows and nodded at the newcomers. Then she pursed her lips, shook her head and nodded at a short dark Frenchman who was talking very fast. The late arrivals knew she would come over when the Frenchman was through.

It was obvious that the talkers were either speaking to Charity or hoping to influence her. She spoke hardly at all. She just sat quietly, glancing around slowly at the figures that were poised around her and her glance made them ripple, rearrange themselves, shift positions, bend forward and peer at her, twist away as if answered in some manner . . .

but no one left. When she stood up and moved, every head in
the group turned with her and no one listened to the Frenchman who had been talking.

Charity was actually not tall, but her long hands and her
leanness made her appear so. There was the suggestion of
boniness about her that was barely eased by flesh; of a small
appetite; of a boredom with food; of a blooded graceful-
ness. There was, however, nothing angular or sharp about
Charity. She had a beauty that was almost ethereal and
this was especially apparent about her eyes. They were large
and dark, changed rather frequently, but always stayed in
the spectrum between black and deep blue. Her skin was flat
white. When she closed her eyes, which she did frequently,
her face deepened in color. Someone had once remarked
to Rodney that Charity looked like a woman who had never
been in sunlight. In fact she often sailed with Rodney, but her
skin never tanned.

Looking at her Rodney thought that she really had the
kind of skin one read about in nineteenth century novels but
actually never saw in real life.

Perhaps she was a prisoner of her looks, he thought. She
looked creative, in good taste, somehow authoritative. People who looked at her asked "what she did." They expected
her to do something and do it well, exquisitely, with talent
and competence. Everything she said was interpreted as
being important.

The guests were arguing about intelligence and intuition in
art. It was a complicated argument and there were elaborate
analogies to biology, allusions to Bergson, decadence, im-
plicit order, the necessity of the grotesque and much else. As
usual Charity did not speak but listened, looking from side
to side.

She reached for a cigarette and at once the group fell
silent, went birdlike and poised in their attention, waited for
a judgment. Charity lit the cigarette. She knew she was ex-

pected to speak. She put the lighter back on the table and smiled up at them.

"It's all a question of individual choice, isn't it?" she said. The guests hissed agreement, but watched her carefully. Her hands moved, the cigarette trailing blue smoke. "And the choice really comes from here."

She put her hand over her heart. Everyone smiled thinly but the argument was over.

Rodney watched her and was puzzled. She was an arbiter and she had decided the argument and all fell silent, but he knew that no one understood what had been decided. She spoke enigmatically, quietly and in a voice that was attractive largely because of its studied flatness. She seemed trained not to win her points by verbal emphasis and this gave her a peculiar and attractive kind of persuasiveness. If her words had been spoken by a Baptist minister no one would have listened. But Charity was something different. Where the hell, he thought, did her authority come from? It was not wealth or beauty or intellectualism. Her words were quite commonplace, but said softly, with assurance. She had aura. Beneath the words one felt that there was a special kind of insight, an aristocratic simplicity that concealed profound knowledge.

She moved across the room and began talking to a highly skilled concert pianist from London, a short wiry nervous man whose eyes were fast-moving, shrewd and knowing.

"Of course, you should study piano," he said sharply. "With those hands you could not fail to be superb." He picked up her right hand, turned it over slowly and everyone was struck at how pudgy, muscular and thick his hands looked next to the long, thin elegance of Charity's hand. "You *must* study with Casadesus. You are lucky he is in Fontainebleau. I will arrange it."

"That's silly," Charity said. "I couldn't possibly. I just want to understand music."

"Just to understand?" he asked. He looked at her, his tough London Jewish Cockney face twisted. He turned her hands over and looked at the polished nails, the perfect crescents, the veins showing blue through the flawless skin. "You could make me into a Communist, Charity. Just by yourself. Because talent is to be used."

Charity looked down at her hands and then at the pianist. She squeezed his ugly hands and Rodney felt restless.

"From each according to his ability," she said. "But who really knows the ability of another? Or even of one's self?"

Most of the guests laughed; a kind of trilling laugh of sympathy; an appreciation of her modesty. The pianist's face changed slightly as he glanced around the room at the others. For a thick insulting second he looked at Rodney. Then he became a businessman. He scribbled down Charity's phone number. He would make the arrangements with Casadesus. He would call next Monday. It would be expensive. He drew her aside and told her it would be between five and six hundred dollars a month.

"Don't be secretive," Charity said, her voice lilting. "You could tell everyone here what it might cost. Money is nothing to be ashamed of."

The man faced the group. He laughed. It was a short mocking laugh.

"It will cost her one thousand dollars a month for piano lessons," he said. "It will be worth it. To the teacher or the student? Only time will tell."

Charity put her marvelous hands to her mouth and laughed.

"She really is modest about her talents," Rodney heard one of the guests say. It was the wife of a French boat designer. The husband did not reply.

The pianist was leaving. He stopped to talk to Rodney, talking slowly, but watching Rodney's face.

"Cut it out," Rodney said. "She doesn't have any artistic

ability. She only looks as if she should. You are very smart to realize so quickly that she has no talent."

"But she looks like a marvelous Pre-Raphaelite. As if she might die of consumption before she has expressed herself," the Cockney said with a quiet savagery. "You are better than you look . . ."

Rodney walked him down the long marble corridor and on the way the Cockney rambled. The Cockney was slightly drunk. He asked Rodney how many artists had pressed easels and canvas and paint on Charity. How many sculptors, he said, standing in front of a statue of de Gaulle, had given her armatures and clay and tools? He did not wait for Rodney to answer.

He ran his hands over de Gaulle's marble features.

"A noble man whom I loathe," he said and trotted along to the door. He did not take Rodney's hand. "You poor bastard," he said and ducked away into the street, running with the enthusiasm of a man who faces a big night. He gave no excuse for not staying for dinner.

The guests had been drinking Canadian Club and martinis for a half hour when a maid stepped in and nodded to Charity. She stood up and led the way in to dinner. It was a magnificent meal. Not only was the food excellent, but it was served on fine plates and there were three wineglasses in front of each person. The smallest glass was filled with sherry when the soup was served. The second was filled with claret when tiny steaks and *béarnaise* sauce were served, along with a huge pastry which opened to reveal a mixture of mushrooms, vegetables and a wine sauce. The third glass was filled later with champagne. It was a very long dinner and very gay.

On Charity's right hand was an American ex-Rhodes Scholar from Illinois who talked about the old days at Magdalen and the excitement of Eights Week. He was an easy speaker and he watched for just the right moment to bring each person into his story. He told how the crew lined up behind one another in the Isis River and winning consisted of "bumping" the boat ahead. The worst part of the river was a narrow placed called "The Gut."

By now he had the table.

"The races are rather dull really," he said. "But when the London *Times* reported that 'Jesus bumped Christ in The Gut' it was too much."

The Magdalen man was very entertaining and Rodney knew Charity would ask him and his wife to stay on when the others left.

He was right. When the soufflé had been served and the champagne poured and the ladies had retired and then returned, the evening ended very quickly. The French left quickly, as if they were intruding on important people. Rodney let the butler see them out. The Magdalen couple stayed behind and he knew that Charity had asked them to wait.

"We should drive through Paris tonight," Charity said. "It is a time for exploring and seeing new things and old things in new ways. And it is cold out. And we should not decide where to go until we have been driving for a long time and have talked a great deal."

Outside the city was cold, blue, pale. The private homes were dark; the shops were shuttered. Almost no one was on the streets. Rodney's limousine, which came with the house and was driven by the butler who had quickly changed into a stiff-visored hat, moved slowly down the boulevards.

The Magdalen man had picked up a bottle of cognac as they left the house and they passed it around, nipping at it. They were all getting somewhat drunk.

Rodney looked at the thin leafless skeletons of the trees which made the buildings look even more heavy and lifeless.

They stopped at the Seine and walked across one of the bridges. The thin hard light caught the sheets of ice that were coming down the river. They seemed hard and glassy, but as they pushed against the barges and the piers they shattered silently, broke up into hundreds of floating particles and then, in some mysterious way, re-formed into a sheet in a few seconds and floated slowly toward the next obstacle.

They were not prepared for this sort of Paris. The cold, the thin grayness of the sky, the massivity of the buildings, the stealth and hurry which cold always induces in people, drained the illusion of Paris from them. They had thought it would be gay, light with music, crowded with excited people. But it was almost empty and there was no music and no one they saw looked gay . . . they looked troubled, harassed, sullen. And it was clear that the city was not built to be viewed under a cold, lowering, gray winter light. The sky pressed down, brought the horizon close, small dark snow clouds scudded ominously by, not more than a hundred feet in the air . . . soaking up the light. The buildings and the street might be majestic and spacious in sunlight, but under such a dim, filtered, ugly light they looked crouched, dunnish. The bony trees, utterly bare, splintered the view in an uncomfortable manner. Both of the couples had spent most of their time in Paris inside of warm rooms.

In the car it was cold. The black Bentley had a heater, but the chauffeur was reluctant to turn it on and muttered some reason which none of them could understand. The windshield wiper scratched at the thin layer of ice on the glass, but could not dent it. They drove slowly down the Champs Élysées, past the frozen dog droppings, the ice-streaked windows of the cafés, the thin outline of the horse chestnuts, saw the shadows of people behind frosted restaurant windows, but that was the only sign of life.

The Magdalen man brought out the flask of Martell Cordon Bleu. It was a flat green bottle. He passed the bottle around. His name was Arthur, he said, but call him Art.

They had eaten only an hour before, but now the bitter cold had made them both bored and hungry. Art suggested

they go to a restaurant he remembered from his Oxford days
and have something warm to eat and drink.

The restaurant was Spanish. As they came in the door the
sound of flamenco singing cut through the smell of roasting
lamb and wine and the sound of dishes and glass rattling and
the murmur of many people talking.

When they went into the main room they could see the
singers. There were two of them. They were both thin muscular boys. Their costumes caught every muscle in their
bodies and when they breathed the blue embroidered cloth
over their ribs stretched and then collapsed. They sang in
high wailing voices, so thin and soprano that they might
have been bred for the job.

As Rodney's group was led to a table he noticed that several heads swung and followed Charity. He was familiar with
the gesture. It was accompanied by a slightly puzzled look as
the person tried to identify Charity. Usually strangers
thought she was a movie star or "a rich woman, like Barbara
Hutton, you know."

The singers accompanied themselves with the hard flamenco clap. One palm was closed into a small cup and then
the fingers of the other hand were smashed into the cup. It
made a sharp exploding sound as the air was trapped between palm and fingers. They did it very fast, their hands
flickering in the air, the sharp explosions ripping through the
room. Rodney noticed that the hands of the singers were
covered with brown calluses and neither of them could fully
open the hand which was slapped by the fingers. They held
this hand tightly curled, like a well-developed and valuable
claw, as they left the little floor in the center of the room,
bowing to the applause.

"It sounds mechanically perfect, don't you think?" Charity
said. She sat very straight in her chair.

The Magdalen man was instantly apologetic. He stated

that he did not really like flamenco music and that this pair were not the best, but it was unusual. Charity did not reply. She smiled at the man.

The sound and the dance *did* seem mechanical, Rodney thought. He could see that Art had already revised his idea of flamenco: it was mechanical. Rodney recalled the scores of times when Charity had interpreted something, just as she had interpreted the flamenco, and had everyone believe her. It was not the wisdom of what she said, he knew. He had discovered the first month of their marriage that she really never thought things out. But what she said was part of a composition . . . her cool elegance, her easy straight posture, the brevity of words, the opaque quality of what she said. She had, he concluded, discovered at some early age that a certain kind of rounded statement which took no sides was also invulnerable to attack. He had never heard Charity in an argument.

They ordered an aperitif and the headwaiter passed menus. A girl stepped onto the middle of the floor and began to sing. She had huge eyelashes, two great shanks of oily black hair which hung down her back and were tied with red ribbons, very full breasts and tiny feet. She lacked any dramatic quality, she merely danced with a quick, highly honed skill. Her tiny feet stomped and clicked expertly, but seemed to have no connection to the big lush body. The castanets were invisible in her hands, which were as big and muscular as a man's, but the clicking intricate sounds poured out effortlessly. The castanets seemed like timers that had been attached to a very intricate machine. Her feet followed the pattern of clicks perfectly. Her eyes, huge and black, opened and shut at regular intervals and she had a fixed smile on her face. It seemed, from watching her face, impossible that she knew what she was doing . . . her body and brain were quite unnecessary to the dance, they were not even a connection between the tiny beautiful feet and the castanets.

"The food is very good here," Art said firmly. "Authentic."

When the waiter came Rodney pointed to an item on the menu which had been written in on the bottom in very black ink. The waiter said something quickly in Spanish and grinned. Rodney could not understand him and neither could Art. The waiter beckoned to the captain who walked over and looked at the menu.

"Those are bull's balls," he said in English. "Fried in olive oil, flavored with rosemary. Very good."

"Fresh?" Rodney asked, grinning.

"Absolutely fresh," the headwaiter said seriously. "From Les Halles this morning. For their freshness I will stand a guarantee."

Rodney ordered the bull's balls and asked about the wine. The captain suggested a very dry Spanish wine. Rodney ordered it. Art and his wife were watching Charity. The wife's expression was frightened; she seemed to be waiting for a suggestion from Charity. Charity looked up at the dancers.

"I'll take the same," she said.

The other couple nodded their heads, the wife trying to smile.

The wine came. It was very dry and Charity smiled at Rodney when she tasted it.

"I like it," Art's wife said. "I need something to sharpen my appetite. I'm so full from your marvelous dinner."

The poor girl, Rodney thought. She's trying to prepare us for the fact that she can't stomach the bull's balls. And she is frightened of Charity.

When the dinner arrived it was delicious. The meat had been cut into thin slices, dipped in some sort of batter and then fried in olive oil. It tasted like very rich veal. The other wife stared at the circles of meat on her plate, her lips working. She sipped the wine and looked at Charity. Charity was eating the meat with no look of curiosity on her face. The other wife drank off her glass of wine quickly and then ran her fork through the vegetables on the plate.

Rodney told Art about the new boat he was designing. With the tip of a spoon he showed the general contours of the boat.

"It won't be big and it won't be as fast as a catamaran, but I think that it ought to win the Trans-Pac race," he said. He looked at the beautiful slim lines of the boat and wished he were back working on her. "She has to be handled right, but in expert hands she will be the safest and maybe the fastest thing around."

He looked up at Art. He was looking at the plump Spanish girls. Rodney felt a slight surge of anger and then relaxed. He raised his eyes and looked around the restaurant.

He had turned back to Charity before he sensed that something had happened. He was not sure what, but somehow his mood had changed. It were as if a gnat had flown across a familiar landscape and in a tiny way changed it.

"Do you like the balls?" he said bluntly to Charity. The eyes of the other couple swung around.

Charity glanced at the plate, then up at Rodney, and then looked at the dancers.

"They are interesting," she said.

She raised a finger to the wine steward and pointed at Rodney's glass. The man filled Rodney's glass with the dry wine.

Rodney almost snapped at her. He felt irritable. But he did not. He was used to control and the itch of irritation he had just experienced was not because of Charity. He had long ago learned how to live with her. And he was really not *that* angry about Art's disinterest in his new boat. Well, sweet Jesus, what was it?

He forced himself to relax in the chair and once more looked around the restaurant. The place was crowded, a mixture of American tourists, Germans with their pink serious faces, and Frenchmen. There was smoke in the air, but even so Rodney was sure there was no one there whom he knew.

But when he looked back at Charity he had as if printed somewhere in his eyeballs a quick glancing impression of a very plain mouth, no lipstick on the lips and the tip of the tongue showing.

He drank some wine, took two bites of the meat and then slowly looked up and around again. Almost opposite them was a couple at a table. The man was very dark and heavily built. The girl had a plain mouth and wore no lipstick. Rodney had the feeling that just before he looked up the girl had been glancing at him.

The couple had just been served caviar, a large mound of it, and the girl was looking down at the black glistening expensive eggs. The waiter was opening a bottle of champagne. The girl shook her head, but the man reached across and spooned caviar onto a piece of toast. As he put egg white and egg yolk and a bit of onion on it the girl sat, slightly bemused, and watched him. Just before he lifted it to her the tip of her tongue came out and ran across her lips. It was startlingly pink against her plain face.

She shook her head again, shrugged her shoulders to indicate she was not hungry. The man held the piece of toast under the girl's chin. She looked directly at him and shook her head again.

The man dropped the piece of toast and said something. The toast broke and the caviar erupted in black pellets across the tablecloth. Rodney started to rise from the chair before he realized that he did not know either of the people. But he felt a real anger at the man.

"You don't really care much about sailing boats, do you, Art?" he said. Why the hell did he always think of him as the Magdalen man, Rodney wondered savagely. Because the bastard was always talking about the damned place. From now on he would get his correct name.

Art looked away from the Spanish girl in surprise. Rodney wondered how a stupid bastard like this, who could drool over a fat mascaraed smelly Spanish dancer, could run one of the biggest savings and loan firms in Illinois. Art had jowls, also . . . the puffy kind. Small, but they would get bigger.

"Sure I do, Rod," Art said. He straightened up in his seat, remembered he was a person of some importance. He sensed the aggression in Rodney's voice. His face showed resentment. He didn't have to take this from a California smarty . . . Rodney could see it going through his mind. Not when Rodney was just turning out a few boats and sailing off to Tahiti and Honolulu and acting generally like a beatnik with a profession. Art's voice toughened. "I don't love the damned things and wouldn't make a long voyage in one if . . ."

"Deep-water sailing we call it, Art," Rodney said.

"I don't give a doodle what you call it," Art said, talking out of the side of his mouth. His eyes glanced away from Rodney's face, looked across the room.

He was looking at the girl with the dark man, Rodney realized. Art's eyes were not even taking in the fat Spanish girl.

The lecherous middle-aged bastard, Rodney thought. First he drools over the fat greasy Spanish woman and now he is playing the field.

Rodney knew that for some inexplicable reason Art felt as combative as he. It didn't have anything to do with that plain-looking girl, it was probably just seeing old friends in a new surrounding.

Art's wife had eaten all the vegetables on her plate, had drunk three glasses of wine and had cut up some of the slices of meat, but had not eaten any of it. She had moved the bits of meat around so that her plate looked picked over.

"Sailing is really more an art form than a profession today," Charity said.

"I've always thought so," Art's wife said.

"I'm no artist," Art said.

The two slim flamenco dancers came stomping back in, their heels hard on the wooden floor, their chins jutting out. Rodney looked past them and at the girl.

The girl was wearing a black dress with a rounded neck and very tightly clutched to her throat was a triple strand of pearls. She brought her hand up and touched the pearls, running her hand along them, barely touching them. Then as her hand reached the nape of her neck her hand jerked away and disappeared under the table.

The man with her was talking to her earnestly and even from this distance Rodney could tell he was pleading. He was old enough to be her father, but he was not. How Rodney knew he could not tell, but no father ever talked to a daughter like that. The man took out a handkerchief and put it to both eyes. Then he leaned back and waited for some sort of judgment.

The girl looked up, stared at the man, then looked down. She shook her head shyly. Strangely *that* gesture was what a daughter might make toward her father. The man's hand shot out, jerked at the bottle of champagne, started to pour into his glass before he was aware it was full. He picked it up, drank it off, and then filled it again.

The flamenco dancers finished another act. They stood, stone-still, stiff, hands over their heads. They did not nod to the applause.

Rodney looked toward them and had a moment of panic: just before his head had turned the girl's eyes had moved. He jerked his head back. The girl was looking at the man, but her head had just ceased moving. She had been looking at him, Rodney was certain of it.

"Art, you want more wine?" Art's wife asked.

He turned, nodded his head and began to look around the room some more. Rodney wanted to stop him.

"Art, you ought to exercise more," Rodney said without the slightest comprehension the words were coming out.

"Pig's ass is pork," Art said with disinterest.

"What does that mean?" Charity asked.

The question brought the four of them back into a general discussion. They discussed Los Angeles and Honolulu and Pasadena and politics, but Art and Rodney were careful not to speak after one another, nor to one another.

Rodney excused himself and went to the toilet. He was upset by his reactions and felt a sense of confusion which he attributed to alcohol. When he came to the toilet it was the usual arrangement; men and women barely separated and entering through the same door.

The plain girl was there, opening her purse and waiting to go in. She turned and looked at him directly. Then she smiled. She held out her hand.

"Do you remember me?" she said. "I was with you in Montauban, a long time ago." She paused. "I think."

Rodney felt an immense relief. He scarcely remembered the girl, but this accounted for all the odd feelings of the last few moments. Yet, in a completely new way, he felt secretive. He looked over his shoulder to see where Charity was. She was sitting straight and beautiful at the table.

"I remember you," he said. "I'd like to see you tomorrow. At the little café at the Place St. Michel. I can't remember the name."

He hesitated, trembling for the first time in ten years, waiting for her decision. It was like that of a little girl.

"The Glace, of course," Nina said. "What time?"

"Eleven or eleven-thirty," he said. Then more firmly. "Exactly eleven-thirty."

"O.K.," she said.

8. Strawberries in Champagne — and Bitters

THE girl was late. Rodney sat at the little table, drinking whisky and soda. Maybe she would not show up. He looked down the street, around the café. He beckoned to the waiter for another drink. The waiter nodded, but did not move. He stared back at Rodney, then picked his teeth with the finger-nail of his smallest finger. Rodney raised his hand and pointed his finger at the waiter. The waiter stiffened and started for the bar.

Oh, for Christ sake, Rodney said in a low voice.

He was acting like a retired general, like a retired German general. He was strung tight. It couldn't just be the girl . . . the one named Nina. He could scarcely remember her name.

In the years he had been married to Charity he had met more than a few girls for a drink. It had been a necessity. Very early in the marriage Charity had told him that she thought sex was "disfiguring" and when he had finally wrung from her what that meant (it was the first and last serious and prolonged discussion they ever had) he knew that he would look elsewhere for sexual satisfaction.

It was not that she was unskillful. Indeed, she brought a kind of expert knowledge to lovemaking which had astonished Rodney. She had done things to him which he had never conceived of. For a few months he had been suspicious of her. She seemed to have the kind of glossy polished style which he had associated only with whores. He was relieved when she told him, quite casually, she had learned the whole procedure from a doctor and a marriage manual.

At the same time she told him she did not enjoy sex because it was not only disfiguring, but it was messy . . . it involved sweat, body excretions, rolling in bed. Quite innocently she also told him that her parents felt she had an obligation to keep her looks and figure intact as long as possible. Which meant she did not want to have children for some time.

Since that talk Rodney had slept with Charity on a rigid schedule which involved her menstrual cycle, but which worked out to four times a month.

Someone was across the table from him.

It was the girl. He was surprised at how small she was.

Rodney stood up and held out his hand. The girl took it without smiling.

"All I can remember of your name is Nina," he said as he seated her. "What is the rest?"

"Faures," she said, "Nina Faures from Montauban."

"Nina Faures, of course. I remember your father. How is he?"

"He is well. He seems very old, as if he is made of parchment, like the books he reads from. But he works very hard and publishes a book a year."

Nina did not look any older than when he had seen her years ago. She was wearing an English tweed suit and her long black hair was pulled back under a small beret. She wore no makeup that Rodney could detect and he thought she was probably shy.

"Would you like something to drink?"

"Coffee, please."

Rodney made an easy gesture to the waiter. He grinned

and came over. Rodney ordered coffee. Nina pointed at his own glass. It was still half full, but he nodded for the waiter to bring another.

"What happened to Rouge?" She looked uncomprehending. "The thin fellow? The one you said was a Communist."

"Rouge? Was he in Montauban during the week you were there?" she asked. The tips of her fingers went over her eyes. She strained to remember. Her fingernails were cut very short and were neat, but not polished.

"I was not in Montauban a week. I was only there a day," Rodney said laughing. "But Rouge was there that day."

Her fingers snapped away from her eyes. The eyes came open. She had a surprise on her face that was very childlike; full of wonder.

"It must have been a week. Maybe one remembers badly, but it seemed as long as a week. It was a pleasant week in my memory, but I do not remember anyone named Rouge."

Rodney felt relief and then instantly wondered why. He felt no guilt over the night in the forest when they tried to escape.

She had probably wiped the whole thing from her mind. He remembered reading somewhere that people who have crushing experiences forget them to keep their lives in balance. Maybe Rouge had been killed . . . and for that reason she could not remember him.

"Forget it," he said, "I was pretty fatigued at the time and it must have been imagination."

He wondered if he should ask her about the capture by the Germans and what had happened. Before he could speak she spoke.

"And what, Captain Cartwright, do you do in America?" she asked and for the first time she brought one of her hands from under the table and placed it alongside the coffee cup. "Are you in business? Are you married? What brings you to Paris? I want to know everything."

"I'm just here for pleasure and maybe a little business," he said. He went on to tell her about his boat designing and his marriage.

Probably this girl had thought of him a great deal, he realized. During the war life must have been dull and the memory of the captain who dropped from the sky was vivid. Maybe that is why she had thought he was a week in Montauban . . . she had dragged out the time and filled it with invented things to ease the boredom of life.

She listened with an intensity that was almost rapt. She was very curious about his boats and why people would pay such big sums merely to race across the ocean. He told her why in detail and felt almost poetic as he talked.

Suddenly Rodney knew he was getting drunk. He looked at his watch. It was close to two. For some reason the waiter had kept bringing drinks and he had talked. He must have had five drinks since Nina arrived.

"We should have lunch," Rodney said. "How would you like to go to a lunch party which a bunch of old Oxford types are throwing? Some of them went there a long time ago and some are undergraduates now, but in any case a friend of mine who went to Magdalen invited me. Let's go."

"I would like it, but should we not pick up your wife?" Nina said.

"No. She isn't in town. She's in Fontainebleau. Taking a piano lesson. Or something."

Rodney paid and left a good tip. Nina looked down at the saucer and laughed for the first time.

"Everyone complains about the big tips that Americans leave," she said. "They say it ruins it for everyone else. I think it is charming. A really fine gesture."

They walked outside and waited for a cab.

"You are the first girl I've ever met who thought a big tip was a nice thing," Rodney said. "Most of them think it is a sign of vulgarity."

They got a cab and Rodney found the address Art had given him.

It took a few moments for anyone to respond at the address. It was a large house and they could hear the bell tinkle far in the rear. The door was finally opened by a girl who was, perhaps, twenty-three.

"I'm Amelia. That's an awful name, Amelia, but my father admired some American female athlete or flier or something like that and named me after her. I guess I'm the hostess, but it's all too disorganized to know," she said. "I own the house so I must be the hostess, but no one else will let me. They are all rushing around, having drinks, answering the door, passing food about. It's a very good party."

Rodney introduced himself and Nina.

The girl led them through a big disordered house, which would have been elegant if anyone took pains with it. She explained that she was Australian, but alternated now between Oxford and Paris because Awn, "you'll meet him, soon enough. A big bloke," and she were supposed to be engaged. And Awn went to Oxford. But now was Christmas vac.

The party was in a yard behind the house. It was a small yard but put together with great taste. There were almost twenty people in the yard, either sitting on the grass or on chairs and all well bundled up. The sunlight was thin. Art saw them and came trotting.

"Absolute smash of a party," he said after he had met Nina. "Really wizard. Nice mixture of old boys and undergraduates. This Amelia is something. Must be the daughter of an Aussie millionaire. Good food and drink . . . mostly drink. You'll see."

Art looked at Nina as they walked out into the cold garden. He started to grin. Rodney turned away. He was certain that Art was about to wink at him.

A waiter wearing gardener's gloves against the cold approached with a tray of drinks. They were all in stemmed glasses.

"What are these?" Rodney asked. He pointed at a glass of sparkling pink liquid in which a tiny strawberry had been dropped.

"Those are Awn's idea. Amelia just added the strawberry," Art said. His English accent was very pronounced. "They are Napoleon brandy and *brut* champagne and one dash of bitters. Bloody good."

"Bloody deadly," Rodney said. He looked at Nina.

"I would like just champagne," she said to the waiter.

"What do they call the pink drink?" Rodney asked.

Amelia had left them and now she was back. She interrupted Art.

"It's called 'The Alice' because there is a place bang in the middle of Australia called Alice Springs and they all call it 'The Alice,'" she said. "When Awn was a boy a trip to The Alice was pure heaven and he thought they would serve things like champagne and cognac. He only made the trip once, on his way from the sheep station to Oxford, and all they had was beer. So he invented the drink they ought to have at The Alice."

Rodney took one. It tasted very good, but mild. The bitters must mask the sting of the cognac.

Amelia pointed out Kenneth Awn. In a quick staccato nervous voice she told them about Awn. First, everyone called him Awn. He had been born and raised on a prosperous sheep station. At first he took lessons over the radio school, but later his mother had a tutor brought out from England. The mother must have been neurotic, Amelia said. She would never let Awn go to The Alice or to Auckland or Melbourne or Sydney for fear he might be corrupted. She was saving him for "English culture" and wanted Awn to have nothing to do with Australians. She failed and without her knowing it

Awn mingled with the jackaroos on faraway stations and
finally even made a few "walkabouts" with the aborig-
ines.

"He was a good student, but all of it was dead except the
movie magazines his mother got," Amelia said. She was eying
Awn. He was almost invisible behind a small cluster of people. "He decided he wanted to be an actor and a director.
And the poor boy had never seen a play. He believed everyone he read in the movie mags."

The big house at the sheep station received a flood of
glossy photos, drama school catalogues, cheap magazines,
brief notes from Eric Bentley and John Steinbeck, a flood of
paper copies of plays and some dramatic criticism. His
mother would let any written thing into the station as long
as it did not come from Australia. Awn taught himself Greek
to read some Greek classics that someone in his patchwork
correspondence had thought would be helpful.

"Can he act or direct?" Rodney asked.

"Look, it's not just that I love the bloke that I say it,"
Amelia said, her voice losing its nervous quality. "But he can.
He's been at Oxford three years and directed two plays and
acted in a half dozen and Hollywood has offered him con-
tracts that are fantastic. But he won't sign. I wonder how he
developed the talent."

"Perhaps it was the isolation," Nina said. "When one is
alone there is the chance to concentrate on a single thing and
do it very well. Especially if one feels that the single thing is
necessary if one is to live."

It was the most she had spoken all day. Amelia looked at
her and nodded.

"You may be right," she said. "I never thought about that.
Whatever it was it's going to make him a famous man, a millionaire, and take him right out of my hands. He's the kind
who will have five wives and not even be able to name the
cast-offs. And I'll be one of the cast-offs. Rather nasty, isn't

it? When I'm thirty-five and old they'll point at me and say 'One of Ken Awn's first wives, you know.' Nasty."

Nina's face turned cold. It was a look so clearly of disgust that Amelia faltered and then stopped talking and finally turned away.

Awn came up out of the cluster of people, laughing at what someone had said and shouting over his shoulder as he walked toward Amelia.

"Huston is like a fish thrown up on a hot beach about twelve hours ago," he yelled. "Still beautiful and fully formed at the moment he begins to stink."

The thin harsh sunlight caught him squarely as he walked away from the table. Rodney was surprised. The man was ugly. He had big hands which looked nicked and bruised and which he held palms forward at his hips as if they were going to capture something. His body was big and lean and obviously powerful, but in that utilitarian stolid way which happened to Englishmen when they were third-generation Australian. His clothes were ill-fitting. He wore a jacket of tweed which was hairy on the lapels, badly worn at the elbows, and frayed at the wrists. He wore a shirt, but no tie.

As he drew near, Rodney revised his opinion. Awn walked with the kind of delicate control which many men feel they have when they are slightly drunk. Usually they are wrong. Rodney knew Awn was not drunk. He *always* felt the way he looked at that moment. There was a stalking, purposeful, meaningful intent in his walking. His nose was sunburned and peeling and separated two light blue eyes which had the kind of hard dispassion, the flinty egoism, which one finds often in children.

He ignored Amelia and Rodney and introduced himself to Nina. His French was excellent. Then he turned to Rodney and shook hands as Amelia made the introductions. Awn's hand was hard and callused.

"How do you keep your hands so tough when you're just acting or reading books at Oxford!" Rodney said.

"I row, mate," Awn said. "I row five bloody fucking miles a day. They want me to row against Cambridge. I tell them I don't like rowing and no one believes it."

"Why do you row at all?" Nina asked.

Awn gave her a long silent look. His face was serious. He pondered.

"Just to keep in shape to be an actor," he said. "Also a director. They both take good physical shape." He shrugged his shoulders. "Most of those Jewish directors in Hollywood get so fat and nervous they can't keep up with the actors. So they wind up pleading with 'em. And then it's over."

The waiter passed and Rodney took another drink. He turned to ask Nina if she wanted more champagne and she had disappeared. He wheeled around and saw her back in the house. A group of guests had drifted back inside.

"Excuse me, I'm going to find Nina," Rodney said.

"Better move fast, mate," Awn said. The soft baby-blue eyes in the big Australian skull caught Rodney's eyes. Rodney revised his opinion: Awn's eyes were not childish.

As he turned Rodney saw a faint worried look on Amelia's face. She was urging Awn to have one more drink . . . just one.

Rodney could not remember ever hearing a woman urge a man to have another drink. It struck him as curious.

Nina was standing on the edge of the group. They were talking politics.

"De Gaulle can bitch it up all by himself," an Englishman was saying. "He gets the *force de frappe* and believes he can use his half-dozen bombs to keep Russia or the U.S. from fighting one another. They both go along and humor him and the moment they can they bang him across the bloody head."

"With what?" a feminine voice asked.

"With the offer of supersonic bombers or another medal or putting up a statue of the old boy in London and one in New York," the Englishman said. "Any little thing. Just so it's honorific. But if they don't give him the big honor before he dies the old boy would think nothing of using his dinky *force de frappe* to start a war. Go out like a Viking. All that sort of thing, you know."

"What's going to do us all in is that impulse for the monumental which exists in all big men," a woman said. "They all want to leave something big behind them to make sure they are remembered."

"What did Hitler leave?" an American said.

The question dangled.

"Ashes and graves," Nina said.

Everyone drank.

Most of the people had drifted in from outside. They sat on the floor chairs or big cushions or hulks outside the circle.

Not quite a circle, Rodney thought. Somehow it was an ellipse. People had arranged themselves in the apparent chaos so that Nina was standing at one end of the ellipse and an empty chair was at the other end. There was no muttering or issuing of orders, but that was the way the group assembled.

Rodney moved over and stood beside Nina. She had drunk only a third of her glass of champagne.

"Would you like to go?" Rodney asked. Then he insisted. "The food is on the buffet, but no one is eating. You must be hungry."

"Hungry? I am not hungry, Captain," she said. She looked into her glass. She was not listening to what they were saying in the room, Rodney thought. "But if you wish . . ."

"No. Let's stay awhile," he said. He moved closer. "Nina, don't call me Captain. It sounds funny and anyway I'm not a captain anymore. I'm out of the service and designing boats. You want to hear about my boats . . ."

He stopped. A flat voice had spoken with a volume which drowned out their small conversation. She did not look away from him as the other voice spoke.

"On balance I would say that Hitler designed a good number of monuments, but they never quite got built," a voice belonging to a solid, bright-eyed and fortyish Englishman said. Amelia reached over to tell Rodney he was an Oxford don and an expert on Hitler. "The minutes of his meetings show he wanted to build a colossal new arch in Berlin, simple Germanic monuments in Paris and London and Rome and then a huge thing somewhere in South Asia to the origins of the Aryan race. Oh, he had the monumental impulse. He just didn't have the chance."

The don finished, rolled a cigar in his fingers, looked at the ash. He waited. The ash was pure white, but not yet long enough to be tapped.

For a group as loaded as this, Rodney thought, they are acting very well. A few eyes are rolling and if they don't eat someone is going to get sick and there will be a few arguments. But they do not talk too much. They seemed to be listening or they were bored by the don's statements.

He looked around the ellipse. Amelia was staring fixedly. She had a drink in her hand and she was drinking it in long steady dignified sips. She finished it and held out her hand and the waiter was there. He maneuvered the tray so her fingers closed on the correct glass.

Amelia's lips smiled, the head nodded to friends, the hands gave directions to servants . . . but her eyes were following someone and it was sure to be Awn. Rodney looked away and, sure enough, Awn was prowling behind the ellipse of guests. He was listening carefully, his big crude head stuck out on a long neck, and his face glacial. His eyes, those sunburned Australian out-back eyes, were almost closed and made his nose larger.

"Dixon, sir, are you sure Hitler didn't leave any monuments?" Awn said suddenly. At the same time he came in from the outside and sat in the empty chair. The big angular body fell into the chair with a grace and muscled ease and sense of comedy which made some of the women gasp and then fall off to a sigh. "He was an actor. Pure, simple, undiluted and superb. He had all Germany eating out of his hand. They loved this Charlie Chaplin type bloke who could look so damned silly . . ." he paused, "and still give them the order to attack Poland, England, America, Russia, everyone."

"Again, Awn, for simplicity's sake," the don said. "Are you arguing he left monuments behind him? Physical things, I mean. Let's don't talk about it all afternoon boring the drinking customers. Name one."

Awn ran his big raw hands through his hair. He closed his eyes and scratched behind his ears and along his neck. He had done this often, for the skin was light red and exacerbated. He bent far forward in the chair and his knuckles touched the floor.

"Is a person a physical thing, sir?" he asked, but did not wait for an answer. "Of course. If a person is a physical thing then Hitler left monuments behind by the millions."

"Let's don't go into the extermination camps," Dixon said. "They are documented and well known and there is a vast literature about them."

Awn rolled in his chair, his hands over his ears, his face working.

He is a big man, Rodney thought, a very very big man. There must be over two hundred pounds and about six feet three inches writhing in the chair.

A pause fell on the group. They looked away from Awn, but did not look at Dixon. They chose new drinks and talked softly, and, mostly, looked at Amelia. She was smiling and there was no easiness in her smile. She took another drink and looked just once at Awn.

"Are humans physical things?" Awn said.

It came sharp and hard. It was a rude question, put that way. Awn knew this.

"Are humans physical things?" he said again.

Dixon looked at him and smiled.

"Awn, if you are asking if humans are physical I must say yes," Roper said. He yawned. "But you ask if they can be made into monuments. Did you ask that? You meant it. Well, then I tell you they cannot. I looked at the bones at Auschwitz and Belsen and heard the pathetic stories. Look, Awn, I saw so much more of this than you that it is preposterous. The secret is this: a monument builder does not build with humans, he builds with the timeless stuff. Granite, marble, silver, gold, stainless steel. Flesh? That goes first. Even bones don't last long."

Awn looked up from the crumple of hair, messy jacket, the joint of neck and chest.

He gave a contented, sure and somehow condescending smile to Dixon.

"If a man can mark a generation of living flesh he can leave a monument," Awn said in a firm positive voice. "If he scars even one generation he has been blessed. It is a sign of his power over the living flesh of those about him."

"Well, yes, I think that's right," Dixon said looking up. He was confused, for Awn was not looking at him. Awn was looking down the ellipse. He trailed off. "Might be that a psychopath would find wounding a generation to be a monument. Not likely though because . . ."

Awn was pointing his finger at Nina.

"What do you think?" he said.

Rodney felt a quick surprise, which he pushed down, and then a kind of cunning. He was drunk. How much he did not know. But he would soon find out. His body tensed and he was squeezing out the booze and the idle concern about the

other people and now . . . right now . . . was the time to
concentrate. He would be sober very soon.

Nina was calm. That did not help.

"You play a word game I don't understand," Nina said.
"Hitler killed a lot of people. So they are no longer physical.
They are dead. Gone. So they could not longer be a physical
monument." She smiled faintly. "If anyone remembered
them they might be a mental monument. Which is not very
satisfactory, is it?"

Awn was confused. He gestured at the waiter, took one
The Alice and drank it off. His big raw hands hung in his lap
but it was not a sign of surrender.

He pointed his finger at Nina and his face was sad.

"Now I will tell you what I mean," he said. "You are a
monument to Hitler. As long as you live you will be a walking
little monument to Hitler."

"Yes. But I am a monument that will last only one generation," she said calmly. "Which is not exactly what Hitler
wanted. All he did was mark me. When I am dead and the
maggots eat everything up the mark will be gone."

Nina rolled back her sleeve. She showed the tiny bluish
number of a concentration camp prisoner on her forearm.
The numbers were almost faded. They looked like a mottling
of veins . . . but not when one looked closely. Rodney bent
forward and could make out 7 and 2 and 3 and four other
numbers.

Her skin was smooth and even and the numbers, once one
looked closely, were perfectly clear.

Awn stood up and walked down the ellipse. He took her
arm and looked closely at the numbers.

"723-5413," he said. He stepped back only one stride. He
was embarrassed. It was really a kind of terrible embarrassment; the embarrassment of a man who seldom got that way
and hated it when he did. Under his sunburn there was a new

flush. Instantly Amelia was at his side. He kept staring down at Nina's arm and twice he gulped.

"Why doesn't everyone eat?" Amelia said. "All my nice food will be ruined. Eat, eat, eat. Come now."

Awn dropped Nina's arm and turned toward the buffet. He walked with his head down.

Art came over and stood beside Rodney and Nina.

"Bloody talk of politics is boring," Art said. "Just hashing over old stuff. Does no one any good. Also Awn has no damned manners. Rude."

"If war is politics then I assure you that politics is not old stuff," Nina said.

Her voice was slightly apologetic.

Awn walked over and joined them. He was no longer flushed and he was holding a plate heaped with scrambled eggs and sausages and a huge dollop of some red jam. He looked at Rodney.

"This is some sheila you have here," he said, jerking a thumb at Nina. "Bright. In Australia we'd hog-tie and brand one as wild as that."

Rodney looked at Nina. She looked puzzled, as if she did not quite understand what he had said.

"Brand her?" Rodney said. "That's a curious thing to say to a girl who's already been branded. You really are a bore, you know?"

Awn began to blush again. Rodney sensed it was a kind of agony for this big man who had always controlled everything around him.

"Awn, you're a damned bloody bore," Art said. "You stand around like a wild stud out of Australia and talk a lot of crap about being an actor and a director when you haven't done a thing. You're a disgrace to Oxford."

Awn did not look at Art, he was still looking at Rodney.

"If that's what you'd do to her down in Australia I suppose I'll keep her out of there," Rodney said.

"Awn, shape up and act like an Oxford man," Art said.

Rodney was sorry he had said what he had to Awn. The Australian was suddenly defenseless. Also he loathed the way Art spoke in crude wounding clichés.

Awn, with a quite unconscious insolence, swung his eyes from Rodney and looked at Art. He shook his head and at that moment Rodney knew he was a great actor. The gesture was heavy with contempt, as offensive as a blow in the face. The gesture and the look were the equivalent of an insult and designed to provoke action.

And Art responded. He swung on Awn.

Rodney saw the blow start. Awn also saw it coming. Awn did nothing. Art's fist smacked against his belly and Awn rolled with it, a clever, half-revolving roll so that it looked as if he had taken the blow directly. The blow made a loud noise because Awn had blocked it with his plate. Eggs, sausages, red jam and bits of white china went in a spray across the carpet. Awn was still holding a triangle of china in his hand. His eyes were now very cunning and very relieved.

"Mate, I forget your name, but you ought not to have such a burr under your tail," Awn said softly. "It could get you in trouble."

"Not from you," Art said. He was poised, fists up, ready for a fight.

Amelia came up, her face full of concern, but hesitant to speak.

"Oh, course not, mate," Awn said. His ugly tweed jacket was shapeless. It was impossible to tell whether he was coiled under the jacket or in pain. "Not from one of the raping Australian athletes. Oh, we spend all our time lusting after virgin women. Bloody awful it is, mate. It's a damned plot by the Australians to repopulate the world. All us descendants of convicts are getting our revenge."

Art swore. He stood with his hands out in front of him. He

lowered his hands slightly as if to ease the situation. Then he made up his mind. He grinned derisively at Awn.

"You're a raw kid, Awn," he said. He brought his hands down and picked up a bottle of cognac from a nearby table. He drank a few gulps out of it. "Just as raw as drinking out of a bottle."

Awn smiled. He pushed away from the chair.

"I agree, mate," he said. "Raw is the word. I kinder like it."

He stood up, stretched, looked around the room. Then he tossed the triangle of china onto the carpet. He looked around the room at the silent guests. Then he crouched slightly and moved toward Art. He paused in his shuffle and looked at Rodney and grinned as if they had an agreement. Still looking at Rodney his hand shot out with the first two fingers stuck out straight and caught Art on the ribs. It made a sharp snicking sound.

Art took a step backward. Everyone in the room looked toward the sound. Art locked his face into a grin. The flesh around his mouth was white and he breathed heavily through the smile.

Although most of the people did not know what had happened they knew it was something violent. There was a quick shifting of position, a soft asking of questions. The waiter paused with his full tray of drinks. Then the movement commenced again.

Rodney saw sweat on Art's cheeks and knew the blow had hurt. It was almost too ingenious of Awn, a bit of clever staging. The blow had been so seemingly inoffensive, made with only two fingers, that it would have been impossible for Art to act as if he had been hurt. Also it had looked playful so that Art did not know what to do. And it had hurt, but only Amelia, Nina and Rodney knew that.

Rodney felt a sense of unreality, as if the whole day were blurred. He had drunk too much, but not *that* much. His mind snatched at something to explain the whole thing. One fragment stuck. It was like King Arthur's days. It was like chivalry and gallantry and flying flags.

But something was wrong. Who were the brave knights fighting for or over? Not Amelia. And surely not Nina. She had hardly looked at either of them and now was staring out the window. But whatever the chivalry was about, Rodney enjoyed it in a way he could not explain.

"Let's go, Nina," he turned to her and said.

Her head snapped up and she nodded agreement.

He knew that Art and Awn and Amelia were watching them very closely as they went out of the door and into the cold sunlight.

Rodney felt solid, muscular, competent. He had kept in shape. He turned again to Nina.

"Where would you like to go?" he asked. "We still haven't eaten."

"To Montauban," she said.

"To Montauban," he said with a false enthusiasm. The town was a full day's drive from Paris. He went along with her joking.

"Can we start right now?" Nina asked.

She was serious. When Rodney spoke his voice was serious and direct.

It was, of course, possible to start right now, he reassured her.

9. The Grease of Excellence

NINA looked across the table at Rodney. The table, which a few moments ago had seated fifteen people, was now empty. There was a debris of pig bones on plates, empty wine bottles, big wooden bowls of sweet butter, the rich smell of cognac evaporating from a dozen glasses. At the head of the table the pig's head still rested on a tray, raised six inches off the table and occupying the place of honor. It had red cherries for eyes, but its mouth was pried open into a smile . . . by a huge truffle. Nina had rejected an apple.

She was twisting a cognac glass in her hand. She had drunk a bit of champagne during the dinner and, as if carried away by the enthusiasm of her old friends, had sipped her cognac.

"This strikes you as barbaric," Nina said looking up at Rodney. "We fell on the food like starving people, like animals. Right?"

"Right," Rodney said. He smiled.

Nina looked down into the glass, whirled the cognac a few times and then with a short defiant gesture which Rodney had never seen before she tossed off the rest of the cognac.

She held up her hands and in the light of the restaurant they glistened with grease. She laughed.

"Normally I hate grease on my hands," she said. "My hands or anyone else's hands. But these are not normal people. They are better than normal people. They are excellent people. The grease on their hands was the grease of excellence."

"Nice phrase," Rodney said. He had drunk a great deal, but he had also eaten a great deal and, as a result, things about evened out. He felt calm and even and very happy. He had been initiated into some strange association and he had enjoyed it. The guests *had* been different. They were the strong, rugged, close-bound survivors of a dreaded ordeal.

Nina tilted her glass slightly, looked into the tiny yellow drop of cognac that remained at the bottom of the big balloon glass. She narrowed her eyes, peered at the drop, smiled and twisted some meaning from it. Rodney knew she was thinking back . . . and so was he. But he was thinking back only something more than twenty-four hours. When they had left Amelia's party and she said she wanted to go to Montauban Nina had meant it. Not in a defiant way, but easily, as if it were quite ordinary to go to Montauban.

They had gone to his garage and he had warmed up the black Bentley and sent the chauffeur for an aluminum heating can. Rodney walked across the street to a shop and got a bottle of cognac and a bottle of excellent burgundy. Then, on a hunch, he bought some bread and a tin of pâté.

He walked back to the garage eating bread and pâté.

He would be better now. He stuffed more bread in his mouth and laughed. It was not clear why Nina really wanted to go to Montauban. Not at all. But Rodney did not feel like questioning her. He was pleased they were going.

"Off to Montauban," he said, tossing the packages in the back.

Nina smiled at him and it unnerved him. She looked, for a moment, quite ordinary and without artifice.

Rodney went out of the garage fast, but a bit shaky, not the usual Grand Prix skid he made into the one-way street . . . which burned rubber for half a block and brought the

car to a skittering halt at the intersection. In the rear view
mirror he could see the chauffeur standing in the street, wiping his hands on a rag, his shoulders hunched with disapproval.

He had driven for an hour and a half without talking. Once
he asked her to open the pâté and she spread some on bread
with a knife from the glove compartment. She passed it to him
without comment.

At some point he knew he must stop and sleep or he would
be in trouble. He turned in at a small inn just after sunset.

As he parked he was not sure what he would do. They
had no luggage.

The woman who kept the inn did not care. She was sleepy
and irritable. She led them to a huge room, three stories up,
with a small coal fire burning and mumbled something about
breakfast.

"I'm tired," Nina said. "And cold." She looked at him in
the small pool of light from the grate. "And very thankful
we came. I was sick of Paris."

"Who was the heavy dark man you were with?" Rodney
asked suddenly.

"He is an Egyptian psychoanalyst and do not laugh," she
said. "He is said to be very good and he is in Paris for some
serious study with some analysts who have gathered from
all over the world."

Rodney did not know how to ask the next question. "Did
you sleep with him?" was the way it would go. But Nina was
busy with her coat. She took it off and walked toward the
huge bed.

She turned away from Rodney and was quickly undressed down to her bra and panties. She rolled into the bed
and sighed. The sigh was a signal. She was sleepy.

Rodney undressed down to his boxer shorts and a T-shirt.
At the last minute he left his socks on. He crawled into bed.

The girl's teeth chattered slightly. It was an oddly erotic sound. Somehow he must stop the chattering. He waited and moved slowly in the bed and then reached out to touch her. She was rigid. She gasped when he touched her.

For years Rodney had not encountered resistance in a woman. Past a certain point in years and experience and previous conversation both partners knew it was wasted time. There was a process of mutual stimulation, of real and sometimes feigned excitement, but both knew the conclusion.

In the stiffness of Nina's body he knew the conclusion was far from inevitable.

He ran his hand over one cup of her bra. The rigidity became ironclad. He raised his hand quickly to her lips. He kissed her and her lips were cold. Even as he ran his tongue over them and moved his fingers over her face the sense of coldness deepened. He pried her lips open with his tongue and met the smooth wetness of her teeth.

"Open your mouth," he said.

He could feel her hesitate. Then her mouth opened. It was very sweet, wet and warm. Her tongue flicked away from his.

She was breathing light and fast. And then Rodney felt a difference. She was frightened. He remembered some episode, bloody and ragged edged, from his youth; the boys in the neighborhood gathered to watch the mating of a rabbit doe and buck . . . strange confusion of signals and purposes . . . the doe frantic in action . . . the buck big and pawing and powerful . . . and the capture and the doe squealing and some white liquid shooting through the air.

Rodney was breathing very hard. At the same pace as Nina, but she was breathing from fright and he panted from excitement.

It was like the first time. He felt the fine shivering of his skin. He tried to reassure himself with the memory of how many times ago the first time had been . . . thousands of times and scores of girls before and years ago. It did not help.

And it could not be the first time for her. That was impossible. A virgin did not go off so easily with a man. And she was living with a god-damned Egyptian psychoanalyst, he told himself savagely.

He ran his hand up her leg. There was the feeling of rigid muscles, cool flesh and then pants and at the edge of these the faintest suggestion of very fine hair. Nina gritted something out, but she did not move her body.

There could not be a first time more than once, his mind told him, but maybe there was a classic first time and it was being reenacted. His mind believed none of this, for his thoughts had slid down to between his legs. He felt enormous.

He remembered what she had gritted out.

"Do not hurt me," she had said.

"Take hold of me," he said.

She shivered, but a word came out, "Where?"

He took her hand and guided it. When her cool fingers touched him they recoiled, snapped back, but he led the hand on. It closed around him and the hand itself seemed to shiver and was very small. Then, without any motion, it began and he was gone . . . his stomach muscles tightened and he moaned. The itch, the ecstasy, whatever it was was beyond anything he had known. And it lasted and lasted.

The next morning was very cold and clear. They left the hotel early. A thin winter sunlight slanted across the countryside without a glitter or the least knowledge of warmth. During the night the Loire had tossed its water against the piers of an old bridge and the ice hung like fragile, green, nightmare cactus. Once, as the Bentley roared along, they saw a horse-drawn cart come out of a field. White jets of steam came out of the horse's nostrils. The lump sitting on the seat of the wagon was like earth, but the lump also gave off twin jets of steam. As they flew by, Rodney had an impression of two living clods, some old blankets, bits of frozen straw dropping, black reins linking the two clods. One eye of the horse was flared slightly, as if barely alive. There was a faint sound . . . maybe leather creaking or a hoof falling or a wheel turning.

"You should remember to call your wife," Nina said. She was curled up in the corner, the aluminum hot water can under her coat. She had taken out a scarf and wound it over her head.

She is the kind of girl who can wear anything, Rodney thought. She has a chic look, just by adding the scarf.

"We must stop for something to eat and drink and petrol and then I will call," Rodney said. "She will not care. I will tell her I have gone hunting with some friends."

Nina laughed. She seemed very happy.

"You are a very relaxed man," Nina said.

"Is that good or bad?" Rodney asked.

"That is good," she said. She reached over and kissed him on the cheek. A light kiss, but even so Rodney felt the glut start to rise in him. It was like a heat, an aroma, a something that drove everything else from his mind. It vanished as she settled back in the corner.

"This afternoon we come to a small town," Nina said. "Would you like to meet some friends of mine? They are all crazy types. All they share is the fact that we were in the German political prisoner camp together. But we keep in touch and they are an interesting group. And very loyal."

"If you would like it," Rodney said.

"It would be pleasant," Nina said. "They live in the same town, but never see one another unless one of the old-timers comes through. Then they come together with loyalty." She shifted in her seat. "Real loyalty."

Rodney was too busy driving to look at her. The road was slick, whitish, and had every appearance of danger.

They stopped at the largest of the three hotels in the town. It was a musty and very sound place and the restaurant was the main attraction. It occupied the whole of the lower floor and the landlady tried to get them to eat at the hotel but stay somewhere else. Nina, with a few words, reassured her and the landlady's face smoothed out and she spoke very fast to Nina about the menu, what should be prepared, the wines, the side dishes, the cheeses. Rodney caught only a bit of what they said. Apparently the hotel made money only on its food. Rooms were a nuisance, what with insolent country maids, mad Algerians trying to escape the police, police trying to catch mad Algerians . . . and did Madame know that some mad Algerians were white? On and on the landlady went. But if they wanted a banquet then that was a different thing.

Nina turned and motioned for Rodney to go up to their room. The landlady threw him a key and he found the room. It was huge and when he opened the door a shiver of dust fell from the curtains and the room was hazy and soft.

Rodney did not unpack his bag and he did not realize it until he stretched out on the bed: he had no bag.

After the intense cold he fell asleep very quickly.

When he awoke Nina was standing in one of the big windows and staring out at the darkness.

He must have made a sound for she turned around.

She looked, in some peculiar way, very courageous and alone.

"They will be arriving in a few minutes," she said. "Poor lonely people."

When they went to the restaurant the landlady closed it off as if some important event had happened. She swung around, her shoulders arched, and she was a guardian.

There were two thin women in the restaurant. They came

screaming at Nina. It was impossible to tell their age, but they had the look of female clerks: ageless. But they also had a quality which Rodney did not understand. Partly it was a reserve and partly it was a sense of heavy gravity. These women had been someplace Rodney had not been. They moved in odd ways which were impossible to understand at once. They were very friendly. It was a friendliness which happened too quickly. Also they were very protective both in what they said and the way they moved: they glanced constantly over their shoulder to make sure they were not overheard.

Somewhere he had read of the training of guerrilla troops. The aim was to make them group, regroup, respond, retreat, attack, disappear, and then emerge solid and victorious. It was an act of virtuosity. These women had it; a curious blend of resiliency and hesitation and probing.

A plump middle-aged man came in.

"Albert," Nina exclaimed and kissed him. He kissed the other two women and then turned to talk to Rodney.

Albert was a dealer in calico exportations to Africa and knew much of African taste in cloth.

"The Jew and the Gentile and the Asian buy by the feel of the cloth," Albert said. He put his finger alongside his nose. "The African entirely by color. The more color the better. You will recall that in the old days Africans dressed only in color; whatever colors they could find in clay or berries or other natural stains. They applied the colors directly to the skin, of course. Now they dress in colored cloth."

"Is it a competitive business?" Rodney asked.

A young man had arrived and then two men of unidentifiable age. The young man had fingers that were lined with black grease wherever there was a line in his hands. He must be a mechanic.

"Competitive? Good friend, it is the most competitive business in the world," Albert said and added, laughing, "and I sometimes think I am the only honest competitor in the business. What some men will do for a franc. My God, some of the calico falls apart after the first washing. I try to combine the best of material with the most durable of dyes and the most sensational of color arrangements."

"Rodney, I want you to meet some of the other guests," Nina said. "Excuse me, Albert."

"No. He must hear this last bit," Albert said. "Do you know the favorite design right now? What design is most popular all over Africa? It is a print of tanks and jet fighters and PT boats . . . each of which shows a black head at the controls. Interesting, eh?"

"Very," Rodney said. He thought he understood what the man was saying: Africans don't want freedom, they want weapons. Interesting idea.

The room now held almost fifteen people. They were drinking cocktails and aperitifs and a surprising number of them were drinking whisky and Perrier.

"Don't listen to Albert and his marvelous integrity toward the niggers," the mechanic said when he met Rodney. "I am a worker. I am a radical. Not a Communist, but a true radical. He sends the shoddiest goods overseas."

Nina laughed.

"It is so like the old days in the camp," she said. A small cluster of the people were standing around her. "We all gossiped and gossiped and talked and talked. And invented stories about one another. And now it is the same. You never see Albert but you invent stories about his shoddy calico."

The mechanic grinned, a tough rowdy grin and nodded his head. He swallowed off his glass of whisky.

"I never drink it by myself or with my comrades because I cannot afford it," he said. "But when I can I drink it so that there will be less for the capitalists. Maybe it will hasten the day of their downfall. More," he said and signaled to a waiter. "I hate the taste."

"Remember the time when we refused to eat unless they let us have the regular half-kilo issue of bread?" a skinny hollow-eyed woman asked. "Remember that, Nina?"

"I remember. And we knew that the guards had sold the bread on the black market so we went on a hunger strike," Nina said.

"A hunger strike? That is very funny. A hunger strike in that damned camp where everyone was hungry all the time," the mechanic said. He swung a glass of scotch under his nose, wrinkled it in disgust.

"That makes no difference. We fought back. A matter of principle," the skinny woman said. "We sat in a row in front of our barracks and refused to work or eat or exercise and the guards were terrified. Scared because the Kommandant might find out they had cheated." The woman dipped a finger in her glass of Dubonnet and sucked it. She talked in a dreamy way, unaware of the audience. "The shit of a guard, the big stupid one from Heidelberg, put a bowl of soup under my nose and walked along the whole line of us, holding the bowl of soup just under our noses."

"It was better soup than usual," one of the other women said. "They were clever. I looked down the line and watched each person gulp as the bowl was held under his nose, swallowing the saliva. Even now when I dream of a rich meal I dream of that bowl of soup. But no one broke. No one put his lips to the bowl."

"And by the next meal we had won," the mechanic said. He was getting drunk. "The lousy damned guards had to go out and buy back the bread. That is what solidarity will do for a group. Not the solidarity of the Communist bureaucrat . . ."

"Come off that propaganda," someone said in a gentle reproving voice. "We all know what happens to solidarity when things really get down to the nasty end."

Rodney felt the group tense. For some reason most of them

looked at Nina. She was unaware of it and smiled at the
woman who had spoken. Albert barged into the group. He
had another story of defiance to tell. His face was flushed.
The story could only be understood by those who had
participated in the event, Rodney quickly realized. They
hung on Albert's words, roared with laughter, smiled when
he told of someone's behavior. On the face of it the story was
meaningless, but it tightened the group. Rodney knew he
was excluded.

The people all took on a gamin quality, became gay and
alusive in their talk, possessed by hilarity. Rodney had seen
this occasionally in tight little groups who had known one
another for years and who seemed to get drunk at exactly
the same point, to laugh at the same subtle joke, to be welded
into a tight organism. The welding was done by alcohol and
by past experience.

Rodney walked from group to group. He revised his opinion. He was not excluded. Indeed each group wanted desperately for him to understand what part of camp life they
were dissecting. Someone would try to tell him the background, but someone else would interrupt impatiently, and
the story would unroll and he never quite understood
it. They looked at him eagerly, hoping he would grasp the
meaning. He tried, but their faces always fell. Without his
saying a word they knew he had not understood.

None of the groups talked about the horrors of concentration camp life. In fact the stories seemed to be events culled
out of a common childhood. Bits of gossip, disconnected
events, descriptions of meals, old impressions, fragments of
experiences were all bound together. Each group told a skele-
tonized story, suggested something larger and more solid,
but never pushed to the point of being specific or complete.
They obviously were enjoying themselves. Even people who
were quite obviously shy and inarticulate here could, with
just a few shreds of episode and a few gestures, call up a

common memory. The faces of the others would light up with hilarity which seemed almost beyond control at times.

Almost all of them apologized to Rodney for their inability to communicate to him the real dimensions of what had happened.

"Charlotte!" one of the women said. "Remember Charlotte?"

"Bitch!" the mechanic said, gazing into the brown eye of his glass.

"For a kilo of bread," one of the other women said with wonderment in her voice. "For a kilo of bread she did it."

A pause fell over the group and several of the men moved restlessly.

"She was a bitch not because of the bread. She was a bitch because she was the first to do it," a man with very thick glasses said.

"You are crazy," the first woman said. "Charlotte did it because she liked it. She wanted a strong man and all of you were too weak."

"Maybe that is correct," Albert said with reflection. "To do it through a barbed wire fence and to do it night after night with any guard who would produce a kilo of bread must have meant she liked it. And surely we were not men enough to satisfy her."

"I was man enough," the mechanic said slowly, not looking up from his drink.

The others paused a moment and then laughed so hard they were at the edge of hysteria. The mechanic looked up and grinned.

"I tried to talk Charlotte out of it," he said. He puffed out his chest. "That is why I was man enough."

The others laughed and pounded the mechanic on the back.

"You are absolutely correct," another woman said heatedly. "You tried to talk her out of it but she was a mad woman.

Absolutely possessed. She even enjoyed all the scratches from the barbed wire that she got on her belly and thighs."

"But later . . ." Albert began.

"Later! Forget later," one of the women shouted. "Later we can all forget. But it was the first one who committed a crime whom we hate."

Oddly enough her outburst of anger made all of them grin. Even the speaker, when she was finished, had a slight smile on her face.

The landlady came into the room, slipped over to Nina and whispered in her ear. Nina announced that dinner was going to be served. They all sat down to one large table.

There were bottles of wine scattered around the table and everyone helped himself. There were also plates of bread and bowls of butter.

The two waiters came in and each was carrying a huge poached salmon on a large tray. The salmon were covered with a layer of rich mayonnaise and were decorated with capers. Surrounding the trays were mountains of asparagus. The waiters started to serve each individual, but Albert interrupted.

"Just put them down in the middle of the table and we can help ourselves," Albert said in a commanding voice.

The waiters put the trays down in the middle of the table and left the room. The mechanic was the first to move. He put his hand, black, laced with grease, over one of the salmon. Then very deliberately he brought the hand down into the salmon, through the thick layer of mayonnaise, pulled off a thick chunk of the salmon, and put it on his plate. His left hand flicked out and grasped a piece of bread. The others watched him with fascination. The mechanic began to eat with his hands, glancing up at the rest of them with a mischievous grin on his face. Suddenly they all laughed; out of control. Then they turned and fell on the salmon. They pulled the salmon apart with their fingers, dropped mayonnaise and bits of asparagus on the table, splashed wine into their glasses, ran thick chunks of bread through the mayonnaise and popped them into their mouths. From the time the salmon appeared until they were reduced to two bony skeletons not a word was spoken although the entire group was laughing quietly. They laughed like members of a humorous conspiracy, sharing some secret knowledge. Occasionally someone would burst into a sharp explosion of laughter and bread and mayonnaise and red spray would shoot over the table. But mostly they laughed quietly.

They all finished simultaneously. There was a sigh of contentment and they picked up their napkins, wiped their hands and all took a drink of wine. At once they began to talk again.

Rodney was sitting next to Nina who was at the head of the table. He had eaten the salmon with his fingers like the rest and had enjoyed it. Nina ate very little. She did not dig her fingers into the mayonnaise and waited until the clean flesh of the salmon was exposed and then picked off a small flake which she ate slowly.

"These are good people," Nina said to Rodney. "They are the innocents of war. Do you not think they should enjoy themselves?"

"Of course they should," Rodney said. In fact he quite agreed with Nina but for different reasons. There was a kind of excitement about the guests which made the dinner entirely different from anything else he had ever attended.

"Do I act as if I did not approve of them?"

"No, of course not," Nina said. "It is just that a lot of people do not understand and think that those of us who were in the camps were made grotesque or deformed by the experience. I cannot stand such people."

The doors to the kitchen opened and everyone fell silent.

The two waiters staggered out carrying a huge tray between them. Guests who did not have a clear view of the doors stood up to look.

The tray held a pig. It was not a suckling pig. It was a good, heavy young pig which had been roasted to an even chocolate-colored brownness.

Around the pig there was an immense circle of vegetables: mounds of french-fried potatoes, neat stacks of marinated string beans, pyramids of peas held together by heavy sauce, solid green rectangles of spinach soufflé, and blending the whole thing together were pieces of parsley and the yellow trail of soft butter.

The two waiters held the tray at a slight angle. The guests were appreciative. The mechanic snapped his fingers in appreciation and rolled his eyes at Nina. The waiters looked at Nina and then at a side table where they started to move with the huge tray. Nina's face had no expression.

"No, no, on the table," one of the women cried. "We can do the carving ourselves."

The room shook with laughter. The people began to pull back wineglasses and plates. The waiters hesitated, looking at Nina, and still she did not change her expression. Finally Albert snapped his fingers a few times and that made the decision. The waiters put the pig in the middle of the table.

As soon as they had placed the tray the waiters turned and trotted out of the room. Rodney looked slowly around the table. Everyone was staring at the pig. They were smiling, glancing occasionally at one another. It was Albert, the one who obviously had become rich and prosperous since leaving the camp, who was able to make the appropriate toast. Staring at the pig his hand scrabbled on the table for his wineglass. He found it and lifted it up.

"I propose a toast to the night when we ate pork under different circumstances," Albert said. He was deadly serious. He looked straight ahead. It was a very English scene. It was as if someone had proposed the last toast after the retirement of a brigadier. "To the night of our ingenuity."

All stood up and emptied their glasses. Then for a frozen moment they simply stood as if they were sharing a memory.

"I remember that Boche son of a bitch when he found the bones," the mechanic said softly. He said it as a benediction. Then looking at the guests around the table he spoke slowly. "I could send for the carving knives. Do we need them?"

Someone laughed. A hand shot out and grabbed one of the legs of the pig and twisted. The leg turned, the brown skin split, grease jutted out of the break in the skin. Later Rodney could not remember whose hand was the first. It was as if the hand were an extension of the entire group. It bent the leg and there was the slow snapping of cartilage. Then came a moment of resistance. There was a solid crack as the bone separated from its joint. The hand held the entire foreleg of the pig in the air. Hot fat ran down the brown hide of the limb onto the skin of the hand but the hand did not flinch. The hand passed the leg to the next person who began to tear it to pieces. Everyone began to laugh. Hands shot out from all directions and began the demolition of the pig.

"I know this may offend you, Rodney, but it is important to these people and to me," Nina said. "It commemorates an event in the camp which I can probably never convey to you."

"Well, you had better try," Rodney said. He was revolted by the sound of the bones snapping, the pieces of crisp brown skin flying into the air, the way in which the vegetables were passed from hand to hand.

Rodney saw the skinny, gaunt woman pick up a handful of french-fried potatoes and toss them halfway down the table to another woman. They flew through the air like a brown fragmented cloud. The woman snatched them from the air expertly. The two women looked at each other and exploded in laughter. They were boasting of a skill which they thought they had lost but which was still with them. With slow exaggerated motions the woman who had caught the potatoes ate them, holding them above her head, turning her mouth up and then lowering them bit by bit into her mouth.

Only a few people remarked her feat. The rest of them were busy tugging at the pig and talking to one another.

"You think this is disgusting, Mr. Cartwright," Albert said to Rodney. He had a foot of the pig in his hand and was chewing furiously. His eyes were serious and he stared steadily at Rodney. "All primitive rituals are disgusting. They are also noble because they recall a time of heroic action or of survival. What we are commemorating here is a night of survival."

"A night of survival for some of us," Nina said softly.

Nina started to explain the origin of the pig story. Toward the end of their time in the camp one of the surviving prisoners had managed to gain the attention of a German guard. By this time several prisoners a day were dying from starvation. The prisoner, who had been a surgeon in his normal life, remarked that it was tragic that when everyone, civilian and military, was suffering from a lack of food, a body which represented perhaps 175,000 calories in nutrition should be buried.

The German guard was horrified. He thought the surgeon was proposing cannibalism.

The surgeon, in turn, acted as if he were horrified. Such a thing had never entered his mind. What he proposed was that the guard should supply the prisoners with a male pig and the prisoners would feed the dead bodies of the prisoners to the pig. As the pig fattened up they would wait for the right time and then slaughter and eat it. All the surgeon asked was for a decent part of the pig.

The guard was delighted. Three days later he appeared with a message for the surgeon. That night they would deliver a pig to the surgeon's barracks. They expected, the note said in underlined words, that the surgeon would supply the nutrition for the pig.

The guard was stupid, but he had the luck of the stupid. A half-grown pig was actually delivered to the surgeon's barracks. Immediately every prisoner in the camp had started to gather food which was not suitable for human consumption but which could be eaten by the pig. They fed the pig grass, acorns, grease they stole from the garage, newspapers, anything that the pig's magnificent intestinal tract could transform into calories.

The pig actually gained weight for three weeks. Then the guard discovered he had been fooled. The "quota" of bodies were coming out of the camp intact and were being buried in the forest nearby. The guard was furious. He had invested a black market fortune in the pig and was now not even certain that it was alive.

On his own the guard gathered some of his fellows and made a raid shortly after midnight into the camp to recover the pig. The Germans charged into the camp as if they were trying to capture a precious gun emplacement or to make a charge in a desperate battle.

The pig was in the fifth barracks from the gate. Word flashed down to the barracks where the pig was tethered. In a matter of seconds a group of prisoners had swooped down on the pig, picked it up, started across to the last barracks in the line. They arrived panting, the pig jerking in their arms and grunting. Automatically the other prisoners in the camp had set up an enormous din of noise.

Someone had to make a decision. They made it together. The pig could not avoid detection. They must kill him and eat him before the Germans found him.

"Does this disturb you, Rodney?" Nina asked. She seemed very placid, almost bored by the story.

"No, it is just so fantastic," Rodney said. Someone had put

a piece of the pig on his plate along with a scattering of vegetables. He carefully did not look down at his plate.

In a wild fifteen minutes the pig, weighing perhaps 175
pounds, had been reduced from a squealing, living organism
to nothing but a stack of clean bones. The pig's throat had
been cut and every drop of blood had been caught. Then it
had been rapidly torn to pieces. A haunch was passed, hand
by hand, to another barracks where it was torn into smaller
bits.

The heart, the liver, the skin, the eyes, the muscle of the
pig were all eaten raw. It was a desperate race against time.
The hundreds of prisoners tore at the pig knowing that this
would be, perhaps, their last chance for fresh meat before
they died. The immense tension brought forth all kinds of
ingenuity. One ex-butcher among the prisoners grabbed
what everyone else turned away from: the intestines. He ran
out into the night with them, squeezed the excrement out of
them, quickly washed them in water at the toilet, ate two or
three feet of intestine. The rest he stored away beneath his
bunk. He ate the many feet at a disciplined rate: two feet a
day. This, added to the regular ration, was enough to see him
through the last days of the camp.

All that the guard discovered were a few fresh white bones
which had been knicked by frantic teeth. He picked the
bones up, one by one, and took them out of the camp. Later
there was a rumor that there had been a terrible fight between the guards and the black marketeers who had supplied
the pig.

"That is a story of what humans will do to survive," Nina
said softly.

Rodney did not respond at once. He looked down the
table. The ribs of the pig were starting to show as the guests
picked away at the carcass. All of the glazed skin had disappeared. The head of the pig was intact. Greasy hands picked

up bottles of wine and filled their glasses. For a moment Rodney thought that the room was hot and fetid, and then he realized it was actually very cool. A dozen mouths showed white teeth as they gnawed at the luscious meat. A few of the people were standing up in their excitement. The rest ate quickly and methodically, as if they were running a race against time. Their eyes bulged slightly with the effort. Rodney knew it was absurd but he had the impression that they were starting to balloon out, to grow fat and gross in front of his eyes.

"I guess I just don't understand why you want to go through this thing again," Rodney said.

Nina looked at him and nodded. She was chewing at a rib of meat. There was a slight smear of grease around her lips.

"To recall an old memory," she said slowly and deliberately. "The trying times are the ones that tell. We are just reminding ourselves of what we went through."

Someone called for champagne. No one responded in the kitchen. The mechanic went over and stuck his head in the door and roared "Champagne, very cold." In a few minutes the champagne bottles were popping around the room. The guests insisted upon serving themselves. They merely received the bottles from the waiters and then opened and poured.

Although they had drunk a great amount few of the people in the room were actually drunk. They seemed impervious to alcohol and capable of engorging endless amounts of food.

The pig was wrenched apart, dismembered, reduced into smaller parts which in turn were reduced to nothing but bones. In fifteen minutes the pig was gone. Nothing remained but bones and grease. The guests were gasping in their chairs. They admired what they had done.

Albert picked up a huge magnificent pear from a plate of fruit that had been placed in the middle of the table. He

rapidly peeled the skin off with a sharp knife, the juice from
the pear running over his fingers, the drops falling onto the
tablecloth. He cut the pear into neat triangles. He stuck several of the triangles into his mouth sideways. Then he put his
chin on the edge of the table. In the bemused silence the
whole group turned and looked at him. Albert rolled his eyes.
Grease reached from his chin up to his eyebrows. He bulged
his eyes.

They burst into a final almost compulsive laughter. Albert
looked precisely like the pig.

They applauded with their greasy hands. Bits of flesh and
vegetable and tiny droplets of grease flew through the air.
They fell on one another in laughter.

Then suddenly, before Rodney realized it, the room had
started to empty. They left in the way they ate: quickly. In a
great rush they were gone and Albert, after kissing Nina's
hands, shook hands with Rodney and made a short rather
inarticulate speech.

Then the dining room was empty except for Rodney and
Nina.

"Tell me about the concentration camp," Rodney suggested softly.

Nina tilted her glass and a tiny yellow cognac drop ran
halfway up the side of the balloon-shaped glass. Her eyes
followed it as if she were mesmerized.

"It seems so long ago," Nina said. Her voice was very soft.
She had an expression on her face which was somewhere
between a smile and a grimace.

"Don't talk about it if it is painful," Rodney said.

Nina looked up at him sharply. The look turned into a
smile. She shook her head.

"Only liars say it is not a pleasure to talk about the concentration camp," Nina said firmly. "It is a pleasure because the
only ones who can talk about it are the survivors. What gives

us the pleasure is the idea that we have survived. Even now it sometimes strikes me as fantastic."

She reached for a half-empty glass of cognac and finished it off. She looked back at the single drop in her own glass. "It was so long ago and yet every detail is so clear."

Book II

Book II

10. The Camp
in the Forest

THE day after Rodney escaped, the Germans had arrested her father and three boys, all of them twenty years old, who they thought were Communists.

Faures, dressed in a neat black suit, looked strangely out of place in the jail. His fragility, his small bones, his pale face all seemed exaggerated. Nina had the quick, sharp sensation that he would never survive a day in jail. There was something about the cold hostility of the Germans and the roughness of the place that suggested that he would be broken just by being there.

"He had nothing to do with all of this," Nina said to the officer in charge of the Germans who were in the room. "He knew nothing at all about the . . ."

The German, a tall thin angular man, shook his head with a short impatient jerk. Nina stopped talking. There was something about the officer's gesture which was so final that it made conversation impossible. She also sensed, and Rouge confirmed her, that the Germans were in a savage mood. It was the first time in the district that Germans had actually been killed and before the report was made to Berlin the

Germans in charge of the district wanted to make sure that they could report the guilty ones had been caught.

Late in the afternoon Rouge, Nina, Faures and the three boys were led out to a truck. It was metal on all sides and the two doors at the rear were fastened shut with a wide band of iron. There was a small grilled window in the center of each door.

Rouge and Faures adjusted most quickly. Faures took off his coat, rolled it into a pillow and stretched out on one of the wooden benches. Rouge sprawled out on the bed of the truck, a half smile on his face. The truck started off with a jerk, but the moment it reached the main route the ride was fairly comfortable.

"Where do you think we are going?" one of the boys asked.

Rouge looked over at him and grinned.

"We are being 'transported' to a camp for political prisoners," he said. "We are lucky. Since the weapons carrier was blown up the Germans have executed, without trial, fourteen people in this area who they believe are members of the Underground. In this case they were not far wrong. Almost half of them were members of the Underground. The rest were just ignorant farmers. One was a doctor who had a copy of Karl Marx' *Capital* on his bookshelf."

"We *are* the lucky ones," Faures said quietly, opening his eyes. "The first reaction of armed men is always to strike out when they are threatened. Shoot or bayonet or kill anyone who might be connected to the atrocity. Then cooler heads prevail and prisoners are taken and the situation becomes more stable. It was the same with Spartacus and Robespierre and the Commune." He smiled as if they were students in a seminar. "Everyone thinks he is an exception, but history knows no exceptions."

Rouge did not open his eyes, but he stirred. Nina knew he was not asleep.

One of the boys was close to tears. He bent over Rouge and shook his arm. Rouge opened his eyes.

"Where are they going to take us?" the boy persisted.

"I do not know," Rouge said. He seemed to be enjoying the dialogue, gratified by his superior information, slyly pleased by his knowledge. "But if the ride takes more than twelve hours they may be taking us up to Germany. In that case watch out. They may put us in Dachau or Buchenwald."

Only Faures was not shaken by the information. The others stared at Rouge, their eyes pleading for relief. Rouge closed his eyes and went to sleep.

Their transport took only six hours. Early the next morning they drew up outside of a wire-enclosed compound in the midst of a large forest not far from Vichy. They got out of the truck blinking.

Against the wild disorderly beauty of the forest, the camp looked small and very precise. There were two rows of barracks, six barracks in each row and a stretch of grass between the rows. Behind each barracks was a small latrine shack. Just inside the single gate was a long low administration building. At precise intervals around the perimeter of the camp there were guard towers. The whole complex was surrounded by a double bank of barbed wire strung very tightly and, perhaps, eight feet high. The wire was new. The whole complex looked somewhat like a new and somewhat austere summer camp; except for the barbed wire.

A loudspeaker was blaring an order in German and people were pouring out of the barracks and forming into neat lines.

"It is an *Appel*," Rouge said calmly. "It is being held in our honor."

Two guards from the camp swung open a large gate and motioned for the six of them to enter the camp. Two guards fell in behind them, two in front of them and marched them to the front of the administration building. Without instruction the prisoners fell into a line. Behind them they could hear the sounds of others prisoners lining up in front of the barracks. The door to the administration building opened and a major came out. He was a tall man and in good physical shape. He wore dark glasses. He moved to face the new prisoners. His head turned, looking them over, but they could not see his eyes.

"You are political prisoners. You have, in addition, committed criminals acts," the major said. He spoke with a slight stammer. "This is not a rehabilitation center. It is a camp for enemies of the Third Reich. Your fate is in the hands of others and will be decided later. Right now I must give you some simple instructions. Do not try to escape from the camp. Prisoners caught attempting to escape are shot on the spot and the guard who shoots them is given two days of special leave and other benefits. Do not steal from one another. Do not make any demonstrations of any kind. Do not show lights, including cigarettes, at night. Keep yourselves physically clean. On this last point I am most emphatic. I will not have humans, regardless of their former way of life, living like pigs. That is all except for one thing."

The major came to attention as a lieutenant who had been standing behind him walked rigidly past him and toward the small group of prisoners. The lieutenant was carrying a gray envelope in his hand. He handed the package to Rouge. He turned, snapped off a salute to the major, walked back to his former position. Nina noticed that his buttocks wobbled slightly. These must be something less than first-line crack troops, she thought.

"In that package are six red triangles, some thread and a needle," the major said. "You are required to sew the red triangle on your uniform. That is all. You will now be taken to your barracks."

A guard fell in in front of them and another guard behind them. When the six prisoners stepped out this time they moved with something like coordination. They had moved only a few steps, however, when the major called them to a halt. The two guards stiffened to attention and the prisoners, without looking back at the major, did the same thing.

"Prisoner Faures and Mademoiselle Faures will fall out of line," the major said.

Nina and Faures turned and walked toward the major. Once out of the small column they walked in a kind of disorderly civilian manner. When they drew up in front of the major, however, they came to attention. Nina thought grimly that they were already prisoners. Without instructions they knew how prisoners were to act. The major looked over Faures' shoulder.

"Professor Faures, in civilian life I teach at the *Gymnasium* level," the major said. He was clearly embarrassed. "It is a very good *Gymnasium* located not far from Berlin, many of our graduates go on to the University. I just wanted to tell you that we have your textbook *Medieval Political Philosophy* in our *Gymnasium*."

"I am honored, Major," Faures said.

The major loooked over his shoulder at the officers behind him. Nina realized he was judging if his staff could hear what he was saying. Obviously they could not. It seemed to reassure the major.

"Professor Faures, I do not know how you came to be caught up with scum such as this," the major said. He paused. "However it happened it is most unfortunate. Please stay out of their intrigues or any ridiculous efforts to escape. I am a humanitarian, but discipline and order must be maintained." He looked closely at Faures as if for confirmation. Faures did not change his expression. The major shifted his feet and his throat worked for a moment before he spoke. "Surely, Professor Faures, you can from your reading of politics and history know that the maintenance of order is the first requirement of any group which is to call itself civilized."

The major's voice was almost pleading. Faures was silent for a moment.

"I shall have to think about it, Major," Faures said. "Between the reality and the theory there is often a great chasm."

The major nodded energetically. Faures and Nina turned and rejoined the other four prisoners. They moved off briskly. They walked past the columns of prisoners who were drawn up outside the barracks. The prisoners stood at a sort of relaxed parade rest, but their eyes followed the six newcomers closely. To Nina the walk meant nothing except a bizarre feeling of exposure to endless unknown eyes. Rouge, however, looked sharply in all directions, muttered to himself, seemed to be almost in a paroxysm of excitement.

They were marched to the last barracks, did a smart left turn and walked into the barracks. The guards left them at the door. The barracks was approximately one-third occupied. There were two rows of double bunks running down the length of the barracks. In the precise center of the barracks was a heavy black iron stove, with black stovepipe reaching up and through the ceiling.

Rouge went to one of the bunks closest to the stove and threw his bag of clothes and objects he had been permitted to take into the camp on the bunk. He was tremendously excited and Nina did not realize it until he had relieved himself of the bag. He stood in front of the bunk, glancing around the barracks, his eyes gleaming with excitement.

It dawned on Nina as a simple reality: Rouge had always expected to wind up in a concentration camp and it was something that he had prepared for.

Rouge looked around at the other five prisoners and his usual reticence was broken. He seemed almost ready to explode with words. They sensed it and waited for him.

"It is a brand-new camp," Rouge said rapidly, his voice full of excitement. "None of the barbed wire has rusted and the buildings are all made out of raw timber. Also it is exclusively for political prisoners. All of them were wearing red triangles on their sleeves."

"What does the red triangle mean?" one of the boys asked.

"The red triangle is worn by political prisoners. Common criminals wear green triangles; people who are merely 'anti-social' wear black triangles on their sleeve." For a moment they were all silent. Somehow it awed them to think that they had been labeled, drawn into a huge system and now left to whatever fate the system meted out.

"What is the difference between criminal and anti-social behavior?" Faures asked quietly.

"A criminal act is something like theft or rape or forgery or murder. Anti-social behavior is being a drunkard, running a whorehouse, telling fortunes, being a gypsy, or just being a cretin."

"A cretin?" Faures asked.

"That is a concentration camp word for a simple idiot," Rouge said impatiently. "A cretin is a person who has no sense of social responsibility or is an idiot or who is simply a delinquent."

"Are men and women allowed to live in the same barracks?" Faures asked.

"Only in a few camps such as this, Faures," Rouge said. "In the extermination camps, for some silly reason, they keep the sexes separated. Here it is considered unnecessary. Exactly why I do not know, but it has bothered me ever since I heard it. There is a reason, I suppose."

"How is order maintained in such circumstances?" Faures asked.

"If everything has gone well the Communists should already have established control of the camp. You will discover that the Germans do not concern themselves with the internal

management of the camp. That is left to the prisoners themselves. I saw a couple of comrades whom I recognized. They
will be coming in to see me as soon as the *Appel* is over."

Outside there was a sudden barking of orders immediately
followed by a hum of voices and the sounds of hundreds of
feet shuffling. Rouge turned away and walked over to an
unoccupied corner of the barracks. He leaned in the corner
and lit a cigarette. Almost at once the door to the barracks
was flung open and three men came in. They glanced down
the room, saw Rouge and moved toward him. They gathered around him and within five minutes they were joined
by half a dozen other men and one woman. Rouge stood
smoking, listening to what they were saying but not speaking,
somehow maintaining the air of a judge. All that the other
five prisoners could hear was the occasional word "comrade."

The other inhabitants of the barracks did not come in.
Nina, her father and the three boys sat down on bunks and
looked at one another without talking. Occasionally a word
would arc out of the conversation in the corner of the barracks. Suddenly they heard the word "Kapo" muttered in a
sharp, aggressive manner. They also heard, for the first time,
the word "kommando" and the word "Trotskyist." Once
Rouge's voice fell to a low murmur and when he had finished
the people around him turned and looked at the five people
waiting on their bunks. The woman spoke up in a low voice
and Rouge nodded at her. Immediately after that the meeting
broke up.

The group dissolved, however, in a peculiar manner. They
left singly. As each left Rouge gave what was clearly an order.
The person made no formal gesture of receiving the order,
but there was a slight stiffening of the body, a sharp nodding
of the head, and exhalation of breath which indicated that
the person understood. Nina knew that Rouge was a man of
power in the camp. She also sensed that his power was being
contested. She glanced at her father. He had stretched out

on his bunk and was glancing idly at the group in the corner. Occasionally he swung his eyes away from them and looked directly at the bunk above him. Then he would glance back at Rouge.

When the last person had left the corner Rouge walked back to the group of five. He looked at the three boys for a moment and then pointed his finger at the shortest boy.

"Who was leader of your cell?" Rouge asked and his voice had a new bite in it.

"Maggot," the boy quietly said.

"Why did he take such a name?" Rouge asked.

"Because the maggot eats away at what is rotten, cleanses it, then grows wings and is able to fly away free," the boy said. His voice was flat and confident.

Rouge smiled. Then the smile wiped off his face. He turned to the other two boys.

"I will talk to you later," Rouge said. The boys nodded. "Right now I would like to talk to Maggot's friend here and to Nina."

The other two boys drifted down to the end of the barracks and out the door. Rouge looked at Faures. Faures looked back at him.

"Do you feel like exercise?" Rouge asked.

"No," Faures said.

For a moment there was confusion on Rouge's face. Then he nodded to the small boy and Nina and went back to the corner he had occupied before. He leaned in the corner. His posture, his ease, his whole demeanor reassured Nina. Rouge was in command. He offered the boy a cigarette. The boy took it and started to thank Rouge and then stopped. Rouge nodded his head in approval. One did not thank a comrade for a piece of property; even a piece of property which would quickly go up in smoke.

"For the time being we will call you Maggot," he said, pointing at the small boy. "Blush we will now call Nina. The

names of others we will decide on later. I will now tell you
the situation in the camp. It is a very new camp, only six
weeks old. The Party has a link to the camp and orders can
be transmitted instantly from the outside. As soon as the
Party learned I had been captured they passed the word that
I was to be the leader in the camp."

Rouge could not conceal his pleasure. He looked straight
ahead, but a grin flicked over his face.

"Remember, Rouge, I am not a Communist," Nina said
firmly.

"We know that, Nina," Rouge said. "But you do not belong to another political party or faction; thus, it is our calculation that you will become one of us. In any case you will
not betray us. I must tell you that the Party thinks one of the
new boys who came with us is a 'plant' by the Germans.
They do not know which one, but neither of them has a
record of political activity. We will find out which one soon
enough."

Nina could not resist a sensation of excitement. Ever since
her capture she had been more apprehensive than she wanted
to acknowledge. Living constantly in a world of rumors and
half truths and gossip and partial information she had grown
increasingly frightened of what she did not know. Now, for
the first time, someone spoke with authority. She had a thrill
of intense admiration for Rouge.

"What are the problems we face inside the camp?" Nina
said.

Rouge looked at her sharply and gave his hard twisted
grin. He nodded slightly and Nina realized that by using the
word "we" she had confirmed his prediction that she would
become one of "them."

"First, we do not have complete control of the camp yet,"
Rouge said. "There are a group of Trotskyists, a few Catholic
Centralists, a large group of Social Democrats, a hard corps
of Syndicalists and a group of independents who belong to

no party, but who apparently fought with the Loyalists in Spain, but are intensely anti-Stalin."

"What proportion of the prisoners are Communists?" Maggot II asked.

"About one-fifth," Rouge said. He shook his head. "That is enough. We will work on the division among the others. The most important thing is to get organized at once. Here is the way the camp operates. Every day except Sunday the Germans require a certain number of kommandos to go out and cut timber or occasionally to build an anti-aircraft emplacement in one of the nearby towns. There are also kommandos who work within the camp disposing of sewage or hauling rubbish or merely cleaning up the camp. The Kommandant is an absolute devil on cleanliness. It is a fetish with him. There is also a stone quarry about ten kilometers from the camp. It is killing work in the quarry. People assigned to the permanent kommando at the quarry do not live more than four or five weeks. Berlin has set a fantastically high quota on the quarry. Probably the stone is used to strengthen the Atlantic Wall. The quarry uses old ammunition which has been rejected by the military for explosives. It is very unstable and goes off sometimes when they are tamping it into place. At present the kommando is driven to the quarry in trucks. But as the petrol shortage grows worse they will probably have to march there and back every day. It is a very short life to be on the quarry kommando."

"We should make a protest to the camp Kommandant," Nina said.

Rouge looked at her. He twisted his shoulders in a gesture Nina could not understand. It was part mocking and part resignation.

"No, Nina, we must see that our enemies in the camp are assigned to the quarry kommando," he said without expression. "The work lists for each kommando are controlled by an *Arbeitstatistik* which is an office located in the adminis-

tration building. This office has a card on each prisoner and
assigns him to different kommandos. The Party thinks that
they have located a soldier in that office who was formerly a
Communist in Germany and who has disguised that fact
from the German authorities. We will know shortly. But this
is none of your concern. Your concern is to try and see which
of the politicals are reliable and which are beyond trust. Your
second responsibility is to survive. Those of us who survive
will run France and Europe after the war."

Nina looked from the corner in which she and Rouge and
Maggott II were talking. Her father was on his back, his
hands in the air, holding a book. He read very quickly, but
his wrists were so thin.

Very quickly Nina began to learn what life in the camp
was all about. She did not try to analyze what she saw. She
merely did what Rouge told her to do and observed. But she
observed very closely.

The thing that astounded her the most was Rouge's complete absorption in politics. He quite literally did not notice
trees, clouds, the color of the sky, the food he ate, the texture
of the early summer days. With a single-mindedness that was
beyond her comprehension Rouge concentrated on politics.
He was the complete ideological man. He would listen to
gossip endlessly if there was any chance of gleaning a piece
of information. He would listen to an aging Frenchman who
had once been a very high politician and had been a Minister
in two different governments run through his catalogue of
misery. The moment that he realized the ex-Minister had
nothing which would help him he spun on his heel and
walked away.

For the first week Rouge spent almost eighteen hours a day
talking to people who slipped in and out of his barracks.
The corner in which he conferred was pockmarked with the

stubs of cigarettes and smelled of fear. No one went near the corner unless they were summoned by Rouge.

At the end of a week Rouge was ready to make his first move.

One afternoon he called a meeting which included Nina, Maggot II and five men from other barracks. He did not introduce them to one another. He simply began to talk.

"The composition of this camp has been put together very carefully," Rouge said. His voice was calm and full of authority. Nina watched him with wonderment for she knew that he had not moved outside of the barracks since he had arrived. And yet he was now telling them about the environment in which they lived. "Everyone here is a political. But the composition of the group is such that we Communists will be wiped out because we are such a small minority. It is clear to me that the Kommandant knows those of us who are Communists. His orders are probably to exterminate the Communists before any other group. If the Allies ever make a landing or the Russians get close we will be the first to go. But he would like to have us exterminated by our enemies within the camp. Everything else is window dressing. The Kommandant is a very shrewd person. He has mixed up the politicals in such proportion that in any kind of conflict, from a vote to a physical fight, they will defeat us."

"Comrade, I do not agree," one of the men said quietly. "The whole program seems to me to be utterly casual. I see no pattern in it."

Rouge cut in quickly and with the incisiveness of a sharp knife cutting through sausage.

"What about the Syndicalists?" Rouge said. "There are only a handful of such political idiots in all of France and most of them fought against our cause in Spain. But here there are almost fifty of them in one camp. Do you think that is an accident? Don't be a fool. Because the Syndicalists are

committed to violence and direct action the Kommandant is
hoping that they will wipe us out at the first opportunity. He
is right. Just out of their romantic impulses and their criminal emphasis on individuality the Syndicalists and the Anarchists might do exactly that."

"They are very innocent people," another of the men said.
"They really hate violence, and the only circumstances under
which they might use violence is when they think a left-wing
bureaucracy might take over. They are simply people who
hate bureaucracy of any kind. They are not really dangerous."

Rouge waited a long moment. He dug in a shirt pocket
and took out a cigarette. He lit the cigarette and took a deep
breath. The acrid smoke came trickling out of his nostrils. He
waved his hands so that it did not obscure his eyes. He was
staring at the man who had just spoken.

"Comrade, one more error in judgment like that and you
will not be with us at the next meeting," Rouge said. He
said it lightly, almost with frivolity, so that everyone would
know that he was deadly serious. The man who had spoken
did not say a word. Without moving a muscle and without
his expression changing he seemed to sag. The firmness went
out of his face and the bones of his body. One moment he
was a hard and tough man, the next moment he was somehow gelatinous. He had not moved his body or his face, but
he capitulated.

Rouge looked around the rest of the group. No one spoke.

"It is very simple," Rouge said. There was a kind of metallic edge of certitude to his words. "The Kommandant, acting
on orders from Berlin, is hoping that the Syndicalists will kill
us off. He then hopes that the Social Democrats will have a
pitched battle with the Syndicalists. Whichever group survives is of no importance. For whoever survives he will match
against the Catholic Centralists. In any kind of physical combat the Catholics will win. You will note that because of their

privileged position before they came to the camp and since
their arrival, they are at least a couple of kilograms heavier
than most of the other prisoners and a couple of centimeters
taller. The major is a very shrewd person. Does anyone have
a question?"

No one spoke. Everyone in the group was looking either at
the floor or out the window. He was ready to go on with his
talk. But Nina interrupted him.

"The important thing is to make a breakout and escape
from the camp," Nina said. "This would cause the Nazis the
most embarrassment and would interfere most with their
military activities."

"No," Rouge said flatly and instantly. "No one in our group
is going to make an effort to escape. First, because it is technically impossible. Secondly, because those of us who stay
here and survive will have an enormous impact on France
after the war is over. Thirdly, the concentration camp is a
form of discipline and a kind of school which all Party members should be glad to endure." Then he smiled wryly. "And
what would you do anyway if you escape? Not a damn thing.
This is where we belong."

Rouge made his hand into a ball. Everyone except Nina
looked up at him and nodded, eyes suddenly alight with
excitement.

Talking very rapidly, Rouge briefed them on life in a concentration camp. Nina was stunned at the lore and information Rouge had at his fingertips. Again she sensed that he had
longed to wind up in a concentration camp, for it was here
that his true genius came to work.

He told them first about Buchenwald. The first Kommandant was S.S. Sturmbahnführer Koch. In a casual voice he
told them of Koch's love of bloodletting. Koch killed for pure
pleasure. A concentration camp which specialized in killing
was a perfect fulfillment of his life. He had married a beauti-

ful German whore, built in the classic mold: blond, tall, methodical, incapable of understanding anything that was not German.

The demands of Koch and his wife upon one another were too much. Koch turned to homosexuality and his Frau turned to tattooed skins. And to sex. Kommandant Koch inspected the new arrivals for promising young boys. Frau Koch inspected the new arrivals for their prowess as stallions. They would walk down the lines of new arrivals, each making notes in their notebooks as to numbers and names. In each case their selected prisoners were given special privileges, fattened up, given an extra thousand calories a day and then finally called into action. In each case the conclusion was the same. Whether they were Kerr Koch's boys or Frau Koch's men they all were exterminated very quickly after they were called. The good family Koch seemed to revel in their decent and symmetrical life.

"Koch was too crude," Rouge said, his voice as flat as ever but his eyes darting around at his listeners. "He was replaced by S.S. Sturmbahnführer Pister who was more canny. At this moment Pister is playing off the French against the Ukrainians, the Russians, the Jews and anyone else he can involve." He paused and looked around the group. "The Nazis are no longer stupid. Frau Koch can no longer take the skins of tattooed humans and make lampshades out of them. They have gone beyond that."

Rouge lit another cigarette. He waited for comment. He knew there would be none. None of his listeners had ever heard such tales before. They stood stunned, suddenly aware of the awful dangers which confronted them. When Rouge spoke again he spoke to a group of followers, a band of believers.

Crisply and very economically Rouge outlined what must be done in their camp.

First, they must develop their contact with the German

ex-Communist who worked in the *Arbeitstatistik* office. Secondly, they must make sure that every Kapo was a Communist. Thirdly, they must clearly identify the political affiliation of every prisoner in the camp. Fourthly, they must make sure that both the central cookshack and the medical center were manned by Communists.

Once this was accomplished they would be able to overcome all of the other political factions in the camp, despite the fact that they were a minority, and most surely, the one that had been marked for extinction.

When he had finished Rouge leaned in the corner. He watched the group, waiting for comment. Nina knew it was a crucial time. If a prisoner spoke he must be sure of what he said. It was a time of testing.

There was a long cool silence. Two or three of the men were older than Rouge. They had been through the Spanish Civil War. They were used to prisons and exile and to hard living conditions. They glanced at one another and finally one of them spoke. He was a man made of cartilage and bone and a great faith in the Communist Party.

"Does this mean, Comrade, that we should exterminate the leaders of the other political factions?" the man said. He looked directly at Rouge while he turned an unlit cigarette in his hand. To Nina he looked like a relic, a museum piece of the perfect, seasoned, toughened revolutionary.

Rouge jerked. It was like a quick spasm of revulsion. Then his face went flat.

"No, Comrade, we do not kill off the opposition," Rouge said. His voice was cold and deep. "The whole technique is to have our opponents kill one another off. We are the defenders of every common man, the supporters of every good cause. We are not murderers. But if others murder in a way that benefits us it is our duty to encourage their behavior."

Quickly and with a kind of urgency Rouge explained what he meant. Nina could not tell whether they were intrigued by his ingenuity or whether they were horrified by his methods. In any case none of them raised an objection.

The next morning Nina went for a walk around the compound with her father. Without a moment's hesitation she told him what they had discussed with Rouge. He listened carefully, his head cocked to one side. Occasionally he asked a clarifying question. He nodded as if he were receiving a report from a bright student.

When Nina had finished they walked for a half hour without talking. Faures identified the trees surrounding the compound. Once he looked at the clouds and reminded Nina of their Greek names. They watched a squirrel dart down from a tree and start to wend its way through the barbed wire entanglements. It was a small, alert and very active animal. It brushed through all of the barbed wire without touching a barb. But when it got to the charged wire it paused, raised itself on its hind legs and sniffed the air. It hesitated for several seconds, weaving its head back and forth, sensing that there was something strange about the wire. Then it turned and made its way back to the forest.

"What do you think of what Rouge said?" Nina said.

"I do not fully understand such a man," Faures said. "If he possessed the simplicity of that squirrel I would trust him more. The squirrel knew only that there was something terribly different between the electrically charged wire and other wires. So the squirrel did the conservative thing. It retreated. I wonder if Rouge has that wisdom?"

Nina felt a surge of irritation with her father.

"We are not squirrels, Father. We are political prisoners who may be exterminated at any moment. Rouge, at least, has a program of action. What do you think of it?"

She really was not interested in his answer. In some way Nina felt their roles had been reversed. Now she was the person who knew more about life and survival and reality than her father. He seemed like a very ancient and fragile child who must be protected. She had only asked him about Rouge so that he would not feel resentful at being excluded from the conference. Also she still had a lingering sense of guilt that her father had been made a political prisoner because of her own activities. His fragility and his abstracted air added to her sense of concern. He seemed utterly incapable of taking care of himself.

"Rouge is really an idiot," Faures said quietly. His voice had an edge of speculation in it, but he also spoke with authority. "Take just one thing. He believes that the Kommandant of this camp is an ingenious and shrewd person. Nothing could be further from the truth. The Kommandant is a typical German bureaucrat. He is ignorant, uncouth, unimaginative and wants only to avoid trouble. When Rouge says that the Kommandant is pitting one political faction against another he is indulging in one of his own fantasies. I guarantee you, dear girl, that the Kommandant has not the remotest notion of the political makeup of this camp. But Rouge must believe this to make himself important, to make his struggle worthwhile, to exact sacrifices from his followers."

Nina felt a flush of outrage.

"Father, do not repeat things like that to anyone else," she said as if she were talking to a child. "You simply do not understand what is going on in this camp."

Her father looked at her, twisting his head on his thin neck for a better view. They walked by four sentry boxes before he spoke.

"It is so strange," he said with wonderment in his voice. "Throughout history it is clear that the cruel ones, the impulsive ones, the ones who act out of rage, the conspirators, the revolutionaries, all share one characteristic. They are stupid. It is only their enemies who endow them with a false wisdom. You are dealing with the scum of Germany and, to make yourselves important, you must persuade yourselves that they are devils and ingenious."

Nina was so angry that she strode out ahead of her father and completed her circuit of the compound two hundred yards ahead of him. Faures walked along casually, looking at the sentry boxes, the trees beyond the compound, occasionally sniffing the resin-scented air with pleasure, three times picking up pieces of grass and chewing on them.

Faures looked, for all the world, like a perfectly innocent and very thin child.

11. Victory
of the Believers

A T THE end of only three days Rouge was ready to take over the internal government of the camp. He outlined it carefully to one Communist selected from each of the barracks.

"These guards are not S.S. troops, they are rejects from the Russian front and men who are unfit for strenuous combat duty," Rouge said. "At heart they are all clerks."

"But they are clerks with guns," one of the Communists said with a twisted smile.

"Precisely. That is why we have to play on their clerkly minds," Rouge said. "As some of you know they have been set a quota by Berlin of one hundred square meters of stone a week. Each Monday a small train comes to the railhead at the end of the quarry to pick up the stone. Making sure that the quota is fulfilled is really all they worry about. Right now it is easy to fill that quota. Because the camp is new they can use all the prisoners they wish at the quarry. But in a few weeks surrounding commands will start to call on the camp for kommandos to go out and do various chores. Then the meeting of the quota will be more difficult. Our task is to make sure that it is impossible."

They looked up at him in surprise.

"Why do we want to sabotage the quarry workers?" someone asked. "I thought we merely wanted to get the people's enemies assigned to that kommando."

Nina was the only one who knew Rouge well enough to detect that he paused for a moment, his eyes came to an unbelievably hard focus on a nail in the floor, and then his face was normal.

"The tactic is changed," Rouge said. "We are going to show the Socialists and Anarchists and the rest of them that we stand ready to help them against the common oppressor."

The others were puzzled.

"Has this policy been cleared with the . . . the outside?" the Spanish Republican asked.

"Yes. Now is the time to stand shoulder to shoulder with anyone, Comrade, who is willing to save the Russians," Rouge said casually. He spoke slogans as if they were slogans and for this reason made a very good impression. "We may ourselves become a fighting group, operating behind the Fascist lines."

Their faces lit up. In the midst of a prison camp their leader was talking easily about their roaming the countryside like the partisans in the Balkans. It was enough to end the doubts.

"Look, Rouge, we make up only one-fifth of the population of the camp," a middle-aged man said. He had been a famous left-wing journalist on the outside. He was soft around the waist, but he had a stubborn little chin and an acid wit. "How can we cut down the stone production just by ourselves?"

"The thing to do is get at least a few Communists on the quarry kommando," Rouge said. "Then it is all a matter of technique, Comrade. With a small pair of pliers you can break several teeth on a saw, let the air out of one of the truck tires so that a few hours are wasted that way. Start a fire close to the explosives dump. Undercut a slope of rock so it crushes a guard. Such little incidents always cause more confusion than one can imagine. By the time the saw is replaced or the tire is fixed or the wound is bandaged there will have been a flap of excitement. The opportunities are endless."

The group looked at Rouge with admiration. A few of them pointed out that almost surely the Kommandant would respond with some sort of punishment. That was precisely, Rouge said, what he hoped would happen. He did not elaborate the statement and no one asked him about it.

"There is another way to irritate the Kommandant and his staff," Nina said softly. She had never attended a Communist meeting. She was not sure who was allowed to speak.

"How?" Rouge asked.

"All Germans are horrified by filth, but this man is pathological about it," Nina said. "I noticed when he makes his inspections that he is always running his finger underneath bunks looking for dust. He also loses his temper whenever he sees a prisoner who has not taken a shower recently."

"What are you suggesting?" Rouge asked, but some of the harshness had gone out of his voice. He showed an awakening interest.

"One kommando a day is responsible for cleaning up the camp," Nina said softly. "I suggest that we infiltrate that kommando and sabotage its efforts. Nothing will frustrate the Kommandant more rapidly."

Rouge leaned back in the corner, closed his eyes, and put his head toward the ceiling. He stayed that way for a few moments. When he looked down and opened his eyes his face had cracked into a smile.

"Very good, Nina," Rouge said. He pointed at Maggot II. "I want you, Maggot II, to make sure that some of our people are on the cleanup kommando. Use your imagination with what can be done."

In two days the camp was in an uproar. The tiny hospital treated a rash of people who had severe cuts in their legs. One-third of the trucks suffered either from flat tires or mechanical breakdown. The prisoners who manned the garage and machine shop were unable to keep up with the repairs to the trucks. They complained of a lack of spare parts, but even when the spare parts arrived, by the time they were unpacked delicate things such as spark plugs or magnetos were broken. Two guards had suffered critical wounds from sudden cave-ins at the quarry. The stonecutting saws lost teeth at a fast rate.

The physical aspect of the camp also changed. The administration building was the only building which had flush toilets and running water. Behind each barracks was a small latrine, the contents of which were emptied each day into a huge container which was mounted on four wheels. This sewage was transported half a mile outside the camp, where it was emptied into large diked fields where it served as fertilizer for vegetables grown for prisoner consumption. Work on the sewage disposal cart was considered the most unpleasant job in the camp. The morning after the meeting with Rouge, the cart, just as it was filled, was overturned directly in the middle of the camp. Two tons of excrement spilled out onto the thin lawn. Immediately the odor was magnified by the sun. There was a great moan of disgust from the prisoners. The Kommandant appeared on the porch of the administration building. He stared down toward the cart and the men milling around it. He barked an order and someone brought him a pair of binoculars. He raised them to his eyes, took one glance, and immediately began to trot toward the overturned cart. Normally when he was excited or performed any physical exercise, the Kommandant's face became red. The prisoners noted that he was, on this occasion, deathly pale.

He stopped at the edge of the great stinking pool and looked at it in disbelief. He swayed as if he might faint. Then he turned and looked at the cart. One of its wheels had come off and rolled to one side and this caused the cart to turn over.

"Clean it up," he said in a voice that was tiny, tense, and overcontrolled. The prisoners looked up, startled. The major was almost catatonic with rage.

"Clean it up with what?" one of the prisoners said. He looked down at his hands and then out at the vast pool of sewage. Then he looked at the Kommandant.

The Kommandant took a white handkerchief from his pocket and put it to his nostrils. His face, quite suddenly, had a stricken, childlike, innocent look to it. Some of the prisoners were sure that behind the thick glasses and the white handkerchief he was sobbing.

The Kommandant turned and walked rapidly back to the administration building. Five minutes later a truck roared up beside the sewage cart. It was full of pails and shovels. Two German guards dumped them out at the feet of the prisoner kommando.

"The Kommandant wants it cleaned up in a half hour or the Kapo in charge will be shot," one of the guards yelled. He put his hand over his nose and mouth and the truck engaged gears and sped away from the miasma of warm, rotting sewage.

The Kapo gathered the prisoners around him. He looked around at them evenly.

"As you know, it is a rule that a Kapo can inflict injury or punishment upon his subordinates to get a job finished," the

Kapo said. Few of the prisoners knew it but he was a Communist. "I want you to take off your clothes and use the buckets and shovels to reload the cart. If you have not finished in twenty-five minutes I will use my shovel to punish one of you a minute until I am shot. The punishment will be a single blow with this paddle." He picked out of the stack of shovels a peat-digging spade. Its edges were as sharp as blades. He smiled around at them. "The blow will be administered with all of my force at the nape of your neck. Now take off your clothes and get to work."

The prisoners were not frightened. They knew they could clean up the mess in that time. With a kind of adolescent frenzy they tore off their clothes, grabbed buckets and shovels, and stormed into the small lake. It was too outrageous, too preposterous, too filthy a situation to be taken seriously. They roared with laughter as they passed the buckets back to the cart. The other prisoners were attracted by the smell and the sound. They gathered in a semicircle on the windward side of the cart and watched the proceedings.

At that moment Rouge presented himself at the administration building. He requested permission from the guard to see the Kommandant on urgent business. The guard grinned and told Rouge this was a bad time to see the Kommandant. Rouge nodded, but still insisted. The guard went inside and then came back out. He led Rouge into the Kommandant's office.

As he closed the door the guard's face had a look of utter astonishment. Rouge and the guard both knew that the Kommandant had never seen a prisoner before in his office. Rouge had gambled that the trauma of the overturned cart would have upset the Kommandant's normal decorum.

The Kommandant was standing at the window watching the men at work. The small muscles in the back of his neck trembled. Once he gulped, resisting the impulse to vomit. Rouge coughed. The Kommandant turned but Rouge was not certain whether the Kommandant really knew he was in the office.

"Herr Kommandant, I have a suggestion," Rouge said quickly. "What has happened with the cart is a real tragedy. But even when the kommando has cleaned up everything they can with the shovels and the buckets there will still be hundreds of pounds of," he hesitated, "maybe thousands of pounds of debris in between the blades of grass and soaked into the ground. With the weather this hot it will leave a stench for weeks over the camp."

The Kommandant stiffened.

"Swine, absolutely filthy swine," the Kommandant whispered. "They told me that the prisoners were inhuman, less than animals, when they briefed me in Berlin, but I did not believe it until now. No German would have allowed the cart to tip over. But no human, whether he were German or not, would play so madly in his own excrement."

Rouge looked down through the window. The prisoners did seem to be enjoying themselves. They danced through the rapidly diminishing pool of sewage, jumping like goats, filthy from their feet to their chins, their shrill laughter screeching into the Kommandant's office.

"That smell, Herr Kommandant, will persist for weeks unless something is done," Rouge said.

The Kommandant looked up sharply, established some contact again with reality. His face lost its paleness and assumed its normal ruddy color.

"What do you suggest?" he said, glancing again through the window.

"Let us use the firefighting hoses to wash it away," Rouge said. "If we can hose enough water over the soiled area the dilution will be so great it will leave no odor."

The Kommandant rocked on his heels for a moment.

"I will think about it," the Kommandant said.

Rouge put the next prod in very carefully.

"The odor will not disturb the prisoners, sir," he said. "We are used to it. But visitors might be offended."

The Kommandant cringed. He looked carefully at Rouge and regained his control. The only visitors here would be his superiors. The Kommandant nodded for Rouge to leave.

Rouge nodded and left the office. He knew the Kommandant would supply the hoses, but he must wait a decent interval so it would look like the Kommandant's decision rather than that of a prisoner.

Ten minutes later a squad of guards began to give orders to the Kapos. All of the fire lines in the camp were to be hitched up to one another and when the men were through the area was to be hosed down. Ten minutes before the half-hour deadline the cart was two-thirds full, the hose was turned on and the prisoners who had been working in the sewage danced in front of the powerful stream of water, roaring with laughter as it washed away the excrement. Finally they were all a dead shark-belly white, only their faces and hands tanned by the sun. They retreated from the soiled area. The powerful stream poured out tons of water and gradually the blemish was eliminated. The stench disappeared. A new wheel was put on the cart and the prisoners hauled it out of the gate toward the vegetable plots.

The next day the Kommandant discovered three garbage cans back of three different barracks which had not been emptied and were already beginning to swarm with flies. At each barracks he called the inmates together and gave them a furious lecture. When he returned to the administration building he discovered that the plumbing had gone awry and the toilets were backed up. Also the water that came out of the taps had an earthen color to it. None of the guards were plumbers, but several of the prisoners were. They were instantly called in and ordered to find out what had happened. They repaired the damage and gave the Kommandant an explanation. Apparently someone had flushed a solid object down the toilet. Owing to a mistake in plumbing some of this water backed up into the pure water supply which came through the faucets.

The Kommandant's face worked with a mixture of disgust and rage as they explained. The thought that he might have been drinking contaminated water frightened him.

"The whole thing was organized by Rouge," Nina told her father. She could not keep the admiration out of her voice.

They were taking an exercise period late in the afternoon. Exercise was optional, but most of the prisoners spent the time walking around the compound, keeping just inside of the guard wire which was about twelve inches off the ground. Any prisoner who crossed the guard wire was automatically assumed to be trying to escape. Any guard who saw him would commence shooting. Faures walked for several moments without speaking.

"It will probably give the Communists control of the camp," Faures said quietly. "Although liberals would like to deny it, every nation has a character of its own. It is one of the sure lessons of history. Germans are obsessed with cleanliness. They are also obsessed by a passion for order and regularity. By sabotaging the stone deliveries and the sewage systems Rouge hit very close to home. What do you think will happen when the Communists have control of the camp?"

Nina had never considered the question. In her experience the Communists had been the most courageous people she knew and the only ones willing to stand up to the Nazis. Somewhere in her mind she had the idea that they would be more generous than the Nazis. She told her father this.

"History has taught us a few other lessons," Faures said. "One lesson is that the former revolutionary who comes to power is the quickest to become an oppressor of the most savage type. Maybe it will not happen in this case. I hope not."

It was Friday afternoon before the Kommandant realized that the camp would not meet its quota of stone for the train that would arrive on Monday. He quickly had the word passed that work would continue over Saturday and Sunday to fulfill the quota. The Kapos ran from one barracks to the other passing out the information.

Almost at once a heavy dignified man who had been the Catholic mayor of a small town was in Rouge's barracks. Rouge was lying on his bed with his eyes closed. The Catholic shook him awake. Rouge opened one eye and glanced at the man.

"Go on," Rouge said. "I can hear you with my eyes closed."

"Do not think we are ignorant of what you Communists are doing," the man said with a quiet ferocity. "We Catholics have met among ourselves and we have also met with the Anarchists and Syndicalists and the Social Democrats. The pattern is clear. It has been you Communists who have sabotaged a smoothly working system. Until this week we were able to meet the quota easily. Now suddenly it all collapses and at every point of collapse a Communist is involved."

"Are you pro-Nazi?" Rouge asked softly.

The mayor hesitated.

"You know that is not so," he said. "I am here simply because I am anti-Nazi. But as long as we are here we should work with one another against the common enemy. Our tactic is to survive."

"*Your* tactic is to survive," Rouge said without opening his eyes. "Our tactic is to attack. Leave. There is nothing to discuss."

The order to leave broke the ex-mayor's composure. He bent over Rouge's closed face and in a low rapid voice began to utter a stream of obscenities strangely mixed with the kind of orders one gives to a subordinate. Occasionally he would glance up and shake his head, as if reality had been distorted, not believing that he could actually be defied by a person such as Rouge.

Rouge did not open his eyes. Once he brushed a fly from his face.

Finally the mayor stood up and walked toward the door. He held his head and shoulders erect, like a mayor leading a procession, but his torso and his legs twitched nervously. They barely carried the rigid head and shoulders out of the barracks.

"What do you think now?" Nina asked her father, leaning over his bunk. Everyone in the barracks had heard the conversation and the mayor's loss of control.

"The Communists will win," Faures said flatly. "A confident and strong tyrant always kills off his strongest enemy. A weak and vacillating tyrant always tries to recruit his aid. The Kommandant has all the weaknesses of the German. He will turn over the internal government of the camp to the Communists. Not because he likes them, but because they seem to him to be the only ones that can assure that his quotas will be met and that discipline will be maintained."

A half hour later Rouge walked again to the Kommandant's office. Again he came to a stiff attention and requested permission to see the Kommandant. He was with the Kommandant for a half hour. No one ever learned what they discussed but two hours later there was an *Appel* and a new list of Kapos was announced. A murmur ran through the prisoners and the guards reflexively raised their rifles. The murmur died away. All of the new Kapos were Communists.

"The task of the new Kapos is to see that the stone quota for the week is met," the Kommandant said. "If the quota is not met by Monday the Kapos will be held responsible."

A groan went up from the workers. In the newly organized camp they had not been forced to work yet on Saturdays and Sundays.

The next morning, a Saturday, the new kommandos were made up with the new Kapos as leaders. The composition of the kommandos was very cunning. The most active and outspoken of the Anarchists and the Catholic Centralists were all put into one kommando. The Social Democrats were scattered throughout the other kommandos.

"Rouge has gotten to the ex-Communist who is in the work assignment office," Faures said out of the side of his mouth to Nina. He listened to the whole proceedings with fascination. His eyes flickered back and forth, observing the Kommandant, Rouge, the guards, the various groups of prisoners. He murmured something to himself.

"What did you say, Father?" Nina asked.

"I'm sorry, my dear. This is the first time I have seen political man in real life," Faures said. "Before he was always a faceless person in a book."

For some reason the statement offended Nina. She glanced straight ahead without replying.

That evening when the trucks rolled back into camp the weekly quota had almost been filled.

Again there was an *Appel*. The Kommandant announced that every kommando except one had equaled or exceeded its daily quota. With half a day's work on Sunday they should meet the weekly quota. Then he turned and pointed at Kommando Number 8.

"Kommando Number 8 did not produce today," the Kommandant said. His voice was troubled, mildly scolding, like a schoolmaster who must address some particularly obstreperous group. He paused and his mouth worked soundlessly, as if he were chewing on some tough sour object. "If tomorrow the stone quarried in by Kommando 8 is not four times as large as it is at the present time the Kapo will designate the man in his kommando who is chiefly responsible. That man will be shot."

Nina sensed instantly that these were not the Kommandant's words, nor was it his idea. This was an instruction he
had received from Rouge. She marveled at the ingenuity
and simplicity of the idea. She could imagine the next day
the battle that would go on within each member of Kommando 8. Kommando 8 was the one in which the anti-Communists had been gathered. Their Anarchist or Catholic
principles would tell them one thing. Their urge for survival
would tell them to work harder. She could also sense the
shame that they would feel if they started to work harder.
Dimly she was aware of the awful gnawing battle which
would go on inside each of them.

The next day Kommando Number 8 had produced not
four times as much as the previous day, but six times as
much. The Kapo in charge had chuckled as he reported to
Rouge. He said that for the first half hour of work they had
done almost nothing, merely glancing at one another. Then
someone had began to saw quickly for a bare thirty seconds.
Instantly the kommando had been transformed. They worked
like mad puppets moved by urgent hands. They had gulped
their thin soup during the middle of the day and had instantly
trotted back to their saws and explosives and shovels. The
stone piled up faster than the truck could haul it away.

By that night the control of the Communists as a group,
and Rouge as an individual, over the camp had been established.

When they exercised that evening Faures was amused.

"Your friend Rouge managed to double-cross everyone,"
he said. "The Communists who wanted to have control of
the camp by eliminating their enemies and, thus, all becoming little Caesars have been betrayed. The anti-Communists
who are supposed to eliminate the Communists have become
deathly afraid of the system. And the Kommandant, who is
supposed to quietly eliminate the Communists, is now working in league with their leader."

Nina walked on without talking. Her father was a fool, she thought. A senile fool who thought up crazy schemes. She did not learn until months later that he was the only one who had guessed the entire truth.

12. Kapos, Hard Stone and Common Criminals

THE sixth of June came. By evening the rumor had spread through the entire camp. The guards moved briskly in their towers . . . and when the prisoners tossed stones over the fences and against the towers there were quick spasmodic spurts of fire. Followed by a derisive laugh from the prisoners. Allied planes flew past in low and lazy flights and maniac prisoners went out to have their pictures taken. There was a bustle about the administration building. The prisoners were ecstatic with excitement. The Communists pointed out that the Allies should have landed the summer before, specified the plot to undermine the Soviet Union. There were rumors that special tank columns were being sent on lightning raids across France to capture the prison camps. There were other rumors of air-drops of paratroopers or at least of food and cigarettes.

A Maqui from the nearby village, inflamed by the excitement, ran to the edge of the barbed wire and threw a packet

of food onto the grass. A nervous guard shot and killed him.
From the nearby forest a bullet caught the guard and tore
away his throat. The guard ran, hobbling and bubbling,
down the expanse of grass between the barracks, his fingers
to his throat, and died just at the first step of the administration building. He died with a silly grin on his face and
at least fifty prisoners ran up to look at the rare spectacle of
a dead German guard. The guards fired into the air in a
quite random way.

The anti-Communists called a rally and were beaten un-
mercifully by the guards. The guards asked to talk to the
Kommandant. They wanted protection. The Kommandant
refused to see them and told them they were close to
mutiny.

Rouge called an emergency meeting of the Communist
leaders and included Nina. He proposed that they at once
make a few demands on the Kommandant to indicate to him
that they expected eventually to dominate the camp. Rouge
assured them the Kommandant had no control over the
camp and wanted none. But he would kill any prisoner
who tried to escape. After all, Berlin was above the
Kommandant. They finally agreed on two issues. The first of
these was a reduction in the weekly quota of stone from the
quarry. Secondly, they were to ask for the right to send and
receive letters. Rouge pointed out that the second request
was really the most important. It would allow them to establish contact with the Underground.

"Solidarity among genuine Communists is now of the ut-
most importance," Rouge said earnestly. "Already the left-
wing fakirs, the false Socialists, those who specialize in mis-
leading the masses will have seen the handwriting on the
wall. They will be flocking to join the Underground but their
real objective will be to maintain political power after
France has been liberated."

The group standing around Rouge trembled slightly.

None of them asked how Rouge had gotten orders from the outside before. The things at hand were too exciting. They shivered with the anticipation of future power, were stunned by the visions that snapped through their heads. The time of fear and apprehension was over. A new time was coming. None of them knew precisely the shape and nature of what was to come, but all felt it would be soon. When they dispersed they walked out of the barracks with their shoulders squared. They watched Rouge and two of their Comrades head for the administration building. For the first time they made no effort to melt in among the other prisoners.

Nina and her father went for one of their long walks around the perimeter of the camp. Nina told Faures what the Communists had decided to do. When she told him of the request to reduce the stone quota for the camp Faures stopped in midstride. He swung around and faced Nina.

"My God, they are fools," Faures said. "I knew they were intense and committed, but I never realized that they were fools. Is there any way to stop them?"

Nina felt, again, an irritation with her father. Maybe, she thought, he is senile.

"No, they are already in the Kommandant's office," she said. "I do not see what is so foolish about their two demands."

Faures walked for ten seconds without responding. He seemed lost in thought. He looked down at his feet. Then he raised his head.

"Nina, my dear, there are only three types of people who are prepared to murder, torture, maim and let blood without limit. The first is the fearful man. The second is the man in the grip of a vision, an idealist. The third is the professional: the common criminal. The Kommandant is a fearful man. He is frightened of disorder and violence. He is frightened at the prospect of not meeting his stone quota. He is paralyzed at what some nameless bureaucrat in Berlin will think of a simple statistic which indicates that his quota has gone down. He wants things to run smoothly. That is why he was willing to turn the internal government of the camp over to the Communists whom he hates. Just because he is fearful."

"You mean that Rouge is the idealist murderer?" Nina said. Her voice was almost sarcastic, but when she looked at the slight bent figure of her father it was impossible. "Is he not better than the Kommandant? The fearful murderer." She really believed none of this; it was a crazy discussion.

Her father walked and pondered. Nina looked at him and realized that he suffered less than anyone in the camp: it was so much like the University.

"No, my dear, you do not understand the difference between the two types. The fearful man will kill only those of whom he is fearful, but the intellectual in the grip of a vision goes far beyond that. It takes an intellectual to plan and work out, with loving detail, the mass murders of the world. It takes sweep and imagination. One must believe in abstractions if one is to kill immensely. One must have thought of it in the library, or the study or the seminar. He can persuade himself, completely, by pure reason, that whole categories of people stand in the way of the vision. Then he will cheerfully eliminate the entire category in the name of the vision. A peasant or a working man cannot kill by category. He will kill his *own* landlord or his *own* employer or his *own* wife. He can murder in passion but not in cold logic. The intellectual has a bigger grasp. He can, by the beautiful refinements of the mind, by its marvelous intricacies, come to have a broad, reasoned and wonderful vision. He puts history, or power, or right, or necessity on his side. Once he has the reason, he can kill. Stalin was an intellectual who wiped out the entire class of kulaks because he had convinced himself intellectually they stood in the way of history. Later he wiped out an entire intellectual class. With all the cunning of an intellectual who had come to power, he knew they were the greatest menace. And he was envied by all of the librarians, writers, professors and coffee shop intellectuals. They smoldered with envy of Stalin even when they banded together to protest his mass executions. Almost any of them would, in their secret hearts, gladly have changed places with him."

"Librarians are the natural murderers of the world," Nina said speculatively. "It is an interesting idea." She hated her father. That was the only thing she was sure of. When she spoke her voice was sharper. "It seems to me that the murdering is always being done by your honest sailors or Cossacks or simple soldiers or some group of workers who cheerfully beat someone to death."

"You do not understand, my dear," Faures said and he raised his finger, held it at chest level as if he were making a serious point. "Of course ordinary people can catch the vision. A vision is as contagious as the common cold. There are times when it can send a whole population into a frenzy of bloodletting. But the shape of the vision, its first advocates, are always the intellectuals. Left to his own devices the simpleminded man will only hurt or murder men that he knows have outraged him in an individual manner. Not that the simple man is a good man. Far from it. He is as evil as anyone else. It is just that his simplicity makes it impossible for him to become bloody-minded in the abstract."

They had completed their circuit of the perimeter just as Rouge and his two companions came out of the Kommandant's office. They walked stiffly, somewhat hunched over, the lightness gone from their steps. They went silently into the barracks.

In a few moments the other Communist leaders from the other barracks had joined Rouge. Nina stood at the outside of the circle.

Rouge looked around at them and they sensed disaster. Rouge cleared his throat.

"The Kommandant has gone quite mad," Rouge said. His voice lacked confidence, he seemed to be uncertain of what he had witnessed. He kept glancing at his two companions for reassurance. They nodded dumbly at him. "He acted like a man possessed. He refused to talk French and screamed at us in German. He said that the Germans would throw the British and Americans back into the sea. When I told him we had two demands he laughed."

"It was hardly a laugh," one of his companions said. "It was more like a scream of pleasure."

"When I reminded him that his own safety was involved and that he would be brought to account when the Allies had won the war he merely laughed harder," Rouge said. The group around him shifted. Their mood of jubilation slowly disappeared. Some were already starting to run for cover . . . except there was no cover to seek. "He said flatly that we would not be given letter writing or receiving privileges."

"What did he say about reducing the stone quota?" one of the men in the circle asked.

Rouge's eyes shifted, looked over their shoulders. He cleared his throat again.

"The man is mad," Rouge said. "He said that rather than reduce the quota he was going to up it twenty-five percent. He also said that we needed more wholesome exercise in this camp. He had seen reports of the work accomplished by kommandos at Dachau and Buchenwald and stated that our norm was far below theirs. He stated that to make sure we went to bed each night and slept soundly we were to be given an hour of compulsory exercise every evening after dinner. This will consist of walking around the perimeter of the camp for a solid hour."

Someone in the group sighed. Another person made a

sound very like a moan. Nina watched their shoulders sag. Also their voices, which for the last eight hours had been almost strident, were suddenly filled with a whining quality.

"What if we refuse to take the exercise or to fulfill the quotas?" someone asked.

"The Kommandant said that any kommando which did not fulfill its daily requirements would have its Kapo shot," Rouge said. "When the exercise period comes, if any barracks fails to fall in for the hour's walk, one person, starting in alphabetical order, will be shot each day."

"Do you think he really means to do it?" Nina asked.

Rouge looked at them and it was an effort. He forced himself to stand straighter in the corner. He nodded his head. Without a word the group dispersed.

In addition to the increased stone quotas and the hour exercise, other things happened very quickly. First, their food supply was cut drastically. It hit savagely. Before the meeting of Rouge and his two companions with the Kommandant, the food had never been good, but it was always ample. Prisoners were given individual rations of margarine, sausage, cheese, apples, syrup, and a liter of flour pap. The central cookhouse, from which all of the barracks were supplied, also received potatoes, vegetables, bread, sugar and coffee or tea. The central cookhouse supplied the barracks with canisters of soup or stew and caldrons of coffee. Also prisoners were allowed to receive Red Cross packages of food or food parcels from their families.

The individual allowances were stopped at once. Suddenly everyone was living on the rations which were issued from the central cookhouse. In twenty-four hours food became the most common topic of conversation in the camp. Previously everyone had been bored by the food, but had been sated. Now, for the first time, stomachs rumbled and the more sensitive prisoners complained of feeling dizzy.

"What do you think of the cut in rations?" Nina asked her father. He was lying on his bunk between the time when the work ended and dinner was served. His eyes were closed. He opened his eyes and smiled at Nina.

"The Kommandant intends to starve us to death before we are liberated by the Allies," Faures said. "For a man as obsessed by fear as he is and with a limited imagination there is only one alternative: destroy the evidence."

Nina turned on her heel and walked back to her bunk. She was furious. What hurt was the sure knowledge that her father had not the slightest notion she was furious.

The second event was the arrival of the Greens. They arrived one day in the late afternoon. Four trucks pulled up to the gate before the camp. The prisoners gathered around as the backs of the trucks were unlocked and the new inmates climbed down. The sun was broken by clouds, but every few moments there would be a hard, bright, dazzling fall of sunlight which swept across the camp like some enormous searchlight. For a moment Nina did not believe what she saw. She thought it was an accident. A trick of the clouds and sunlight.

The men getting out of the trucks were Frenchmen, there was no doubt of that. But they seemed to be a dangerous essence of Frenchmen. They were smaller, darker, more active than any group of men she had ever seen. They moved with quick energetic gestures, argued with one another, smiled, acted completely unlike prisoners, and moved rapidly. They were not the least curious about their new surroundings. They ignored the other prisoners. Nina had an antic thought: these were men from a circus, the clowns, the entertainers, the tumblers, the dwarfs. Then as they came closer she saw the triangles on their sleeves. They were green.

"They are common criminals," Faures said. He looked at

them with great interest. "They have been sent here to break the Communist control of the camp."

This time Nina did not feel angry at her father. She felt a sense of quick black depression.

She watched the new prisoners playing and pushing one another. Like members of a carnival they uncoiled slowly and moved in a rowdy column between the two rows of barracks. Her father was right, Nina thought. Here were the thieves, rapists, bank robbers, forgers, embezzlers, every criminal that the web of French justice had managed to sweep together during the strange time of occupation. Two things were immediately clear about them. First, they felt no sense of guilt. They were banded together in a kind of riotous spontaneity and enthusiasm. Secondly, it was clear that they had leaders.

They came in the camp like Crusaders who were slightly drunk. In hard fact, some of them were drunk. Somehow they had managed to smuggle cognac onto the trucks. They made no effort to conceal the bottles as they walked along.

Even those without alcohol were in good humor. They swore, hit one another on the arms and back, looked casually at the wire fences, made loud remarks about how easily the camp could be escaped.

Only one incident marred their progress. A short swarthy man was carrying a bundle on each shoulder. One of the Greens came at him from the side and tripped him. The man fell, the two bags rolled in opposite directions. The man rolled over on his back and looked up at the man who had tripped him. He ripped off a hard short cursing sentence. He had also produced something in his hand which flashed. The man who tripped him said something which was placating, but not apologetic. The rest of the Greens walked around the couple, carefully ignoring them. The man who had tripped the shorter man picked up one of his bags and held it to-

ward him. The man climbed stiffly to his feet, still tense and
wary. The knife vanished. The two men joined the caravan.

"That is their only defect," Faures said.

Nina turned and stared at her father. She did not understand him. Somehow she did not feel like asking.

13. The Days of
1500 Calories

NOTHING is private in a prison camp. The hard public eye catches everything and everything goes into the
flood of rumor which sweeps back and forth. Even what a
person thinks of what the public eye has seen is known.
Not even the mind can be kept private.

The Greens were housed in a single barracks. It took two
days for the political prisoners to discover that the Greens
were being given superior rations. Rouge at once called a
meeting of all factions among the politicals.

They assembled quietly in the rear of Rouge's barracks.
The other prisoners went outside. Nina eyed the group.
They included Syndicalists, Anarchists, Trotskyites, Catholic
Socialists. There was even a short energetic man who was a
Fascist, but a Fascist in the style of d'Annunzio . . . before
he was imprisoned he had worn a small dagger on his belt

and gave flowery savage speeches to tiny crowds. The Nazis
had arrested him at once and when he asked why he was a
prisoner he was told his crime was "Romanticism."

"It is clear that Berlin has decided to starve all political
prisoners to death before the Allied troops or the Russians
can overrun the camps," Rouge told the group. "All of you
are aware that our food ration has been already cut. Before
it was barely adequate. Now it is a starvation diet. The
Camp Kommandant is personally opposed to this, but he
must carry out orders. The Greens have been sent in because Berlin expects us to put up a resistance. They expect
the Greens to break us and to split our discipline. The German guards will not intervene . . . they are under orders.
If we survive it will be only because of what we are able to
do by ourselves."

"Under Communist leadership?" one of the Catholics
asked, his voice tough and implacable.

"Or united leadership," Rouge said blandly. He turned to
a French doctor who had been an active Communist before
coming to the camp. "Dr. Mauriac, how many calories do
you think we are getting now?"

"About 1600 per person," the doctor said. "Before we were
getting around 3000 per person. If a person did not move or
work he could live forever on 1600 calories. But the stone
cutting and other work mean that each of us is running a
deficiency of about 1400 calories a day. On that you will lose
weight fast."

"I can also tell you that very shortly an hour of compulsory exercise will be instituted," Rouge said. "It will be no
more than walking around the perimeter of the camp, but it
will be at a set pace and the guards will enforce it."

"Ah, if that is done then we will fail quickly," the doctor
said. "The first ones to go will be those who already are
thin."

"It is inhuman," the Catholic leader breathed, but he stared hard at the doctor. "What happens to the body when it runs such a deficiency?"

"The body automatically tries to protect its most vital organs," the doctor said quietly, as if giving a lecture to interns. "First subcutaneous fat will be used. Then mesenteric, perirenal and epicardial fat will be consumed. By the time this is exhausted the body will have lost approximately forty percent of its original weight. If malnutrition continues, the fat around the essential organs such as the heart and brain will be consumed. Last to go would be probably the fat in the marrow of the bones. Soon after that the vital organs would cease functioning . . . precisely like a lamp which has run out of oil. Death comes rather suddenly. At that stage even the least exertion can cause one or another of the organs to malfunction and then almost instantly and quite painlessly the person is dead."

"What happens to the testicles?" one of the Anarchists said, grinning.

"You will not worry about them long," the doctor said. "The body does not tolerate such luxuries. You will have neither the desire nor the capacity. Eventually you will suffer from azoospermia . . . an absence of sperm."

It was the last effort at humor.

"We are luckier than in the camps for Jews or the camps actually in Germany," Rouge said. His voice had gone as clinical and disinterested as that of the doctor's. "There they have been conducting experiments on prisoners. They have experimented with malaria and typhus as well as mustard gas and phosgene gas. Almost all of the prisoner subjects die. In some camps whole kommandos of prisoners have been dumped into tanks of freezing water to see how long German pilots can be expected to survive if they parachute into arctic waters."

"That's enough," the Anarchist said. "We understand."

Little of what Rouge mentioned was new to the prisoners for they had heard such rumors constantly. But they had never been given with the authority with which Rouge had spoken and backed by the authority of the doctor.

The Catholic leader, a slightly overweight man, was breathing hard, as if the air were being exhausted from the room. Quite unconsciously his hands surrounded the layer of fat around his waist, as if it were a sort of protection. The mood of the group had changed. They had come prepared to do battle with Rouge and now, quite subtly, they seemed to be pleading with him.

"What do we do?" the Catholic said.

"We discipline ourselves, we bury political differences, we fight back," Rouge said. "We will 'organize' food and distribute it equally." He paused. "Organize" was prison camp jargon for stealing. "We will organize on a big scale. We will organize food from the Greens, from the forest where we cut wood, from the surrounding villages, from the guards. From now on we are all Reds. It will be a battle of the Reds against the Greens and the Fascists."

He began to explain how the "organizing" would be operated. The others nodded and when they left, the political prisoners had, for the first time, a firm agreement among all factions.

The plan to "organize" food worked well for a few weeks. The kommandos in the forests brought back mushrooms, edible shoots, an occasional snared rabbit, chestnuts, occasionally even a handful of truffles. Rouge dropped notes from his truck whenever it passed through a village. The notes were carefully written, but if they were picked up by a partisan they would make sense to him. In three days Rouge had made a contact and asked the Underground to leave food in the various forest areas in which the kommandos worked. Soon the work parties were coming back with whole cheeses, thin loaves of grayish bread, packages of

brown sugar. Within the camp some of the Reds became
skilled at stealing food from the special barracks in which
the Greens were fed. Sometimes it was a kilo of rice, other
times a big chunk of margarine.

The mood of the Reds soared. Their caloric intake was
still not high, they were still losing weight and ribs were
beginning to show, and wrists looked gaunt and a few of the
weaker people were already beginning to get the "Mussulman" look . . . the nickname given to men who had become so emaciated that they looked like the European's notion of an Arab dervish. But the "organizing" was growing,
becoming more skillful with each day. There was the possibility that they could survive.

The Greens remained quiet. They watched the Reds with
a detached, almost amused, look on their faces but most of
the time they sat in small circles and gambled. The Greens
were not sent on work parties. They made no effort to talk to
the Reds and when they had to speak to a Red the Greens
treated the Red with a kind of amused contempt, in which
there was no malice. They made no effort to clean their barracks, but they spent a good deal of time retailoring and
pressing their clothes. Most of them wore dark sharply
creased pants and ties. They also wore felt hats. In a prison
camp their attire, dandified and self-conscious, seemed insane.

Some Reds began to believe that the Greens had been
imported for no special purpose. There was something childlike and antic, almost innocent, about the Greens when
viewed from a distance. They looked like children busily
playing at games. Occasionally there would be a short vicious fight, precisely like the fights that occur among children, but it would be over quickly.

Rouge was not one of those who thought the Greens were
innocent. He was right. Two weeks after the Greens arrived
Rouge was called into the Kommandant's office.

The Kommandant handed him a piece of paper, then turned and walked to the window. He spoke quickly over his shoulder.

"Prisoner, you have controlled your people well up to now," the Kommandant said and his voice was half-strength. "We did not fool one another. I knew that you were running the prisoners by proxy. I have made a careful study of prison camps and always it is the prisoners who take over their own discipline. As long as the camp was clean I did not mind. Now all of that has changed. The central office of *Arbeit-statistik* has sent out a directive. You hold it in your hand. Read it, but do not repeat it to anyone. Understood?"

The Kommandant took off his dark glasses. Rouge looked at him and nodded. He understood. The Kommandant would not hesitate to kill him, but at the same time the Kommandant wanted to live after the Allies had won. That was why Rouge was being shown the letter.

Rouge's eyes skipped the first paragraphs which were mere formalities. His eyes lit on the significant paragraphs which were clearly labeled as orders.

Studies made on prisoners in other camps and the recent experience from other camps indicate that by now 10 percent of your prisoners should have died if they have been restricted to the 1600 calories a day, forced to work eight hours, and given an hour of forced exercise. Your quota of deaths by starvation should, based on other experience, now be starting to go up very sharply. Our Inspector General reports that, to the contrary, the political prisoners in your camp seem in very good health. You are hereby directed to carry out the following steps:

1. The recent group of criminals transported to your camp is to be split into groups so there are at least four of them in each of the other barracks. They are to be given instructions that henceforth their caloric intake will be zero cal-

ories a day. They must obtain food from the political prisoners.

2. There are to be no medical excuses from work. As of this date the doctor serving in your hospital will certify every person, automatically, as ready to work every day. Those unable to work will be classified as malingerers and summarily executed.

3. As much as possible various elements should be manip-ulated so that Communists are the first to die of starvation.

4. As usual the high German standard of cleanliness must be maintained. Outbreaks of filth-related diseases have, by special direction of the Führer, been reported directly to his office.

"In Berlin they just do not understand," he said. "I have tried to explain to them but they just do not seem to understand."

Rouge handed him back the letter.

"They understand well enough," Rouge said abruptly. There was no longer any need to be courteous to the Camp Kommandant. The two men were equal. For this information Rouge knew he would be obligated to save the Kom-mandant's life at some point. Rouge turned and left the office.

The Greens came into the various barracks that afternoon. They came as quietly as cats, their eyes filled with curiosity as they looked at the strange surroundings.

Four of them came into Nina's barracks. They were young men, with tiny almost waspish waists, and they were finely muscled. They took the personal effects of the former occu-pants of the four beds which were closest to the stove and threw them on the floor. They arranged their own things neatly.

Their pants had been altered so that they clung tightly to their legs. They did not wear boots, but thin-soled shoes made of what looked like genuine leather. And they were very vain about their hair. They wore their hair long and each of them combed his hair at least a dozen times a day, glancing into a small mirror which he carried in the pocket of his jacket. Their notions of cleanliness, however, ended with their own bodies. In anything which was public or did not touch their own skin, they seemed oblivious to dirt and disorder. In some undefinable ways, a few hours after they had entered the barracks it seemed to have a quality of squalor which had been missing before. Often they did not trouble to go out to the latrine but simply urinated in the corners of the barracks; they never bothered to clean off the common table which the occupants of the barracks shared.

That evening when dinner was served there were four extra rations. The person who had been appointed by Rouge to measure out the food filled the Greens' tin cups with a measuring cup. It was a thin vegetable soup, with a few drops of grease floating on top of it. There was also a single piece of bread for each prisoner with a neat yellow square of margarine placed on it.

The Greens sat down with the Reds and ate quietly, but with atrocious manners. They bent over their food and ate very rapidly while the Reds, as usual, tried to prolong the period of eating. The Greens ate without talking, their eyes glancing around at the other prisoners. Once, one of them muttered to the person who was obviously their leader. The other man laughed but none of the Reds could hear what had been said.

When the hour of compulsory exercise began the Greens climbed into their bunks.

When the hour was over and the Reds returned to their barracks the Greens were playing cards at one end of the table. Their mood had clearly changed. They laughed and joked among themselves. The catlike quality about them was accentuated. The Reds fell into their beds, gasping for breath, their eyes closed. Somehow intense fatigue arouses a pain which centers behind the eyeballs.

One of the prisoners slapped his cards down on the table and laughed.

"We need another player," he said. The Reds opened their eyes and looked at him. It was the leader. He was a small, powerfully built, very graceful man from Marseilles. The other Greens called him "Speed." Speed looked around the barracks.

"Come on you. The one who divides up the food. You look like you would be good at poker."

The man who divided the food sat up on his bunk. He was a large man named Raymond and he had been a pharmacist outside. He was also a member of an obscure Socialist sect which believed in the precise equality of all men in physical things. They claimed to be the ideological descendants of Babeuf and when the millennium came they proposed that everyone wear uniforms so that there would be no vanity in clothes. Also everything, including luxuries like champagne and caviar, would be divided precisely among the entire population.

"I do not play cards," Raymond said calmly.

"You say you do not play cards?" Speed said. He shook his head as if the answer were unbelievable. The other three Greens laughed. Speed shook his head again, his arms held forward and dangling in a clever imitation of Raymond. The Greens laughed harder. Speed looked up and said in a droll voice, "What if I told you you must play cards?"

"I would say that I do not know how to play cards in the first place," Raymond said. "In the second place I have nothing to play with. I have no stakes."

Speed mimicked Raymond, rolling on the outsides of his shoes with his legs bowed, his hands hanging apelike between his knees.

"The rules of the game anyone can learn in a few moments," Speed said. "And as for stakes let me assure you that you have a stake. Your life is at stake."

"How can my life be at stake?" Raymond said. He slipped out of his bunk and stood quietly, quite unafraid.

"Because I say so," Speed said and stood slowly erect. Visibly he tensed. "Because all of our lives are at stake. You are the person who divides the food. You decide who will live and from now on the four Greens in this barracks are going to get a double ration of food. If you win you can divide the food as you have always done in the past. But if you lose you will have two alternatives. Either you will give the four of us Greens double rations or we will 'dance.'"

The Greens stopped laughing and looked curiously around at the Reds. A silence fell over the barracks. Raymond stared at Speed. He shook his head once, as if to clear his mind. The Reds looked at one another, their eyebrows raised in puzzlement.

"What does it mean 'to dance,'" Rouge asked suddenly.

"Well, if I were to dance with the divider of the food here we would have our right legs tied together from the ankle to the knee and then we would dance," Speed said looking at Rouge as if he were an idiot. He laughed flatly. The other Greens grinned softly; they were watchful.

The Reds remained quiet, aware somehow that they were being threatened. Around the word "dance" there was something ominous. Those Reds who were leaning on their elbows or who had sat up in their bunks slowly, by almost imperceptible little motions, drew themselves back into their bunks as if into a fortress.

"Only one person survives the dance," a harsh un-French voice said from one of the faraway bunks. A small figure bounced out of an upper bunk, walked to the middle of the aisle. "Each of the dancers is given a knife and as they dance they fight. Only one survives the dance. He cuts his leg loose from his dead partner and the dance is over."

The Reds were suddenly motionless. What they had sensed was now made concrete. Speed looked speculatively down the aisle at the man who had spoken.

Nina moved over to Rouge. She whispered in his ear. "It is Tony, the Corsican," she said in Rouge's ear.

Tony was the most devout, the most intense and the most silent of Rouge's hard-core Communists. At a meeting no one stood close to him. He had an aura of rage and anger that surrounded him like an invisible membrane. He never spoke, but his Yes and No votes were given with a savage shake of the head.

Tony had been born into a poor agricultural family in Corsica. He was born with only one gift. He had a magnificent body. Eventually his physique had landed him a job on a luxury liner, the *Ile de France*, as an assistant to the chief masseur. He had been fired from that job for being too brusque to fat and hung-over passengers. He had finally wound up as a pastry cook in the galley.

Every day Tony had gotten up two hours before his shift began and exercised violently on the fantail. Then he went in and prepared pastry for the anonymous passengers up above. He worked beautifully but with anger. Day after day, month after month, year after year, the river of rich and exquisite pastries that he made flowed into the bellies of the fat and soft passengers above.

There was something maddening about the job. That he, lean and well muscled and taut, should prepare these marvelous delicacies for the people who had only become fat and sluggish from eating them was maddening. He loved the perfection of the delicacies, the curlicues of whipped cream and spun sugar which he laid over them, the rich red color of a strawberry glaze. Yet he knew that these beautiful pastries would form the soft shark-white flesh of the fat men and the wrinkled skin of the women who were passengers. He had dug his own fingers into their flesh and, with disgust, had felt the snail-like quality of their bodies. Tony was not an analytical man by nature. But he was caught in a very simple trap: he loved pastry making and he loathed the people who ate it.

One of the cooks, a confirmed Communist, had one day made everything simple for Tony. He had talked about "the bloated Capitalists" and the "oppressed Proletarian" and, as if the magician had performed a conjuring trick before him, the scales fell from Tony's eyes. He had joined the Party eagerly and with complete dedication. He was probably the only person in the camp who did not complain about the food. Although he was several kilos lighter than when he went into the camp there was something Spartan, frugal and satisfying to Tony about the thinness of the food they were given. Tony still exercised constantly and one of the reasons he spoke little was that the plan of action of the Communists was, to him, so utterly simple: they were preparing to throw themselves upon the engorged bodies of the Capitalists when the revolution came. Everything else was a froth of words. Communism, for Tony, was so simple: people should eat less and exercise more.

Speed looked down the aisle at Tony.

"So, little man, you know what the dance is all about?" Speed asked.

"Yes, in Corsica I have seen the dance done many times and other things besides," Tony said flatly. He was squeezing an old tennis ball in his right hand. He reached a certain number of squeezes, changed the ball to his left hand and began to squeeze again.

Nina understood instantly the strategy of the Greens. Each group in each of the barracks was probably at this moment selecting someone, on some pretext or another, who would be a likely victim. Raymond had merely seemed the most reasonable one and had the additional advantage of being the person who divided the food. She looked at Rouge. He also understood.

"You are nothing but a common murderer," Rouge said in a hard voice.

"I have been called nicer things," Speed said smiling. "But only by the police. In fact, friend, you sound like a policeman."

A few of the Reds laughed and Rouge gave them a pitying look.

"To fight Raymond would be murder, the act of a coward," Rouge said as if Speed had not spoken.

Nina sensed instantly that Rouge had made a mistake. Speed tensed at the word "coward" and color moved up on his neck. He still smiled, but he arched his shoulders forward and rolled up onto the balls of his feet.

"What would be fair?" he asked and now his voice was icy.

Rouge hesitated.

"What would be fair is for you to take your equal share of the food and not come in here and set yourself against your fellow man," Rouge said and his voice reflected his uncertainty.

"You are not my fellow man," Speed said. "You are scum. Not one of you would last a day in a real prison; a prison which had real men in it."

There was pride in his voice. Nina realized the man was actually proud of himself and of his fellow Greens. Also he had not the slightest notion of the enormity of what he was proposing.

"We are all in the same boat," Rouge began but Speed pointed a finger at him.

"You, shut up," Speed ordered. "All of *you* are in the same boat, all of you with the red triangles on your sleeves. We with the green triangles are not. You are going to die in this camp and you damned well deserve it. Now one of you is going to come over here and play cards and who will it be?"

For a moment there was hesitation in the room. Everyone was looking at Rouge. Nina could feel the uncertainty in the man, it came off him like a thin acrid sweat. Then he licked his lips and spoke.

"Tony, you play the game," Rouge said.

Nina knew that this was the second mistake. Rouge had now given sanction to the game.

Tony walked easily down the aisle and joined the four Greens. Speed rapidly shuffled the cards. He announced they would play draw poker. He dealt each of them five cards. Tony watched Speed's fingers with a detached air. When Speed had finished he looked up.

Tony did not pick up his cards.

"How many cards do you want?" Speed asked.

"None," Tony said quietly. "You cheated on the deal. You will cheat on any cards I might ask for."

Tony said it without accusation. It was a simple statement of fact. This time the flush rose from Speed's collar and climbed to just below his eyes. When he spoke his voice was hoarse.

"How many cards for the rest of you?" he said, trying to ignore Tony's composure. The three Greens looked away from Tony. Their eyes were slightly confused. They drew cards and shuffled them restlessly, looking at them secretively, as if the game were really important. Between glances at the corners of their cards their eyes shifted over to Tony.

Tony simply turned his cards over. He had two pairs. He glanced down at them and the expression on his face did not change. The other three players left their cards face down. Speed, some of his composure regained, but his eyes still

very hard and glittering, turned his hand over. He had three
deuces. Tony stood up.

"What do I fight with?" Tony asked. "I do not have a
knife." With no attempt at irony he went on. "Would you
like to fight bare-handed? Then it would be the man that
could strangle the other one to death."

Later her father told Nina that this was the critical moment. If Rouge had acted quickly the Greens, the common
criminals, would have yielded. The common criminal has a
very tight and well-developed code; all of them know it.
They have one standard of courage and one measure of loyalty. Tony had torn away the standard of courage; he introduced a new way to kill.

Speed was confused and uncertain. At that moment,
Faures said, Rouge could have swarmed over the Greens
and they would have cheerfully died.

But Rouge was trained for a different game. Speed flushed
and shuffled his feet and swore softly and then did the only
thing he could do: he tossed Tony a knife.

Tony turned the knife over in his hands. His fingers handled it in an unfamiliar way. The knife was somewhat
thicker than an icepick and slightly curved. Speed took a
knife out from his waist. It was thicker than the knife in
Tony's hands, but no longer. He walked up to Tony and put
his right leg out. One of the Greens whipped out a length of
rope and began to tie their legs together. He did it skillfully
as if he had done it many times. The rope made deep creases
in the cloth of their pants, it clearly was biting into their
flesh. When the Green was finished he stepped back, raised
his hands and said, "Go."

Instantly Tony threw his whole body sideways, taking
Speed with him. As the two men fell in a slow arc to the
floor Nina felt a moment of terrible exultation. Then it died.
For even as they fell Speed, in mid air, switched his knife

from his right to his left hand and with his free hand grabbed Tony's wrist. It was the reflex of a man who had been exposed to every trick of the game. But Tony's un-schooled reflexes had not been exhausted. He saw Speed's knife switch and the moment he hit the floor he rolled up like a ball and his free leg pinned down Speed's knife arm. For a moment they were quiet on the floor, their bodies straining, but neither making any great gestures. Then very slowly Tony brought his free left hand into the air toward Speed's throat. His powerful short fingers inched up Speed's chest. Speed bent down and tried to bite the fingers. Tony jabbed his fist up. It was a sort of judo blow and it caught Speed squarely on his Adam's apple. His eyes bulged and his throat worked and a trickle of soup, yellowish and acrid, came out of the corner of his mouth. At the same moment Tony's hand closed on Speed's throat. Speed's eyes bulged. The Reds clapped. A few of them uttered low savage en-couragement. Speed turned his purple face toward his three comrades.

Without a signal one of the Greens stepped forward and began to pry Tony's fingers loose.

"The fight is with the knives not with the hands," the Green said, staring calmly about at the Reds.

If they had, any one of them, started toward the Greens they could have flooded over them and killed or wounded them. But they were so stunned by the ferocity of what they were seeing, they were so unused to violence, that they merely nodded their heads at the Green.

The three Greens, holding the hands of the two comba-tants, lifted them again to their feet. Again one of the Greens said "Go."

Then it was all over very quickly. With an incredible speed, an almost invisible flash of action, Speed's right hand came up to deflect Tony's thrust. His own blade disappeared into Tony's stomach. There was a slight sound as if the blade were passing through heavy silk, then a slight snick as if it hit harder material, and then the blade passed through Tony's sternum and was pulled free.

Tony slowly straightened up. The front of his shirt was turning red from the waist to the collar. Nina knew that he was already close to death. He smiled at Rouge and there was neither fear nor remorse in his face.

The edges of his mouth turned up in a slight smile. Then in a gesture which was totally out of character with the smile, his knife lashed out. The long slightly curved blade caught Speed in the shoulder. The blade went completely through the shoulder and stuck out on the other side.

Tony let go of the knife. He sank back to the floor.

That was the last day of Communist sovereignty over the camp. In each barracks a similar fight had been performed. In each barracks a Red had been killed. In most barracks the fight had been quick, quiet, and very easy. Speed was the only Green to be wounded.

The time of literal anarchy had begun.

Only a small group of hard-core Communists remained loyal to Rouge. The rest of the prisoners began a chaotic and individual struggle for survival.

Terror, which had been subordinated, was now a live thing in the camp. It came like a shrill monsoon wind which one could neither feel nor hear, but which drew nerves to the thin point. And with the rise in terror the most important organ in every person's body became his stomach.

The brain, rationality, logic, loyalty, ideology, politics and reason all disappeared. And the stomach grew and grew. Faures watched with no surprise. It had always been so.

Nina finally accepted the truth.

14. The Days of Long and Short and Love and Hate

THE days became palpable. They were like stones. But stones of a peculiar quality. Stones that rested on top of an enormously high cliff. Huge, round stones, which could be pried loose and launched into the abyss of the day. At the beginning of the day everyone ached for the day to be over. In the morning they strained and pried against time, wanting the day to fall soundlessly and without interruption into the blackness of the abyss. And each day they were partners with the day. They traveled with it; bound up in the day as integrally as every molecule of the stone.

But the days never passed as quickly as a stone falling into an abyss. They passed slowly. There was the agony of waking up with the full bladder and the empty stomach and the aching muscles and the wild delicious memories of dreams. One wanted to fall back into sleep. It was the ultimate narcotic. Sleep, sleep, let me sleep, a dying man would scream, and he would be prodded into agonizing wakefulness and the doctor would snap off the judgment, "Fit for work. Send him off."

Down the day each person stumbled. Each thing was an agony. Even the food was an agony for when it was gone, the thin gruel of it, the stomach roared back and screamed and racked and begged for more. And, oh Christ, how the body wanted to give a sweet answer to the stomach. But by then it was time to crack stone or saw stone or explode stone.

The next sensation was the rattle of the truck. With a fat body it would be nothing; the body would take the little blows easily. With a body where the bones were held together by the skin, the nerve system was expanded and immense and very tender . . . every rattle hurt. Grown men, their eyes shut and their faces strained, pissed in their pants as the truck rattled along to the quarry.

The work in the quarry was somnambulistic and lunar. No one understood how it was accomplished. They moved untold tons of stone, but they did it in a dream. And they moved the stone across a landscape which was not real. It was moonlike. They whispered jokes to one another about the unreality of the whole thing.

The one joke, the central joke, revolved around the fact that this whole thing was taking place on the moon. The things they did could not take place on earth . . . so they must be on the moon. And with that understanding, and the rifle butt of an apologetic pimple-faced guard, they beat a great chunk of stone into tiny pieces with wild goatish cries.

The exercise period, the weird hour of walking together in a long ellipse, was, at first, the most unbearable thing. Finally it became the thing they lived for.

A man became a "Mussulman" in a single day. He saw his face in a piece of mirror and knew it. He killed himself cunningly. He pulled out a loose tooth and sawed at the flesh on his wrist. Eventually he opened an artery and with a sigh of relief lay back. The next morning he was cool and dead. Some thought he smiled, but others said it was merely the drawn, fanged, starved look which made all Mussulmen look happy in death.

*

A boy seventeen years old, a Catholic and a virgin, became obsessed with sex. He dogged older men for information which they were too tired to divulge. He described his wild fantasies to them in detail. Finally they referred him to the women. The first woman to whom he made an approach was willing. But the boy's body was too far gone. Sex existed as a marvelous warm and abstract and detached idea, but not as a reality. He left the woman's bed and with the measured cadence of a Boy Scout walked toward the danger wire which marked off the fence from the compound proper. The guards hesitated, called softly to him, said that he was like a sleepwalker. They shot at him with a hundred and twenty-five bullets, only six of which hit his body. The Kommandant was disgusted with their marksmanship, but insisted on a decent burial, with ceremony, for the boy.

This puzzled the prisoners, the Reds, for other Reds who died were merely carted away quietly and made a statistic in the neat and jubilant report of the Kommandant.

A woman fifty-three years old, a hard and toughened Communist, saw Jesus Christ. For thirty seconds she described how he was soaring over the camp. She described his face, his beard, his luminous eyes, his robes. Then she became catatonic. She sat down on the ground, her head twisted in the direction in which she had last seen Christ. She did not change her posture by even the slightest gesture. She was frozen as hard as wood. She was placed in her bed and stayed in precisely the same position. She refused to open her mouth for food. She died from starvation. There were those Reds who thought her glittering eyes had consumed all of the sustenance in her body. Some of the Greens found the woman intriguing. They brought food to her while she lived (she did not touch it) and flowers when she died. They wept at her name and they made a neat petition to the

Vatican to have the woman beatified. She had, they said, given up the horror of Communism. They were convinced the Reds had killed her.

The stone quota was up 10 percent, but no one noticed it. Their bodies were already drawn so fine, their exhaustion so complete, that another 10 percent meant almost nothing. Except a joke.

The Greens were disgusted. The bizarre performance of the Reds horrified them. The Greens became the proper bourgeoisie of the camp. They spat upon the unkempt rabble. They became much more meticulous about their clothes. As the Reds became disheveled the Greens became impeccable. At least three times Greens told Reds that the Reds did not deserve more food because they were so dirty and thin and undeserving. The Reds had trouble in answering.

Rouge called an emergency meeting of the political leaders. They stood around him and he faced them with his back to the corner. But now they swayed. By the time he had finished his opening statement two of them had fainted. Two others had fallen asleep. Most of them did not hear the answer which the doctor gave to Rouge's question, "The camp is receiving food for everyone who has died. If the Greens did not take so excessive a share all of us could maintain our present weight."

Six prisoners saw an angel ascending to heaven. All of their descriptions tallied. She was long and white and somewhat overweight, but she had swirled over the camp and then risen straight into the sky until she was a dot and then a mote and then a speck. Then she vanished and the six

prisoners were ecstatic. They were undismayed when a
Green told them that it was a meteorological balloon and
not an angel which had whirled over their camp.

A black market developed in religious emblems. Oddly
enough the Communists, from the orifices of their bodies
and their clothing, produced the most of these forbidden
objects. Once, however, they had bargained away their religious emblem for food or a cigarette they would immediately try to buy it back and the price would be twice what
they had paid.

There was a seminar, called by a serious Protestant minister, upon the subject of existentialism. In fifteen minutes
the seminar was discussing the morality of cannibalism. It
ended dismally. One of the Kapos informed them that no
dead body would be left in the camp long enough to give
the matter serious consideration.

The Greens made outrageous proposals to the surviving
women. Universally they were accepted. And universally the
Greens reneged. They were only teasing. The shrunken
women they saw were incapable of arousing their sexual ap-
petites.

The Kommandant took long walks through the forest
when the prisoners, minus the Greens, went through their
hour of forced exercise. After several weeks of this, he had
lost a few pounds, his complexion was clear, and he always
arrived when the prisoners had collapsed into their barracks.
He talked seriously to the guards and a few leaders of the
Greens about the fact that the camp was a healthful place.
He had received a report that heart diseases had dropped
radically in the prison camps. Germans eat too much fat and
so do Frenchmen, he said severely.

Faures said to his daughter, "It is astonishing how quickly hunger, real hunger, will break down a political ideology. Is it not?"

Nina stared back at him.

The Greens were bored.

The Kommandant was euphoric. The camp was producing the proper number of corpses. At the same time he had received a report from Berlin that his camp was one of the most healthful and hygienic in Western Europe.

All the German trucks were requisitioned for use at the fighting front. The stone quota was cut back 10 percent, but the prisoners had to walk to the quarry and back. The French Fascist cursed the Allies for taking away the trucks of the prisoners. Tears ran down his face. The other prisoners nodded numbly. They did not know their precise motives. Rouge spoke softly, but with a grating voice, and a few remembered what he said. He told them to prepare for something worse. The rations demanded by the Greens meant that the Maquis were going to great lengths to feed a bunch of common criminals. The "organized" food would stop. Rouge was ordering it stopped. The Reds hardly understood what Rouge said.

The Greens were bored. The Greens were also restive.

There was a rumor that a homosexual guard had been appointed to one of the sentry boxes. Two-thirds of the men looked up eagerly to see if they could identify the newcomer. Alas, it was only a rumor.

The Greens agreed to fatten up two of the Red women who would then serve as whores for the rest of them. There was a terrible clamor for the two positions. One Green was killed during the deliberations. Most of the other Greens were for the selection of a very tall and half-dead redheaded girl who was the daughter of a titled family who had picked up radical ideas.

The idea of screwing a tall and aristocratic girl excited the Greens. But one Green had a wife who was redheaded and the whole thing was a terrible affront to him. The Reds watched as the decision was made. The Green with the red-headed wife talked a good deal and then, thinking he had won, asked for a vote in his favor: no redheaded whores. Someone, a thin pale forger from Paris, challenged him out of boredom.

There was a "dance." The forger lost. So did the redhead.

A tiny segment of the Camp, the Greens and the guards and the Kommandant, were doing setting up exercises every morning and every evening to lose weight. For some reason which no one could explain they did their exercises publicly.

Three Allied P–47's made a pass over the camp. Prisoners, guards, Greens and Reds, ducked for cover. Except for one person. To the pilot's eyes the camp was utterly deserted. But suddenly there was a dark figure standing in the center of the compound, his arms jerking at the plane. He was a Catholic Centralist who had learned semaphore. On their next pass the three planes shot him to death. His arms looked as if they were cradling a machine gun.

He had been semaphoring, over and over, one phrase: "Save us. Christians. Save us. Christians."

Autumn came and winter came and the trees were bare. No prisoner noticed the trees. All they noticed was that they were colder in their bunks. The Communist doctor drew up endless charts of calories and physical activity.

*

A middle-aged Socialist asked to be shot. His grounds were that he was beginning to believe in God. The request was forwarded to Berlin.

The camp began to smell. The Kommandant was infuriated. But nothing could be done about it. A visiting German doctor pointed out to him that starving people were not continent. The doctor also added, with approval, that diarrhea was encouraging. It was a symptom that usually preceded the last spasms of life.

The Greens employed their two whores to let out their pants and blouses. They were gaining weight. Neither of the whores were good seamstresses. They were astonished at the ferocity of the Greens' reaction. They quickly recruited, and gained special privileges for, two female prisoners who were skilled seamstresses. The Greens were very dapper.

A man died in midsentence. He was talking to Nina and several others and saying he had a peculiar lightness of the body. Still speaking, the words drifting back from his mouth, his eyes closed and the body pitched forward. By the time Nina put her hand to his chest the heartbeat was gone.

Then a final thing happened. Nina and her father were in a kommando which was walking back from twelve hours of chopping wood. One of the prisoners asked if he could go into the bushes to relieve himself. Beside the guard was a Green who had walked out to the woodcutting site merely for exercise. The Green proposed that the guard agree to allow the man to go into the bushes. However, if he were not back in thirty seconds the guard would give his gun to one of the prisoners. The prisoner would either shoot the man who had gone into the bushes or he would shoot any other prisoner of his choice. The guard would be protected because he had a Luger pistol in his belt with which he could cover the prisoner entrusted with the rifle. The prisoner with diarrhea made it back with five seconds to spare. A shiver went through the file of prisoners. They marched back to the camp. It was Faures who told Nina that the prisoners walked like SS troopers as they came back into the prison camp.

That night Nina's father walked over and sat on the edge of her bunk.

"They have gone just the slightest bit too far. They have passed over the line and are asking humans to be subhumans." He smiled at her. "I know I sound like a professor. But I must tell you that the whole sweating, miserable and awful effort of millions of years of mankind have gone into avoiding what we witnessed this afternoon."

Nina stared at her father and nodded. Anything to get to sleep. She was not quite sure she understood what he said next. It had something to do with the destruction of the Greens. She heard the words "anti-social" and "evil" and "against the natural law" and she smiled. They seemed like words from another planet. She fell asleep.

15. Time of
the Solitaries

THE compulsory exercise period was an agonizing low-pitched pleasure. The Reds knew it was killing them, but it was the only time they were all together, could gossip and exchange rumors, could judge how well they were doing as compared to the rest. They became exquisitely attuned to what the protruding bone of an elbow meant, what a yellowish face portended, could judge a silence precisely: either the silent person was a Mussulman and doomed or he was conserving energy and was healthy.

Round the ellipse of the barbed wire they walked. By an unspoken agreement they all walked as slowly as possible. Even so not a day went past that two or three figures were not sprawled on the trail of brownish grass. The others walked around them, flowing past them as a crowd will flow past a dog's droppings on a sidewalk. No one had the strength to help another to his feet. It was enough to stagger through the hour and then, blindly and with a huge relief at having survived, walk back to the barracks.

Nina always walked with her father during the exercise period. They talked more than most of the other Reds, for Faures was fascinated with the camp and the prisoners. Because of his slight body he did better than most of the prisoners on the slowly reducing diet. He was gaunt, but he had always been gaunt. The numbing fatigue which the others felt did not affect him. He talked because he had the energy to talk. And this was one of the reasons Nina walked with him: the others resented his cool detached and incessant conversation. They stared at him dumbly, hating his energy and also the abstract general tone of his conversation. The others would talk, but only to exchange rumor or to bargain. A conversation about the outside world was offensive. It cut like a rasp into the minute talk of the immediate environment which obsesses starving and imprisoned men.

Nina really walked with her father because no one else could tolerate him. His comments brought out the most murderous in the prisoners.

"The Greens are no longer interesting," Faures said one afternoon. "It does not disturb me that they broke Rouge's control of the camp. That was interesting to watch. But now their percentage of the food is so great that technically none of the rest of us have a chance to live."

"Father, you can be very amusing at times," Nina said. She was tired and for the first time she felt the results of starvation. Her bones seemed too large for her skin. It was a painful sensation.

"What is necessary is that the Greens' control be destroyed," Faures said.

Nina laughed. A few people in the column turned and looked at her.

"That is what we tried to do for weeks," she said. "Father, there is no way to destroy the power of the Greens. They have beaten us. Once and for always."

"No, no, Nina. You do not understand such things," Faures said.

He did not talk for the rest of the exercise hour.

Nina did not discount her father's ingenuity. During the summer, when everyone was excited by the news of the invasion, he had begun to think of how to survive the winter. He had gathered rags from all over the camp; a scrap here, a scrap from the guards, a pair of ancient pants that someone had thrown away. Then he had persuaded an ex-tailor to stitch the rags between two shirts. The result was a thick ugly jacket which had amused the tailor. In the summer the jacket was a joke. When the cold came the jacket became beautiful. Faures had made one for Nina also and she wore it day and night.

Also when the cold came there was a quick hysterical search for rags to make into jackets. By some precise law of economics no one could, any longer, accumulate enough rags to make a jacket. And no one would give up the rags he had. Each person lived in the hopes of getting enough cloth to make what everyone in the camp called a "Faures jacket." And none, after Faures, succeeded.

But there was a great difference between having the foresight to gather material for a jacket, at a time when everyone expected to be rescued the next day, and breaking the power of the Greens to control food distribution.

Three days after Faures had spoken to Nina about destroying the Greens a small squat man with the nickname Sailor came into their barracks. Sailor was a Green and he was also a physical fitness enthusiast. He exercised constantly and his body was knotted with muscle. He was said to be very suspicious.

When Sailor came in the four Greens were playing cards at the table.

Sailor walked over to them and began to talk in a low, rapid voice. Speed and his Greens smiled at Sailor. Then Sailor bit off a word and it hung in the air loud enough for the Reds to hear it. The word was "alcohol." Speed put his cards slowly on the table, face down. He looked narrowly at Sailor. Then he shook his head.

Sailor was suddenly angry.

He stood with his legs apart, his thumbs hooked in his belt. It was an overly dramatic posture; almost insolent.

Sailor spoke again in a low voice and bent toward Speed. He was delivering an ultimatum. Suddenly the other three Greens were staring at Speed. Speed tensed, leaned forward, and then shrugged his shoulders. He made a deprecating gesture. He started to deal out a new hand.

Sailor waited for a moment and then walked out, pounding one fist into another.

"What do you think the talk about the alcohol means?" Nina asked.

"It is something I started," Faures said. "I took four cigarettes to one of the Tabacs and asked if he could trade them for potatoes. I told him we needed the potatoes for an alcohol still which Speed was operating."

Making alcohol in the camp was impossible. Next to cleanliness the Kommandant was obsessed by the notion that the prisoners might lay hands on alcohol. He was himself a total abstainer. He often said that one of the benefits of the camp was that it took drunkards away from the blight of alcohol. Every few days he sent special squads on surprise raids on the barracks searching for alcohol stills. Nina was certain that no one in the camp was operating an alcohol still, including the Greens.

"Why did you say such a thing?" Nina asked.

Faures turned on his pillow and looked at Nina.

"The Greens are the only organized government left in the camp," he said. "The rest of us are savages living outside of any law and incapable of organized activity. The Greens are held together by two things: the pleasant task of exterminating us and the peculiar bond which exists between all criminals."

"What does all this have to do with alcohol, father?" Nina asked.

"The mentality of the criminal is simple. It is based on a childlike kind of pride. Even when it is practiced by very intelligent criminals. This is why the criminal resorts to

nicknames, has elaborate initiation rites, takes pleasure in
his defiance of law and authority, would rather go to prison
than betray a fellow criminal. The criminal will go through
the most degrading kind of deprivation as long as he knows
his comrades have not betrayed him or would do the same
thing for him. They will even willingly die for a fellow as
long as they are certain the fellow would die for them. One
can see the same thing among children. They also constitute
an underworld of their own, using cabalistic words, games,
obscure songs and crude toy weapons, all of which are obviously aimed at the destruction of the adult world."

"Father, you see this as a game," Nina said. "It's not a
game. These are vicious men. Men who could kill you."

Faures looked at her and smiled.

"Nina, my dear, you can be remarkably obtuse when you
choose to be," he said sharply. "What does the child do
when he is betrayed by his comrades? He cries or throws a
tantrum. These are the psychological equivalents of violence. He does not have the muscle or real weapons to
express his violence. How does the adult criminal react
when he is betrayed? By violence." Faures' voice became
more even and less scolding. "Criminals kill and maim many
more of their kind than do the police. They do it because
their pride has been offended."

"But how does the alcohol figure in this?" she asked.

"Because the instant one of the Greens believes that another has alcohol it will not be their thirst for alcohol which
will be aroused. It will be a more terrifying thing. It will be
a blow to their self-esteem. And that is all the criminal has.
In fact, in political life that is all that anyone has: self-
esteem. Or so it seems to me."

Nina did not know whether to cry or laugh. Her father
was a strange one. He was pompous and contented and abstracted and, at times, he sounded very practical and even
shrewd. But he always arrived at the practical conclusion

through some long involved search which took place entirely in his mind.

She laughed. Her father pitched against the entire force of the Greens was ridiculous. But the laugh, almost against her will, came out as an admiring laugh.

Raymond, the former pharmacist, walked over and leaned down toward Faures.

"Is tomorrow the time?" Raymond asked.

Faures nodded his head. Raymond walked back to his bunk, pulled his blanket up to his neck, and was promptly asleep.

The next day as they started on the exercise period, Raymond was a transformed man. The other prisoners walked in their usual manner, their heads down, trying to keep the pace as slow as possible. But Raymond walked with exuberance, his cheeks flushed, his voice loud and strident. At the sentry box closest to the Kommandant's office Raymond raised his hand and waved and then yelled a friendly obscenity at the sentry. The sentry gazed at Raymond in astonishment. As they continued their circuit Raymond staggered occasionally. He laughed, corrected his stride, wove back into the column. At first the prisoners thought he was having a convulsion; a flaring of energy before he died. They avoided him. Then someone said Raymond was drunk and it was so startling a statement that a flurry of conversation began. They were stabbed with a furious envy.

The next time the column approached the Kommandant's headquarters the Kommandant was standing on the steps watching them. Raymond waved to the Kommandant, bowed deeply, invited him to join them. The Kommandant's face tightened.

"The man is drunk," the Kommandant said. He gestured at two guards. "Take him out of the line and into my office."

Raymond went willingly, dancing between the clutching

hands of the two guards, his voice cheerful and exuberant. He disappeared into the headquarters building.

"We will not see him again in this camp," Faures said to Nina quietly. They were walking at the rear of the column.

"They cannot execute him merely for being drunk," Nina said.

"He is not drunk," Faures said. "He is acting drunk. Also he will have the smell of alcohol on his breath. He stole a tiny vial of alcohol from the dispensary. Like all of the medical alcohol it has been treated so that it cannot be drunk. But he has rinsed his mouth with the alcohol and the odor will last for hours. He will tell the Kommandant that he can tell him the source of his alcohol supply only if he is not returned to the camp. Raymond will point out that if he is returned to the camp after informing he will be killed. The Kommandant will agree and will transfer Raymond to another camp. In his way the Kommandant is almost as childish as the Greens. What he considers a strength, his detestation of alcohol, is really a form of weakness."

"Who will Raymond say is manufacturing the alcohol?" Nina asked.

Faures looked quietly at her for a moment. There was something appraising in his glance. Then he made up his mind.

"He will say that two of Sailor's men are making the alcohol," Faures said.

Two hours later there was an uproar from the administration building. The floodlights surrounding the building caught the lanky solemn figure of Raymond walking to a car accompanied by two guards. The car went to the gate and was passed through. There were a few sparks from the exhaust. Raymond had left.

Almost at once a group of guards came from behind the building and walked down the parade ground between the two rows of barracks. They were led by the Kommandant. He was a man transformed by rage. He walked with all the assurance and arrogance of an SS officer.

The Kommandant turned into the barracks occupied by Sailor. He and his squad disappeared into the barracks. For a few moments there was silence. Then there was a din of noise, lowing of voices, the sound of wooden things being smashed. The political prisoners came shuffling out, black, gaunt, emaciated shadows, wrapped in their blankets. Some guards came out with two of Sailor's men.

Sailor and the Kommandant emerged and stood at the head of the steps.

Sailor's voice was thick with rage. The Kommandant was silent and very pale. Suddenly the Kommandant wheeled and slapped Sailor across the face. Sailor's voice snapped off.

Nina, watching from a window, could see the terrible shame which showed in Sailor's face. The man trembled and crouched. He glanced at the Greens about him and then turned, ready to kill the Kommandant. A guard's rifle butt shot out and caught Sailor on the side of the head. He shot down the steps. He landed in a sitting position. He put his hands to his ears, as if his head were ringing. From hundreds of open windows around the camp a low laughter emerged. It took Sailor several seconds to distinguish between the laughter and the noise in his head. He sat there, his head glancing from barracks to barracks. He slowly stood up. The Kommandant and his squad marched the two Greens to the front of the administration building. Suddenly the two Greens were standing alone watching the squad walk away from them. The squad wheeled and formed a firing squad. The Kommandant barked out the order. The two Greens were amazed.

"All right, soldiers, the game is over," one of them said. He laughed derisively. "Put the popguns away and take us back to our beds."

"We'll report you to the boss," the other said. He was cocky and relaxed. "You're supposed to be shooting those lousy politicals. Not us honest crooks."

They looked at Sailor. Every person in the camp felt the fear in their look. They did not think they would be shot. They would be saved by Sailor.

The Kommandant spoke. The smack of the bullets only deepened the look on the two Greens' faces. Even as they staggered, regained their footing, scrabbled for stability they thought Sailor would save them. And then the look of astonishment, the most complete astonishment which can occur only once, crossed their faces: they were dying. It took several seconds and it was not, Nina thought, like the motion pictures. In the pictures the men were slapped to earth the moment they were hit. But real bullets did not act that way. They did not knock a man flat. They sapped the life out of him gradually.

The two Greens sighed, staggered in small circles, collided, one coughed blood, the other fell to his knees, one moaned and the other took it up, their eyelids dropped and then flickered open desperately, they stared and saw nothing, they got closer to the ground and finally they scratched and clawed their way into the grass. They jerked for minutes after they were prone.

The firing squad was fascinated. No one vomited.

By the time the kommandos had returned from the forest the next day six Greens had been killed in formless, sporadic battles that raged through the almost empty barracks.

"It is not fast enough," Faures said softly to Nina as they took their exercise. "It must not just be gang against gang but the members of each gang must come to suspect one another."

"How did the Kommandant decide to shoot two of Sailor's men?" Nina asked.

"Because Raymond said Sailor's group was making alcohol," Faures said.

"But no one is making alcohol," Nina said.

Faures looked at her and did not respond. He had the look which came over him when he delivered a paper to some academic association.

That night Speed discovered a note close to the iron stove. It was addressed to one of his subordinates. It asked for help and it was signed at the bottom, "Sailor." Instantly, with no intervening stages, Speed was in an utterly cold and irrational rage. He asked the Green to whom the note was addressed for an explanation and did not listen. He stared implacably at the man.

"You scum," Speed said. "You shit-bird of a scum. I save your life a dozen times. I take six months rap for you. And you deal with Sailor. Just because you want a glass of alcohol."

Suddenly the accused man turned and went to the bag which had his personal effects. He rummaged for a few moments and came out with a small glittering meat cleaver. He walked back to the table rolling up the sleeves of his left arm. He put the arm out on the table and looked up at Speed.

Nina could see the man's eyes. Faures was right. The accused man's eyes glittered with injured pride. Speed made no sign. The man turned and brought the cleaver down with a sharp flashing blow. There was a tiny gritty sound. The man had cut his own left hand off at the wrist. He pulled his arm back a few inches from the detached hand. Blood jetted out on the table. He stood looking at Speed. Speed still did not move.

"Bandage up his arm," a voice pleaded from one of the bunks.

Speed did not move. The other two Greens gazed easily at their companion. In thirty seconds blood was running from the end of the table. In a minute and a half the man was beginning to sag about the shoulders. Two and a half minutes later his eyes lost their glitter, dulled, he sagged sideways and fell forward on the table.

The next night the two remaining Greens killed Speed in his bed, using knives. The next night one of them was killed by someone from Tabac's gang. The next morning the last remaining Green committed suicide.

The barracks suddenly had no Greens left. But no one turned to Rouge for leadership. In fact, they turned to no one for leadership. The race would be too close for the luxury of ideology or friendship or loyalty. Also their bodies were past the point where they could respond to such appeals.

16. The Time of Love

THE camp was the same except that hoarfrost glittered on the barbed wire.

The camp was the same except that its inmates were fewer.

The camp was the same except that the Kommandant was meeting his quotas. There was even the hint of a medal.

The camp was the same except that none of the prisoners

spoke any longer; instead they gasped at one another; gave signals to save calories.

The camp was the same except that no one had muttered the word "ideology" for weeks.

The camp was the same except that it was utterly quiet.

The camp was the same except that the Greens were like everyone else and got the same ration and asked for no more.

One thing was the same: the exercise period.

They stumbled in. Each of them a scarecrow of knees, elbows, shivering, gasping, rags pinned together, obscene words used sparsely, hands reaching for a bunk, eyes closed, lips chapped raw, sores, moans which they could not control, a terrible awareness of bones pushing against skin, a taking of pulses, a calculation of calories expended, a sigh as fingers touched bunk, a vertigo of relief that the day was done.

And all of it was done autonomously. No one spoke. No one made plots. That time was past. The toothpicks of people did not offend one another. They moved like ants. Each to himself. Each in line. Each to his bunk. Each to his own misery. Each aware that pride, dignity, rumor, gossip, community, begging and fighting were not worth the price. Not any longer.

One night a man moaned and said aloud, "How long until the Allies get here?"

"The day after the last of us is dead," a voice replied.

It was part of the vast design. They all knew it. They immediately fell asleep, somehow contented.

Nina hated the moans she could not control. No one noticed them, but somehow she detested herself for making them. And still, she knew, she and her father were better off than most. Just because of the Chinese-style padded clothes and the fact that her father had saved food and was so light that he could maintain his weight on two-thirds of the ration. She got the rest. She envied him his wispiness.

One night as they came in from the exercise period a large-framed middle-aged woman, who had been a famous actress before she became a Communist, spoke up.

"By God, how I would like to spend that exercise hour up in one of those warm sentry boxes," she said, her hand holding on to the bunk for support. She was gaunt, but her eyes were magnificent . . . huge and softly glowing. "I am beyond it. But some of you girls still have a chance. The Germans are not eunuchs. Not if you can make yourselves attractive."

With a natural and quite exhausted grace she rolled back into her bunk.

The moans and stirrings stopped. There was a sudden silence. Usually the barracks creaked with the reflexive sounds of agonized bodies. And the silence was suddenly thick. For everyone was calculating. Like a spider's web, part of their calculation was collective: how far will the guards go for sex?

It was a massive and subtle calculation which they all made simultaneously. Which guards would be susceptible? What would the Kommandant do if he found out? How could one make the first approach to a guard? Did one have the strength to climb up the tower if the guard nodded? Should one ask for more than just the warmth of the sentry box? What would the other women ask? What could the other women give? Round and round the speculation went, with each of the women covertly watching the others.

Nina wondered why none of them had thought of it before.

Then she thought how difficult it would be to make any of

the women attractive. They were too thin, too listless, too poorly dressed.

Without a word being spoken the men in the barracks were dropped from the collective, intense, almost frantic prescience which existed in the barracks. None of the guards gave evidence of homosexuality. The men relaxed and fell asleep or moaned or whined or belched or felt their organs and limbs. But the women, without exchanging a word, soared on.

"It is possible," a voice said. "They have been away from women for a long time."

There was a sigh of agreement.

"The Kommandant will do nothing," another voice said. "The end is too near."

There was a sigh of agreement.

"Are any of us attractive enough?" a voice asked.

And that was the end of the collective, weblike, spidery, searching, intuitive collective moment. They felt it snap. One woman sobbed.

Each woman began to make her own calculations.

When the lights were out Faures tapped Nina on the shoulder and they walked to the doorway of the barracks. They slipped through the door and sat on the steps.

For winter it was a mild night. It was very clear and the stars were visible. There were no clouds. The barbed wire was dewy and it caught the light that had traveled a million light-years and made spectacular little orbs around each barb.

"The actress is right," Faures said suddenly. "The Kommandant has orders to starve all of us to death before the Allied troops arrive. Because he is a bureaucrat he will do it precisely that way . . . by starvation. Therefore if anyone can get extra calories he or she will survive. Also the

Kommandant will not interfere with guards who take women into their sentry boxes. He goes to sleep promptly at seven and sleeps with the conviction of a person who knows if he stays awake he will lose his mind. He sleeps fourteen hours a night. It is a common sympton of psychosis."

"But will the guards be aroused enough by the female prisoners to take the risk of inviting them up to their sentry boxes?" Nina asked.

"I do not know," Faures said. "But I suspect they will. Because the sex impulse died long ago in most of the women they think it inconceivable that the guards can still have sexual thoughts. Until now the guards have probably not seen anything among the gray column which passes beneath them to . . ." He paused and cleared his throat, "To arouse them. Tomorrow all of that will change. The women are ingenious. They will find ways to excite the guards."

Nina glanced at her father. He was so pompous.

"What happens to the men?" she asked.

"They will die," he said. "Except for me and possibly Rouge. I will survive because I have been prudential and have saved food. Also because I am so small I can live for a long time on the ration. Rouge will live because he must. He is a fanatic. He wants to see what will happen. He cannot resist his curiosity. The others are already Mussulmen, even if they still have a few pounds of fat to lose."

"And what of us women?" Nina asked and her voice was puckish, slightly taunting.

"I do not know. If you can obtain extra food from the guards you will survive." He paused and cleared his throat. "Everything hinges on how the sexuality of the female prisoners is used." He paused again and then went on relentlessly. "If you can make yourself into a successful whore you will survive. It is as simple as that."

The sky tilted. Nina was gripped by embarrassment. The

blackness above them wheeled and stars slid away in long flicks of light.

"I am a virgin," Nina said. "I am ignorant."

Orion slipped again, pelagic seas of stars whirred around. One star seemed very bright, but as she fastened her eyes on it it grew dim, became elusive. Her attention became very sharp. She was immensely intrigued with the stars. She could not remember the last word she had said to her father. She raised her finger, traced the motion of the Pleiades.

"I cannot help," Faures said in a grating voice, a voice she had never heard before. The sky was suddenly dark and blank. "I do not know what sex means to a young man today. Or even to a middle-aged man. Such things are fashions. But you must discover."

Nina had a suffocating sensation and could not remember precisely what they were talking about. A shooting star saved her. By some fantastic communication as it blazed and died it gave her a permission: she could breathe. She took a deep breath and was again human.

"I will probably learn," she said laconically.

"Learn from the others," Faures said in his usual voice. "Do not commit yourself. They will rush out to seduce the guards for warmth and food and they will make mistakes. Also they will imitate one another. And so they will become boring. Wait as long as you can and use your intellect." He gripped her arm. "Intellect is everything. Intellect and prudence."

As he pulled her to her feet and they walked back into the barracks Nina was curiously lightheaded. She had not thought it would happen this way.

The next day a P–38 came over the camp at dawn. It came so fast, shattering the silence in all directions, at so low an altitude that the guards could not even raise their guns. It dropped a canister attached to a long nylon streamer. In the canister was a message. It was delivered to the Kommandant and ten minutes later he ordered an *Appel*.

"The message from the Allied Commander of the Allied Expeditionary Forces has just been delivered to me," the Kommandant said. He was trembling. "The message orders me to assemble all prisoners and state that you are to do no further work outside the boundaries of the camp. The Allied fighters will fire on any and all columns moving outside the camps. I am held personally responsible for your safety." He paused and his hand went to his forehead. "It names me by name. It also orders me to assemble all prisoners and give you this message." He paused again. His trembling grew worse. "I have done so. There will be no work details today. But there will be the compulsory exercise period."

The prisoners cheered. A ragged, weak, coughing cheer. Then they dispersed.

Faures followed Nina and drew her aside.

"The prisoners are fools," he said severely. "They do not understand what is happening. The Kommandant is like one of Pavlov's dogs who suddenly has had his signals reversed. He probably does not worry about the stone quarry for the Allied planes have so disrupted the trains that there is a huge surplus at the railhead. But he still must meet his quota of persons who will die from starvation each week. So we will no longer work, but our rations will be sharply cut."

That day they received warm water for lunch. For dinner they received a half pint of vegetarian soup. There were no fat globules on the surface of the soup.

It was a cut of 75 percent in their ration, the Communist doctor estimated. Four people died that afternoon. They were all men.

The exercise period that night was unlike anything which had happened before. As the diminished groups trickled out

from their barracks and formed into a column Nina could
see that at least six of the women had changed. The change
was so abrupt that it staggered her. The six women, all from
different barracks, were wearing what seemed like well-de-
signed street clothes from a Paris couturier. Their faces were
made up. Their breasts were high and firm. Although it was
bitterly cold their arms and necks were exposed. They
walked with the careful casualness of wealthy women.

False breasts, girdles, lipstick, dressed, carefully done hair,
rouge, eye shadow, shoes with heels had all been manufac-
tured in a single day.

The first guard, a heavy man who drowsed through most
of the day, did not detect the difference. Between that sentry box and the next one of the women skillfully maneuvered
herself to the outer side of the column.

The next guard, a young boy, noticed her.

A strange look of confusion went over his face. He stared.
He pulled back the window and let the cold air pour in.
Then he looked again. The woman glanced at him. Her hips
moved and in the white light her breasts were very promi-
nent. She glanced away. The boy did not collect himself until it was too late. He shouted something and the woman's
laugh floated back to him.

Within the column there was a quietly ferocious maneuvering for position, for now the made-up women knew
where they must be to be seen. By the time they had passed
three more sentry boxes they had made their way to the
outside of the column. With the drab column of gray stick-
like figures behind them the women looked colorful, sexual,
gay. The guards began to call one another on the phones.
Their faces were a mixture of surprise, desire and confusion.

By the time they passed the young guard for the third
time the surprise and confusion were gone from his face.
Apparently he had been assured that the Kommandant was

asleep or that some unanimity had been reached among the guards. He whistled.

"Invite me up," one of the women called. "I'll show you something you never saw before."

"Come on," the boy called. He laid his gun aside. His eyes were bright with excitement.

Nina was walking directly behind the woman. She could see that the woman's dress had been thrown together out of the smooth blue thin lining of field coats. Her buttocks wobbled unnaturally. The woman did not hesitate a moment. She turned out of the column and walked to the guard wire . . . she lifted her skirt and went over it delicately, aware that the entire column was watching to see if she would be shot. She walked gracefully across the forbidden zone. The column came to a complete halt. In the darkness at the foot of the sentry tower she lifted her skirt and plucked away two pads of cloth which had been wadded up and fastened over her buttocks to give them more size. Her legs were thin and white, even in the darkness. The column shuffled on as she began to climb the ladder.

She rejoined them forty minutes later, just as the hour was ending. Her cheeks were flushed and she was holding four chocolate bars, a package of cigarettes and a large meat sandwich in her hands.

"How was it?" one of the other women asked over her shoulder.

"Warm," the woman said and her voice was silken. "He went for my breasts but I had to divert him because my bra is stuffed to make them look bigger. He diverted easily. He said to come back tomorrow night. The other guards are waiting to see if he was caught."

The next day almost every woman in the camp was working furiously. All except those that had lost so much weight that they already resembled Mussulmen and had lost all hope. Nina watched a twenty-eight-year-old girl working with something in a matchbox. It was flour and the girl cautiously added iodine from a small bottle to the mixture. She put it next to the stove to let it dry out, but stood very close to the little box.

Nina realized that the girl was making rouge.

"I'll help you put it on," Nina said to the girl. The girl looked at her sharply.

"I can't give you any of it," the girl said. "There is barely enough for me."

"I don't want any," Nina said.

The girl was still suspicious, but she allowed Nina to apply the rouge late in the afternoon. It worked well. Two spots of rouge took the hollowness of her cheeks and made them, rather than badges of starvation, into seductive highlights. Nina suggested that she moisten some of the flour and iodine mixture and use it for lipstick.

"It will powder away on the guard's lips if I have to kiss him," the girl said. She looked up apprehensively. "He will be able to taste it."

Nina stared at the girl.

"Let's add sugar to it," Nina said. "Then if it powders it will taste sweet." She paused, something reaching up from below for recognition. "How is your breath?"

Without a moment's hesitation the girl lifted her head, opened her mouth and allowed Nina to smell. As the girl expired, the faint smell of an almost perfect breath came to Nina's nostrils. It amazed her. She thought of the rancid food they had eaten, the rotten meat, the stale vegetables, and marveled. (Later the Communist doctor told her it was probably due to the fact that all of them were living off their own body tissues. The food they got was so slight that it almost instantly was absorbed by the alimentary canal and did not have a chance to build up gas in the stomach.)

The addition of sugar helped. As the lip rouge dried up it had little glittering crystals in it. When they assembled for the exercise period the other women glanced at the girl and were startled. Her lips seemed to glow in the harsh light of the floodlights.

That night the guards were alert, attentive, and very much alive. They studied the women as they went by. By unconscious agreement the men and noncontesting women walked on the inner part of the column. The made-up women formed a single file on the outside and nearest the sentry boxes.

The fat German, the perpetually somnolent one, who had the first sentry box was on his feet and studying the girls. His honest middle-aged face wrinkled with concentration. He had the opportunity of first choice. Although the window to his sentry box was open the sweat stood out on his forehead. His head swung back and forth. He looked, somehow, like a serious inspector of some commodity of great importance. The girl whom Nina had helped make up turned and smiled. The guard's face firmed up.

"You, the one with the lips," he said. Four of the women stepped forward and moved toward the box. The guard's face went red. "No, no. None of you. That one. The one with the lips that glitter."

The girl murmured across a file of prisoners as she broke out of the line, "Thank you, Nina. It was the sugar."

She crossed the guard wire. This time the column did not stop to see if she made it. They knew she would.

Nina was walking beside her father on the inside file. She was the only woman not resembling a Mussulman who had not put on makeup or false breasts or pads for her hips.

"It is a strange thing that women who are starved or deeply troubled are, even without the makeup, for a time more beautiful than in their normal situation," Faures said. "Up to a point, of course."

"Up to the point where they look like scarecrows," Nina said and she was neither irritated nor mocking. "Maybe it has to do with the endocrine system. Maybe in desperation their eyes have more sparkle or they hold themselves more tightly and these things might be sexually attractive."

"That is almost surely part of it," Faures said. "The physiology of the system works, maybe out of some unknown survival instinct, to make the female most attractive just when she is most in danger. It would be worth a little time to investigate." His voice in the span of a few seconds became speculative. He put his hands behind his back. "A sophisticated physiologist teamed up with a sociologist might do research which would prove Darwin right . . . even in this regard." He chuckled and then cut it off abruptly. They were coming to the next sentry box.

The helmeted face peered down at the women. Abruptly an arm shot out and pointed at a tall blond woman.

"You, the tall one," the invisible face said. "Come up."

The blond woman was a Catholic Socialist and was unmarried. Outside she had been intensely dedicated to Catholic trade unionism, which was not strange for her father was a savage anticlerical entrepreneur who had died when she was sixteen, leaving her only a fortune, an intense resentment of private enterprise and a blind devotion to the good works.

The blond woman went across the guard wire, climbed the ladder quickly. Before the column had passed, Nina could see the guard kissing her. She was a foot taller than the guard. He looked like a squat midget being engulfed by a great wiry spider. He twisted her savagely and Nina could see the blonde's dress come as high as her breasts. The guard, without lowering his head, put his mouth to her left breast. He gurgled with an insensate wild blubbering sound. The blonde's eyes followed the column; her head swung on her elegant stalk of a neck: the lower part of her body twisted and ground: she moaned as the guard penetrated her.

Nina remembered the moan. It was wholly artificial. Sounds, Nina said to herself, are important.

When they got to the young guard's sentry box the woman who had gone up the night before quickly stepped across the guard wire and moved toward the ladder. The young boy nodded, but his eyes looked at the new women, the additions since last night.

Each of the guards took a woman that night. But there were only six guards and over twenty-five women. The moment that the last guard had made his choice the women relaxed into a sullen silence. The whole column slowed to a dawdling walk. They knew they were not being watched. No one looked up at the sentry boxes. They had no curiosity. They talked about the rations, about the possibility of a further reduction, about the rumors of an Allied advance. Rouge, now a skull-head walking on spindly legs, asked what the Kommandant would do if the camp did not meet its quota of dead at the end of the week. The column fell silent. They realized that the food given by the guards to the chosen women would drastically alter the balance. Now all were not equal.

Rouge proposed that they establish a committee to share whatever food the women gathered. He proposed ways in which the food could be collected and distributed so that each of them might have a chance to survive. The liberation could not be far off. The women did not listen. The men walked ahead, eyes down, conserving energy, placing each foot carefully, breathing hard, making the endless internal calculation of what was happening to the organs of their bodies. Organization, planning, sharing, politics . . . all of that seemed impossibly far away. They marveled that they had ever cared about anything but food.

The food ration remained at an implacable 800 calories

per person. A few of the Mussulmen died during the week. But the women who were successful with the guards returned to the column each night with small bundles of food and some of them began to put on weight.

The nightly exercise period went from a silent and bitter competition to a kind of grotesque promenade. The guards had, after a few nights, become selective. They looked for variety. At first it was merely for a different woman. But one night a woman who had not yet been chosen and who was tottering with weakness yelled at a guard, "Ah, handsome boy, how about the French way?" The guard, an older and very fat man, was suddenly interested. His eyes flared with interest. He motioned to the woman to come up.

She returned, trembling and swaying, but with a small bundle in her hand. She had cognac on her breath. She was drunk.

"They have started to bring in cognac to the sentry boxes," she said proudly. "It is just like a party for them. They are either boys who have never had a woman before or they are older men who are just becoming curious about their potency. Christ, he was heavy."

Watching from the outside of the barbed wire, a stranger might have thought it a kind of extended carnival. Each day it grew more frantic. The guards, past the point of worry about the Allied invasion, were drunk almost constantly. And they became at first discriminating in their sexual tastes and finally bizarre, shouting their sexual inventions to see which woman would meet the challenge . . . and one always did. One woman had a long talk with the doctor about sexual perversion. She learned about masochism and sadism and an older guard became interested. The only difficulty was that he was inexperienced and too strong. He strangled the woman and she died before he realized what he had done.

The Kommandant ignored everything except cleanliness.

With a simple Teutonic thoroughness he went through each barracks, each latrine and the unused hospital each day sniffing for odors, searching for dirt. When he found dirt he gave the entire barracks a shrill chastisement and then returned to his quarters. He did not come out after nightfall and therefore did not see the drinking among the guards.

Nina kept her weight at around ninety-nine pounds only because her father gave her part of his ration and because he had stored away in tobacco tins several pounds of bread which he had squeezed and dried into tiny flat biscuits.

For two weeks the only fatalities were among male prisoners, and the quota for the prison camp was low. The Kommandant knew it, but he also knew that his communications with Berlin were so uncertain that he could escape attention. Mail trains were being blown up by Allied planes, telephones did not work, letters were delayed, reports were confused. He yielded to his weakness. He could not bear to keep inaccurate records or to falsify a piece of paper so he merely reported from time to time to Berlin that he had received no response to his last weekly report. The records he did not forward were meticulous. They recorded the name, sex, weight of the prisoner at death, cause of death, reason for detention.

Except for the deaths and the quiet silent shuffling of the male prisoners the camp had a gala appearance. There was no petrol for the trucks so no one worked at the stone quarry. Everyone was at leisure and the men sat in the thin sunlight like patients at some cheap resort. The women used their long daily hours to build false breasts and hips, to manufacture lipstick, to barter information about the desires of the different guards; even, toward the end, one of the women found a way to make perfume to kill the slightly rancid odor which comes from a starving body. As the dinner hour approached the women became more active. They were nervous, like actresses about to be auditioned. They gulped their dinner and waited impatiently, but with a terrible pressing anxiety, for the exercise hour to begin.

Nina was the only woman not involved. But she watched carefully. She walked on the inside file with her father. She studied the faces of the guards, glanced at the gestures of the women, listened to their words. She was astounded at how soon, under the compression of hunger and war and fright and cognac, the sexual shrewdness of the women increased. They were as learned as the most sophisticated courtesans of Rome or Pompeii. They knew as much about the prostate gland and the recuperative powers of the male and the erotic zones as any doctor.

Nina sensed, dimly at first, but then more surely, that this would be their undoing. They would, between their skills and desperation, exhaust the guards. She tried, as calmly as possible and with a kind of cold neutrality, to guess how the thing would end.

Eventually Nina was proven right. The economics of choice and physiology began to operate. A few of the guards began to pass up even the most imaginative forms of perversion. They were uniformed and bored satyrs who had reached boredom. They shook their heads or glanced away and barely managed to stay awake. Also the gifts of food to the women became smaller. Then the night arrived when her father passed her a bread biscuit and told her that it was the last one.

"How many more weeks do we have until the Allies arrive?" Nina asked.

"No one knows," Faures said. "The winter will slow things down. It may be three months."

"None of us can survive that long," Nina said slowly. "Not without some addition to our ration."

Faures nodded agreement.

That night Nina moved to the outside file, the one nearest the sentry boxes. She was wearing a plain skirt, a heavy winter jacket and boots. She was neat and clean, but she wore only the slightest bit of makeup . . . something under her eyes to make them look larger.

As the exercise hour began she put her head down for a moment and a shudder went down her body. It was not fear or remorse or even apprehension. It was the gesture of shaking off a past, of sliding from one reality into another. Her teeth chattered.

It is important to no longer think, she told herself. Now I must act. Act without ever having acted before. The best way is to be nonrational, to depend on the clues and hints and lore she had learned from the other women.

The shuddering stopped. The column stepped off. The women began their waving of arms, the offering of charms, the swinging of hips, the lifting of eyebrows. The first three guards watched without responding. The women's offers became more explicit, detailed and profane. Nina kept her head down, but her body was straight. Her arms were crossed over her breasts. Occasionally she swung her arms as if to restore the circulation.

The next three guards selected women out of the line. They disappeared up the ladders.

On the third circuit of the compound the young guard called to Nina.

"Eh, you. The one in the jacket," he said. "Up here."

Nina did not look up. The woman behind her hissed at her. The boy called again.

Nina looked up slowly. The boy jerked his thumb toward her. Nina hesitated, her stride broke, she stood still for a moment. In the hard light she blushed. Then she shook her head as if there had been a misunderstanding. The boy's eyes were bewildered.

"Quick, while he's still in the mood," the woman behind Nina whispered. Her voice was pure agony.

Nina picked up the pace again. She had taken only a few steps when the boy's voice came down on her.

"You think I meant it? You skinny duck," he said. "I didn't."

The column moved slowly, quietly, dumfounded. Nothing like this had happened before. In their surprise the women in front and behind Nina drew away from her; their senses numbed, they only knew that she had broken some rule. Later one of them told her it was as if Nina had shouted, "No, I do not want to live."

The ambience around Nina communicated itself to the next guard. He watched her and was on the phone to the boy instantly. The boy must have revealed his confusion at being rejected. The guard called the next guard.

"Hey, you, the skinny duck," the guard called confidently. "Come up."

Nina glanced at him. Again she blushed, her tongue showed at the corner of her mouth, pink and moist, and then she bent forward again. She regained her stride. She made walking a very serious thing.

On the next few circuits Nina was not sure what she did. But at each sentry box it was slightly different; something she had absorbed from watching the other women plus some intuition plus some deliberate thought. She remembered that the next time the boy talked to her she crossed her arms over her breasts and twisted slightly away, but at the same time glanced at him. Her eyes, she knew, were wide and frightened. The boy's words changed instantly. He was still abusive, but he no longer meant what he said. His voice went gentle, almost apologetic.

The next night all six of the guards ignored the other women and made approaches to Nina. Carefully keeping the rational part of her mind buried, acting only out of impulse, Nina ignored them. But each time she gave a flicker of recognition . . . a tiny spasm of shock, a blush, a sideways glance, a twisting away with the shoulders, accompanied by a slight undulation of the hips. One guard, an older and very drunk guard, became abusive.

"How would you like a bullet through that skinny ass of yours?" he said.

Nina said nothing. Made no response.

On the next circuit the guard was weeping. He mumbled something incoherent. It seemed to be a reference to his wife and children.

The next night Nina moved back to the inner file. None of the guards took any of the other women. They argued on their phones and looked over the column. They called for "the little duck." One ordered the column to stop and for "the little duck" to move back to the outer file. Nina did not move. The guard was confused. He blustered for a moment and then fell silent. The column waited gratefully. After ten minutes he ordered them to move on.

That night two of the women told Nina that she must make a selection among the guards. Somehow the uncertainty about her was denying the rest of them any food. They stared at her quietly as they talked, both of them women who, in normal life, were intelligent mothers of children and, perhaps, devoted wives. They tried to make out the reasons for her sudden upsetting of the old order.

"I will choose tonight," Nina said.

In fact the choice was made for her. When they passed the first guard he yelled at Nina and his voice was hard and demanding. Nina sensed that the guards were in conflict over her. When the column reached the boy's sentry box he ordered them to stop.

Then the unbelievable happened. The boy climbed down the ladder and *he* walked over the guard line, his rifle at the ready, swinging over the column. It was the most unorthodox thing that any prisoner had ever seen any German do. He walked around the column and pulled Nina out of line by the shoulder.

He took her a dozen yards from the column.

"These other guards are pigs," he told her bluntly. He stared over her shoulder. "They are married men who have become brutes. They will . . . they will . . ." He paused, hesitated. "They will hurt you."

"I cannot leave my father," Nina said with the ingenuousness of a puzzled girl. "Also I am afraid."

The boy's head moved. He looked closely at her. She blushed and then lowered her head. He put out his hand and wiped a finger harshly across her lowered cheek. He looked at the finger.

"The others all come apart like chalk," he said unevenly. "As if they are not women, but something made out of false materials."

Nina kept her head down. Her shoulder blades shivered. Her mind was blank. It was nothing more than a kind of sounding board, a sponge soaking up the moods, motions and gestures of the boy. Something told her it was a time to sob. She sobbed.

"They are good women, but they are desperate," Nina said into her jacket. But she knew the boy could hear. "You have made them that way. I do not want to become that way."

Somewhere deep in that spongelike part of her head, she uttered a rule: a woman's cry is taken by a man as interest in him.

"I do not want you to become that way," he said and his voice was steady. She looked up. He had tears in his eyes. She made tears come to her eyes. The boy's face worked. Then for some reason, and Nina later knew it was his shame over his tears, his face hardened. "If you cannot leave your father I will shoot him. He will die in the end anyway. Which one is he?"

Nina's tears stopped. She stared steadily at the boy. Now she must wait, pause for a moment until intuition told her what to do. She fought back the impulse toward rational action. From somewhere the instructions came.

Her hands raised to her breast. She glanced down and then back up at the boy. The tears came again, but her body, with an almost invisible and quite reflexive gesture, seemed to lean toward the boy.

"I will stand in front of him," Nina said. "When you shoot, the bullet should have enough power to kill both of us."

Nina, the rational part of her, was astonished at how little surprise she felt at what happened. She knew how it would end, her lips almost made the words which came from the boy's mouth. He seemed like some marvelous ventriloquist's dummy whom, by an elaborate system of linkages, she could control.

"I was only testing you," the boy said. He was suddenly bluff and masculine, sure of himself. "I want to make sure you are not like the rest. I can take care of both you and your father." He hesitated and she knew what would come. She prepared to cry. "But . . . but, you must be only with me."

Nina bent her head and wept.

She hardly heard what the boy offered. He would give both her and her father food. He would give her father a faked medical excuse for not exercising. If an order came for extermination by shooting he would smuggle them out of the camp.

Nina did not nod. But she followed him when he went back across the guard wire and up the ladder. The box was a shock. It was warmer than anything she had experienced in months. It had the same effect as an enormous draught of cognac. Through the glass she sought her father's face. He looked at her and when the boy pulled the glass back to tell the column to move on, her father nodded. She was proud that he was not looking down. That would have made the next hour much more difficult.

When the first Allied tank swung in front of the administration building and the long barrel swung gently into position and the Kommandant walked out with a little white flag in his hand the camp had changed. Nina and five other women were still alive. Rouge and Faures were in reasonable shape and could walk erect. Four other men were Mussulmen and could only shuffle and stare.

Yet it was strange that when the American lieutenant and the Kommandant made their inspection and the Kommandant turned over the camp to the Americans it was the four Mussulmen who somehow found the strength to fall upon the Kommandant and strangle him. They waited until he had explained to the lieutenant how clean he had kept the camp. Then the four walking skeletons creaked in upon him and with a maniac strength and a great rasping of lungs strangled him. In the struggle the Mussulmen suffered broken arms and legs, for their bones were fragile and the marrow was almost exhausted. One of them died immediately afterwards of a heart attack, but he laughed with genuine laughter as the pains gripped his chest.

The lieutenant looked on coldly. He had liberated three other prison camps, one of them for Jews, and he was old for his years. He was, by now, an expert on handling such situations. Besides, he had two other camps to liberate.

Book III

17. The Rabbit
Hunters

RODNEY jerked awake as he became aware of the silence.

Nina had finished talking. She looked into her cognac glass. The sun was just coming up and through the dirty windows of the hotel it was turned into flat reddish slabs of light.

She must have drunk a great deal, Rodney thought, but she did not show it. Then he remembered that she drank almost nothing. She had been talking for hours and it had taken her all that time to finish the single glass, taking it up with tiny flicks of her tongue. Her voice had a mesmerizing quality, even when she spoke of unpleasant things. And he thought she had spoken of some very unpleasant things. What were they? He had not remembered all she said because the cognac had gradually gotten to him. After the ex-prisoners had left, Nina had started to talk. The fat congealed on the bones of the pig whitened the plates like rind-ice. Silence flowed like a substance through the empty hotel, broken only by the lulling rise and fall of Nina's voice. He stared at a cluster of wineglasses which had distinct finger-

prints of grease on them . . . two of them had crescents of
red lipstick around the rims. He tried to recall precisely
what Nina had said.

Rodney was intensely curious, but for some reason there
were parts of her story which almost automatically, as if a
nerve had been tripped, he had forgotten. He sank into a
mood which was part drunkenness, part a vast wonderment,
and part a kind of envy for those who had been in the camp.
He felt a sense of self-pity.

"That is a fascinating story," he said, pulling himself up in
the chair. The waiters had not touched the table because the
party had run far past their working hours. He looked
around for wine and found a half-empty bottle. He delicately poured himself a glass. He drank it off.

"Not fascinating," Nina said. There was a blue smudge
under her eyes. "It has happened to millions. But only a
small fraction survived. For each who died, however, there
is a large group who understand. Who really understand a
concentration or political camp. Maybe because they had
relatives in a camp or because they were almost imprisoned
themselves or maybe just because they had the nerves which
told them what such a life was like. That is the way the
world is split now, Rodney. Those who have been in a concentration camp or can understand what it means to be in
one . . . and those who have neither been in one nor can
understand what it means to be in one."

Rodney swung his head toward her. He felt a mixture of
shame and anger.

"I was neither in a camp nor do I understand them," he
said, making his voice hard.

Nina laughed.

"You are droll, Rodney," she said. She reached over and
took his hand. "You understand. Even though you were not
there."

Rodney wanted to believe her. Her hands felt very small

and reassuring over his. She had strength, he thought, she had sat up the entire night talking and much of the time he had drifted off to sleep or into a dangling condition just short of sleep . . . maybe his eyes were open, but he had not comprehended everything. In an odd, twisted and quite irrational way the things he had forgotten made him envy the people who had been prisoners in the camp. They, at least, had something to draw them together; they understood something he would never know; they had *experienced*.

"You are sleepy," Nina said.

She stood up and they walked past the immense debris of the previous night's dinner. In the glancing early morning light everything flashed with the slight patina of grease . . . it dulled the glasses, glistened on the napkins, was slick over white gnawed bones, had even soaked into pieces of bread and was smeared over apples and pears.

Rodney ran his tongue over his lips. They were slightly greasy. He rubbed at them with his handkerchief.

He undressed and fell into the bed naked. He ground his face into the pillow. He was very sleepy, but he also knew the thick familiar sensation in his chest and thighs. He felt Nina throw back the bed covers and get into bed. At once her hand fell on his forearm and patted. He felt a slight resentment. She had said something last night, during the long liquid hours, about sex and herself and the camp. He could not quite remember it. Then she spoke a few words he could not make out and they sufficed to put him to sleep, although he could not remember what she said.

Rodney woke up in the afternoon. Nina was gone. He washed his hands and face, felt the last film of hard grease wash away, and quickly got dressed. He went downstairs. The landlady was waiting for him. She smiled, her yellow big teeth showing, and presented him with the bill. He quickly translated the total figure into dollars and realized it

was close to three hundred dollars. Obviously he had paid
for the meal.

He took out a book of traveler's checks.

"Your friends are big drinkers and big eaters," the landlady said. There was no apology in her voice. "They are
funny ones."

Rodney paid and asked where Nina was. The landlady
shrugged. The lady had gone out, that was all she knew. She
had her coat on and she had gone out.

Rodney moved quickly out through the front door. It was
a very cold day and starting to grow colder as darkness approached.

Rodney found himself trotting toward the car. Nina was
not there. For some reason he ran entirely around the building. Then he trotted back up the road. He looked north and
the road was empty except for a truck which was moving
away from him. To the south the highway was unbroken
except for a tiny black formless knob. He paused, holding
his breath, trying to tell if the knob was moving. Although it
was far away and without features it looked somehow familiar. He kept using the old flier's trick of moving his eyes
from side to side to try to catch an identifying liminal impression of the figure.

Panic started to rise in him and then, anxious for control,
he started to laugh. He had only known this girl a few days.
This was preposterous. He had just meant to pick her up, as
he had scores of girls before, maybe have a brief affair and
be gone . . . also as he had done scores of times before. But
before the laugh had stopped in his throat he was running
for the car.

Usually Rodney was gentle with a car. He liked to bring it
to life slowly, not flood the cylinders with raw gas but coax
it into a slow low purr. For the same reason that he had a
respect for his boats, he had a respect for mechanical things.

There was a proper way to handle them. He hated to see them abused. But now, suddenly, he was in a rush. His foot jabbed at the accelerator and he choked the car full-out. He winced as he heard the screech that came from the engine, but finally it lunged into a ferocious overheated life. He backed out of the parking place and started down the high-way.

It was growing darker and he was a hundred yards away from the moving object before he was certain it was Nina. He drew up beside her and rolled down the window on her side.

"Going someplace?" he asked, his voice bitter. She looked at him with surprise, as if he were a total stranger. She also seemed somewhat frightened. Instantly Rodney's voice changed.

"Jump in, I'll give you a ride."

Nina waited for a few seconds, staring through the open window at Rodney, then she smiled. Rodney swung the door open and she got in.

Rodney reduced the choke and evened out the engine. He was uncertain.

"Would you like to go back to the hotel?" he asked.

Nina shrugged her shoulders. She smiled at Rodney. He started down the road. There was nothing to go back to. They had paid their bill and they had seen Nina's friends. It grew dark fast and Rodney turned the lights on. After twenty minutes of driving they were on a highway which ran beside a river. Odd refracted lights flashed off the river and gave the highway a ceremonial and frivolous look. The lights from the river caught the icicles on the trees, lighting the road. It was like the illuminated approach to a carnival.

"That was not a lost day," Nina said. "A day spent with friends is never lost."

"Well, maybe it wasn't lost, but if you are serious about

getting to Montauban we are going to have to move along faster," Rodney said. "Also I've got to buy some new shirts. This one is getting a bit high."

Nina laughed delightedly. She reached over and kissed Rodney on the ear. Only when he felt a slight breath from her nostrils in his ear did he realize it was very cold in the car. His hands tightened on the wheel and his foot went down on the accelerator.

"Rodney, you really are magnificent," Nina said. "You have a marvelous sense of humor." She hesitated a moment. "Also you are very good with people."

"You are very generous, Miss Faures, but when and where do we stop to eat and get back on a regular schedule?" Rodney asked.

He glanced over at Nina. She looked very small in the corner. He realized he had not asked where she was walking to when he overtook her. Now, somehow, it made no difference.

"A few kilometers along, maybe fifteen or twenty, there is a very good small inn," Nina said. "At this time of year it caters to hunters." She reached over and touched his arm. "And you do not have to worry about my running into any friends from the concentration camp. As far as I know none of them lives in this area. So you can have a good dinner and a sound night's sleep."

The tavern was at the edge of the river. It was really an old castle which had decayed from the extremities and now only a solid squat central building remained. Reaching out from the building were the broken limbs of castle, caught in the black glittering night-lights. It looked like something injured.

Rodney was surprised at the pleasantness of the main rooms of the inn. There was a large combination bar and public room and beyond that was a kitchen. In the main room was a huge fireplace which heated both of the rooms and also illuminated them. There was a small bar along one side of the fireplace. There were only three people in the room. There was a woman, wearing an apron, who was working in the kitchen. There was a man putting linen and silver on the half-dozen tables in the dining room. Leaning against the bar was a small dainty man with a figure that was slim everywhere except around his waist. There he had a small firm potbelly held in by a wide brown leather belt. He was drinking and talking to the woman in the kitchen.

"Madame, you have guests," the man at the bar said. Then he snapped his finger. The woman came out from the kitchen wiping her hands on her apron. She wanted to know if they were spending the night or just having dinner. Rodney said both. She brought her red chapped hands away from the apron and asked about luggage. She called over her shoulder to the waiter.

"We have none," Rodney said, smiling at her.

"None?" the woman asked. "It is very cold in the rooms. You should have some nightclothes." She paused, pondered the situation, and then her face relaxed. "We can take care of it. Rico, my husband here," she said, jerking her thumb at the waiter. "Rico is a pack rat. He is like all of the Spanish. He has enough nightclothes to outfit a regiment. He can take care of that."

Nina glanced at Rico. Rodney sensed the intensity of the look as Rico straightened up and came to a sort of low-pitched attention. His face was protective, veiled, almost as obviously as if he had protected his head with his hands.

"Why do you accumulate things?" Nina asked.

"An old habit," Rico said. Then he relaxed. He went back to placing the silver. "Something picked up in prison during the war. Save everything . . . it may have a use. You would know."

"But I save nothing," Nina said laughing.

"That is the way some of us became," Rico said. "Either

we saved everything or we despaired and saved nothing. I never despaired."

Rico did not look up from the table; his fingers worked rapidly, but his shoulders shook with laughter. Rodney felt a slight irritation, the slight twinge of exclusion. Nina glanced at him and shrugged her shoulders.

"I did not know he was an ex-political until he stood and looked in the funny way that prisoners adopt," Nina said as they walked toward the bar. "It is a thing of absolute neutrality; waiting to see whether one is safe or threatened."

Rodney and Nina walked over and sat down at a table. The man at the bar walked over. He introduced himself. His name was Péguy and he asked if he could buy them a drink. On close inspection Rodney noticed that he was wearing a hunter's leather jacket and had a small mustache.

Nina suggested martinis and Péguy walked back to the bar, stepped behind it and began to mix a pitcher of martinis. It was obvious that he was an old and trusted customer.

He brought three glasses to a table. He put the glasses down and then darted out of the door carrying the pitcher. He was back in a few seconds. He had stuffed the pitcher full of icicles and was swirling the pitcher in his hand.

"Just like in America, eh?" he asked looking at Rodney. "Iced."

Rodney grinned.

When the mixture in the pitcher was blue-white Péguy poured the drinks. They were excellent. Péguy eyed Nina and Rodney closely and was satisfied with their reaction. He mentioned casually that they were made with English gin.

"Soon there will be more company for you," Péguy said. "It is the hunting season and the really energetic hunters stay out until the last possible moment. They are not back yet."

Péguy drank at a furious speed. He would fill Nina's glass

and Rodney's and although he would put only a few drops into their glasses his would always be empty. He would promptly finish off the liquid in two or three gulps and then start the ritual again.

In fifteen minutes they had finished the pitcher and Péguy was mixing a new set of drinks. Three hunters had drifted in, all of them empty-handed. Péguy invited them to the table with Rodney and Nina. Slowly, so slowly that it was noticeable, as gradual as the change from drizzle to rain, the room began to pick up speed and tempo. Everyone began to talk a bit faster, to gesticulate more, to drink a bit faster. All of the hunters identified themselves indirectly. Two were lawyers in Paris. Péguy was a manufacturer of rubber stamps. He said proudly that it was the most rapidly expanding business in France. Even schoolchildren now carried rubber stamps to smack onto the hundreds of papers they had to fill out every year at school. Another of the hunters was a writer who also raced sports cars in his spare time.

"What do you write about?" Nina asked.

"About racing cars, of course," the writer said.

They all laughed and instantly Péguy was serving more drinks.

Because Rodney's stomach was somewhat sour from the drinking and lack of sleep the night before, he swallowed off three martinis with large glasses of Perrier water before he began to feel much better. The three hunters and he and Nina were seated around the table and the man Péguy had by now brought over the bottles to the table. The woman came in from the kitchen carrying a chilled block of pâté, a wooden bowl of butter, a bowl of radishes, and two loaves of bread.

Somehow the arrival of food excited Péguy. He got up and began to do a whooping, odd little dance around the woman. He danced with very precise, almost mincing, steps, but his face was drawn up into a quite severe smile.

The woman started to laugh, but Péguy silenced her with a hard look. She held her laughter in, a tear rolling with glycerin perfection down her chin while she swayed with her arms loaded.

The hunters roared encouragement to Péguy.

"I've known him for fifteen years and I never saw him do that," the woman said.

"He comes here every year but this is the first time he has ever danced. It is absolutely comical," the writer-racer said.

Leaning back, looking at the man with eyes mellowed by three drinks, Rodney suddenly understood him completely. He had not danced for years. Now he was doing one of the dances that was a courting dance when he was very young. He stood stiffly, arms outspread, his proud little belly jutting out, the arms flexing. He danced very precisely. His eyes flashed with an unbelievable pride.

Rodney sensed something else. Péguy was circling the cook as a camouflage. He was moving with all the aggression of a rooster. It was the dance one would do at a bacchanal. Easy, he told himself, don't let your imagination run away with you. But he was not quite sure what he was imagining.

The woman put the bowls of food on the table and Péguy ended his dance with a flourish. The hunters howled with delight and Rodney and Nina applauded. Péguy, with an exaggerated pride, walked to the table, picked up a raddish, split it in two with his thumb and forefinger and spread butter over the two halves. Slowly, as if it were a ritual, he popped the two halves of the radish in his mouth and crunched down hard on them. Then he turned and smiled at Rodney and Nina.

"Even after walking all day with a shotgun in the cold there is still some power in the old carcass," Péguy said disarmingly. "I should dance more often." He reached down and cinched in his belt, threw back his shoulders. Miraculously the tight little belly disappeared. Péguy seemed really astonished.

"This is the first time in years I have really thrown my shoulders back and danced," he said.

He continued to stare at his flat belly. He ran his hands over the belt buckle. He reached over for a piece of bread and cut off a thin slice of pâté from the block.

"I wonder where his belly went to," Nina said, glancing at Rodney. She spoke in a very soft voice.

Rodney shrugged his shoulders.

The other hunters ripped into the food. One of them tore a *baguette* of bread down its entire length with his fingers and then sliced off four pieces of pâté which he placed along the half-*baguette*. He ate it as if it were a gigantic open-faced sandwich. With his free hand he poured himself some wine. His eyes rolled in his head with excitement and pleasure. Everyone, except Nina, dug into the food and for several minutes no one spoke. They were joined by Rico.

Spatters of yellow butter appeared on the table, crumbs fell onto the pâté, knives hacked into the block of rich pâté, occasionally someone grunted for a bottle of wine or for more bread. No one had bothered to light candles and the only light was from the huge fireplace. The light tumbled and fell, swelled and then diminished.

"This must have been the way it was when the castle was first built," Nina said in a soft voice which everyone heard. "Back in medieval days when the men came back from their fights or hunting or wars or whatever they were doing."

Everyone at the table glanced around. They seemed to be appraising themselves and the others. They smiled at one another. They were pleased with what they saw.

In ten minutes all of the food had been eaten and the men fell back in their chairs staring at the empty bowls.

"Best day I ever had here," the writer said. "Didn't shoot a damn thing but it was still a good day. It's like when you are racing a car with everything in tune and floating into the turns with perfect control."

"Friend, you are becoming poetic," the lawyer said.

The writer looked at the lawyer and then grinned. It was a muted grin which was meant to be sheepish but which came out tigerish.

"I feel poetic," the writer said. "Also I feel powerful. Do you know the American game of Indian-wrestle?"

"None of that," the cook shouted. She had been circling the outside of the table, watching them with an astonished look on her face and estimating when they would be ready for the next course. "The omelet is ready and I cannot delay it another minute. Be heroes at some other time than dinner time."

She brought the omelet out slowly. They all breathed appreciation. Rodney felt as if he had been in the inn for months.

The omelet was in a huge omelet pan which the woman carried in her right hand. In her left hand she had a large white serving plate. She put the hot serving plate on the table and held the omelet down for them to examine. It was a crisp brown on the edges and bubbles of butter came through the surface and ran over the soft yellow center. She picked up a fork and with a quick expert motion flipped the omelet over a third. Then she ran a knife under the remaining two-thirds. They waited breathlessly. When she was satisfied she turned the pan over and the omelet fell neatly into the plate, all folded and tiny jets of steam coming out of it.

"It is wonderful," Nina said softly.

The woman turned her eyes away from the omelet and smiled at Nina. She sucked air through a tooth as a signal to her husband and he jerked to attention. He trotted over to the kitchen and came back with warm plates. Expertly he began to serve the omelet. The woman went to a window beside the fireplace, pushed it open and reached outside. She brought in two large pitchers of white wine which had been chilling in a snowbank. She began to pour wine for all of them. The wine was imperfectly chilled; it had rivulets that were icy cold running through it while other parts were almost room temperature, but it had a marvelous bouquet.

This is not an ordinary dinner at a small inn, Rodney told himself, straining a bit to push back his sense of hilarity and well-being. He had never seen a French restaurant where the drinks went uncounted, the meal appeared spontaneously, and the owners seemed to have decided for themselves what would be served. It was a very pleasant sensation. This was the heart of France, he told himself, the place where the soul of a nation exposes its real generosity. He reached for his glass and drank half of it.

They ate the omelet slowly. The hunters talked about their bad luck at hunting. Péguy questioned Rodney about America and what Americans thought about de Gaulle. Rico ate slowly and systematically and without talking. His wife moved slowly around the table watching the face of each person as he bit into the omelet.

When they had finished the last of the omelet Péguy stood up over the serving plate with a piece of bread. The plate was as clean as if it had been washed. Then he bent forward slightly and, as if he had done it a thousand times, he devoured the piece of bread. Everyone applauded.

"My friend Péguy, this is a marvelous and hospitable inn," Rodney said as Péguy sat down. Péguy seemed abstracted but he understood what Rodney had said. He brought his head slowly sideways and looked at Rodney and then his eyes focused with understanding.

"I have been coming here for years, my friend Cartwright, and I have never seen it like this," Péguy said. "Usually this bitch of a woman and her stupid husband cannot cook a single thing worth eating and they skulk around waiting for tips. Tonight, somehow, things are different. Maybe it is because you are an American and they are excited at having you here." He paused a minute and reflected. "Oh, shit, that is not the reason. They have American tourists here in the summer and they give them the worst food and the highest prices I have ever seen. No, it is something else."

Rodney turned to Nina and saw the pink edge of her tongue disappearing back into the corner of her mouth. Her head was bent forward, her eyes looking down at the table. He had the impression that she looked like some sort of rare painting or a snip from a motion picture he might have seen.

Without reason he felt a flare of anger at Péguy. The man had been offensive to Nina. The old bastard is probably a roué, Rodney thought. This inn has probably seen a thousand parties like this and all of them are aimed at gratifying his roosterlike tendencies. There is nothing as decadent as a fading Frenchman.

Nina looked up and smiled hesitantly at Rodney. He did not quite understand the look, but the resentment at Péguy was heightened.

The woman arrived with a great earthenware bowl of jugged hare. She explained that the hare had been marinated for days in wine and then slowly simmered on the back of the stove for almost three days. She had not known when to serve it, but now she felt was the right time. She held the bowl high so they could not see the contents. When she had finished talking she put it in the center of the table.

Rodney stared at it for a few seconds without understanding what he saw. The contents of the bowl looked like brown glazed objects. He could see what looked like a rabbit's leg or a rib cage but it all seemed cold and almost sculptured.

The waiter reached over and stuck a serving spoon into the brown mass. He seemed to have pierced the skin of a volcano. Jets of brown liquid shot into the air. A magnificent aroma arose from the bowl. He served them quickly. His wife brought serving plates of hot vegetables.

The jugged hare was delicious. At first Rodney had thought that the pieces of hare would be as hard as stone, but they fell apart easily. The concentrated sauce was beyond anything he had ever tasted. The hare tasted of herbs, wood fire, the essence of some wine and it was very delicate. Rodney used the fried potatoes to sop up the gravy.

Rico had brought out bottles of Châteauneuf-du-Pape. It was a heavy red wine. No one sipped it. They all took it in gulps.

Briefly, so fast that it never hardened into an impression, Rodney felt a slight nausea and remembered fragments of the night before. He had the feeling he had been eating for days with a kind of gluttony, and then he forced the thought from his mind.

There was a period of silence. The only sound was the occasional snapping of a small bone, the suck of wine going into a mouth, the clink of a utensil against a plate. Again Péguy repeated his feat of gathering all of the gravy into a narrow area and then swooping it up on a piece of bread. They all applauded as he ate the bread.

For several minutes they all sat back in their chairs and looked at the table and one another. None of them were drowsy. Their eyes glittered. They made small nervous gestures.

One of the hunters suggested that they dance. He went up to his room and brought back a portable record player. He also brought a handful of Twist records, old Glen Gray pieces, and a few recordings by jazz groups in Paris. He set the record player upon the bar and put a Twist record on.

Péguy was instantly at Nina's side. He said something about never having done the Twist, but never too old to learn.

Everyone at the table stood up to watch. It was clear that
Péguy had never done the Twist before. It was also apparent, however, that he learned very quickly. He watched
Nina do a very mild Twist. For perhaps fifteen or twenty
seconds his feet and body shifted as he got the sense of the
dance. Then in midstride he went far past Nina. The hunters
stared. The cook put her hands to her mouth in surprise.
Péguy was doing a wild extravagant Twist that Rodney had
seen done only by professionals before. And his belly had
disappeared and his shoulders were back.

When the record stopped playing the hunters did not ap-
plaud. All the men at the table, as if by a common instinct,
reached out for their glasses and drank. Péguy led Nina
back to the table. His shirt was sweaty and he had a hard
confident grin on his face.

Nina sat down quietly in a chair. Péguy stood, his legs
astride, looking down at the table. The woman had put out a
wheel of Camembert cheese. The surface of the cheese was
cracked and the cracks were oozing the soft interior cheese.
Beside the marble platter which held the cheese there was a
basket of French bread and also a basket of North African
pears.

Péguy picked up a knife and cut a wedge out of the
cheese. The other men jerked their heads to look at him. He
glanced around at them with a slight contempt. Rodney
glanced at Nina. Her eyes were wide and glistening. Her
mouth was opened slightly as if she were tasting the cheese
herself.

When Péguy's teeth closed on the bread and cheese, her
mouth closed and there was just the slightest moisture in the
corners of her lips.

One of the hunters, the writer, swore softly. He looked up
in surprise, astonished that he had spoken aloud. Then his
lips set and he went on talking.

"I can dance," he said defiantly. "At least I can dance as well as Péguy."

He turned to Nina. He looked at her full-face, but she glanced away. She looked down at her hands. The writer moved out toward the floor and Nina got up, obediently, and followed him. The writer slammed the player-head down on the record and turned toward Nina. It was apparent that he had never danced the Twist before either. But in a few seconds he was dancing as well as Péguy. In addition he was doing some improvisations which would have been ridiculous if they had not all drunk so much and if Péguy had not danced. Some of the steps took inventions of Péguy and went far beyond them. At one point the writer was bent completely backwards with his legs cocked under him, and his whole body from the neck to the ankles writhed. Only the feet and head were utterly still.

Nina laughed. It was a laugh of embarrassment. When the record ended they came back to the table. Her cheeks were flushed.

Rodney felt drunk, but with an added quality he had never experienced before. Somehow this dinner seemed to be linked to the evening before at the inn and also to Art back at the party in Paris.

It had something to do with Nina, but, at the same time, he knew that was impossible. With the slow, sluggish accuracy that comes with drunkenness he focused his eyes and attention on Nina. In one way she looked more virginal, more restrained, more proper than any woman he had known. There was, indeed, a certain primness about her. She seemed almost disdainful. No, he corrected himself, not disdainful but almost digusted at anything physical. Part of the coolness came from her simple dress, her unpainted well-shaped nails, the sparse use of cosmetics, her face that was almost plain, but not quite.

An idea kept probing into Rodney's odd mood. He fought
it away but could not put it down. It came sharp across his
consciousness "her breasts would be perfect." How and why
he knew this he could not tell. He had never seen them. But
they would be perfect. They would be firm, slightly
pendant, girlish but suggesting they were just at the edge of
ripeness.

At that moment Rodney felt a gripping concupiscence, a
kind of hot sluggishness that was very powerful. At the same
time that his body seemed lax and possessed, his mind
seemed very clear and independent. He was going to take
Nina out of this room.

He pushed back his chair, stood up and walked over to
the waiter. He asked him where their room was. The waiter
gave him directions. He walked back and took Nina by the
hand. She looked up at him with a quick startled look. At
once every other man around the table tensed. Rodney
looked around the circle, waited for one of them to move.
They look puzzled and baffled.

Rodney led Nina from the room, and as they left the room
he had a delicious sensation. He knew that with them they
had sucked out the entire excitement and delight of the
evening. Now the men would be violent with one another,
become quarrelsome and mean.

As they walked up the stairs into a huge hall which was
illuminated by the single candle Rodney was carrying, he
had another sudden thought: Nina was possessed by lust.

The candle shook in his hand.

18. The Flight
and the Capture

RODNEY awoke with a sense of disappointment. Part of it came from the sure knowledge that he was hung over and would feel worse before he felt better. But it was more than that and he could not put the rest of it together.

He rolled over. Nina's face was inches from his. She was sleeping, her lips parted. They were in a huge disarrayed bed and a faint light came in from the narrow window.

Rodney studied Nina's face for a moment. It was not plain. It was too well formed for that. But it was not the kind of face one would turn to look at on the street. She had a beautiful nose and generous bowed lips, and a very even complexion. She made little of all this and yet Rodney had the feeling she was composed, put together with intelligence, ruled by some model.

He rolled and put his head down into the pillow. The night before came back to him in vivid disorganized swatches of time and place. The eyes of the hunters all staring at Nina, the strange euphoria which gripped all of them, Nina's tongue showing briefly between her lips, the incredible dance by Péguy, the sense that all of them were strutting and preening, Nina's modest dancing. What the hell did all of this mean? And the night before? What did that mean?

He had hauled her from the dining room as if he had won her in some primitive battle. He had placed the candle be-

side her bed and had undressed her with complete
confidence. She bent her head and permitted it, but she was
lifeless. A few times as he almost faltered he could feel her
flesh tremble under his hands and his own fingers felt
scalded. As her breasts were exposed her hands came up to
cover them.

Rodney finished the undressing, stripping off her stockings
as the last move. She did not lift her feet so he left them
about her ankles. Crouched before, the smells of her body
coming to him and the smooth skin of her legs only inches
from his eyes, he was afraid he had lost her. He stood up
quickly. He reached over to pull a hand away from her
breast . . . aware that the room was very cold and her skin
was gooseflesh. Their bodies burned like two engines in the
big cubicle of coldness. Her hand did not come away at first
and then gradually she yielded. At the same time she lifted
her head and looked at him for a moment . . . and then
down.

She was, for some time, very rigid in the bed. She was like
a mannequin that was not quite sure of its movements. But
the resistance only excited Rodney.

A thought, as firm as words, but with the violence of a
shock, passed through Rodney's mind: Nina, beneath everything, is lustful. It was a discovery; a kind of smashing insight.

He forced her legs apart and her breathing rose and she
then screamed. It was a peculiar scream. It was stifled, it
was not a cry of protest, she did not seem to be screaming
for relief, but from something else. Perhaps, Rodney
thought, it was excitement.

He was also aware that her hands were on his back,
gently pushing him forward.

When he penetrated her she went, for a terrible second,
absolutely rigid, her legs straightened out and she stopped
breathing. Then as he moved forward once she came back at

him with a savage kind of release. She sobbed into his ear, but her body was locked tightly around him. She rose and fell with him.

She was, he realized, unskilled. Her pelvic thrust was instinctive, irregular, restrained. *He* was teaching her. The knowledge made him dizzy and almost unbearably sensitive. His entire body seemed to be caught in a low grinding orgasm which he tried desperately to withhold from a climax. He was aware of every awkward movement which Nina made, of her breasts, of her increasing skill, at the sounds which had changed from surprise and pain to moans of pleasure. He put his hands around her breasts, pressed on her nipples with his thumbs and she gasped. Her motion stopped and she slowly arched her body and a sound came from deep in her throat.

He passed a climax and was only dimly aware of it. He continued as if there were a fire within the girl which must be extinguished. Occasionally her body went into a quick racking movement and she moaned.

At some point, perhaps a half hour after he had penetrated her, she lifted her mouth and put it against his ear. She spoke in a hesitant, almost experimental voice. He was sure she had never used the words before. They came from her lips with utter novelty.

"You cock, you big terrible cock," she said.

Hearing the words Rodney could not distinguish his precise sensations. The entire thing was now like an orgasm. He rose on his arms a few times and screamed a few words at the girl and although her face was flushed she winced as she heard them.

When he had stopped from simple exhaustion the center of the bed was moist with sweat. The candle had flickered down and was beginning to gutter. He fell asleep on top of Nina.

Now, digging his face into the pillow, Rodney revised his

opinion. He did not feel disappointment. What he felt was a
sense of anxiety. He had not been certain Nina would be
there when he had awakened. Now that she was there he
felt relieved.

For a moment he thought of Charity and her love making.
She was far more skilled than Nina. Charity did odd things
with her hands and mouth and there was no part of his
body which her tongue had not explored. She made love to
him in every conceivable posture and place and there was
no experiment which she would not attempt. But there was
nothing wanton in her sexuality. It was as cool as illustra-
tions from a marriage manual.

Nina, for all of her inexperience and hesitancy, had lifted
and excited and then drained him in a manner he had never
known before.

Half asleep he remembered a strange episode with Charity. He had told her about Japanese girls who caressed a
man with a feather-light brush and crooned to him as they
stroked his body. The words were not understood by the
American occupation troops, but the combination of strok-
ing and words finally produced a frantic twitching and writhing and, in the end, a body-wide orgasm which left Americans limp and numb and, in most cases, quite frightened.

Charity had listened and asked a few questions. A week
later Rodney awoke to the gentle swoop of a brush down his
back. The brush worked over his back and thighs and neck,
but never approached his genitals. At some point, when he
was simultaneously relaxed in all his muscles and scream-
ingly taut in his mind, the brush was changed. A tiny gentle
hairlike brush worked at his ear . . . stroked, entered, withdrew, circled behind the lobe, picked up in tempo and then
backed away, swirled back to enter the ear and go almost
into his brain, withdrew and became hauntingly delicate
with only a few hairs moving about the orifice. Rodney was
astounded and scared and delighted. His ear had, in some

perverse way, become the center of all his sexual hotness. He had an erection, but it seemed far away and almost casual: it was his ear which was burning to the point of boiling over, to the point of climax.

She had laughed and thrown the brushes across the room. She was asleep almost at once. They never repeated the experiment. Both knew that Rodney had been humiliated.

Rodney looked once more at Nina and then turned on his side.

Rodney fell asleep. Without waking up he knew that Nina was still there. Later he was aware that the light had deepened to a dim yellow. At the same time he felt a vague uneasiness, a sense of subtle alarm. The hair rose on the back of his neck. He resisted opening his eyes. Then slowly he let his eyelids slide open.

Nina was sitting up in the bed, crouched slightly forward. She was entirely naked. Her eyes blazed down into his and her face was not six inches from his. He shut his eyes, waited for a few moments and opened them again. Nina was still in the same position, her eyes glowing. He wondered how long she had been crouched like that, staring at his face. He had no notion what would happen if he smiled or spoke. Her eyes were focused in a hard mechanical way, her lips were drawn back slightly, the perfect white tips of her teeth were slightly separated.

For five or six minutes they stared at one another. It was still very cold in the room and Nina's skin was puckered and very blue. She scarcely seemed to breathe, as if she were devoting all of her energies to the passion that had gripped her.

Slowly he closed his eyes. With the greatest self-control he had ever exercised he refused to open his eyes. He tried to think what it meant.

For a moment he thought she might be after his money. He always had four or five hundred dollars in neat twenty-

dollar bills, close to ten thousand francs in thousand-franc
notes, and $1500 in traveler's checks. This was a good deal
of money. Rodney was not conspicuous in his display of
cash; it was always apparent however that he could afford to
pay.

Almost at once Rodney discarded the idea that Nina was
planning to rob him. If she were really after his money staring at him like that would only serve to alarm him. Also
Nina seemed to have not the slightest interest in money.
Rodney was sure she was not a thief.

He felt a kind of shame. Here is a girl who has suffered
and been through the wringer of life and I at once think she
is a thief. Jesus, when will I ever get to the center, the *real*
center, of things in the way she has? Not sailboats or Los
Angeles society or the great swirling galaxy of cheap American sentiment, but down to what was the real thing between
people. He felt dirty and soiled and Nina seemed so clean.

He dozed again, still unsure of what was happening. He
heard a truck go by on the highway. He stirred.

Nina's hand fell on his shoulder and ran down onto the
arm, over the biceps and inside his closed elbow. The elbow
was half closed, but she forced her fingers in, very gently.
There was something about the caress which was very lulling. She was curious about him and his body. She was speaking softly to herself; words which he could not quite make
out. But the meaning was clear. They were the words one
might use when examining a painting. The words were admiring.

Rodney rolled over on his back with his eyes open.

"What are you doing?" he asked.

"Looking," she said. She pulled the sheet up above her
breasts. "Is that wrong?"

Rodney laughed. He reached over and pulled her down
on the sheet. He saw her eyes as she disappeared beneath
him: apprehensive, willing, limned with curiosity. He hung

over her, dominating her completely. Then he moved more closely and her eyes opened and then went wide and as he entered she was halfway between terror and excitement.

"Nina, I am going back to Paris today," Rodney said during breakfast. "I have some business to do and I must be getting back. I will go on the train."

Nina was eating a white roll and drinking coffee. The hunters had left early, but they had ordered the waiter to give Rodney and Nina a half-dozen *fines* with breakfast. Rodney had drunk three, but Nina just shook her head.

"You are so crazy," Nina said. She shook her head over the coffee. "You are just going to leave the valuable car here and go back to Paris. It is marvelous."

Actually he had forgotten the car, but he said it would be no problem. He called over to Rico and asked him if someone could be persuaded to drive the Bentley back to Paris within the next few days. Rico rolled his eyes as if it were a stupid question. Everyone in the village would be ready to drive it back. Just tell them where. Be assured it would be delivered in very excellent shape.

"Good," Nina said. "We shall go together. I will call a cab when we are ready to go to the station."

It was the first loop in the snare. A silky, almost inaudible sound, it fell on Rodney's ears and he recognized it. He was frivolous with the cognac in his stomach, but he knew that the first loop was cast. Looking in Nina's face he knew that she also knew it and also that she was feeling very much like a fowler that morning. For a few very lucid moments the common knowledge was there between them and Rodney thought slowly of the importance of what he had to do now. He knew that he could break the one loop; a sharp sound in his voice would be sufficient. It would take an effort, but if he refused her it would all be over.

Then the warm marvelous cognac fumes came up out of

his chest, redolent with coffee and unsalted butter. He felt
enormously confident, sure, able. It didn't make any difference where they separated. He had found her in Paris.
Why not take her back there? She thought it was a loop of
the snare and she was right, but he could break the loop as
well in Paris as here. He was delighted with the sudden insight into himself. He ordered another *fine,* smiled at Nina
and told her they would go on the early afternoon train.

They walked to the station, got tickets for Paris and
boarded the train that afternoon. They went at once to the
restaurant car and had a long lunch. Nina was delightful
and told him a very elaborate story that was quite humorous.
His attention now was mildly alerted to the consistency of
her stories and he realized that she had now told him that
she was born in three different places: Dijon, Montauban
and the Argentine. Now it did not matter, but he realized
for the first time that she was either a very talented liar or
careless. He did not have time to think about it, for the train
was almost to Orléans by the time they finished lunch.

They were eating cheese when someone mentioned they
were ten minutes outside of Orléans. They had drunk a bottle of white wine and Rodney felt prescient and very much
in control.

This girl is too much for me, he said to himself. Now I can
face it. She has a kind of quicksand energy which will suck
me under and consume me. Oh Christ, it would consume
any man. She is skewed a bit, different from any other girl.
She sets everything on fire and feeds it with alcohol and
excitement. Every man knows he can dominate completely
any woman, but it doesn't work that way. This one is too
much.

Suddenly he signaled for the waiter and ordered champagne. Something tore inside of him, rebelled at what he
had told himself. He looked at Nina again. She was eating
cheese quite calmly. He could see no marks of the previous

night on her. She pointed her finger out the window where a group of colts were racing around a green pasture, excited by the passage of the train.

The harmonic rhythm of the train, the stress of glass against steel, the shimmering and shattered sunlight, the quick flux between brown coltskin and pure green grass and some unknown tree was wonderfully exciting. It hit the eyeball with novelty and complete freshness.

Rodney felt silly. He had merely looked away from Nina with cheese on her lips and now he was convinced that the whole world was reflected in the confluence of her pink lips, yellowed cheese, uncommitted eyes, white teeth and exquisite bubbles of saliva in the corners of her mouth.

He swung his head away from the glass window of the train.

For a moment Rodney thought that Nina was like one of the colts. Then he knew that was not so. He thought of Charity. She did not come through very clearly to him. She had one quality that was appealing: she was not dangerous.

Nina laughed, looking over her shoulder at the vanishing pasture, and Rodney was terrified. He must get off the train. Very quickly he made a plan. He had no idea of why he was so desperate.

Rodney planned to slip off the train in Orléans, catch the next train to Paris and then get on the Métro without leaving the station and be home in ten minutes after his arrival in Paris.

He stood up and for the last time he looked down at Nina. "Excuse me for a minute," he said. "I must go to the men's room."

He chose a men's room which opened directly onto an exit from the train. He was in the toilet when the train slowed for Orléans. He had left his overcoat in the compartment with Nina and it had 5000 francs in a pocket. Nina would find it and it would be more than she had had when she met him.

As the train slowed, he felt a sense of swelling relief; as if he were stepping out of a high-pressure area into normality. He was ending it so well.

He opened the door and Nina was in the corridor facing him. She was standing casually, her arms folded. But her eyes were focused into black pits of brilliance. One forefinger made a deep white pit in her arm and at the bottom of the pit a drop of blood appeared. Rodney stood for a moment, staring at her eyes, then down at the fingers digging into her arms. If it had been possible by any means to have raped her at that moment he would have done it. He felt the now familiar sensation of warmth that crept throughout his lower body.

They stood there while the sound of airbrakes squealed in their ears, people pushed out of the exit, hucksters came down the platform with bottles of water and fruit. At that moment, as clearly as if it were a physical act, Rodney felt another loop of the snare fall about him. He could shrug it loose by merely pushing past her, throwing her aside and walking off the train. He knew she would not follow him. He did not push past her, however, and he could feel the loop tighten and so could Nina.

Nina took him by the arm and her fingers were soft. She guided him back to their compartment.

"Rodney, you are frightened," she said. It shamed him instantly. "I can see it in your eyes and face. Are you frightened that we are going back to Paris together?"

"You know that I am married," he said, and grinned. The grin never developed. It was too contrived. Somewhere he had missed something important and this thin elegant girl knew it. Also she *knew* what he had missed. He wilted.

"What difference does that make?" she asked. "That you are married?"

He wondered if she knew he had intended to get off the train in Orléans.

"But . . ." Rodney started to say.

"Yes, I know. You are already married, but one can always get a divorce. That is an easy thing for Americans." Then incongruously, with flowering innocence, she turned to him. "What we did last night. It means we are bound together. It means a great deal."

Rodney started to laugh, but it got no farther than his throat. He looked at her suspiciously, knowing he was still somewhat drunk. Did she really not know that millions of men and women slept with one another every day and were not married and that it meant very little?

He took her by the arm and led her back to the dining car. The champagne was waiting. The champagne excited him and the sharp edges of the time and place began to dissolve. She had absolutely no legal recourse; she could not blackmail him; she was powerless. All he had to say to her was goodbye and if it were said firmly enough he could walk away. It was more difficult now than it would have been that morning, but still he knew that he could handle it when the time came. The thought of Nina going into a tantrum or raising her voice against him was impossible. He would avoid it.

Rodney felt a marvelous sense of control. He ordered another bottle of champagne, only a split this time, and smiled across the table at Nina. She smiled back.

Rodney took Nina home with him. As the train approached Paris and he drank more champagne he became increasingly convinced that this was just the sort of thing Charity would appreciate. They had always been very liberated and several times Charity had urged him to have an affair if he thought it would help his work. She was a very tolerant person and he would put it in a light Hemingway mood. Once he thought of introducing Nina to Charity the idea seemed very clever and he was suddenly impatient to

be in Paris. He was anxious to return to the big calm house
in the Tuileries; to the long quiet hours; to the patter of
Charity's voice.

He did not think of what he would do with Nina. He had a
notion that after she had met Charity he would keep her
around for a few days and then send her off. Or he would
introduce her to a few rich Americans he knew. Or he would
give her the money for a small apartment and put her there
and then just not drop around. On that afternoon, as the
train sped through the darkening Paris landscape, the orderly fields swept up from the horizon were jumbled by the
nearness of vision and then swept away; that afternoon it
seemed to Rodney that he possessed all of the opportunities
one could wish. He would worry about the exact problem
later.

19. The Guest

C HARITY did, in fact, take it very well. Rodney called
her from the station. He spoke fast, putting the story together humorously, as the sort of thing that could happen to
anyone in Paris. Charity seemed reserved, uncertain and she
said nothing. But when they arrived at the house Charity
was friendly and even enthusiastic. Nina walked calmly be-

side Charity, her coat over her arm, wearing the same clothes she had worn when she left Paris. Once in the hall she turned up the light under a Cézanne . . . ran her finger over the surface, discovered it was an original and nodded at them. At some point Charity decided to take it as a joke.

"It's so much like a novel," she said. "Does she speak English?"

"None. You can say anything you want in English in front of her and she just smiles."

"Was it fun?" Charity paused and chose her words carefully. "I mean getting out in the countryside and being with the French people."

"Christ, yes, it was fun," Rodney said. He was relieved, although he was not quite sure that Charity fully understood what he had been doing. "Let me tell you about one of the characters we met in a hotel." Rodney told a very good story and Charity was delighted. She caught the mad, antic, compulsive character of the trip and for the first time since she arrived in France she felt certain that life in Europe was not the same as life in Los Angeles.

Charity called the cook and they had a late supper. They ate fruit and cheese and Charity had gotten some Canadian Club whisky from someone at the British embassy so they had several highballs. It was the first highball Nina had ever had, but she enjoyed it.

"She can stay for a few days, can't she, Charity?" Rodney asked. "I don't have the slightest idea what she does here in Paris or where her family is, but I don't think she will want to be around too long."

"Why of course she can stay," Charity said. "Don't be small-minded. I'll put her in the front bedroom; the one with the view of the gardens."

The next morning Rodney woke up early. His head ached, an acid taste welled up from his stomach. He was not hung over, he had simply slept badly. The ways in which he could send Nina off did not seem as easy as they had the night before. Evenings with Nina had fallen into a pattern. Early in the evening he saw her rather clearly, half understood her shy gestures, felt no deep attraction to her, even wanted to get rid of her. But with a few drinks and the presence of other people the mood changed and he became sure of Nina and of himself. The feeling grew during the evening into a kind of hard certitude that had the strange air of reckless-ness about it. In the morning he felt uncertain about her again. She slipped from the precise focus of the previous evening. With alcohol and a crowd she was sharply defined, easily understood and desirable.

Sitting in bed he felt the urge for a drink. He seldom drank before lunch and never before breakfast . . . until he had met Nina. But he could think of no way of getting to the liquor cabinet without being seen by the servants. He discarded the idea as being both silly and dangerous. He reassured himself that it was only a matter of being firm. His shoulders went square and he slid out of bed. Charity was still sleeping in the other bed. One arm hung from the covers . . . perfect, almost waxen, laced with a tracery of light blue veins, the fingers long and exquisite.

Charity's arm stopped the growing optimism he felt. It was perfect, but it was lifeless.

When he got downstairs Nina was having breakfast in the dining room. She was reading *Le Figaro* and smiling.

"Roddie, you must give me a few thousand francs," she said, putting down her coffee cup. "I need some clothes. These are too rough to wear around here." She waved her hand and took in the whole house . . . it was a strange ges-ture that was proprietary, possessive, self-assured and very confident.

Rodney did not speak for a moment. He watched Nina's hand and arm. *Her* arm and hand were not sculpturally per-fect, but they possessed authority. Quite by themselves.

Quite independently of Nina. Rodney knew he must move hard.

"Nina, you can't stay here longer than tonight, you know," Rodney said. "It would be silly to have Charity and you both living here. It is impossible. Look, I'll give you ten thousand francs, you buy some clothes and then you leave. All right?"

Nina took the ten thousand francs, smiled at Rodney, kissed him on the cheek and left.

A half hour later Charity came in. She walked with her elegant, boneless, yet poised stride, a peignoir swirling around her hips. She was made up in her usual spare manner. Unconsciously she turned her right profile slightly toward Rodney.

"I talked with Nina last night after you went to bed, Rodney," Charity said. She was glancing at the paper. "She is delighted with the house. She said she was going to stay. Did you invite her?"

"I did not," Rodney said. "In fact I just told her to leave and she has left."

"You mean you ordered her out?" Charity asked. She turned and faced him directly, her far-apart eyes curious, her posture suddenly tense.

"Of course," Rodney said. "Look, Charity, I'm not apologetic about Nina. She's an interesting girl and there is that fantastic bit about her picking me up during the war. It was just an experience. Now it's over."

"I'm pleased, Rodney," Charity said. "Not that I object to what happened. But the girl is strange. She is obviously upper class. She bears herself well and has nice manners and dresses well, but any girl that would go off with a man at the drop of a hat. Well, it just might have gotten sticky."

"And you hate sticky things," Rodney said.

Charity's eyes hardened and Rodney smiled. Charity sat down and opened a paper. The maid brought her her usual breakfast: a small glass of orange juice, two poached eggs looking very white and aseptic on a piece of toast, a small pot of coffee. She ate without looking up. As always she ignored the toast. She was a very precise eater. Her eggs were always hard because she disliked the sight of yolks dripping.

"I don't quite see what you saw in her," Charity said when she had finished the paper. "She is not what one would call a ravishing beauty. Young and fresh and good bones, but that is about all."

Rodney grunted. He felt desolate and confused. Nina had been a victory, but he could not explain it to Charity.

Nina came back late in the afternoon. She was wearing a quiet gray dress with a rich look about it. Her breasts were demure and tiny and her hips seemed muted under the material.

Nina was very gay when she came in and kissed both Rodney and Charity on the cheek. She went over to the bell and pushed for the butler and asked him for a Canadian Club and Perrier.

"Rodney, would you like a whisky and soda?" she asked.

Rodney was surprised at her reappearance. He nodded, not quite sure what she had asked. He felt he must make a move of some sort. Charity was glacial in her chair although she smiled at Nina, somewhat the way a mother would smile at a precocious daughter.

Nina had simply ignored his order to leave. Now she was offering drinks to them as if she were the hostess. Rodney waited tensely to see what Charity would do. Charity accepted it. She took a whisky and Perrier from Nina and nodded thanks to her. Rodney wondered if Charity was frightened by Nina.

They sat and drank and in a few hours they had finished the bottle of whisky. And it worked its wonderful chemistry on Rodney. At some point his annoyance with Nina vanished and he began to talk quickly, almost feverishly. Nina insisted on telling the cook to stop dinner so they could go out. They went to Fouquet's for champagne and laughed in the cold Paris air. Later they went to the Tour D'Argent for dinner and had three kinds of wine, climaxing with a very cold *brut* champagne. It was a very exciting evening.

The next morning Rodney and Charity had hangovers. Nina brought them a *fine* before breakfast and Charity took it eagerly while Rodney hesitated for a long miserable moment before drinking it down. An hour later four packages arrived full of clothes and hats for Nina. Also a tiny elegant packet of perfume for Charity and a box of chocolates with her initials on each piece. For Rodney there was a very excellent tie. Rodney paid for the whole shipment and it was over 100,000 francs. The *fine* before breakfast and a few after breakfast kept Rodney from feeling too angry. But he was now quite decided that Nina must leave.

But in the end the house defeated him. For the house was huge and very old. It was on three floors and the marble floors picked up the sound of one's footsteps and gave off ringing dulcet sounds. The tricks of some long dead builder trapped Rodney.

The afternoon of the day when the clothes arrived, Rodney met Nina in the hall.

"Nina, I must talk to you," Rodney said.

"Of course, Rodney darling," Nina said and stood expectantly.

"Look, Nina, you must leave. This is preposterous. Charity does not like it and I do not like it. If you need money I shall give you as much as I can. I am not rich, but I can give you something. Then you must leave."

He looked at her and she was in a new mood. Her eyes were large with pain and under her lashes enormous tears gathered and rolled slowly down her cheeks. Her throat worked convulsively. She nodded dumbly.

"Yes, you are right," she said. "You are absolutely right."

She took his hand and they walked down the marble corridor. In front of one of the statues she stopped and looked up at him.

"I will go," she said. "But give me a goodbye kiss and then I will leave."

Rodney kissed her carefully on the cheek. As he bent forward he was certain he was safe. It was midafternoon, the sun was out, people were moving through the house. Whatever it was that Nina did to him could not be done in broad daylight. He bent forward to kiss her cheek. But there was a slight withdrawal of her cheek, her head must have moved a fraction of an inch. Rodney's lips searched for her mouth. Her lips were closed, but he could feel a tiny trembling beneath the skin. He forced her lips apart and ran his tongue along her teeth. A sound came from her throat, a smothered moan. Reluctantly her teeth separated and their tongues met. Rodney ran a hand over her thighs and could feel the flesh tense.

He drew his head back and looked down the hall. Somewhere there was a bedroom, but he could not remember where and it was impossibly far away. At that moment Rodney knew he was snared. A painful, hot, insane pattern was established in the house during the next few days. Rodney talked to Charity about her piano lessons, about his boat-building, about Southern California. She responded in her usual manner, but he knew she was puzzled by Nina's presence in the house. Her parents had taught her to leave decisions to her husband and Rodney had always been the one to make the public decisions . . . the situations which visibly called for a decision.

In Los Angeles their friends had always said that Rodney

was an ideal husband: quick to make decisions, but never humiliating her.

"I suppose there is no reason she *has* to leave, is there?" she asked abruptly when Rodney was talking on some other matter.

"Oh Christ, I forgot. Of course there is a reason," Rodney would reply. "Charity, we are not running a free boarding-house. It's just that she has no place to go and I think that she likes the house. I'll go get rid of her right now."

He would confront Nina and calmly tell her why she must leave. He told her that he would have a lawyer in, would have her removed from the house by force. But always by some accident they brushed together. She would reach out to shake his hand, their arms would touch, and at the moment she touched him the whole thing collapsed.

Rodney could no longer identify the emotion. It was something perverse and unique and he had no defenses. Contact with Nina always produced the powerful and overriding urge. He came to recognize that the slight physical contacts were not accidental: *he* brought them about. He was sickened with himself. A dozen times he walked with Nina down the great echoing halls toward her farewell. They had never made it to the front door. He made love to her in all the recesses in the hall, in the attic among the dusty trunks, in the garage with the smell of grease and motor oil in the air, once in the kitchen and when Nina stood up there was a smear of butter and crumbs across her back and her eyes were sparkling.

After these quick compulsive moments Rodney would move instinctively for a drink. It was not that liquor made him feel better but it transformed the memory. As the alcohol hit his stomach the whole experience was changed. It became something wild and adventuresome; had the air of excitement.

He was not sure Charity understood what was happening. She spoke to him less frequently and mostly he saw her fine profile bent over a book. She did not practice any more on the piano.

There were days when none of them left the house and the curious cycle would repeat itself. There would be the hurried and sympathetic conference with Charity, the prowl through the house looking for Nina, the denunciation and the threats. Nina would always agree. Rodney would steel himself for the farewell. And then, in ways which he did not want or understand, the departure would fall apart. It was not always physical contact which started it. Sometimes it was nothing more than watching Nina walk down the long corridor to the door. Something in her walk or the way she held herself or some word she uttered would be enough. His voice would go a bit thick, Nina would continue along the corridor and a fear would grow in him that he was losing her forever. Once she got all the way to the door, was turning the handle and Rodney had a quick searing rage toward someone outside the house. In each case it was Rodney, assuring himself this was the last time, would pull her back . . . to the attic, the niches which held the statues, anyplace. Then the long walk back through the house and he would stand before Charity and without speaking she would look at him. She listened calmly to his explanation and then went back to her book.

20. The Big House

INCREDIBLY, life in the big house settled down to a routine. The most puzzled members of the household were the servants. They talked incessantly about the situation and found endless refinements to discuss. They eyed the three occupants cold-bloodedly, the way a person might look at a cow or a horse that was being offered for a very high price.

Charity was quiet and reserved, much the way she had always been. It never occurred to her to snoop and she was startled when her maid told her of the wild encounters between Nina and Rodney in the niches along the hall. The maid put it deftly, rehearsing it with the head cook, making sure that she led up to the event in just the right manner. She expressed a concern for Monsieur Cartwright's house, suggesting that one of the statues might fall on him and crush him to death. When Charity asked how this might happen it took her several minutes to realize what the maid was saying. She dismissed the girl from the room at once and went back to her book. She did mention it casually to Rodney and he flushed. For a moment he was furious and suggested that they fire the maid. Charity merely gazed at him quietly. Finally Rodney muttered something about it being a "piece of servant's gossip" and left the room.

Nina moved about the house a good deal. She did not bustle but she was very attentive. The first day she gave an order to one of the servants it was almost a request. She merely asked that a cup, which had been laid out for tea, be returned to the kitchen and wiped with a clean cloth. But in several days the servants knew who was giving orders in the house. The requests hardened into orders. The orders were not given in an arrogant way, but they were always given firmly. Suddenly Rodney and Charity and the servants were aware that the huge house had become somewhat dilapidated. Silver had gone unpolished, stretches of marble floor had not been washed, dust had gathered on high ceilings, some of the fabric on the huge chairs was wearing. All of these things changed very quickly.

Rodney, glancing in the mirror one morning, saw that his face was thinner. In fact his face looked gaunt. He was astonished. He had the impression that since meeting Nina he had eaten enormously, was almost wallowing in food. His mouth never seemed fully empty from the last meal or drink or sandwich or piece of fruit he had eaten. Somehow it had to do with Nina. She ate little herself, but merely by being around her one became interested in food . . . or food appeared in great quantities . . . or the preparation of food became a paramount topic of conversation. And yet Nina never opened the subject herself. It was that she dropped signs of avidity when food was mentioned. Rodney was not sure how she did this, but he was sure that it happened.

It distressed him to be so thin. And it was a mystery. In Los Angeles he had sailed and played tennis and squash and swam. Here he exercised hardly at all. He did walk around the house a great deal. He walked down the halls, climbed the stairs, poked around in the attic, and into the kitchen and quietly watched the help, then down into the cellars. His wandering seemed pointless and was very irritating to the servants. In a few weeks, however, they learned that Rodney did not even notice them as he passed.

"That man is like a cat, with those big crazy eyes," one of

the maids said while standing in the kitchen. "He makes me nervous and the poor boy looks so thin."

"And for a damned good reason," the head chef said, mashing the flat of his cleaver against the meat-cutting table. He was a huge, sixty-year-old man of very conservative views. He allowed no one on the staff to steal food or liquor and his language was always very proper. He also did not exercise the ancient prerogative of chefs to have love affairs with the maids. "The man is haunted. You are stupid. All of you," he said quietly. "But that does not surprise me. What surprises me is that you do not understand that this Nina girl is the cause of Monsieur's thinness. She has the kind of madness for which they used to burn witches." He paused and looked at them. His face went bitter. "None of you understand. Back to work."

The mood in the house was orderly and even, but it was as frangible as a piece of fine crystal. All moved in a calm deliberate way, almost holding their breath, just to make sure they would not crack the eerie crystalline mood of the house.

One day Nina asked Charity to go shopping with her. Charity was surprised, but for some reason she welcomed the invitation. Nina had talked to the chef and he had agreed to let them shop for the food for the day.

Nina insisted that Charity wear a scarf, for it was still very cold outside. They had only walked a half block before Charity realized how really cold it was. For weeks she had been exposed to the open air only when moving from the front door to a taxi or the chauffeured car. Now she knew her cheeks were pink, almost blood-red against the whiteness of her skin. She felt a kind of gay recklessness. They had not talked since they left the house. Charity glanced over at Nina. Again she had the feeling that she had tried to express to Rodney. Nina was not plain. Much more she gave the impression of a person who was trying to *appear* plain. Her

features were excellent, but she did nothing to accentuate
them with cosmetics. Also, her clothes were not plain. They
might give that appearance from a distance, but if one got
closer it was a much different thing. The dresses were exquisitely made and they were made for an effect. Precisely what
the effect was, Charity did not know. Somehow Nina reminded her of the nuns at the high school in Los Angeles.
But the comparison was ludicrous and it embarrassed Charity.

"How did you meet Rodney?" Nina asked suddenly.

"I don't really recall. I think it was through the family,"
Charity said laughing. "During the war Father used to invite
a group of officers from all of the Services for cocktails on
Saturday afternoon. Then he would ask a half dozen of them
to come to lunch on Sunday. Actually my father had known
Rodney's father for a number of years and all I remember is
that Rodney was a steady guest at our Sunday lunches. I
suppose we just drifted together."

Charity put her left hand to her cheek. She was not wearing gloves and the single large diamond on her hand had a
bluish quality. In fact it had the slight blue tinge of Charity's veins, and it seemed almost a part of her body rather
than an artifice.

"The exercise is good for you," Nina said and then
abruptly changed the subject. "Did you know other boys
before you met Rodney?"

Again Charity laughed, but this time the laugh was somewhat uncertain.

"Well, I went out with other boys," Charity said. "During
the war Los Angeles was all mixed up. Young officers from
all over were passing through on the way to the Pacific or
were being trained at airfields in Southern California."

"What kind of boys?" Nina asked.

"Princeton boys, Yale boys, and there were also boys from
Harvard and Stanford," Charity said and then paused. "In

fact, they came from all over the United States. Some of them even came from overseas. You know, Poles and Frenchmen and Dutchmen in exile who were being trained in the United States."

"No, I did not know," Nina said. "We got very little information."

"I really do understand how it was in France, Nina," Charity said. "Father used to remind all of us that the French champagne and cognac that we drank would soon be exhausted if France was not liberated. He was very conscious of the terrible time you people were having here on the Continent."

Nina glanced sharply at Charity and then away. They walked to the first shop without speaking. It was a *boulangerie.* The shop was small and in gold letters on the glass window it said "Boulangerie. Pierre et fils." Inside on the marble slabs Pierre and his youngest son were working on a side of beef. An assistant was cutting up a whole lamb. The marble slabs glistened with fat. There was a steady plinking sound as the bare bones, every sliver of meat cut away from them, rattled into a large metal can. Pierre's daughter sat behind a small raised counter with a box of change in front of her. She glanced at Charity and Nina and then back at the movie magazine she was reading.

The aprons of the men were covered with blood which had hardened into a thin purple layer and then had been glossed over with newer layers of fat and white splinters of bone.

"Good morning," Pierre said. He finished tying up a veal roast and stepped toward them. He eyed them cautiously, not sure he had seen them before.

"We would like some *tournedos,*" Nina said and smiled. "We are from the Cartwright house. I think you know what the chef likes. He likes them small, well aged, very tender, but not too thick."

Pierre scratched his nose and his hands were surprisingly white, cleansed by the untold thousands of pounds of suet that had passed through them.

"I have a very good piece of filet, Madame Cartwright," Pierre said. "There are really only six *tournedos* left in it, however. That is the best I can do."

"I am not Madame Cartwright," Nina said. "This is Madame Cartwright."

Pierre's eyes did not blink. He merely nodded at Charity.

"Madame Cartwright, if you need more than six filets you are making a mistake," Pierre said grinning. "Just forget invitations to the men until you have the group down to six people. Women always like to think that they enjoy a dinner where there is an excess of men. But they forget such affairs very quickly and for a good reason: they do not know if the fervor of the men was due to the fact that there were so many of them or whether the women really were attractive. On the other hand women never forget a dinner in which there is a shortage of men. The shortage of men, Madame Cartwright, is the best sauce that you could give to my *tournedos*."

Charity understood what Pierre had said, but she was confused. She turned and looked at Nina. Nina was glancing at the great sleek, red and white and purple color of the side of veal.

Charity felt that she was being insulted, but she did not know precisely how. She decided it was the man's way of joking.

"Yeah, yeah, yeah, Papa, all right. Shut up," Pierre's son said in embarrassment, his face glowing. "They are in a hurry. They don't want a lecture from you. I'll deliver the *tournedos*."

The son was staring at Nina. Pierre rolled his eyes comically, held his head in his hands and pushed it from side to side. He winked at Charity.

Charity suddenly felt relieved. She hated embarrassing situations; situations in which she did not understand what was happening. Then she realized something was strange in the shop. The men looked as if they were holding their breath. Pierre was not looking directly at her, but his eyes were angled toward Nina. Charity turned and looked at Nina.

Nina's hand, strong and well shaped and not particularly beautiful, had come out from her coat pocket. She was taking the glove from her hand. Charity was unable to identify exactly what Nina did, but whatever it was it brought the men all rigid. The sound of a saw on animal bones stopped. Nina's hand came out of the glove and there was a sigh in the shop. She reached out and touched a side of veal. With a small motion she pushed it and the whole carcass shivered.

Charity looked away quickly. Pierre had now moved his head. His eyes bulged from their sockets as if he were watching something very extraordinary. Pierre's son was the same. Charity glanced at Pierre's daughter. She merely looked confused, uncertain about what was happening and then back at her magazine.

Charity cleared her throat and told Pierre to deliver the *tournedos* by the middle of the afternoon. Instantly, at her first words, a seismic shock ran through the other people in the room. They snapped to attention, grinning, exaggerating their motions, strangely like people who had been too suddenly awakened.

As Nina and Charity walked back Charity's sense of well-being and physical excitement vanished. The cold had an odd effect upon her. She felt an unidentified bitterness. She looked at the trees and the frosted cobblestones and ice-glazed windows of the houses and they seemed oddly distorted.

That afternoon was the first time that Charity discovered Rodney and Nina at their lovemaking.

Rodney had been working in his room, doing some sketches of rudder detail on the new sailboat he proposed to build when he got back to Newport. He was restless and his finger shook slightly so that the work not only went slowly, but it looked messy. Two things kept breaking across his mind. First, he was aware that he could not recall the look or feel of life in Newport. Normally he had a sharp memory for places and people and events. But now he could not recall Newport at all. It was as if a map in his mind had just been painted a dull, even gray. Secondly, he realized that since they had returned to the house he had never once made love to Nina in a bed. All of their lovemaking had been quick, feverish, performed in awkward postures, Rodney bent over the small body of Nina, Nina's face always frightened and her eyes surprised and her hands reluctantly coming up from her sides and finally, at the moment of climax, pressing savagely into his back.

Rodney was sick of himself. He pitied himself and he knew that he did and that added to his self-revulsion. He never recalled before having been aware of himself or examining his motives. This turning inward and racking himself with questions was childish, he tried to convince himself. And the questions never found answers. The whole thing was crazy, he told himself. He looked at the sketch. It was shaky and amateurish. When he had started he had a clear vision of what the rudder should be like and it had been exciting and novel. Somehow he could not now remember the novel parts to it. He slashed the pencil across the sketch and felt a twinge of satisfaction as the soft lead broke and made a scrawling, rough wound through several layers of drawing paper.

He stood up and began to pace the room. In a few moments he was out in the corridor. He heard footsteps and turned around. It was Nina walking toward the door. She was wearing a coat and hat.

"Where are you going?" Rodney asked.

"I thought I would go for a walk and maybe visit an old friend," Nina said.

"A friend like the Egyptian psychiatrist or that crazy Australian Awn?" Rodney snapped out.

He was surprised at the ferocity in his voice. But behind that there was an even deeper surprise: he was suspicious of Nina. He moaned softly, cut by the humiliation. For weeks he had been trying to get her out of the house and now he realized that he really would not let her leave.

This is the way a man must feel at the moment he knows he has a sickness like cancer or alcoholism or something fatal, Rodney thought to himself.

"It is a girl from Montauban," Nina said. "She is sick. Would you like to come along? The exercise would do you good."

Rodney shook his head. He didn't want to speak. He knew his voice would be hoarse.

They walked slowly down the corridor. The inevitable happened. In a hot, sluggish, joyless mood he forced Nina into one of the niches. It gave him a dull pleasure to pull her coat up and hear two of the buttons pop loose. As he penetrated her, he heard a sharp click—far away, but very distinct. It took him a few seconds to realize it was a door opening. Slowly, without interrupting his motions, he swung his head in the direction of the sound. Charity was halfway through the door. She looked the other way and then in Rodney's direction. He knew he should stop, that even now, in the dimness of the corridor, he would be able to bluff his way past the whole incident, brush it off as something fanciful. But he could not stop.

Charity was very distinct because she was standing opposite a window. Her long, elegant hands still rested on the doorknob and her face was expressionless. Then slowly her eyes widened. She was staring directly into Rodney's face.

Her eyes did not seem to comprehend what they were seeing, but her lips drew back as if staring at something very strange.

At that moment the climax came. Charity's face wavered and dissolved as Rodney's body shook. In the odd light of the corridor her face became a kind of mask of contempt. He felt a perverse delight.

When he pushed himself away from Nina the door was closed and Charity had gone back into the room. Rodney, still trembling, got on his hands and knees and looked for the two buttons. He found them and handed them to Nina. She thanked him and then turned and walked down the corridor toward the door.

Rodney walked to his room and very quickly finished the sketch of the rudder.

Only when he was done and looked down at the simple perfection of the rudder and realized that he had recalled the novelty that had escaped him did he think about Charity.

Rodney walked down into the room in which Charity was reading. He did not quite know what he would say, but he did not feel as revulsed as he had a half hour ago.

"Charity, I think we ought to get out of the house for a few days," Rodney said suddenly. The words surprised him. "It would do us both good. One of the Frenchmen who helped me out of France in 1945 was named Proudhon. He lives at Portivy. He was a wonderful character of a man. I'll call him."

Charity did not speak. She gazed at Rodney. One of her fingers was placed under a word on the page. She seemed prepared to wait forever. It was this coolness that had always put Rodney off before. At that moment, however, he felt neither angry nor nervous.

"If he is there and can see us I'd like to leave this afternoon," Rodney said firmly.

He had almost closed the door before Charity spoke. He stopped, standing outside the room, the door open only a few inches. Her voice came to him distinctly.

"I could hear the words she was speaking, Rodney," Charity said. "She has a lovely voice. A very nice diction."

21. ". . . *This Warlike Puppet*" (*Byron*)

RODNEY was not certain how Nina was included in the trip to Portivy. Probably it was because of Proudhon. When Rodney had called Proudhon the Frenchman had instantly asked if Rodney had ever driven to Portivy from Paris. Rodney said no and was given orders to stay where he was. Everything would be arranged.

Charity caught some of Rodney's enthusiasm as Rodney talked about Proudhon. When he had walked out of Montauban in 1944 he had been passed from one man to another, each man taking control of Rodney as he was moved through the area the Maqui knew best. The last man, and the most crucial, was Proudhon. He was the man who must make the contact with either a French fishing boat willing to sail to England or an English rescue boat or submarine. Proudhon was the expert on the coast of the Quiberon peninsula.

Rodney had spent a week with Proudhon and it was probably the most dangerous week of his life, but he did not realize that until much later. Proudhon had a simple philosophy about escape: if you look as if you are escaping you will be caught; so look as if you belong where you are.

Proudhon had casually taken Rodney to a German officer who was a security specialist. He introduced Rodney to the officer and told him Rodney was a nephew of his from Montauban. They split a bottle of wine. Proudhon knew the German's French was so imperfect that he could not detect Rodney's American accent.

Proudhon forced Rodney to walk boldly through Portivy, took him to restaurants, aboard the fishing boats, along the beach where the German defenses were being perfected. He was openly so contemptuous of the Germans that they thought he was joking and accepted it. No one believes the truth, Proudhon said, so just tell them that and they will think you are a comedian.

During that week Rodney learned that Proudhon had been given a fairly good education and although he professed to hate books and bookish people he read a great deal. He had opinions on everything. Even more surprising he had information. And he loved strange words.

The next morning Proudhon was in Paris. He was a long thick root of a man. His body was muscular, the kind that would never go to fat. Although he moved with a slow deliberation he exerted enormous control. It was clear to Rodney that Proudhon had also lost a leg since they had last met. There was a shoe at the bottom of his left trouser leg but the whole leg moved mechanically and the shoe slapped down with a dull sound.

Proudhon wore a dark, very old woolen suit with a fisherman's brightly striped shirt beneath the jacket. He also wore a black bowler which he took off only when he was indoors.

Proudhon came into the house like a presence. They were

all to stay at his hotel in Portivy, but meanwhile he wanted
to show them some sights along the way. His black eyes
darted around the house and in a few moments he excused
himself and went to the kitchen. When he returned two
things were certain: first, he had ordered a picnic lunch for
them and, secondly, Nina was to accompany them. He had
not yet met her.

He had also had a talk with the chauffeur and made it
clear that he, Proudhon, was to drive the car. The chauffeur
was to have a vacation of a week or so. Proudhon asked
permission for none of these things. He simply did them.

"They have treated you badly, Rodney," Proudhon said,
grasping Rodney by the shoulders and shaking him. "They
have softened you up. For a man as young as you you
should have more zip and vigor. We will take care of all of
that."

Proudhon wound up driving the car. He drove fast,
casually and with great expertness. He crouched in the corner of the driver's seat, his right hand alongside the leather
of the seat, his left hand gripping the wheel and his head
moving rapidly. He did not hesitate to interrupt anyone
with an observation about a landmark or a curiosity, but he
was not a bore.

They all sensed that he was the perfect commander for
such an automobile. It moved quietly through the noisy
Paris traffic and all of the small chittering cars slowed as
they faced a collision with this monster. It was a spacious
car. It was a combination of luxury and mechanical perfection. The leather had been saddle-soaped endlessly, the motor was in perfect adjustment, everything looked as if it had
been rubbed and rubbed. Facing the rear seat was a small
collapsible bar which pulled open to expose a decanter of
scotch bound in leather and six crystal glasses.

The car was a prewar Bentley and Rodney was surprised

that his father would invest in such a car. In Los Angeles he insisted on small inexpensive cars for his family and seemed to dislike public display of any sort. The Bentley was a complete reversal, for its very age and the exquisite care made it more conspicuous than a sleeker newer car would be.

"This is a marked day," Proudhon said. "It is cold and overcast, but I guarantee you that it will be warm enough to have a picnic."

Outside rain whitened the grass and foliage and the Parisians scurried along in coats and mufflers. When they got into the countryside the farms seemed frozen. Steam came only from piles of manure, and horses which were working gave off jets of white from their nostrils.

Rodney felt euphoric. The Bentley moved at enormous speed over the flat land and the other cars looked small, beetlelike, slightly antic. Also the large old-fashioned windows of the car and its ponderous, swaying motion gave the impression of being aboard a circus vehicle. Rodney, who was riding in front with Proudhon, reached back and asked Charity to pour him a glass of scotch. She broke one glass because of the swaying motion, but on the second effort, helped by Nina, she poured Rodney a full glass. Proudhon took his eyes off the road and grinned at Rodney. Without a word he reached over and took the glass from Rodney's hand and drank it off. Rodney laughed and passed the glass back to be refilled.

The kilometer posts passed at a furious rate, making a visual click and condensing distance. For an hour or so no one talked except Proudhon. It did not embarrass him in the least. He spoke only when he had something to remark and the rest of the time he relaxed and drove the car at its outlandish speed.

"This is not like the last time we met, eh, Rodney?" Proudhon asked. "Then you were scared and we walked the whole distance. I was scared too, but I was not allowed to show it to you." He flung his head back and for an instant stared at the women in the back seat. "There was a moment when we almost ran into a German patrol when I went pi-pi in my pants. Your friend here was too ignorant to even be frightened. That is a nice commentary on man, eh?"

The two girls smiled at him. Nina dug out a thermos jug of coffee which was laced with cognac and poured Charity a cup.

They flashed by a farmer digging in a compost heap and Nina laughed. Proudhon shot her a glance of approval.

"He is pulling out a Camembert cheese which has been sufficiently ripened," Nina said. "I wonder if Anglo-Saxons would eat Camembert if they knew it had been matured inside of . . ."

"Cow shit is what she means," Proudhon said triumphantly. "Yes, Nina, they would love it even more. I have read some of those crazy books written by Americans and Englishmen who have read that German Freud. They love to punish themselves. They even take Freud seriously. To eat something matured in animal excrement would delight them. Whoever promotes the sale of cheese in France should be at once told of the idea for overseas advertisement."

Rodney passed the glass back to be filled. This time Proudhon drank half of it and Rodney drank the other half.

They laughed and then fell into another silence. Rodney enjoyed the silence. He glanced at Proudhon. The man made him happy. He was muscular, content, healthy and very assured.

"Is this good Calvados country?" Charity asked suddenly.

Rodney looked back at her. She had asked it innocently. It was a question that really meant nothing. It was no more than a remark that one might read in the *Guide Michelin*. But somehow the remark infuriated Rodney.

"Yes, madame, this is good Calvados country, but it has been very well cleaned out by the alcohol shortage which happened after the war."

It was almost noon when they came to Châteauneuf-en-Thymerais. Proudhon had been right. The day had warmed up. At first the sun had a flinty quality to it but now it was almost luscious. Proudhon pulled off at the side of the road and into a copse of trees which grew on the top of a hill. Inside the copse it was cold, but the moment they stepped out onto the top of the hillside it was almost too warm. They spread out the Scotch rugs and put down the hampers which the chauffeur and the cook had placed in the trunk. Proudhon took off his jacket and threw it carelessly onto the grass.

"Now is the time for some of your famous American martinis which I had the cook put in one of the hampers," Proudhon said. "I run an inn. Always Americans ask for a martini. Always they are disappointed. Finally I give them pure gin over ice and still they say it is too sweet. Americans just do not trust Frenchmen when it comes to making a martini."

Rodney poured the martinis. They were steel colored, with the merest hint of blue which came from the ice and the crystal glasses.

Proudhon sipped at his drink. He pursed his lips as if he were going to spit.

"Too sweet," he roared. "Less vermouth. What is wrong with you Americans? Cannot you not make a good *dry* martini?" His face twisted with laughter. They all laughed with him.

On the hill across from them a farmer was plowing a field. He used a big plow, which was obviously brand new, the red paint glinted on it and the tongue of the plow was bright and shiny. The plow was pulled by two oxen which wore little plaited rectangles of white wool over their eyes so that they would not shy. The earth seemed to crack under the plow as if it were still frozen, but when it was turned over it was black and rich. A half-dozen birds followed the plow, diving at worms, cawing, spinning in black circles. The farmer never once looked up at either the birds or the picnickers. He seemed mesmerized by the uncurling lip of land; as intense as if he expected a fortune to be uncovered. He walked carefully behind the plow, a small dark man in a business suit and high rubber boots and a felt hat, every bit as proper as a banker.

"Proudhon, the martinis are at least one thing that the Anglo-Saxons have given to you," Rodney said.

"Absolutely," Proudhon said without looking at Rodney. "The object in drinking is to take in the alcohol. The only merit of a martini is that it flavors the alcohol with a small dash of French vermouth."

"I had forgotten what a patriot you were, Proudhon," Rodney said, grinning.

"Me and every other Frenchman," Proudhon said. "Never forget that, Rodney. We say we are citizens of the world but we are great liars. We are citizens only of France." He turned to Charity and Nina. "All right, ladies, let us begin to eat. Why not begin with the pâté?"

The two girls dug through the hamper, unwrapping various objects, putting them aside, turning to others, placing plates, unwrapping silver. It was Nina who finally found the can of chilled pâté. She opened the can and slid the long triangle of pâté onto a plate. She sighed as she did it. The pâté was a rich, brown color. Down the center ran a solid piece of turkey breast and on each side of the turkey there was a layer of truffles. Nina began to slice the pâté with a small sharp knife. Charity sat back calmly and watched the farmer on the opposite hill.

"Charity, we will need wineglasses, four plates and some place there should be some hard bread or toast," Nina said softly.

Proudhon looked around at Nina and then watched Charity get to her feet. He smiled at Rodney, shaking his head slightly. Rodney did not know what the look meant.

Eventually everything was assembled. Proudhon opened the wine and poured each of the glasses a quarter full. Nina placed a slice of pâté on a piece of toast, placed the toast on a plate and passed the plate to one of them. When they all had a plate she paused and looked up smiling.

Rodney was suddenly very hungry. He bit into the pâté. His mouth was watering and the mixture of toast and pâté and turkey meat turned to a delicious pasty morsel which spread through his mouth. He was disappointed at how small the portion seemed. It left an aftertaste in his mouth. He waited impatiently for Nina to spread some more pâté over toast.

"Pâté is a marvelous food," Proudhon said, passing Rodney a glass of wine. "Do you know how they make pâté de foie gras?"

"*Non*," Rodney said.

Proudhon described the production in great detail. He started with the way geese were selected. Then, when the summer sun was hot, they were buried in sand so that only their necks weaved above ground. The farmers would then force-feed them, a handful at a time. They fed corn, pushed it into the goose's mouth and when the goose stopped swallowing because it was full, the farmer would grab the weaving neck and force the handful of corn down the long throat with a smooth stick.

"It sounds a little disgusting," Charity said.

"No, it is not," Proudhon said firmly. "The geese actually come to like it. They are stupefied with pleasure. Finally their necks come to sway with pleasure. All a goose thinks about is food and for a goose it must be paradise. The goose does not have to move and it has a full belly all the time. Of course, the goose does not know that the lack of exercise and the enormous amount of food and the hot sun makes its liver grow as big as a small melon. The goose is happy, he dies, and we have this marvelous result."

Charity had stopped eating. She had a slight smile on her face, but she was watching the farmer on the other hill with a very intense look. Proudhon had a wolfish grin on his face. He went through the hampers until he discovered four heavy linen napkins. He tossed them each one and then, opening his own, wiped his mouth and face with it. He finished off the last of the wine.

Proudhon crouched on his haunches beside Charity.

"Now for the rest of the meal," he said. "Madame, it is hard for you to believe that we are animals and that one of our few primary needs is food. Even when we overeat and kill ourselves prematurely there is a certain pleasure about it. You Americans like to undereat and deny the instinct and stay skinny and live long. It is all ridiculous. The only result is that you live a miserable life and finally die of the frightful diseases of old age."

Charity nodded at him. She brought a chicken wrapped in a napkin out of one of the hampers. The napkin was stained yellow by butter and when she opened it, the smell of fresh tarragon rose from the chicken. The skin of the chicken was crisp, almost black. Charity took out a knife and handed it to Proudhon. He sliced neatly into the leg joint. A yellow liquid gushed out onto the napkin. They all stared at it for a moment. Then they all laughed, although Charity's laughter began somewhat behind that of the other three.

In a few seconds Proudhon had sliced up the chicken until only a white skeleton remained. While Proudhon passed the chicken around, Charity unwrapped thin little sandwiches of Yorkshire ham. They were seasoned with a sharp mustard.

Proudhon complimented Charity on the picnic lunch.

Charity said that she had had nothing to do with it. She had
merely ordered the lunch. Proudhon began to remark how
nicely the thin sandwiches complemented the chicken.

"The mustard is just enough to take the greasy taste off a
fat chicken," he said.

"Can we talk about something else than food?" Charity
asked. "Let's just let the food speak for itself."

Rodney agreed with her. He was aware of an odd cycle of
gluttony and then abstinence through which he had been
passing in the recent weeks. It had something to do with
Nina. He turned and looked at her. She was eating very
little but her eyes moved around watching the hands and
mouths of the others. She was like a child who, in some
fantastic way, was catapulted into the company of adults.
When someone looked at her she smiled; a tiny hesitant
smile. Rodney could not identify precisely what she did, but
in some subtle, quite invisible way, people around Nina became very interested in food. He had a quick flashing recollection of the enormous meals they had eaten on the short
trip.

Oddly enough the recollection did not end his hunger. Instead he became ravenous. He finished off a breast and thigh
of the chicken and ate four of the thin sandwiches. Then,
his hands still greasy and clumsy, he opened a second bottle
of wine.

Proudhon pointed a chicken bone at Nina. He spoke
through a mouthful of chicken.

"What do you do for a living?" he asked.

Nina looked back at him and went on chewing. When she
had finished the sandwich she wiped her mouth with the
big, heavy linen napkin.

"I travel around," Nina said easily. "I do not have any
definite—"

"A wanderer, eh?" Proudhon asked.

"Yes, a wanderer, I suppose."

Proudhon nodded his head in approval, but in his eyes there was still a look of questioning and curiosity.

Rodney was slightly drunk and he knew Proudhon was the same. Charity and Nina had barely finished a single glass of wine.

"Look at that farmer over there," Rodney said abruptly. "He is dressed like a little businessman, turning over the black soil of France. That is what makes France great."

"The little bastard is a businessman all right," Proudhon said flatly and without emotion. "But he is not what makes France great. I'll bet he hasn't paid taxes in years. Farmers are always the first ones to desert in a battle. They are also the first ones to be collaborators."

Rodney felt somehow rebuked. He shrugged at Charity and Nina to hide the chagrin. Suddenly he was anxious to be on the road again.

Rodney scurried around putting things back into hampers and in another five minutes they were on the road rushing quietly down the straight empty highway. Occasionally a car would approach them, a tiny beetle of a thing which grew into a black monster and rushed by with a great noise and the sudden smell of gasoline fumes. Each time a car passed they were all aware of how quiet their own car was.

"Remember the Calvados that Charity wants, Rodney," Nina said.

"At the next town," Proudhon answered.

The next town was small but it had a prosperous-looking café. Proudhon and Rodney got out of the car and entered the café. The proprietor was a sharp-faced man who was wearing a thick topcoat and rubber boots which were splashed with mud.

"He is the kind that farms in the morning and runs a café in the afternoon and evening," Proudhon said with no effort to lower his voice.

The proprietor walked over to the table at which they

were sitting and faced them. It was very cold in the café.

"We would like a bottle of your best Calvados," Rodney said. "Perhaps a bottle of Mézidon, 1927."

The proprietor gave the thin, mocking laugh of the small hard-dealing merchant. He looked over his shoulder. His wife had come into the café from the kitchen.

"As if anyone had Mézidon 1927," he said, his eyes wrinkling with laughter. His wife smiled at him and shook her head.

"Monsieur, it is easy to be funny about such things," Rodney said in a cold flat voice. "But any man who keeps a café and was not a collaborator would have a bottle of Mézidon about someplace. He would sell all of the poor stuff to the Germans and the American soldiers. A collaborator might have sold the Mézidon to German officers unless he were a fool. You do not look like a fool."

The proprietor's face froze in mid-laughter. There were two tears of laughter on his cheeks and instantly they became tears of real tragedy. The man's bony fingers came up, daubed at the tears on his cheeks.

"Collaborator?" he said shrilly. "Collaborator? You come in my inn and insult me. This I do not have to endure."

Proudhon laughed contemptuously.

"Yes, I call you a collaborator or a fool," Rodney said. His voice had a quality to it which he admired. He was also confident that Proudhon approved of his conduct. "I wonder how many of the people in this village would be willing to testify that you were a collaborator?"

"Insults I do not take, not in my own place," the proprietor said, but he was making tiny, bewildered gestures with his fingers. Slowly the gestures became a pattern of conciliation, a begging for pity.

Rodney noted that the wife had ducked, as if bullets were ricocheting around the café.

"Come on, bring it out," Rodney said. "Enough talk, unless you want to tell us what fine upstanding people the Germans were."

The proprietor walked back to the bar, his shoulders shaking. He made a sweeping gesture and threw a sleeping cat off the counter. The cat sprawled in a corner, spitting with alarm as it woke up. The proprietor walked behind the bar and then turned and faced them.

"As I said we have no Mézidon in this inn," he said. Now there was a wheedling sound to his voice. "Not, and believe me, because I collaborated or any nonsense like that. It is just that there is no demand for such an expensive Calvados in a little café like this. But I will send my wife out and talk to some of the people in the village. Perhaps, no one can be sure, one of them will have a bottle of Mézidon."

Rodney smiled at Proudhon. Proudhon grinned back at him and then reached over and slapped him on the shoulder.

"You are a hard man, Rodney," Proudhon said. "A good hard man is difficult to find these days." He turned and glanced at the proprietor. He ordered two whiskies for them.

In a few minutes the proprietor's wife returned. She was carrying a dark green bottle that was covered with gray dust.

"We are in luck," she said, smiling at them.

"Open it," Rodney cut in.

The proprietor opened the bottle very carefully. The cork came out black and musty, shiny on the sides, dark green on top from old mold.

Proudhon took the bottle carefully from the proprietor's hand. He brought it within six inches of his nose and inhaled. Although Rodney was farther away he still could smell the Calvados. The odor spread like some magnificent gas. It smelled very slightly of apples, of fine Normandy ap-

ples hanging in the sun and very fresh. But it also had the
odor of age and dim cellars and fermentation and decanta-
tion. Proudhon turned and looked at Rodney with admiration.

"Pay the man, Rodney," Proudhon said as he walked out
the door slowly, holding the bottle carefully before him.

The proprietor, his face downcast and avaricious at the
same time, muttered a price. Rodney paid it without hesitation. But just as the proprietor reached out for the notes he
picked up the top one. He winked at the proprietor and
turned and followed Proudhon.

"It is magnificent," Proudhon said. He was standing just
outside the door. The two girls were looking at them from
the car. "The only way to tell a really great Calvados is to
smell it in the open air. Even the odor of a cigarette can kill
it. This is magnificent."

Proudhon nodded approval of Rodney. He walked to the
car and asked for four clean glasses. Charity brought them
out and he filled each of them half full. Nina laughed. Proudhon looked sharply at her.

"Proudhon, you are like Pan doing some mysterious ritual
out in a forest glade," Nina said.

Proudhon grinned at her.

"I thank you for the compliment. It is a ritual. Now each
of you can drink this one glass and the rest we will save
tenderly until we have come to Portivy."

The liquor sent a vagrant scent up Rodney's nose. It was
an aftertaste, a thin essence of apples smelled at a great distance. But the liquid on his tongue was pure and rich. He
washed it around his mouth and let it trickle slowly into his
throat. To his surprise an alcoholic shock ran from his stomach, his backbone, into his brain. He felt, almost instantly,
much drunker than he had felt before.

Proudhon and Rodney finished off their glasses in five min-

utes. Without a word they got into the car and Proudhon
started off down the highway. He hummed to himself.

"There is my town and toward the very end, at the right,
you can see my hotel," Proudhon said. They were, perhaps,
three miles from the ocean. Out to sea there was the small
dark shape of ships with smudges of smoke behind them.
Closer inshore were fishing boats, moving toward shore with
their sails still up.

The town curved around a small indentation in the coast
and at one indentation was a quay. Proudhon's hotel was
close to the foot of the quay.

"It all seems so very clear, the air I mean," Nina said.

"That is the effect of the Calvados," Proudhon said with
authority. "Calvados makes the eyesight better." He turned
and grinned at them. Then he turned around and patted the
dashboard of the car. "Now we will get this big hound of a
marvelous automobile going at full speed."

Proudhon traveled the last three miles at close to ninety
miles an hour. He knew every turn in the road and he drove
with the easy relaxed posture. A few minutes later they were
at Proudhon's hotel and were unloading their bags.

The hotel itself was built half on land and half on water.
It walked out into the water on thick log pilings. It was a
heavy-timbered place that smelled of the sea and tides. It
was not beautiful nor was it well kept. In the fading
sunlight, however, it looked very attractive. Behind one of
the windows there was a flickering light which indicated a
fireplace and warmth.

22. By
the Seashore

"PROUDHON, you are drunk," a woman said the moment they walked into the big dining room of the inn. She stood with her back to the fireplace, warming her hands.

"Again," Proudhon acknowledged, holding the Calvados bottle delicately in his hands and bowing his head.

"Like always," the woman said. Her voice warred with her eyes. She spoke in a hard way, but her eyes were warm and they seldom left Proudhon's face.

"Friends, my wife," Proudhon said, flinging one hand toward her while the other held the bottle absolutely level. "As you Americans say, my ever-loving and dutiful wife. Charlotte is her name."

Charlotte laughed. She put on the shell of the hard-driven wife as an act. She was younger than Proudhon, in her early thirties, and she had a slim firm figure which the shapeless dress and sweater she wore could not conceal. She wore slippers, flat woven black things, and when she moved they flip-flopped on the floor. Her hands were warm and strong as she shook hands with them.

"This we will attend to later," Proudhon said, placing the Calvados on a bar which ran along one wall of the big room. His wife sniffed as he described the Calvados and Rodney's skill in pulling it loose from the stricken café owner. "A marvelous tactic. Superb. The poor man, used to spitting on

American tourists, suddenly thought he was going to be tried as a collaborator . . . which he must certainly have been."

"Let's leave the talk for later too," Charlotte said. She took Nina and Charity up a circling staircase like that aboard old passenger liners. She explained that the bedrooms were all on the second floor. Her voice faded and Proudhon and Rodney were alone in the big room.

"You are feeling a bit sour in the stomach about now," Proudhon said. "Me also. I have a cure."

He went into the kitchen, part of which was visible through a large aperture at the end of the bar, and took the lid off a huge copper pot. A bit of steam puffed out of the pot. Proudhon stirred in the pot with a big wooden spoon.

"Come on over here," he said. "Sit at the bar. Have a little wine, a little soup. This is a special soup. Made of the best parts of the fish and seafood. Very nourishing. Fish livers, jowls, tails, hearts . . . all of the rich and good parts. Sometimes some mussels, crab legs, seaweed, peppers, fish eggs. Anything. Sometimes even sand."

Rodney's stomach was suddenly hard. He smiled thinly at Proudhon. He shook his head.

"Can't touch it," he said. "The wine maybe. But not the fish."

"Good. Taste the wine and the soup will then be possible. It will not be so bad. It sounds terrible . . . the entrails of fish. It makes you think of your own entrails, eh? But wait until you have tasted the wine then the smell of the soup will be bearable. That I predict."

Rodney sat down and poured a glass half full of wine. Then he poured some Perrier water into the wine. It bubbled slightly. He drank a gulp, without looking into the glass. It hissed down into his stomach and like some strange beneficent acid cleaned his throat of the faint nausea. He belched and felt much better. He drank off the rest of the glass.

The soup did smell good. He looked at the bowl of it on

the bar in front of Proudhon. It was a light red color, flecked
with coils of butter. He took a small bowl from a stack and
ladled out a helping of the soup.

It was rich, he knew that with the first taste. But it did not
contract his stomach. It was rich with the flavor of iodine,
the strange salty richness of the sea.

"I told you you would like it," Proudhon said. "This is
very good for a person . . . any person. For a person who
has drunk too much it is incomparable. I read your American magazines . . . The *Reader's Digest, Time* . . . all of
them. They talk constantly of vitamins and minerals. In this
soup, which Britanny fishermen have been eating for centuries, is everything that a person needs. A person could live
on this and nothing else. I have done it myself . . . for
weeks at a time I have eaten nothing but this. During the
war . . ."

Then he paused, glanced at Rodney and stopped talking.
He bent forward over his bowl.

Rodney felt better. The wine and soup affected every part
of his body. He felt revived and energetic. He was surprised
that he could eat after the huge lunch they had consumed.

"What does one do during the day here?" Rodney asked.
"What should we do?"

"One does what one wants to do," Proudhon said. Then he
grinned savagely. "Or what he has to do. The fishermen
have to fish and they have already gone out. I do not have to
fish, but I must drink and eat. So I have drunk and eaten
and now I will drink some more."

"And that is all?" Rodney asked.

"That is all."

"You must be bored by noon."

"I am bored by ten o'clock. In fact I am bored now. But
that has nothing to do with it."

"If one is bored that has a lot to do with it," Rodney said.
"If I were bored I would do something. Anything."

"And I would guess that is what you do . . . anything," Proudhon said. "But too much of anything and that is also a bore. In fact I would guess that you are very bored." He paused, listened and evaluated his own words. "No, you are not bored. Right now you are screwing yourself silly. Right, eh?"

Rodney shook his head.

"Just screwing," he said. He took a few more spoonfuls of the hot soup.

Proudhon winked, nodded.

"It is no mystery, Rodney," Proudhon said. "You can see it on the faces of the two girls. One is well laid. The other is not. They both look to you. Soon it will be boring. Do you know what those crazy existentialists in Paris say about a man like you? I read their crazy magazines and books."

"No I do not know what the existentialists say about a man like me."

"They say you lack engagement. That is the great fault with any man," Proudhon said. "Screwing is not engagement. It is merely a form of exercise. Exciting, but not really serious. A man must be committed to something, must work like hell day and night for some cause. They are right, those crazy bastards. Who can make screwing a holy cause?"

Rodney was depressed by what Proudhon said. For a few hours that afternoon he had the sense of being very close to a real man, a hero of the war, an activist. Now he had been cut off.

"You take things too seriously," Rodney said.

Proudhon swung around on his stool. His face puckered with concentration.

"Me take things too seriously?" he asked. "No, that is not so. I take nothing seriously. But you do. You are looking for the thing to become engaged about. But not me. I do not feel engaged and do not need to feel that way."

"Everyone then is engaged," Rodney suggested. "It just

depends on whether or not the thing is important enough to satisfy the existentialists."

"No. Not everyone. Your wife, the tall white one, she is not engaged. Not that one."

"What about . . ."

"The French girl, eh?" Proudhon interrupted. "She is very much engaged. Plenty."

"About what?"

"About what? Who knows? I don't. All I know is that she is engaged. And with her it is like a disease. She's got it very bad. But about what I cannot tell. Maybe she is like you. No sense of what to be engaged with or about . . . but just a feeling that one should be engaged. Why don't you ask her?"

He grinned when he said the last words. He banged his hand on the bar as if it were a joke.

"You understand. You understand everything except yourself," Proudhon said. "And that is just exactly like the rest of us. All right, no more serious talk like this. It depresses me on a night like this. So we will stop talking about it."

Nina came down from upstairs. In the gray, even flat light which came in off the beach Nina was apprehensive. She came down the stairs quietly, looked through the window at the beach for a moment, worrying over the weather. Then she came to the bar and slipped onto one of the stools and nodded at Rodney and Proudhon.

She did not have lipstick on and her face lacked definition, was almost boyish in cast.

"The building smells like salt water," she said. "The rugs, the furniture, even the smell from the kitchen."

"That is because you are over the sea," Proudhon said carelessly. "It soaks into everything."

"There should be a way to get rid of the sea smell," Nina said.

She sounded waspish. If she were like this all day, Rodney

thought, it would be easy to pack her off, to leave her. Maybe if just for a single day she was like this I could get rid of her. Take her to a station, put her on a train, watch her face disappear down the track. When Nina was quiet she had a kind of tenderness, a vulnerability, that Rodney could not bring himself to destroy. But when she talked like this it was something else again.

In his mind, with his eyes almost closed and his stomach growling over the wine and rich fish soup, he had a quick mental image of Nina looking out the rear window of a train as it sped down a narrowing gauge of steel track. Tomorrow he would do it. Put her on the train and watch her leave.

Just then Charity came down. She was wearing a beige-colored cashmere polo coat and it made her face even paler than usual. She smiled at everyone and asked for coffee.

"No Calvados?" Proudhon asked.

Charity shook her head. Proudhon brought her a cup of coffee.

"Where is Charlotte?" Rodney asked.

"She will be out by the boats, buying what she wants for dinner," Proudhon said. He poured himself some Calvados. "You must all have dinner here. It will be good."

Charity turned from the window. She nodded, her face serious and, somehow, slightly puzzled.

"Fine, but I will ask Charlotte if she has a piece of beef or just some cheese and bread for me," Charity said. "I cannot face fish. I'm sorry, but I just don't like fish."

"I'll tell Charlotte," Rodney said.

"I'll walk with you," Nina said. "I need the air."

Charity's expression did not change, except that she smiled at Proudhon because he was looking at her so directly.

The odor of iodine and salt water and wet rocks and washed-down fish scales pervaded everything. The fishing boats were in and the fishermen were hanging out nets to

dry. They swore at one another, comparing their catch, cursing at the sea, asking what the prices were in the Paris market. They groaned at everything and then broke the mood
by swearing.

Charlotte was sitting on an upturned box talking to several fishermen. They passed by with baskets of fish and she
asked to look at them. They laughed and without bargaining
picked out what they said were the best fish and threw them
in the basket in front of her. She made a figure on a notebook and joked.

When she saw Rodney and Nina she stood up. She explained that she had just finished her purchases. She had
what she wanted.

"Let's go to the café at the end of the quay and have a
beer or a glass of wine," she said suddenly. "One becomes
tired of one's own bar."

The café was half full of fishermen, but there were very
few women in the place.

"Do not take the old man along if you go walking tomorrow," Charlotte said firmly as soon as they were seated. "His
leg is bad in the sand. If you ask he will go along, but the
sand will hurt the stump. He will go just to show you he is
young, but I know that the leg hurts him when he walks
through sand. Leave him here."

"All right," Rodney said. He paused for a moment. "What
happened that he lost his leg? It is none of my business, but
I am curious."

"Why don't you ask him?" she said.

"Sometimes people do not like to talk about these things,"
Rodney said. Now he wished he had not brought it up. "I
was just curious, but I will not ask him."

"He wouldn't tell you if you asked," she said and there
was pride in her voice. "He is a stubborn man. He thinks if
he talks about the leg he is asking people to excuse him and
he wants no excuses."

"I know that."

"Maybe he would talk to you," Charlotte said. She turned to Nina. "He is very proud of his war work. He took out at least fifteen escaping men and he remembers each of them. I knew Rodney before he was introduced . . . just from having heard of him so often."

The waiter brought a large carafe of red wine and three glasses.

Charlotte picked up her glass, swirled it gently, looked into the redness. She smiled; a quiet smile, just around her lips. She made a decision.

"He lost the leg because he is a radical," Madame said. "The old man . . . you know he is not so old? Only in his thirties. He looks older. So do I. We look older, eh? Well, we do. But Proudhon lost the leg because he is a radical. Or maybe an anarchist. But he has always hated the authorities. Oh God, how he hates authority and the people who represent authority."

"Which authorities?" Rodney asked.

"Any authorities. Whoever is the authority he hates. It is his anarchism. He thinks that political authority is evil. Anything that overthrows it is good. When he fished he always violated the fishing laws as a matter of principle. 'What does a bureaucrat in Paris know about fish?' he would ask and go ahead and do what he wanted . . . take more fish than is legal, any size lobster, oysters any season of the year. Ah, you should have seen him in the old days. He would be in a rage over these things. Really he would almost foam at the mouth . . . he would be that angry," she said and her face was limp with the recollection, her eyes dazed with the good memories.

"And his leg?" Rodney asked. He wanted to get back to the dining room. He wished he had never asked the question.

"Yes, the leg. I am coming to that," she said. "He hated

the French government and he hated them worse when they
went to war with Germany. He was delighted with the military victory of Germany. It made him uproariously happy to
have those fat little silly generals and politicians in Paris
running around screaming about the honor and dignity of
France. 'Honor and dignity of France,' he used to say. 'I piss
on the honor and dignity of France. Men have honor and
dignity, some men, but a government — that is impossible.' I
tell you I was scared. I thought the villagers would shoot
him, they were so angry. You know, monsieur, most men are
patriots whatever they say. But not Proudhon."

She paused, smiled once more into the wineglass.

"Then the Germans sent a platoon of troups and a lieutenant to occupy this town and to set up defenses and also to use
the quay for E-boats," she went on, smiling. "So Proudhon
had a government anyway. And in addition it was a government by Germans who believe in government very deeply.
Ah, Good Lord, they were efficient. Ration cards, regula-
tions, curfews, instructions, inoculations, even a German
guard on each of the boats so they could not escape to England. For a while Proudhon delighted in taking the boat to
the roughest fishing grounds just to see the poor German get
seasick. He would fry pork just to nauseate the man. In the
end he told the authority, the lieutenant, he would not go
out with a German aboard, that it made the boat unsafe.
Proudhon argued with the lieutenant, who turned out to be
a very shrewd and bright young man, but in the end the
lieutenant became very excited and nervous and threatened
to shoot Proudhon if he kept up his opposition. Proudhon
told him to go ahead . . . shoot. Then, and this is how
crazy people are, the villagers came to love Proudhon. They
thought he was anti-German and they liked his courage, but
he was only anti-government. But it made no difference. He
became the center of the Underground here. Really he was
perfect, if I do say so. He was so outspoken in his criticism

that no German could believe he would actually be the leader of the Maquis. They were convinced it would be some lesser person . . . someone unknown, anonymous. But it was Proudhon all the time."

Proudhon had been excellent, she said, at organizing the Underground. He had refused to let the Underground have the usual rigid hierarchy of leaders and followers. He wanted what he called an "anarchist democracy" . . . which meant that no one had to go along with a decision by the group if he did not want to. Also no one was leader. Proudhon refused to acknowledge that he was, in fact, the leader. He persisted in believing the fiction there was no real leader . . . just a group of comrades. And he fought the Communists in the Underground as rigorously as he fought the Germans.

"Oh, that was a wild time," Charlotte said, her fingers firm on her cup, her face gleaming, her eyes black with recollection. "The Germans must have thought they were faced by the most clever Underground in Europe and actually it was the most ignorant and poorly organized. Proudhon with his 'anarchist democracy' was so absurd that no respectable German officer could believe that his forces were really facing such an array. And, Proudhon, of course he had to make it clear, in small ways, that he was the leader . . . strutting through town with the little heavy boxes which the English used to parachute supplies to the Underground, grinning at the German lieutenant sitting in the café. The German was convinced it was bravado, that Proudhon was a big braggart. And would not search him.

"The lieutenant was a university graduate and he used to invite Proudhon to drink with him at the café. Proudhon would accept, but he would bring his own wine so that he would not be taking anything from the chief authority. The lieutenant said Proudhon was trying to model himself after some little-known nineteenth century anarchist with the

name also of Proudhon. Proudhon laughed and called the
lieutenant an 'educated fool,' a fine example of how learning
could make a man absurd. Proudhon would always end by
mocking Hitler in a loud braying voice that carried over half
the square. It embarrassed the lieutenant, especially if any of
his troops were about. The lieutenant told the men that
Proudhon was an idiot, the town buffoon, but he was never
quite sure."

Charlotte told them of one of Proudhon's big "communal
direct action projects," as he loved to call them. It was a
term he had gotten from some syndicalist novel of the nineteenth century. He loved to use the term because it lacked
the military flavor and the mysterious jargon with which the
regular Maquis apparatus liked to surround their operations.
It was a phrase meaning violent action against the Germans,
but as Proudhon used it the phrase seemed to sound like a
project to grow radishes for the whole community.

The Germans were bringing in a convoy of trucks loaded
with 200-kilo mines that were to be fastened to the Underground obstructions along the beach. The convoy consisted
of six huge trucks each carrying eight of the mines . . . big
round evil black eggs packed in excelsior and wired firmly
down. The convoy came into town proudly, the trucks roaring and each one guarded by three young German soldiers.
Motorcyclists formed a watchful vanguard: a soldier with a
submachine gun sitting in each sidecar, staring through gog-
gles for enemies.

The German lieutenant, bright-eyed and enthusiastic,
was proud of the powerful mines. The efficiency of the caravan. He turned to Proudhon and made a great proud gesture
toward the caravan and did not have to say a word. Proudhon spat once and walked over to the trucks which were
waiting for orders from the lieutenant on where to unload.

Proudhon reached across the knees of one of the guards
and patted one of the mines.

"Ah, those are little beauties," he laughed. "Take them out of town before we blow them up. No self-respecting Underground man can resist such a luscious target. What an explosion these would make. Please, Lieutenant, take them away before I blow them up. Down the road to the beach where they will be safe."

The lieutenant roared with laughter. It struck him as very funny. He banged Proudhon on the arm, exuberant over the massive show of power that rode on the trucks.

Proudhon, when the lieutenant hit him on the arm, was just shaking loose from his fingertips a tiny phosphorous bomb. The little bombs were really no more than fire starters which would burn for ten or thirty seconds or one minute depending on a time setting. When they went off they simply popped open and burned with a savage flame which only grew worse when water was poured on it. The bombs were supplied by the English air-drop. This particular bomb had a one-minute time setting. It fell into the straw on the bed of the truck. Proudhon and the lieutenant stood together in the street watching the convoy of trucks pour down toward the beach. The trucks went right onto the sand, moved in a precise line toward a concrete blockhouse.

"It was a beautiful day. Sun bright, blue sky, sea gulls flying around, like a festival," Charlotte said softly. "When the trucks were a half mile away the line suddenly stopped. Flames were coming from the first truck. Little orange licks of flame and a bit of black smoke. Soldiers poured off of the trucks and began to mill around. One of them ran to the ocean with his helmet, came back, threw water on the truck. Proudhon watched the lieutenant stiffen and then call for his personal car.

"But it was too late. It was like a beautiful picture. Suddenly the first truck seemed to disappear in a great orange ball that made absolutely no noise. The ball spread to the other trucks and one by one, with incredible speed, they all went up. It happened so fast that the trucks had disappeared, the beach had become a big churning cloud of sand and water and debris, before we heard the sound of the explosion. But, damn it, when we did feel it and hear it what a shock. It almost blew us down. Proudhon grabbed the lieutenant and held him upright in his arms to keep him from falling. When he looked at the lieutenant he could see that the German was in tears . . . great big tears like a little boy. His face all screwed up into a rage and anger and confusion."

"But how did Proudhon lose his leg?" Rodney asked.

"Later that day he lost it," Madame said. "The lieutenant wanted to commit suicide. He drank a liter of schnapps, called his superior officers and told them what had happened, although of course he did not know what had happened . . . he thought one of the mines had been defective, and then prepared to commit suicide. Proudhon tried to talk him out of it. Proudhon argued that it was silly to believe that the lieutenant was to blame. Really I suspect that Proudhon was trying to make a convert to anarchism . . . he kept talking about the rottenness of organization and government, suggesting that any government that did not know how to pack bombs tightly and safely did not deserve the support of its citizens. The lieutenant just did not listen. He was determined, he had made up his mind."

What happened, of course, was that Proudhon finally, in desperation, had to tell him how the explosion had occurred. The lieutenant would not believe it. Then Proudhon showed him one of the little phosphorous bombs. The lieutenant almost died on the spot. His face grew red, then white, then blue. He stared at Proudhon and at the villagers and at his soldiers.

The German lieutenant had felt it was unsoldierly to be

defeated by so casual and disorganized a force. As shocking to him as the loss of the mines and the trucks and the men was the fact that he had lost all this because of a tiny bomb dropped into the back of one of his trucks by a man he had said was an idiot. As the lieutenant stood facing Proudhon, all the expressions of a lifetime went across his face: a wave of humor, of despair, of self-deprecation, of awareness of the absurdity of the whole thing, of hatred, of something like jollity. But in the end the expression was one of mute despair. The lieutenant was so absorbed in his despair that he did not even attempt to arrest Proudhon . . . he just stared at them and then stumbled off down the beach, to the open mouth of the armory.

"Down the beach he went like an intoxicated rabbit that had learned to walk on its hind feet," Charlotte said. She was hunched forward, warming to the subject. "His feet dragged in the sand, leaving a trail behind him. He walked right by the smoking trucks without even looking at them. He kicked over pieces of flesh, stumbled against hot wreckage, plowed through broken glass and went, like an animal to a lair, into the mouth of the armory. Then Proudhon realized that the man was really going to commit suicide and he ran off down the beach toward him. That's where he was a fool . . . why didn't he let the damned Boche go off and kill himself? But not Proudhon, he had to give us a thirty-second harangue on the fact that a single man is better than the most magnificent government and then he tore off down the beach to rescue the single man who represented the government we all hated worse than anything else in the world. And that is justice, you think, eh, monsieur? Justice, eh?"

Nina was staring intently at Charlotte. Rodney felt a pang of jealousy or something very close to it. Again he had the sense of being isolated from a kind of life in which people faced real experiences, lived more vividly, felt more deeply.

This was part of his feeling toward Nina . . . the dim feeling she had experienced a great many things, big things, important things.

"Yes, Charlotte, I think in a way that is justice," Rodney said.

Nina swung her head and looked at him without expression.

She told them about the leg, but for her it was an anticlimax. What was important, from her view, was that Proudhon would go down the beach to rescue a man who, until a moment before, had been an enemy. Rodney could see that she saw in this action a quixotic, crazy attractiveness. The actual loss of the leg she described quickly, almost coldly and in boredom. The run down the beach after an enemy in the name of humanity was what fascinated Charlotte.

Proudhon went to the black hole that was the entrance to the beach armory five minutes after the lieutenant disappeared into it. The lieutenant, with Teutonic thoroughness, had lit an eight-minute fuse that led to a phosphorous canister and the canister, in turn, was buried in a small mountain of mines and bombs. When it went off the whole armory would go up.

The lieutenant screamed to Proudhon to leave the armory, told him that it would go up in a great explosion in a moment. Proudhon grinned at the lieutenant who was draped over the small heap of munitions and walked toward him. The fuse had already burnt most of its length away and there was no longer a possibility of stamping it out. All that could be done was to haul the lieutenant out before the armory exploded.

Proudhon was strong, stronger than the lieutenant. He wrestled with the lieutenant for a moment and then had him slung over his shoulders. The lieutenant screamed in protest and embarrassment. He twitched wildly on Proudhon's shoulders, his toes kicking Proudhon's calves, pleading to be allowed to die sensibly in the armory. They were just at the entrance, stepping out into the clear day, when there was a soft low puff of sound from inside the armory and then a deeper, booming roar.

"For a moment it was like one of those posters urging men to join the army and fight for France," Charlotte said softly. "The two men, one carrying the other gently over his shoulder, safety in front of them, danger behind them. The entrance to the armory actually turned red and it was like a magnificent motion picture. We could all see it so clearly. We did not believe it, but we looked at it. We stared. I think I felt very proud. I thought he had rescued the damned German and knew how great a gesture that was."

Then the full blast hit the two men. They shot across the beach, their toes barely skimming the sand, moved by invisible blast forces. They sailed ahead of the gout of flame and smoke, jetted almost to the water's edge. The two bodies entwined with one another, like black rag dolls, turning and twisting, smoking slightly. The lieutenant's body caught most of the shock of the explosion and shredded away in flight. By some accident of explosives, some queer fateful dispersion of force, Proudhon was hardly touched by the blast. He was lifted to the edge of the surf and sat up in the water, hardly stunned, and perfectly aware that his left leg was torn entirely off and that he was covered with gobbets of the lieutenant's flesh.

When the villagers reached him Proudhon was slowly pulling himself up out of the sea leaving a long stain of blood that went out like a tongue of color into the clear foamy water. He was not in shock, nor was he close to unconsciousness. He was swearing softly and his face was disillusioned. The village pharmacist, with the help of two others, trimmed up Proudhon's leg, bandaged it neatly after sprin-

kling it with sulfanilamide which was taken from the first
aid kits which had been dropped to them by the English.

Of the lieutenant there was nothing left but the stripped
skeleton, fresh and reddish white, but even the hairs of the
head stripped away, down to the bare skull.

The explosion had broken Proudhon's eardrums and he
could not hear, but he could talk. He was weeping for the
lieutenant.

When Charlotte had finished she sat quietly, looking
down between her powerful work-stained hands. She picked
up her glass, swirled it and drank off what was left. She was
smiling slightly, a smile of recollection and nostalgia.

"A man like that is really a hero," Rodney said softly. "A
real hero."

"A hero to whom?" Charlotte asked dreamily. "A hero
must have a public to whom he is a hero. But everyone in
the village thinks that Proudhon was silly to try and rescue
the German lieutenant. They think he was not a sensible
man."

"Such a man is a hero to a lot of people," Nina said in a
small controlled voice. "But it is hard for people to step forward and say they admire a hero. Especially if what he did
was something that they might have done. Every man that
saw Proudhon that day knows he is a hero, but each man is
also envious."

"To you he is a hero," Rodney said. "Maybe a public of
one person is enough to make a courageous man a hero."

Charlotte looked up, glanced shrewdly at Rodney. She
nodded her head.

"Maybe you are not as dumb as you look," she said softly.
"Maybe Proudhon now has a public of three — you and me
and her. You are wise to see that he is a hero." Her voice
was edged with wonder.

"There are others. I'm sure of that," Rodney said.

The woman's head jerked up and she grinned.

"Oh, yes. There are others all right. Some of the women in the village see Proudhon as their secret hero, but for a strange reason," she said, her voice cold. "There is an old fishwives' tale that a crippled man is more sexually potent than a whole man. The feeling is that his body compensates by making him more virile. So those women admire Proudhon and are envious of me. So you are right. His public is bigger than just the three of us. But it is not a public that I like." Then her voice softened, her face relaxed into a grin. "That is not completely honest. Actually I like to see the admiring look on their faces. It gives me a secret pleasure to know that they think Proudhon and I lead a scathing red-hot sex life."

They got up, Rodney paid and they left the café. It was dark outside and the cobblestones were beginning to mist with the night chill. They walked without talking to the inn.

Proudhon was talking to Charity, his left hand turning the stem of a glass which was half full of Calvados. He glanced at Rodney, smiled and then drank the glass off.

"The old woman told you my secret, eh?" he said in a loud mocking voice. "I can tell by the look on your face. Not a nice story, eh?"

Rodney flushed. He started to protest but Proudhon had already swung off the chair and was pouring him a glass from the green bottle.

23. The Fire Inside

"I AM a man who likes things very simple and straight," Proudhon said. The corners of his eyes were slightly blood-shot, but his eyes were focused. He was steady and, apparently, not the least bit drunk, although he drank a good deal. It was past midnight.

"That's what everyone wants," Rodney said. "For Christ's sake, no one wants things complicated and twisted."

Proudhon turned and looked at Rodney to make sure he was saying what he meant. Rodney was angered by the look.

"Rodney, I knew you only for a few days when we walked to the coast during the war," Proudhon said. "At the time I thought you were sometimes very cunning, sometimes very smart, sometimes very . . ." He snapped his fingers, searching for the word. "Sometimes very dull. Right now you are being dull. About yourself and the two girls."

"And you are very sure about yourself and Charlotte, eh?" Rodney said. "Look, Proudhon, we are not old friends. We don't know one another. I think you are full of shit, but in a peculiar way. You act like a knowledgeable old bastard, full of Gallic cunning, smart so hell won't have it. Love to rob the English and American tourists."

"And the Germans," Proudhon said. He was looking back at his glass, swinging his head up occasionally to see how the fishermen who had come over to see the visitors were behaving. "We screw them as much as we do you."

"Let me go on," Rodney said. "You talk too much and don't listen enough." Rodney paused, knowing he was dishonest. Proudhon did not stir. "But you don't know anything more than I do or a lot of other half-assed men staggering around the world know. You just curl your lip and all the foreigners freeze, thinking you know what the hell you are talking about."

Proudhon nodded agreement.

"Well, then stop this crap of telling me that you know something I don't know," Rodney said. His voice was irritable.

Proudhon looked at Rodney blankly. Then he nodded. He looked around the room again.

The big room of Proudhon's inn was, considering the late hour, noisy. A group of young fishermen had come into the inn after dinner and started to drink. They were attracted by the two women, Proudhon said. Nina and Charity were sitting at a table against the wall and behind Rodney. Rodney and Proudhon were sitting at the bar.

"Now you are in a clever mood, Rodney," Proudhon said, almost as if to himself. He closed his eyes, shook his head in wonderment, then opened his eyes and looked at Rodney.

"I am not in a clever mood," Rodney said. "I just want to know what you think the whole thing is about. Not just about the two girls, but about life. Oh, Christ, how can a person put it without sounding like a fool?"

"It is not a foolish question," Proudhon said. "It is only that Americans and Englishmen are afraid of asking it. 'Duty,' they say; a man should do his duty."

Proudhon carefully poured the Calvados.

"What I want to do is make a straight, vertical, black, unerasable, pure mark as I walk along," Proudhon said.

"Why not horizontal?" Rodney said. Instantly he was embarrassed. Proudhon looked at him, saw the embarrassment and looked away.

"Horizontal, perpendicular, ninety-degree angle, parallel, obtuse, oblique . . . I don't give a shit," Proudhon said without anger. "All I want is to make the mark. To know it is mine. I don't want to be a waggling line. Like those French generals and politicians who turned and weaved and wanted to end up with their villas and châteaux in the country and their apartments in Paris." He paused and drank off the last of the Calvados. "A man is a line in time and space, eh? A real man is. A fake man is a nothing. He works for a big organization or a law firm or a bureaucracy or a Métro or a soccer team . . . and what does he get at the end? A pension."

"And a gold watch," Rodney said.

Proudhon did not understand. Rodney explained the institution of the gold watch upon retirement. Proudhon found it very funny. He laughed until tears ran down his cheeks. His imagination ran away with the idea. He talked of a special room in the big New York corporation skyscrapers where little men would be busy chiseling away at the backs of watches, putting on the names of the people who would have a retirement dinner the next night.

"They all weep at these dinners, eh, Rodney?" Proudhon asked. "They must. It is silly, giving a gold watch as one gives a dog a pat on the head. But the one who gets the watch weeps for a special reason. He is bitter over his senseless life which is now over."

"Most people drag themselves through life without leaving a line or mark behind them," Rodney said. "Maybe they are scared of making a mark. They want to disappear into the landscape, not be visible, not leave a track by which they can be traced. For such people the watch may be a good thing."

"That is truly unbelievable to me," Proudhon said. "To *not* want to leave the straight line behind. The watch, Rodney, is a reward for being nothing. Can you conceive? A man wanting to be nothing?"

Something about the statement angered Rodney. He had never thought of leaving a line behind him. And, perhaps, that was why he was angry. He felt that everything he had done until this moment was shapeless and without meaning. He was experienced enough, however, to attribute most of it to the Calvados. But not all of it.

The hair rose on his neck. He was trying *not* to think of Nina. He could feel her like a presence. For two hours he had been sitting against the bar, his back to Nina and Charity and looking at Proudhon. Behind Proudhon were the six young fishermen. They alternated between the bottle of pure white gin and the bottle of stark red wine.

The fishermen were mostly in the young twenties. They had discarded their pea coats because of the heat from the fireplace and were wearing thick dark sweaters. The arms of the sweaters were sequined with fish scales which caught the light. Gradually they took off their sweaters and were down to their striped short-sleeve shirts. Their arms were crusty with dried fish blood to above the elbow. Occasionally, like a flat jewel, a fish scale would be caught in the dried slime and blood on their arms.

As he had talked to Proudhon at the bar Rodney could hear Charity and Nina talking behind him. For over an hour their talk had been fast and chatty. For the last half hour they had been silent.

It was then that the six fishermen began to play their game. At first it was a sort of arm wrestling, with elbows on the table. They wrestled a pair at a time, the winner then taking on the next man. A short dark man with large white teeth was winning. He had a huge biceps and an unnaturally long forearm. This gave him the advantage of leverage.

By the time he had arm-wrestled with four of the others, however, the sweat was cutting through the crust on his arms. He lost to the fifth man and when his knuckles cracked down on the table he was instantly on his feet protesting.

"I had no time to rest," he said in a joking voice.

Rodney suddenly understood something which he had ignored before: the man was speaking to Nina, making her an apology and defending himself, but was quite unaware of it. Only once did his eyes casually glance in Nina's direction.

"You lost and that's the end of it," the man who had beaten him said. The others nodded coldly.

The loser bristled. He claimed a right to arm-wrestle the winner after a rest.

"You are out. The first loser. Now I will wrestle until I beat everyone or am beaten. And so on," the winner said.

He said it with a flat hostile implacability. And with pleasure.

Some old well-known pattern was forming, Rodney thought. Now, somewhat drunk, he could sense it. The fishermen were already gripped in an invisible and tightening net. They would go through the stages of swaggering, suspicion, more drinking, and finally the last act would happen: violence.

"What do you think of the girl?" Rodney asked.

Proudhon looked over Rodney's shoulder. Rodney knew Proudhon was not gripped by the strange rising feverish mood of the room. Proudhon looked at Nina carefully. He watched for a few moments and then started to speak and stopped. His eyes narrowed slightly and his mouth worked with confusion. He looked over his shoulders at the fishermen. Sweat, effort, strength, muscles, curses, energy rose like an almost visible aroma from the table.

Proudhon's eyes glittered and he came to a kind of rapt attention that Rodney had not seen in him before. His big head moved on its strong neck like some outsized cobra, focusing on some distant and, perhaps, dangerous object. He licked his lips.

Rodney reached out and tapped him on the chest . . . in mid-gesture his intention had changed. He had started to grasp Proudhon by the shirt and shake him . . . for what reason he did not know. But his fingers became civilized in mid-air.

"Come on. Talk," Rodney said.

"All of them, those stupid fishermen, all of them have an erection," Proudhon said. He pounded the butt of his hand against his forehead. "How could I have missed it?" He stared over Rodney's shoulder.

"Why?" Rodney asked.

"Why? Why do you think, you silly bastard, you dumb Yankee cuckold?" Proudhon said in a savage detached voice. "Because of Nina. That's why and you knew it all the time. Or you are more nutty than I think."

"Why did you say 'cuckold'?" Rodney asked. Somewhere a logic was forming in his mind, fugitive pieces fell together, a pattern almost formed.

Proudhon was startled. He looked at Rodney as if trying to remember who he was. He looked like a man who had been startled.

"Did I say that?" he asked. "I take it back. No, I do not take it back. You are fearful of being cuckolded. Not legally, but who gives a shit about legality. But really you think all of these men want to lay Nina and you are absolutely right."

In a soft voice Rodney told him about the last weeks. Proudhon barely listened, but he listened. He watched Nina all the time.

"It is no mystery, Rodney," Proudhon said finally. The light faded in his eyes. Almost literally something within his skull went dim and the eyes lost their glitter and took on their normal look. He glanced back at the fishermen and nodded as if they confirmed something he had expected to find. "Nina is crazy. Or maybe she is more clever than other women. But she is the cause of the fishermen acting the way they do. And she is the cause of all those other nights when you saw people act in crazy ways. She puts men in a sexual frenzy."

Rodney swung his head and looked at Nina. She had her head down and one hand was held across her breast as if she were embarrassed. It was the way a young girl is both embarrassed and proud of her breasts. Her other hand gripped her leg. He felt sobered and he studied Nina. There was nothing lascivious or sensual about any one part of her, but the total effect was, in some inchoate way, very exciting. He realized dully that *he* had an erection. This outraged him, made him the equivalent of the fishermen, forced him into a community which he did not want to join. There was something deliberate and composed and very subtle about Nina's posture. She felt him looking at her, raised her head and was startled. She flushed.

The flush. That damned flush, he thought. He remembered something about it . . . but what.

"She can make herself blush," Proudhon said harshly.

"That's impossible," Rodney said sharply. "No one can make himself blush."

"Well, she can. And there are a lot of other things she can do and she does them damned well," Proudhon said. He took another glass of Calvados. This was inferior to the Mézidon, but by now neither of them really cared. "I don't know how she does those things. She is like a magician. One knows they are tricks, but still one is mystified and maybe even frightened. That girl is a magician at giving erections to men. But one cannot see how she does it."

"Then, why are you so damned sure she is the cause of the erections in this room?" Rodney demanded.

Proudhon looked at him full-face, then glanced away.

"I look at things more honestly than most men," Proudhon said. "I have my reasons, but I know it is a fact."

The fishermen had finished the arm wrestling and the short dark man was still protesting. The one who was the victor was grinning, but the other four merely stared at the dark man and the victor, restless and angry.

Suddenly, with no warning, one of the four hit the stocky man on the biceps. The blow made a harsh splatting sound and on the dark skin of the man's biceps was the imprint of a fist. He stared down at it with his eyeballs bulging and his skin turning a red tinge under the darkness.

The fist mark slowly disappeared. The stocky man turned to the man who had hit him. The man turned sideways, pulled his sleeve up, exposed his own biceps, grinned at the other man and wordlessly invited him to strike him. The stocky man gathered himself into a tight-curled position, his lips drew away from his teeth. He uncurled like a short powerful spring released from enormous pressure. His blow took the other man off his feet and the man wound up in a bent posture, his feet scrabbling for dignity. He was still grinning, but his lips kept quivering, fighting back a look of pain. He slowly came upright. The skin on his biceps had been flayed and a trickle of blood ran down his arm.

The stocky man laughed and turned toward the man who had won the arm wrestling.

"It will go on until there is real trouble," Proudhon said. "And all because of her. Let me tell you how she does it, Rodney. Or that part of it I can see, but you cannot. Take her lips."

Rodney laughed and then, abruptly, stopped. Proudhon was giving him the cold hard glare.

"Take her lips," Proudhon began again. "Up close they are good full rounded lips. A young girl's lips. But she compresses them. Makes them very thin. She cannot conceal, however, that they are rich lips that have been pressed thin. Why? Why does a girl with rich lips make them poor?"

Proudhon paused, but Rodney knew he did not want an answer. Proudhon gazed over Rodney's shoulder at Nina, as one might gaze at a museum piece . . . the look of an unloving cool expert.

The fishermen were exchanging blows on the arms with a kind of abandon which concealed a very rigid order. Thin sprays of blood shot across their table and their shirt sleeves were becoming tattered by misplaced blows. But each man had to take his turn. No man wanted to miss his turn to hit the biceps of another and no man wished to miss his turn at being struck.

"A girl with rich lips makes her lips poor and thin so that she can arouse the desire in each man to make them rich and red and thick again," Proudhon said. "Oh, sweet Jesus, what I would give to go over and rip her off that seat and make those lips open and turn red and show a mouth and finally teeth and at the end to make my tongue go into her mouth. Ah, and her tongue. One barely sees a bit of it. A triangle of pink moist flesh that flicks out and disappears. Or is drawn carefully, like an old maid about to give a lecture, across the lips. Just enough to see that it is a probing eager and too much controlled tongue."

Rodney tried to laugh, but the sound got only to the middle of his chest and turned into a cough.

"Maybe you're oversexed," Rodney said, searching for something to say. Then more aggressively, "I'm damned sure you are."

Proudhon gave Rodney a look that was pitying. Rodney looked down at their empty glasses, but he did not feel like drinking.

Rodney knew he had heard some of this before. He had dreamt it or someone had said it to him. He struggled for recollection and it slipped away; hot and elusive, it vanished. Like physical excitement sweated into a frigid air.

"Now take her breasts," Proudhon said. "For some reason we all regard the breasts of a woman very highly. I am not sure what Nina is doing . . . it is a kind of quiet coverage, a suggestion of embarrassment, a bowing of her shoulders to protect her breast. But the result: one knows that her breasts are tiny, firm, white and have never been bitten or sucked by a man. And how does that make you feel? Or how does it make the heroic fishermen, those dumb clods of the earth who go to sea out of habit, those miserable wine-soaked bastards feel?"

"I don't know," Rodney said. "I don't even think they think a thing about her breasts." He gulped on the lie.

Proudhon was controlled, but one of his hands pounded on the bar like a pile driver. He glanced at Rodney and a sneer started over his face and quickly died.

"Well, good friend, you are wrong," he said. "They are thinking of that and a few other things and not a damned other thing. The girl is a wonder, a kind of fantastic thing." His voice was full of awe. "Take her hips. Don't turn around, Rodney. Look at the fishermen and see what they think they are feeling. They *think* they are fighting with one another and getting drunk and being sailors on shore leave. In fact they are *not* thinking . . . they are doing a crazy dance for the girl. Sailors and fishermen on the beach do not give a shit about *one* girl. Normally. But this time they do. And part of it is those pulled-back decorous mean hips, which, just because they are so pulled back, assure you that they will give a thrust and a jolt which will take you into another world."

"Another world?" Rodney said, laughing, riding on the strength of anger. He was fighting to recall something that told him about the whole thing. "When you say another world, you are romantic."

"Almost surely you are right," Proudhon said. He looked

over at the fishermen, yawned, nodded at Charlotte, glanced
once more at Nina and Charity . . . but, Rodney knew, did
not see Charity. Then he leaned forward and pulled Rodney
by the front of his shirt. "You are too good to be so obtuse,
Rodney. Every man dreams of the next girl. The girl who
will give him the pelvic thrust or the tickle of the hands or
the lick of the tongue or the scream of coming which will
make the final conquest. Right?"

"Right? How the hell would I know?" Rodney said. Anger
was gathering. He made himself relax and smiled at Proudhon. "All I know is that the girl loves me. And I satisfy her."

"You do not know that for a minute," Proudhon said
calmly. "You are as scared as a man can be that you cannot
satisfy the girl. And you see every man in the street as a
threat." He gave off a savage kind of laugh. Then he spoke
softly. "You don't think for a moment she is satisfied. Not
with the way she bends forward over her crotch and guards
it and is startled when a man looks at her." He took Rodney's arm. Rodney shook it loose.

"Proudhon, you are a nosy old man," Rodney said, and
despair gripped him. Why did he lie so much? Why did he
always attack what he knew might be a threat? "I take that
back, Proudhon."

Proudhon was not even listening. He was watching Nina.

"Those hands," he said in a wondering voice. "Like one of
those sculptured things at the Louvre . . . cold and smooth
on the outside, but you feel the blood flowing underneath.
She turns them over, looks at her palms . . . why? Because
if you scratch a girl's palm and she doesn't pull her hand
away she is yours. Then she writhes the hands together
. . . why? Because it looks like agony, like a tortured person trying to bury some evil impulse, trying to keep from
grabbing something on a man."

Rodney laughed and for a moment he was relieved. He
laughed because of Proudhon's odd, arcane, almost hu-

morous use of words. Proudhon was well read and he was
bright, but he also wanted to hide his knowledge beneath the
skin of a tough old veteran of the Maquis: a man with a
wooden leg.

The fishermen were a shuffling shifting indistinct group
now. Their fists popped on one another's biceps. The
sounds bounced in the room, as palpable as tennis balls or
pieces of earth. Rodney, now perceptive, could detect the
quick little unconscious glances they shot at Nina. Their
tempo was picking up.

"Now she brings her twisted hands up under her chin, her
elbows covering her breasts," Proudhon said. "Christ, it is
enough to give me an erection."

The fishermen's weird contest changed abruptly. Someone
missed a biceps and hit a man on the chest. It was a sharper,
bonier sound. The man winced and whirled around looking
for his attacker.

"She is like a conductor," Proudhon said softly. "The men
react with grunts, blows, puffing, cursing when she raises
her hands to her chin. She is a miracle, Rodney. A miracle of
tensed, balanced, scarcely buried, barely controlled lust." He
laughed, but the phlegm dulled the purity of the sound.
"But a miracle. She plays them like a marvelous conductor,
leading soundless music, to some score that is sunk deep in
each man, but which he doesn't understand." He paused,
made his face owlish to take away from the extravagance of
his metaphors. "And the poor bastards don't know what they
are doing. They just react. Just stumble around and around
and don't know what the hell they are doing."

"Where did you get so smart about music scores and reactions and things like that?" Rodney asked. Quite suddenly
his French was very poor. The words kept slipping away
from him. That, and the elusive memory of the night when
all of this had been plain, gave him a sense of futility.

"A French school boy learns those things, Rodney," Proudhon said tapping his chest. "We don't have to go to college like you Americans to learn things any civilized man would know."

His face softened and the harshness of his voice dropped. Then he looked away from Rodney and stared, openly now, at Nina.

"Did you know that the woman's mouth is like her sexual organ?" Proudhon said, as if to himself. "Each has lips. Each has a tongue. Each is moist. Each is bottomless . . . but in one we put food to fill it and in the other we put . . ."

"Look, Proudhon, I don't want to hear any more," Rodney said. "You're crazy. I don't want to listen to all the crap."

"No. Not crazy," Proudhon said. His eyes glittered again, came back to life; starting far back in the black liquid of the eyeball were flashes of diamond sharpness which swam to hard focus. "Every man thinks that about the woman's mouth and her sexual organ. It is just that we never say it. Just as we never say that we think nuns become nuns to escape their overpowering lust. If we said it then something would be loose in the world of men, eh? Then we could not kiss a woman because we would be thinking of her sexual organ and we could not nod to a nun . . . we would be attacking her. But just the same, that is what we feel."

When Proudhon mentioned the words "nun" and "lust" the toughly resistant memory fell into place. Not all at once. It came hard. It took time. Perhaps five minutes. It was like pulling flesh away from his own bones and trying to recognize and identify and assemble them. A lot happened in that five minutes. Rodney was thinking of the other inn, the one after the ex-prisoners had left and of a table on which every plate glistened with pig fat and bottles were everywhere, and not far from his nose was a half wheel of Camembert which, over hours, oozed out from its whitish skin and onto the plate. But his eyes were watching the fishermen just over Proudhon's shoulder.

The fisherman who had been hit in the ribs had found his adversary. They circled one another. One of the other fishermen took up a glass of wine, drank, and glanced toward Nina . . . and red bubbles appeared in the corners of his mouth. It was because the lips turned up and were savage. He swallowed without moving his head, although his eyes went back to the two fighters. The bubbles were sucked away from his mouth.

"And now, Rodney, for the eyes," Proudhon said. Rodney was scarcely listening. The fragments were falling into place. "Nina never takes a steady look at a person. What she does is to glance directly at a man, just long enough to hold his eyes and engage his attention. Then the eyes go frightened and she looks away in panic. What does this tell the man? It tells him that she is frightened of her own lust for him. And so she glances away."

Rodney pulled himself away from reassembling the recollection.

"I think you are right, Proudhon," Rodney said slowly, not wanting to lose the hard-won memory, the slow beginning he had made. And he did know that Proudhon was right. He was terribly tempted. He wanted to look back over his shoulder at Nina. But he knew what he would see and it would make him furious. More than that. "You are right about the eyes. It can give a man an erection at twenty feet. But not if it is done by *any* woman."

"No. Not by any woman. That I don't understand yet," Proudhon said. He looked away from Nina, glanced down the bar. "Any woman could do these things, but none of them do. Except this one. And why? Why would she do it?"

"I am beginning to understand," Rodney said. "Or remember."

He put his hand out in front of him; a soft gesture asking for time to think.

Almost dreamily Rodney put the memory together. Now

he recalled all of that first evening with the ex-prisoners
. . . the last part of the evening . . . the lonely part
. . . the part where he was drunk . . . the part where she
was talking . . . the part where he listened and dozed and
forgot . . . the parts, fragments, gobbets, shreds, pieces,
shards. Now he remembered.

The two fishermen were circling one another. The mood
was part puckish, but part of it was deadly . . . a small part
and none of them knew it. They played it like a game.

It flowed back to him. It came like a quiet secret. The details were there . . . exact and suddenly remembered.

"I could make a guess," Proudhon said. "I could guess
why she has the magic. She must have been cornered at one
time . . ."

"Cornered by what?"

"By anything. But it has to be something very very important," Proudhon said.

Caught on the fluid of Proudhon's bright glittering eye, by
odd refraction, was a tiny diminished picture of Nina and
Charity. The picture was too small to make out details of
lips and eyes and hands. Rodney could, with a hard steady
stare into Proudhon's eyes, make out only the general difference between the girls.

Proudhon went on talking, impetuously, with a kind of
mesmerized and metal-hard attention.

"Something had to take that girl and put her in a crucible
so hot, a pressure so high, a situation so dangerous . . ."
Proudhon stopped. He put his finger against his nose. "I talk
a lot. True. But I see a lot. I exaggerate. I brag. I swagger."
He paused and his face went slightly white. "But I understand that girl. She is that way because she had to do it to
live."

He snapped his fingers, beat his palms against his forehead.

Rodney felt a sensation which was half exultation and half

bitter. He could tell Proudhon something . . . but he did not want to tell him what had reassembled in his mind.

"You're right," Rodney said. He hesitated, afraid to go on and say the words. Something was flowing behind his eyeballs . . . and in his ears . . . a perfect recall of that greasy, horny, piggish, drunken, spilled wine, the dirty napkin, bread-crumby, pâté-slicked lips, quick gossip, hard innuendos, and brutal night. He had slacked against Nina and had heard what she said, but had not thought of it until now.

"I think she was going to be killed if she could not fuck a guard in a prison camp for politicals," Rodney said, holding up his hand for Proudhon to be quiet. "She told me about it. I remember, right now, I remember everything."

Proudhon was attentive.

"That's what it would take," he said, his voice sad and low, like that of a professional undertaker. Sad. But not really meaning it. The glitter in his eye indicated he did not take it seriously. Rodney was not quite sure what was serious and what was merely excitement. "If she had to live in a political camp . . . ah, then, of course, then everything is imaginable. That is the crucible, the pressure, the hard burn of simple survival."

Rodney's mouth was dry and his lips suddenly needed his tongue. Very deliberately, making it casual, he licked his dry lips with a dry tongue.

"Once more and it is serious," a voice said very loudly.

Rodney felt a great relief.

"This the last time to hit me on the arm," one of the fishermen was saying. "If you miss and hit the ribs then we are in trouble. I will not wait around forever." The man paused and made a search for the contemptuous thing to say. "Not for a little nigger like you."

The small dark man grinned at the larger man. He looked at the five of them and their blood-speckled arms with the dark spatters on their blouses. Then, very slowly and as if it were very important, he looked around the room.

Rodney felt the man's eyes pause when they met Nina's face, but he could not see her. It was only a feeling. He was sure he was right.

The small dark man uncoiled. It was painful to watch. He did not even aim for the biceps. He struck at the man's rib cage. As the fist went into the man's ribs several things happened . . . some ribs snapped with a rippling brittle sound . . . the man's breath came out of his lungs in one puckered-mouth surprised gasp . . . his knees buckled very slightly . . . vomit came out of his mouth and the others danced away from it . . . and he broke wind. And he blushed.

And then he gathered himself.

The bigger man, with the broken ribs and vomit over his blouse and the rolling eyes which ached for control and the humiliation on his face, gathered his body and mind together.

Softly, so softly that Proudhon did not hear it, the stricken man purred out the litany of hate and vengeance and blood. The small dark man waited, smiling.

"All right, Proudhon, what do you make of it?" Rodney said. He was not listening to anything. He knew that Proudhon knew they had gone beyond the point of connection. "Now what do you make of it?"

Proudhon never had a chance to answer.

The larger fisherman with the broken ribs swung on the small dark man. The bigger man was in shock. His eyes were glazed and he had a weird look about him.

The large shocked man connected. His knuckles cracked and so did the neck of the surprised dark man.

There was a marvelous suspended moment when everything was still, quiet and unmoved. Then the dark man was lifted off his feet and brushed past one of his friends, scraped glasses from the table, and wound up on the wall. For a moment he hung there like a crucifixion . . . spread-eagled, neck limp and gentle, face benign, blood showing on his palms. His eyes started to roll up into his skull. He smiled at his friends and sunk to the floor. He said something, but no one heard him. He maintained a wonderful unconscious dignity and from the corner of one glazing eye he saw that it was appreciated. His collapse had something of the theatrical in it, but his bone-cracking smack into the floor was honest.

The large man, the victor, was agonized. He had won a small fight and lost something much bigger. Rage washed over his face and mixed with other emotions like confusion and surprise and uncertainty. But from no eye did he catch a sense of approval. For a moment he pulled his big feet back and forth across the floor, the rubber boots making a surprisingly harsh sound. He fought for dignity and lost. And then he was murderously negative. In every motion and every gesture a very pure hostility poured from the man.

It was beyond the comprehension of the others. He was a man who was part animal and his pawing gestures were like those of a hurt bull. And the words were incomprehensible; garbled and twisted, they came like hard fragments which were obscene, but not reasonably so. They were insane words, like screams from a nightmare.

"Pure," that was the word, Rodney thought. That was the word Nina had used. Suddenly he could remember almost everything she had said about the concentration camp. The desire to survive was pure, selfishness was finally pure and uncomplicated by concern for others, lust became pure and peeled off the fears and manners of centuries, hunger was pure, the cold was pure, warmth was pure. And all else was impure . . . hatred was a luxury, camaraderie was insane, gossiping was a waste of calories, reading a book was narcotic and nothing else. An appeal to morality was the only humor in the camp although no one took the time to laugh. Each person, Nina had said, moved carefully, concentrating, maneuvering toward the pure things. They moved with zombie faces, heedless of one another, through an atmosphere which seemed thick and retarding. They plotted only for the pure things which would keep life going. To mix the pure things such as stealing two ounces of food with the impure and putrid things such as giving a Marxist answer when a Nazi answer was called for . . . that was evil and insane.

And she had, Rodney realized, learned how to live in the unlivable, to exist where existence was impossible. She became desirable. She had become desirable in the basic long-forgotten hidden ways in which female animals made themselves attractive to males. She walked alone through all the artificially cleansed and conditioned women of the world with a secret knowledge and she used it when she became bored or frightened or when she merely wanted to reassure herself.

The dark fisherman came off the floor. He gasped like a fish, but it was impossible to know whether he was breathless or in a stupor. The others glanced at him and then in an insult that was too extreme to be deliberate they turned away, talked among themselves. The dark man fumbled at the table, pawing over the silverware, his hand knocking plates together . . . all the while staring madly at the man who had struck him. Rodney understood suddenly what he was doing: he was searching for a weapon.

"He's looking for a knife, Proudhon," Rodney said.

Proudhon wheeled on his stool and came off the chair at the same time. He moved in a quick blur and his wooden leg was no handicap. He swore at the dark man. But the man already had the knife, a large blunt knife, and he was darting toward the man who had hit him.

The dark man swung the knife in a huge arc, as if sensing that he must compensate for its dullness by a harder blow. Just as he swung downward Proudhon lashed at his waist with one arm . . . tried to sweep him backward in an improvised tackle. Proudhon only partly succeeded.

The knife entered the right part of the large man's back just below the shoulder and swept down to his buttocks, tearing a piece of cloth from his shirt, knicking through the belt and stopping with the blade sticking from the man's buttocks. A clot of cloth, flesh and leather stopped the knife's downward passage.

The long wound opened for a moment, clean and white and showing ribs and odd bits of gristle. Then it flooded with blood. The injured man turned his head and looked down at the knife sticking from his buttocks. Proudhon had carried the small dark man to the floor. The dark man did not resist. Instead he started to laugh. A hard biting mocking laugh. The large injured man, his nerves still not feeling pain, looked at the dark man who was rolling in Proudhon's arms and laughing like a fiend.

The injured man started to blush. He glanced unconsciously at Nina, then down at his exposed white buttocks with the knife, the clumsy table knife, sticking out like a metallic tail. He blushed deeply. Then he pulled the knife out, brushed away the gobbet of blood and flesh and cloth and tried to pull his pants up. The belt had separated and when he pulled on the front of his pants the cut in the back only opened more widely, showing white flesh.

He lost his temper.

"You unspeakable bastard," the injured man roared, glaring at the man whom Proudhon was slowly releasing. "You are insane. I will never sail with you again. You are lower than a . . ." His face winced with pain. The narcotic of shock was wearing off. It made him more angry. He could no longer swear in the vernacular. He fell back on old classic child-remembered expressions. "You are lower than a dog. A filthy rotten dog." The fiend, the small dark man, now released, was rolling on the floor, drumming his heels onto the hard wood, convulsed with a humor which was hysterical.

He gave the large injured man the obscene finger. Then he was off pounding his feet and laughing.

"All you think about is women," the big bleeding injured man said. He was close to crying. "You are . . . really . . . you . . . are obscene."

He drew himself up, holding his pants, one hand in front, the other in back. One of his friends took off his shirt and stretched it over the wound. It clung instantly, soaking up blood.

"Get out. All of you," Proudhon said. "I will call on the telephone that you are going to the doctor's. Take him in a car. If he walks he will open the wound more and maybe bleed to death. Not that it would be a great loss."

The five men left the inn. Proudhon made the phone call. Rodney walked over to Nina and Charity. They were pale, but Nina's eyes were excited.

"Nina, you are leaving tomorrow morning," Rodney said. He ignored Charity completely. "You caused all of this and I finally understand how and why. Now you must leave."

"You did not understand before tonight?" Nina asked in a surprised voice. The excitement went from her eyes. Her voice was cool. "I told you about it before. That first night."

"But I did not understand then what you were saying," Rodney said. His voice was surprisingly level and even. "Maybe I did not want to. I don't know. But now I know. I know you are sick to the point of being crazy. You have a secret and maybe when you learned it the secret was necessary for life. But now you use it as a weapon."

Nina's eyes moved away. Rodney hesitated.

"Not as a weapon," she said softly. "As a confirmation that life means something. That it means an evil thing." Her voice was puzzled. "I told you all this. I went into the camp when I was very young. When I came out I was ageless. But most of all I was empty. Empty of anything except the 'pure' things which I mentioned to you. What people call normal is insane." She smiled at Charity. "I do not say this to excuse myself. It is just that I must, from time to time, make sure that *I* am something. I must assure myself from time to time that all of you who live in the carefully prepared and pampered and easy and fictional world are false. I have only one way to do it. By making you equal to me, I can live on." She smiled and turned her elegant white hands palms up, gazed down at them. "Not that living is all that important."

"You are going tonight," Rodney said. His voice was simple and powerful and very sure. Nina sensed the new quality. She nodded.

"As soon as you like," she said.

She turned and walked up the stairs. Rodney could not bring himself to look at her. He turned to Charity and looked at a complete stranger.

24. The Last Escape

OUTSIDE the day was beginning to brighten. Rodney felt it through his closed eyelids. It would be an overcast morning and then by noon the fog would be burnt off and the sun would appear. The quay would steam, perhaps, and the steam would smell of fish scales and old rubber boots and the thin strange smell of drying nets. He did not open his eyes. The whole picture in his mind was invented, he said savagely to himself. He invented scenes to fill his mind, but they were only things he had read about. Or they were ways he had been told to view things. Nothing was his *own*.

"She's leaving," a voice said. It took him a moment to realize it was Charity. "Want to see her off?"

Her voice had that even flat quality. He could not tell if she were mocking.

Rodney's eyes jerked open. He looked at Charity full-face. "Yes I do," he said.

"Proudhon has started the car," Charity said. "I heard it just a moment ago. While you were sleeping."

He wondered why she added things like the remark about his sleeping. He had never been sure that her flat even comments were bitter or merely the remarks of a disinterested person.

"Did someone teach you that by remarking that others sleep hard it suggests you are a light sleeper and thereby delicate and thereby aristocratic and thereby doomed to death from consumption?" Rodney said.

Charity stared at him blankly. Rodney felt a quick biting despair. She didn't know what he was talking about. Also he knew that whatever had been between them; affection, respectability, the sure knowledge they were a striking couple, a low-pitched urge for success . . . whatever it was it was gone.

When he got outside Proudhon was listening to the Bentley. He had a smear of the rich red fish soup on his chin. He saw the smear reflected in Rodney's expression and casually wiped it off, licking his palm.

"This is the best way, Rodney," Proudhon said. "I guarantee it. The girl is bewitched. She is fatal for a man . . . any man. Don't feel it is just you. She is a casualty of the war.

One of the invisible casualties with the power to really spread her affliction. She will never stop. She will work the trick, that fantastic trick, again and again until she is killed or goes crazy."

"Where is she?"

Proudhon went wary.

"Rodney, don't bother to say goodbye," he said, his eyes down, listening to the engine. "It's easier that way."

Charity had told Proudhon about the times before, the countless attempts, the miserable wild failures, Rodney knew. He was not certain how he knew Charity had told Proudhon, but he was certain. He felt shriveled and smaller.

"I'm over it," Rodney said. "I can stand it."

Nina came out, walking briskly, carrying a small bag and wearing a shawl over her head. She could have been any one of a thousand girls who walked down the street of a provincial town. She was attractive, but not beautiful. Her figure was exceptional, but she never dressed to take advantage of it.

Watching her Rodney thought it impossible she had almost torn his life apart. She was like one of those little girls who glance in endless reproduction out of the windows of Parisian buses . . . neat, controlled, bored, hoping to escape into something exciting. It had all been in his mind; something that he had imagined because of a loneliness or inadequacy in himself. He had glazed her over with an attractiveness that she really did not possess. Now that she was certain to leave, had been delivered into the final and sure hands of Proudhon, Rodney could even feel pity for her. He felt the urge to do something to express his pity . . . give Nina a big check, kiss her before she left, say something reassuring. He thought of the bleak life to which she would return: the thin gray life of clerking or of living in a village waiting for some doltish country boy to marry her. In the end, however, Rodney did nothing. He shook Nina's cold hand, stood beside Charlotte as the Bentley started to move and waved after it. Proudhon's tough round fist came out of the driver's side, jerked up and down in a farewell salute. He blared on the horn. The big hulking body of the car slid around a corner with a screech of tires that could be heard for miles.

Rodney felt a quick stunning sense of wholeness. It was like the point in an illness when one becomes well again; the tingling moment when one has passed from disease to health.

He went back to the room and Charity was asleep. He undressed and got into bed and woke her by moving his hands over her body. She awoke and looked at him with a cool eye. She moved her body under his, stroked him, went through the expert preliminary motions. Once he glanced at her face and she was, as always, staring straight up at the ceiling. He jerked his head aside and went on with his eyes closed.

When he got out of bed he had lost the fresh feeling of having escaped from disease. He wanted a drink.

Proudhon should have been back in time for lunch, but he was not. If he had taken Nina to lunch in Auray and put her on the afternoon train, he should have returned in time for dinner. But he had not. At eight o'clock Rodney called the railroad station in Auray and the stationmaster reported that he had seen a girl and a man who filled the description Rodney gave, but they had not gotten on the train. Rodney asked the stationmaster if he had seen a black Bentley. Yes, he had seen such a car parked in front of the station earlier in the day but it was not there now.

"He is probably spending the night with a friend in Auray," Rodney said to Charlotte. He did not tell her that Nina had not gotten on the train. "He will be back in the morning."

"Probably drunk in some bar and showing off the car to

his friends," Charlotte said. "Those Auray roughs are a tough bunch. Proudhon worked with them during the war. Most of them are mechanics now. Then they were demolition men. I can see them driving around in your fine car, drinking whisky from the bottle. A sorry lot."

Proudhon did not return in the morning. In fact he did not return for five days. Rodney went into Auray but could find no trace of them. He asked the police if they had seen Proudhon or Nina but they had not. He returned to Portivy and he and Charity waited at the inn . . . for what they were not sure. They were only sure that they should not return to Paris until Proudhon showed up . . . they were responsible.

Charlotte went on with her work around the inn almost furiously. She joked with the fishermen who came in, but there was a hard quality to her voice and after a few days most of them did not come around.

At first Charlotte was furious only about the car. She was sure that Proudhon was driving it around the countryside, lording it over his old friends.

"He is a child," Charlotte said the first two days of Proudhon's absence. "He will drive the car around, speeding up and down country roads to show them the fine car and how well he can drive it . . . he likes to anger people. I can see him now, driving fast, drinking a lot of cognac. Oh, the dirty bastard. Wait till he gets back," she promised.

When Rodney came back from Auray without Proudhon or the car or any word of them, Charlotte stared at him, wet her lips and withdrew into silence. For five days she cooked exquisite meals for Rodney and Charity without talking to them. Her anger and then her fear went into the cooking.

Then on the fifth day, in the evening, Proudhon returned. Charity and Rodney were sitting in the café of the hotel drinking coffee and cognac. They heard the odd sound of his leg creaking across the stones of the quay and then he quietly opened the door and came in. At the same moment Charlotte came in from the kitchen, for she had heard the sound too.

For a long moment they merely looked at one another: Proudhon in the doorway, Charlotte in the doorway of the kitchen, Charity and Rodney looking up from their table. For the moment there was a long quadrangle of tension in the room; an almost tangible curiosity and fear and anxiety. Charlotte's face was angry and red, but there was anxiety about her mouth. As she looked at Proudhon the anger loosened and then vanished and then concern and a gentleness went across her face.

"Sit down, Proudhon," she said and there was a softness in her voice, a gentleness that Rodney had never heard before, had not even imagined her capable of. "Sit down and I will get you a little wine. A bottle of good cold hock."

Proudhon was a wreck. Only the tough belligerent look around his eyes was the same. Beneath his eyes the skin was dark and punchy, the eyes themselves were bloodshot in an intricate terrible way. His teeth had yellowed and his lips were dry and bruised. His shirt was dirty and the neck hung away from the flesh as if he had shrunk inside the shirt. His hands which had been big and powerful now looked withered and delicate, like the hands of a very old man . . . somehow ineffectual and clawlike. Strangely, Proudhon looked as if the cheap black suit were holding him up, giving shape and structure to his body that it would not otherwise possess. He sagged in the doorway, grinning his tough grin which was weakened by the thinner lips and yellow teeth, held erect by the black suit, the eyes sad.

"Welcome home, Proudhon," Rodney said. "We were wondering where you were. Now we can go."

"No. Stay awhile," he said softly.

"We'll go," Rodney said, anxious to leave the Proudhons together. "I have to get back to Paris."

He wanted to ask about Nina, but he assumed that Proudhon would say something. Even if he said nothing, Rodney thought, we will leave. He was suddenly desperate. Like fat drops squeezed out of a sausage, the fear came to the surface of his mind: he didn't want to hear about Nina. It was better left unsaid. Rodney stood up, reached down for Charity's hand.

"No. Not yet," Proudhon said.

Under the suit the body rustled, shivered back into size, took strength, energized the black serge suit and brought it wisping across the floor to their table. He moved quickly, but in a crabbed fast way, as if uncertain how long he could maintain balance. They smelled him as he sat down: a faint odor of cognac, sweat, hotel bedsheets, and something else as salty and ageless as the earth. He smiled at them, aware of his appearance, his smell, his defeat.

Charlotte came with the bottle of wine. It was cold and tall and she took the cork out with a quick jerk and poured Proudhon a glassful. He sucked it in with a sharp sound and Rodney remembered something: when he had been in the hospital for his burns every seriously injured man in the ward sucked in liquids as if they were the key to life . . . as if ordinary gulping and swallowing were too slow and haphazard. Proudhon was like that, like an injured man, sucking in the nourishment, desperate for survival. Proudhon waited for a moment, looking straight down at the table, waiting for the wine to take hold of him, to stiffen his mind, strengthen his body. He looked up slowly, so very slowly that it was agony to watch him. But he had courage and he looked squarely up at Charlotte.

"I thought I was beyond pride, but I was not," he said in a strong, utterly determined voice. "She got at me . . . in just the thirty kilometers to Auray . . . she got to me. Like one of those worms that enter an Egyptian's foot and work straight up through the body to his liver and then feed on his liver until the man is dead. And it was not her fault. It was me . . . the worm was attracted to the liver." His voice was full of wonder, a lingering strangeness. He bent his head and looked at them. "Except it was not the liver, but the crotch and she is not a worm."

"Just drink the wine and then go up and get in bed and I will bring you some of the fish soup," Charlotte said. Her hands touched his shoulders, felt for the man beneath the dirty cheap fabric, reassured by contact. "The soup is good this time, Proudhon. Mussels in it . . . beautiful fat mussels that I gathered myself. It will be good."

"No. In a minute, but right now I have to tell Rodney the whole thing," he said. "Later I will forget part of it or my memory will try to protect me by remembering only the noble parts of it. Right now I can tell you the whole thing."

"All right. Tell us," Charlotte said. She turned and waved Rodney and Charity into their chairs. She poured them some of the cold hock.

"For twenty kilometers nothing happened," he said. His eyes half closed, focused on some inner memory. "I drove fast, really enjoying the car. It's a big beautiful brute of a car . . . I leaned it into curves doing eighty and it roared into them, took them with pleasure." He looked up at Rodney with something like gratitude. "Whatever else happened that car was beautiful. That I really enjoyed. In fact if I had just concentrated on the car, if I hadn't looked over at the girl, everything might have been all right. But I looked at her once . . . just to see how she liked the drive. I was going like hell, screaming along the road, big as anything in the leather seat of that car and I looked over at the girl."

Proudhon paused and Charlotte automatically reached for the bottle and filled his glass. He looked down at the glass, twisted the cool stem. His face was puzzled with the recollection . . . as if he were recalling the impossible and unbelievable.

"It is impossible to tell in words what I saw," he said softly. Rodney sensed what was coming. "I looked at the girl and she was sitting straight in the seat looking right ahead at the road. She felt me looking at her and she turned and stared at me. A pretty little face, big eyes, slight lipstick on her mouth . . . the face of a very innocent young girl. Then the corner of her mouth turned up, very slightly, and something like fear went across her eyes. She shrank away from me, but with a peculiar motion. I turned back to the car and thought about what I had seen. The girl thought I was viewing her as a woman, as something to go to bed with. And she shrank away from that and that was why there was fear in her eyes. But her shrinking away was not really a shrinking away . . . it was slow and hesitant as if she really had thought for a moment of falling toward me in the most wanton way possible. Crazy, eh?"

Rodney stared at Proudhon. It was like having a dim, barely articulated, quite vague feeling translated into the hard, bitter currency of words. Proudhon was saying what Rodney had felt so many times. Rodney looked at Charity and her eyes were opaque, told him nothing. He was not sure she understood. He hoped she did.

"Crazy, but very stirring," Proudhon went on. "I felt that the girl was scared of me, that she thought I might stop and rape her under a tree or in the big back seat of the car. But at the same time she seemed to yearn toward me, to fear herself and what she might do if this were to happen. It was like something I felt when I was very young and for the first time the older boys told me of girls . . . of what a boy did with a girl. I was scared. Really scared. But behind it was a curiosity so black and hard and intense that I thought of nothing else for months. I was scared of the girls, but I wanted them so badly that it was unbelievable. I have never known a desire like that since. Love and sex, good sex, I have known. Charlotte knows that," he said and nodded at his wife. She nodded her head solemnly back at him. "But desire, pure raw desire, that is something I have not known since youth. And once one knows a girl that kind of desire vanishes forever. Maybe it is partly made up of the secrecy, of the unknown. But I felt that this girl, this Nina, had something of that about her. She had innocence and she wanted the innocence violated."

"There is no sense in talking about it," Rodney said. "It only makes it more painful. This happens to every man . . ."

Rodney did not want to hear any more. Proudhon's words slashed into him and he felt panic. Proudhon twisted his head and then shook it; the way a bull shakes its head, the movement gaining momentum. Abruptly he stopped. "The hell it happens to every man," Proudhon said savagely. "It doesn't happen to one man in a million or we would all be insane. It only happens when a man sees a girl like that. In the time it took the Bentley to cover two kilometers I changed. I was a new man . . . or rather a new boy. Everything was just the same . . . ah, the words make me sick. Really sick. I've heard them so many times . . . no one is ever able to really tell a great change. A crazy boy has a vision and becomes a priest and finally a saint and all it does is make me hate the church. A man gets a leg shot off and he says it feels just the same, nothing has changed, but he has a quiet inner notion that everything has changed. We witness a great catastrophe and notice only the color of a girl's hair and it is because we fasten on something small and steady and known to keep our senses. Well, this was the way with me. I was astonished that we were still piling along in the big car, that the kilometer stones still popped up, that grass still grew green, that the black wheel still responded under my hand. I was astonished at all of this because I felt inside as if I were on fire, at the same time, breathless. It was actually hard to breathe . . . I was really panting out of desire for that girl. Instantly it seemed to me the most important thing in the world that I go to bed with her, ravish her innocence, spark her hidden lust, and her virginity."

Rodney stopped hearing the words. One at a time, taken literally, they were too incredible and hard. It was like a tiny, almost invisible fire which produces thick smoke of very complex and amazing designs and of dark violent hue. Rodney was hardly aware of the words, but the impression was vivid and strong.

"Now there is one thing you must know," Proudhon said. The skinny neck brought the big head to attention. He glanced at the hock and then at Charlotte. She shook her head. "Yes. Otherwise Rodney will never understand. Charity I think will never understand in any case. But I must tell them. When my leg was blown off a piece of iron also took away my balls. That was the end of sex for me."

Charity blushed. Rodney felt nothing for a moment except an understanding of why Proudhon had been so quick to perceive the tension which Nina could generate. In a sense he was a spectator to what she did while every other man was a participant.

Proudhon went on, telling of the trip.

He sat numbly in the Bentley, feeling like a very young boy who first senses the desire for a woman. He trembled with the intensity of the desire. When he glanced at Nina she had hunched into the corner of the seat and he could see nothing but her hands and her head. But underneath her coat he could imagine a prim cool mysterious body; a body that was controlled for too long and well managed, but which hid a deep private rage to know a man. He could almost feel the way the flesh would writhe away from his hands and then, quite unconsciously and against will, writhe back at him . . . be eager to have its innocence destroyed.

The Bentley whined into a hard curve, Proudhon's hands
slipped on the wheel and he realized that his palms were
sweating. His body was rigid, tense with excitement. He
thought for a moment of stopping the car right there alongside the road and turning on the girl. But he thought of
difficulties of concealment and with a sudden cunning he
realized there was not adequate cover alongside the road.
But also on a more fundamental level he was for the moment frightened: what if the girl just said no and stared at
him. What he did not think of was the fact that he was
incapable of taking the girl in any case. That he had lost his
testicles was swept out of his mind, was totally forgotten.

He was caught in a fever which was heady. He laughed at
anything. He felt *whole*.

For the last ten kilometers into Auray Proudhon lived
through a whole criminal lifetime. He planned like a rapist,
a seducer, a panderer, a kidnaper. It was criminality of a low
order, but he knew that and still could not help the way in
which the details of the crimes came ringing through his
head. It was like the time he had watched a printer throwing handfuls of old type into a huge pot of hot lead . . .
they hit the surface precise and individual and clear and in
an instant they were melted away, vanished utterly in the
white-hot flatness of the melted lead. In the same way tactics came from the blackest recesses of his brain, emerged
perfect and precise to the surface, and vanished away utterly in the hotness they met there. He shook his head, stub-
bornly resolved to work out a sensible plot for being alone
with Nina, for seducing her, for arousing the greatest passion in her.

But it was a failure. As they drove into the outskirts of
Auray his mind went blank, fighting for control, for tactics,
for a plan . . . but nothing came. He drove aimlessly about
for a few minutes but Nina said something to him and

he turned, in despair, and headed for the train station.

Without a plan he got out of the car, unpacked her bags, carried them to the station. He even walked toward the ticket booth with her knowing full well that at some moment he would have a plan, not a great plan perhaps, but a plan. He knew that his very desperation would give him a plan.

When his lips finally spoke the plan it was unbelievably thin and sad. He would not have believed himself capable of such absurdity.

"Why go to Paris right now, on this train, Nina?" he said. "There is a château on the edge of Auray which has the best remaining formal garden in France. Box hedge six hundred years old and so thick that it is like solid wood." Nina stared at him uncomprehendingly. "They say the hedges are so thick that a man can't shoot a bullet through them. We could drive out in the Bentley and then have an omelet in the Hôtel du Nord." She was looking at him, not understanding what he said. His mind, dumbly, blindly, desperately, reached for something concrete and yet startling. He found it. "When the English queen was here she did just that . . . saw the château gardens, and then an omelet at the hotel and she said it was the most beautiful garden and the most magnificent omelet she had ever known. Besides, we can put you on the afternoon train and it is a better one."

Proudhon at that moment was more frightened than he had ever been before in his life. Nina turned away to buy the ticket, she already had the franc bills in her hands. Proudhon had a small stunning premonition of what his future life would be . . . a black falling away from this great moment, this chance to live again, to recall his youth. Everything after this, if Nina went on the train, would be bitter and trivial. He stood and stared at her, waiting. He could do nothing now. He had made his ridiculous appeal and all he

could do was wait, his body wanting to scream, his breath
shipping in and out like a dog panting. With all his will he
willed her to stay.

Nina turned the francs in her hand, looked at the two
women ahead of her in the line. She looked puzzled.

"What is the name of the château?" she asked.

"Château d'Hermitage," Proudhon said and he almost
screamed the words. "It is beautiful. I have seen it. Nothing
like it in the world, I tell you. Magnificent."

"Could we see it and get back in time for the next train?"
she asked.

"Easily. I guarantee it." He sagged with relief. Words
could not help him now, but if he moved she would follow.
She did. She walked slowly back to the car.

Proudhon got back in the Bentley and leaned against the
fabric of the seat cushions with his eyes closed. He gathered
his strength and then opened his eyes and started the car.

"Do you feel all right?" Nina asked.

He looked at her quickly, trying to see if she was honest in
her question. She was looking at him closely, concern in her
eyes, but nothing else.

"I am fine," Proudhon said. He licked his lips, swallowed a
huge lump down his throat. "The motion of the car sort of
excites me. That's all."

Nina reached over, took the handle of the door and
slammed it shut. The door closed with a muffled, honed,
snug sound . . . an expensive sound. Nina pulled the coat
around her neck again and leaned into the corner of the
seat. Her eyes caught Proudhon's, then she ducked her head,
looked straight ahead and Proudhon felt the lust grip him
again.

The day passed in hot misery for Proudhon. They walked
through the grounds of the Château d'Hermitage and they
were the only people there. It was true that the grounds
were beautiful . . . small box hedges, tiny geometrically

trimmed shrubs, neat walks . . . everything angular and perfect, reproduced from some rational drawing board. They walked up a small stairway and looked back down at the gardens; they were perfect, linear, trimmed, rectangular, balanced, harmonious, geometric. With a kind of wanton enthusiasm Proudhon thought that this was the time and place to take Nina . . . here in the midst of all the carefully balanced beauty of the garden the act would be sharpened and heightened . . . the wetness and hotness and erraticness of sex would be a crude satisfying contrast to the garden. His mind played with it so long that they were leaving the garden before he could make up his mind to act.

As they drove back toward the city he knew that action would not be easy. He was not sure how Nina would respond to his taking her in his arms. She might go hot and limp at once. She might, and his mind grew red and frenzied with the possibilities, claw against him, find release in his gesture and initiate him to acts of frenzy and excess that only the innocent can know. But, on the other hand, she might turn hard in his arms and laugh at him. Or not respond at all. And this would be unbearable.

When they were back at the hotel having the omelet Proudhon knew he must make his move quickly or Nina would be on the train to Paris. The omelet was good and he insisted that she eat most of it while he drank Calvados. He drank a great deal that first night. It was just as if it was alcohol poured on fire; it flared up and burnt in his stomach and then was gone. It gave him neither courage nor insensibility. It left him just as he was before.

He watched her eat the omelet until there was only one more bit of yellow egg, folded neatly around the black knob of a mushroom, and then he spoke, knowing that waiting would not help.

"Stay in the hotel overnight and I will drive you to Paris tomorrow," Proudhon said. "I don't have to be back at any certain time and there is business I could do in Paris. How about it? I'll drive you tomorrow. It will be beautiful. We'll stop and have a picnic, drive along at a nice pace, but not too fast. It will be wonderful."

Nina looked down at her hands and then up at Proudhon. She pondered for a moment, then looked down at her hands, turned one over and looked at the white palm, the short delicate reach of the fingers. It was a little girl's hand, but the way she closed it and then looked up again at Proudhon made the hair rise on his neck. That closed feminine innocent hand seemed capable of the most extreme sexuality.

"This sounds crazy, eh?" Proudhon said, looking at Rodney, Charity and Charlotte. "Me. Proudhon the tough guy; Proudhon the cynic. But when she closed that hand I almost fainted. It was the most obscene and exciting gesture I had ever seen. Why? I do not know. By then I was delirious. Like a man who had escaped from reality and was living in a new hot world."

It took them four days to drive to Paris. The days took on a blurred, chaotic, pell-mell quality. He made approaches to Nina, revised tactics, pushed liquor on her, was kind and then brusque . . . and all of this done with the awful pressure of desire like a huge hand at his back.

In flashes, in rips of memory he could piece the days together. There was the moment when he had stopped the car on a slight hill and beneath them a valley stretched away in a long unrolling of trees and greenery with a white band of stream and sand down the middle. He turned and reached for Nina and kissed her and her lips went soft and yielding under his and he could feel her breath come up hot and strained through her throat. He let her go, drove quickly for a hundred yards where he could park the car and reach back for a blanket in the rear . . . and Nina sat there looking coldly at him and, with his face flushed, he dropped the blanket and put the car back in gear. Another time he took

her in his arms outside of her hotel room and she stood
rigidly and he stood back and then turned and walked down
the hall . . . and he had taken a dozen steps before he
sensed that her hands had butterflied over his back in a kind
of message. He turned and walked back, but her door was
locked. Later that night, or another night, he knocked on her
door and it was unlocked and she was sitting up in bed with
the sheet pulled up around her neck. She was naked under
the sheet and as Proudhon told her that he loved her, that
he would leave his wife for her, that he would work for her,
she let the sheet drop and he saw her tiny breasts and the
sweep of white flesh down to her belly. He stopped in the
middle of his speech, his throat so congested he could hardly
speak. He went toward her dumbly, his hands reaching out.

She stretched up to meet him and in a quick flashing view
he saw her entire nakedness down to the naked toes. She
pressed his head down on her neck and later to her breasts
and his mouth seemed to be engorged with the softness of
her breast . . . and he had to draw back to breathe.

"She sobbed then," Proudhon said. Charlotte had brought
him some fish soup and his body was expanding into the
suit, taking on more substance. He held a finger against his
nose in wonderment. "I have never been moved by a woman
crying. Never. Not even by Charlotte. Maybe it is a defect
in me. But that cry made me hate myself and to desire her
beyond my belief."

They were all very quiet in the big room. The fire cracked
softly, but it was muffled with a deep layer of ashes. Charlotte had her head cocked and watched and listened. Occasionally she would smile. Once Proudhon began to pound
his fist on the table and was obviously unaware of how shattering a sound it was. Charlotte walked over and stopped
him and he glanced at her and nodded.

"That's the way it went for four days," he said. "Me like a
damned dog chasing a beautiful and endlessly exciting

bitch. I did it with the energy of a boy, like a crazy man."
He ran his hand across his chin, his mouth wide with
wonderment and disgust. He spoke in a low harsh voice.
"Like a boy . . . I keep coming back to that. Like a boy,
with all the gross, leering, insensitive lust of a boy, but with
the shrewdness and drive of a full-grown man. I panted and
drooled and fawned and crawled and screamed after the
girl. For four days. Like a crazy man. I argued with her
when she rejected me and then I pleaded with her and
finally I even wept in front of her. Me, so old that my tear
glands had dried up . . . me, I wept. Big tears that I was
astonished to feel on my cheeks. The first tear came like a
drop of iron squeezed out of a narrow passage beside my
eye. I looked at the tear, caught on my finger, as if it were a
strange substance. It hurt terribly to cry. The pain was physical. But I had to cry to convince the girl. I hoped it would
move her and perhaps it did."

"Proudhon, be quiet," Charlotte said. "Don't talk about it.
Drink the wine, drink the soup. Don't talk."

"This hurts," he said. "I know it hurts. I know that, Charlotte. But it's the truth and so I say it. It is all so startling
that I do not even yet feel shame. Maybe I never will. The
last day we were driving to Paris and my heart dried up in
my chest as I saw the city come into sight. Once we were
there I knew I would lose her. It was as simple as that. She
would just say goodbye and be gone and I couldn't stand
that. I hated the look of the city that morning. It loomed up
out of the dust and heat like one of those cities that they tell
us about when we are kids . . . the beautiful big city on
the plain, all glistening and spires glinting in the dust. I
hated it. I would have obliterated the whole city just to
spend another afternoon with that girl. I was possessive. I
wanted to keep that girl away from everyone, from every
other man. I was . . . I was . . . look, it's hard to say it.
Very man. I am an abnormal man, I see a number of things,

I enjoy things. Then suddenly in one afternoon all of my energy, my life, my thirst, my hunger, my thoughts, my body . . . everything . . . focus down on that one tiny thing . . . the body of that girl. In a way it was unbelievable. I didn't notice the road, the car, the trees, the food, the wine. I just saw that girl. Everything else was cut out from vision."

He looked up and around at them, his face in despair at communicating the enormity of what he felt.

He paused and drank off his glass of wine. Charlotte filled the glass again and Proudhon drank it off and took more. He was very thirsty. Rodney had the impression that Proudhon's body was like a burnt-out shell, like a sponge, like some kind of sea animal that was used to the deep cold waters of the ocean and had been suddenly thrown up onto a rock where a queer dazzling misunderstood sun burned and burned at him. The burn showed around his eyes, his lips . . . the skin brown and desiccated. His neck was gaunt, his head a dried out shell. He prospered under the wine as if he had taken no moisture for weeks.

"How did it end?" Charity said when several minutes had passed and no one had spoken. "How did you ever leave her?"

Proudhon looked up at Charity with gratitude.

With a sharp prescience Rodney realized that Charity had sensed the most startling thing about Proudhon: he was a man purged of the disease he described. There was something of the convalescent about him . . . the absorption of the invalid with a sickness he has completely dominated and subdued. Indeed Proudhon was almost happy, shed of a great burden, almost relieved.

"It happened instantly," Proudhon said. He stared down at his glass, narrowed his lips, forced himself to concentrate. Clearly he was reaching for precision, with the exactness and hesitancy of the saint who wishes to tell the shape and

detail of a miracle. From his eyes one could tell he did not
expect to be believed . . . but it was terribly important for
some internal reason that he be most exact at his first telling.

"It happened instantly," he said again, "and in a way that
is hard to describe. I stopped the car outside of Paris beside
a little restaurant and insisted that we have lunch. It was a
delaying tactic. I wanted to have time to think of how I
could still keep her even if we went into the city and my
mind refused to grapple with the problem. My skull just
glowed with heat and thoughts tumbled crazily over one
another and I could bear down on nothing. So I insisted that
we stop. The restaurant was beautiful. The leaves made an
agreeable speckled shadow that softened everything about
the place. We sat down at a table on a porch on the rear of
the restaurant and could see down the slope of a tiny valley
that caught everything of the countryside . . . a hayrick, a
tiny silvery stream, a horse, a row of corn. Up close, in the
trees nearest us, I could see squirrels and once a pheasant
strutted out from the brush . . . turned and walked back to
invisibility."

Proudhon begged Nina to go off with him. He told her
extravagant stories of how he would make money in North
Africa catching fish and raising wine grapes and starting an
import business. He told her of his age and strength and
painted a picture of the future which he knew was fantastic
and absurd . . . grotesque in what it claimed. But he
hoped desperately that some fragment of the vision would
catch her imagination, spark her affection, make her decide
to go with him. Once she did that, everything else in the
world *might* become possible. If he could possess her, have
this body always next to him, be the owner of it, of the eyes,
and breasts and slight hips and little smile and awful innocence, then he might do anything else.

Out of the side of his mouth, and quickly so as not to

interrupt the flow of argument, he ordered champagne and a very expensive lunch. Nina sat quietly watching him talk. When the waiter came with the champagne and held the bottle low and pulled the cork out with a sudden pop she was shocked. Proudhon watched her sit up straight, look around as if she were dazed and then she shook her head.

"In that instant it was all over," Proudhon said. "She changed right in front of my eyes. The façade of innocence overlying lust, the glow of evil about her, was gone . . . as sharply as a sound is gone. She looked perfectly ordinary, like a moderately attractive girl. I stopped in midsentence and stared at her. Something in my body or my brain caught a new signal. I felt muscles relax, go soft, the tension eased. She lifted up her glass and drank the champagne thirstily, the way a little girl might, but this time there was no hidden meaning in her gestures. I was trembling, my hands shook, my stomach quivered . . . my body realized before my brain that I was free of the sickness. I looked away from Nina and studied the little valley in front of us."

"What had happened?" Charlotte said and this time her voice was angry and demanding. Rodney knew that she felt the danger was over, she could be harsh again with Proudhon, not handle him so delicately. "Don't sit there like a damned idiot. Tell us what had happened."

"It had stopped," Proudhon said. "My desire for her. Just like that. It was all over. She was just another girl. Another woman. I asked her what had happened as if she were an utter stranger who had seen me through a sickness. And she understood. 'It is a trick, Proudhon,' she said. 'I am ashamed to tell you that all you have felt for the last four days is just a trick that I learned and which I cannot help using. I used it against you out of boredom. But it was only a trick.'"

"But what was the trick?" Charlotte asked shrilly.

"I do not know and neither does she," Proudhon said. He

was very weary. "All I can do is tell you that I felt the trick. But once it was over I had no notion of what caused it. Neither did she."

"She is not too hard to understand," Charity said. She was very confident. "The girl is nothing but a bitch."

Proudhon did not move for some time. He turned the glass with his fingers. Then slowly he looked at Rodney.

"Do you think she was a bitch, Rodney?" Proudhon asked. "No."

Proudhon smiled, a thin replica of his normal smile, but the real sense for the first time that day of humor in the man.

"No. Nina is not a bitch," Proudhon said slowly. "I do not understand her fully. But she is one of the accursed of our time. She is one of those who went, in a few months, from being a girl to being as wise and evil and hard-driven as women can get. She learned some things which allowed her to live. If she could not do those things she must die. She learned a terrible game. Which we taught her to play. I am not a philosopher, but Nina has been taught to play a game of games if she was to exist during the war. War is the funny game the nations play. The game that Nina played is the game that a little girl had to play to survive while the nations were at the bigger game."

"Proudhon, you are a very sentimental man. You do not understand . . ." Charity said.

"No, Charity, let the man rest," Rodney said. "He is right. Maybe he is sentimental, but it makes no difference." He paused. "Listen, during my escape I stayed in a village where the sign of goodness was to be able to drink a wine just down to the last layer . . . and then it became a bitter foul thing. That is what we have made Nina do . . . drink all the wine and then live on the last bitter rejected obscene layer of wine. And she can never forget."

Charity looked at him without understanding.

25. The Last
of the Wine

THE separation was not hard. Rodney left their room at six. He looked out the window, saw the summer fog, smelled the redolence of the fishing boats and heard the muffled clank of shortened lines and men swearing.

He turned to Charity to wake her up, but she was leaning on her elbow looking at him.

"You were going to wake me up," she said. She smiled. Her marvelous smile, her beautiful features falling into cool perfection. "I'm glad. I thought for a moment during the night that you might leave without saying goodbye. But you were going to wake me up. Goodbye, Rodney. I just wanted to see if you would. Even though I knew last night before we went to bed that you would."

She rolled over and instantly was sleeping easily.

That was when the separation was easy. There was a mixture of despair and hope in Rodney as he realized that Charity could not have cared less. She was almost affectionate. But, most of all, she was sleepy. That was more important than Rodney or Nina or Proudhon or the yacht business back in L.A. or what Mr. Cartwright would say or, even, what her good parents would say. All of this was hope.

The despair was what he could face during the next day. Or week. Or how long it took to do the thing.

Proudhon was waiting down by the car. He was pacing

back and forth, a bowl of soup in his right hand and a flask
of cognac in his back pocket. He watched the fishing boats
preparing to put out and muttered criticism to himself.
When he saw Rodney he went into the kitchen and came
out with a bowl of soup. He offered Rodney the cognac, but
Rodney refused it. He took the soup.

"It went all right with your wife," Proudhon said with no
doubt in his voice. "It may not go so easily with Nina. She is
frightened, but only the way that a very tough person is
frightened. Will you know the difference?"

"Yes. I will know the difference."

"A foggy morning is no time to give advice, Rodney, but I
must just the same." He took an apologetic pull at the
cognac. "Neither Nina nor Charity have ever known love.
With Charity it does not matter. She is past needing it. She is
like a million other women who have been made sleek and
secure by the way they are raised. They really do not need
love. Oh, Christ, Rodney, I was only teasing when I told you
that American women had that varnished empty look. There
are women like that in France and England and, for all I
know, in India and Russia."

"What is the difference? What makes such a woman?"
Rodney asked. In a quite satisfying way he felt as if he had
passed through a boyish period. "Boyish" was exactly the
word to describe his work, his life, his conversation, his inter-
ests. And now all that was over. What was to come would
not be more happy, but it would, he knew, be more solid.
He thought of the word "manly" and then laughed softly.
Proudhon smiled. "Would you say it is because Nina has
been through the camp and Charity has not?"

Proudhon rocked on his good heel. He sucked the soup
from the side of the bowl. He looked at Rodney and tried to
appraise him. Rodney turned his head at the same moment
that Proudhon turned away. They were both embarrassed at
the mutual exploration. Then Proudhon made a fumbling

gesture which caught Rodney's attention. Proudhon was moving his hand toward his hip. His eyes intent on the fishing boats, he pulled at the bottle.

"Rodney, I do not know what you mean," he finally said.

"Maybe the world today is divided into those that understand how brutal others can be and those that have no conception," Rodney said. He spoke crisply, with a new assurance. "The idea is not mine. Nina told it to me. She said that she could tell those who understood the concentration camp and those who could not. And something about those who could not. And something about those who could not understand she had to arouse or humiliate or try to understand."

Proudhon's eyes sharpened and then he understood. He knocked his hand against his forehead in the gesture of understanding. He stood stock-still for a long moment. It was the posture of the boxer who has been hit very hard.

"It is something like that," he said. "Last night you talked about the slime beneath the little wine. That is what it is all about. Most of us swim through the rich good wine above and never taste the slime. But those that do, those that must humble themselves or are broken by concentration camps or tortures or the madness of fighting with rifles or tanks or flamethrowers or dropping depth charges on men caught underwater in a metal cigar . . . those that taste the slime at the bottom are different. Forever."

"They are not better," Rodney said.

"No. Not by necessity. But they have been forced to go to the very bottom and then their mouths pucker and they want to vomit from what they have seen. Most people simply roll over and die," Proudhon said. "There are hollow-eyed veterans wandering America who have wives and children and jobs and do not believe in any of it. They have tasted the bitter slime and forever after they are marked by it. They are not better. They are just more capable of wonder and of delight and, maybe, of bitterness."

Proudhon stopped and felt again for the bottle. Rodney started to speak and Proudhon shrugged and Rodney stopped.

"Better? Why would you ask such a question?" Proudhon asked. "Even so; whatever you say, I am proud of you. It is a good question to ask. It has never occurred to me for years. Another lie. It occurred to me when I told you about those madmen in Paris. Those existentialists. How can a man be better than another? By seeing the worst of every man and every situation?"

"Without being better they have been to the bottom and seen the worst and are merely more complete. Ignorance of something that is in each of us merely leaves us incomplete. Charity is incomplete in a way that most Americans and other humans are. I was, but I think I am not any longer. You are completed. You have seen the worst."

Proudhon grinned, that tough knowing grin which Rodney remembered from the war.

"I am not complete here," Proudhon said, putting down the soup bowl and gripping his crotch. "But I am complete up here in the head. Look, Rodney, I saw it in all forms. I saw the good honest Jews who went to pieces as they were forced into the slime at the bottom . . . and realized that their dream of a nice respectable life, protected by law, was ruined by savages. And I saw your American GI's caught by the same madness come unstuck. Those American soldiers that survived it were those that had 'buddies.' Sweet Jesus, what a word . . . a good word. Soldiers with their eyes bulging and still wearing bloody bandages went fleeing in search of their 'buddies.' Even if it meant going back into combat."

"Nina is a special case," Rodney said. He thought about it. "She is caught halfway. She has learned to live in the abnormal world of peace and manners and style. But she also has been in the slime and knows the tricks of survival one learns there. She is half abnormal and half insane; and she must practice the tricks she learned in the slime against the normal world."

The fishing boats were moving out. Their masts disappeared into the low fog, bodies scurried and worked at lines and pulled nets into tubs with quick movements. The smell of diesel oil came, thick and unnatural, to their nostrils.

"You think there is a normal world?" Proudhon asked. His confusion was genuine.

"No. That is, not a normal world. There are only different forms of mad worlds. And then there are individuals who have to find a place to rest or stand still or connect or come to know someone in one of these worlds. One cannot float in the mad world. One drifts too long and one dies. Choose a level, whatever level, but whatever the level is you must come to know or love another person . . . touch someone else. That is what I can do with Nina. And that is what I cannot do with Charity."

The boats slid by the breakwater, the stones irregular and greenish, the boats misty and obscured, the men motionless. They caught the pitch of the ocean waves and the men moved their bodies without moving their feet.

Proudhon sighed. He took a pull at the cognac. He looked into Rodney's soup bowl and sighed again because it was empty.

"It is hard to talk," Proudhon said. "You are educated. I am clever and well read and hide the fact that I am well read and clever. I am a silently clever man among the country people. The peasants. You are like a peasant among the people who are varnished and very glistening, but they do not perceive it. So you are safe. The talk we have made is not satisfactory, but we reach one another." He paused. He put his finger against his nose. "Now you have the problem with the women. I am a eunuch." He raised his hand, anticipating objection. He was surprised when Rodney said nothing. "Ah, the innocent pilot from the airplane falling into France has learned. One thing he has learned is not to perform for me."

"Because you are a eunuch you can tell me something which will be helpful," Rodney said. He was finished with the soup and ready to move. "That is a bitter thing to hear and to take and to absorb. It must hit very close to the center of a man. To be told you are a eunuch and be asked for advice in the same breath is hard. It must hurt."

"It does. And I can tell you very little. I can tell you that this Nina girl is two people. She must be each to live. She must be the innocent schoolgirl who went into the Maquis without knowing what it was about. And she must be the woman who tore me apart while I was driving her to a train-head. Between the two she is beyond belief. She has the strength of the maniac and the limpness, the turning away, of the schoolgirl."

"What you say is that it will not be easy with her. Right?" Rodney asked.

"That is exactly what I have said. You said she is two people," Proudhon said and he was angry. "Correct. Now you must make her one person. You are not the perfect man to do this, but it is your job. Years ago I could have done it better. But forget that. Now it is your desire. Why do you think you desire to make her one again?"

Rodney watched the last boat pass the end of the breakwater. Somewhere a milky white light was giving way to a rich dull orange shape which could only be the sun. The houses across the bay were taking form, hardening into real buildings with windows and roofs and women washing the stone stairs . . . dull glints of light came from glass, fogwet rock, a skinny boy's spectacles, a shattered wine bottle, the rubber apron of a fish dresser, the headlights of old tired trucks.

"It is not because I feel responsible for her going to the

camp," Rodney said. "Nor is it that I think that she loves me. She is frozen solid and cannot love now, but that will change fast. Nor is it because I think she will be endlessly a sexual thing. Nor is it . . ."

Proudhon laughed.

"Thank God, you do not expect the endless and timeless and gut-grabbing sexual thing," he said. "Even without the loss of my balls I know that is impossible."

The sunlight broke through. In a few dazzling moments, which hurt the eye, the whole town was clear and visible.

"I have to leave," Rodney said. "Charity is perfectly all right. She will know how to get back to Paris and to the States and to Reno. That last word, Reno, means a divorce."

"Easily. She will do all of that easily. The divorce is the last thing that will trouble her. I will be helpful and offer to do anything. Except, maybe, I will not offer to drive her to the train station."

They laughed and Rodney got into the car. Proudhon turned quickly and was back into the inn before Rodney could start the engine. The door slammed shut. It was oddly like a greeting.

It took time. All things take time, except the things which are not worth doing.

Rodney went to the house in the Tuileries. Nina was not there. He slept and then ate a solid meal. He did not drink. He questioned the servants. They did not know what had happened to Nina.

Rodney went to the flamenco restaurant and asked. No one had heard of Nina. He gave the owner a box of American cigars, for he had learned not to buy important things with money. He simply told the owner what he wanted. The owner did not quite believe him for several minutes, but finally he took the box of cigars. As Rodney walked out the owner gave him a bottle of cognac. He did it casually. He did not utter a word, but a waiter asked Rodney for his phone number.

Rodney called Montauban and talked with the police; a very civilized man who kept records in a municipal office; the man who lived in the house which Nina and her father had formerly occupied; the headmaster of the school Nina had attended. None of them had ever heard of Nina Faures nor had they heard of a Professor Faures. And all of them were very curious why he called. Rodney knew they were lying.

"I am her lover," he said to each person. "From my accent you know I am an American. I can only assure you I am sincere in wanting to find her. We have had a difference. I want to make it up."

They took cover slyly. Over the phone who could trust a strange voice? But they promised to help if they could.

Rodney talked to a private detective who was reputed to be an expert in locating missing people. The detective was a squat toadlike man with very kindly eyes. He was candid. He had taken on the profession because his parents, then his sisters and brothers, and, finally, his schoolmates had told him he looked like a private detective. From a scientist he had learned that he had only missed a gene, which gave him the squat look. His brothers were all tall and blond and very stupid and well connected. He was not optimistic. He stated a minimum price for making the search, but emphasized he could not guarantee results. Then, inexplicably, he said that he would not charge unless he found the girl. He said, looking over Rodney's shoulder, it would be costs only.

Rodney walked around Paris and went to every place where he could think Nina might go. He went to restaurants of the highest class, to meetings of veterans of various concentration camps which were announced in the papers, to the cafés where Americans gathered, to the George V. In the papers there was an announcement of a lecture by a Dutch psychoanalyst on "Concentration Camps and the Lack of Life Thereafter."

Nothing worked.

Rodney waited.

It was the owner of the flamenco restaurant who finally helped. He called Rodney and said that a girl he thought was Nina was in the restaurant the night before with a very tall man who spoke with a hard English accent. The owner had tried to talk to her, but the girl had looked at him with cold eyes and complete hostility. Yet the owner was sure she was the girl.

Rodney went to Amelia's house without calling. When he rang the door Amelia answered and for a moment she did not recognize him. She was slightly drunk and she hung on the edge of the door, smiling and trying to identify him.

"Rodney Cartwright, Amelia," he said. "We met before. It was a party some months ago. A garden party."

Her face was a peculiar balance of muscle and early fat. She was alternately soft and very hard, understanding and quite beyond understanding. She flirted and then was scornful. Finally she identified him. Then she laughed.

"Of course, the American who brought Nina," she said. She swung the door open. "It's just like the last time. A party and Nina is running things. You've come in on the same act, same scene, same lines, same action."

Rodney eased into the house and the first thing he saw was Nina's trim neck and head. She had her back to him. She was not moving, but the whole room was moving about her. The young Rhodes scholars were talking in big strident voices and Awn was proposing a new game: a game where they could quickly decide who was the most powerful man in the room. The women in the room were very quiet. A small tough Jewish Rhodes scholar baited Awn. His accent

was strong, but his remarks were sharp and biting. He did
not look at Nina, but Rodney knew he was talking to her.
Awn, big and flushed and drunk, was pacing up and down,
anxious to get to the game and contemptuous of the Jew.

Rodney moved a few feet. The Jew was in the game as
much as anyone else. He was using his only strength. He
was very confident. He hardly glanced at Nina.

"The girls are either drunk or puzzled," Amelia said in a
soft rasp with her lips against Rodney's ear. "They don't
know what's happening. Matter of fact, neither do I. But it
hasn't happened since that girl was here before. Funny coin-
cidence, isn't it? You here again and her here again? That
grammatically correct? Who cares?"

"I do," Rodney said.

He walked slowly around the room. The whole thing was
now familiar. It was different only a bit. Now he understood
what was happening. And he was the only person in the
room who did.

The men were squaring off and starting to warm to Awn's
game. It was some intricate game in which each of two men
held a coin outright in his left hand and faced one another.
Apparently either man could throw his coin into the air. The
man who won would be the man who managed to both
catch an opponent's coin, evade his blow, and then strike
back.

Awn was winning. That was clear. It was also clear that
everyone was drinking very heavily. Even the women. The
only exception was Nina.

Nina sat in the half-light of a lamp. Her hands were
folded in her lap. Her face was barely visible. She was not
talking to anyone. At first glance she seemed very lonely.
But she was the center of the game. Like iron filings above a
magnet everyone, men and women, had looped around her
and she was the blank spot where the loops met.

That was it, Rodney said to himself. The place where the

power is greatest the drama is least; there are fewer human iron filings about; the blankness is very very blank . . . and just because it has the power.

Rodney went to the far end of the room. Someone offered him a drink, but he refused. Awn threw a coin in the air, ducked to his left, spun and caught his opponent's coin and instantly struck out with his hand. It made a dull, splatting and very unpleasant sound. No one remarked Awn's dexterity and he stood for a moment, flushed and uncertain. He was confused, but he was certain of one thing: he had moved too soon. His big body moved restlessly.

Fifteen minutes passed. Nina shifted in her seat, glanced around the room. The human iron filings shifted and re-shaped. Rodney knew she had not yet seen him.

He did not feel the gripping sensation, the odd swirling involvement, the swell of pride, the harsh studlike commitment.

Nina finally saw him. He watched her eyes. She was searching for the break in the unanimity of opinion, the exception to the excitement which gripped everyone in the room. She looked directly at him.

As if sight had been reversed, he knew precisely what she saw: a familiar face, but one she did not want to recognize. She smiled and then the smile vanished. He was not smiling back.

Rodney brought his hand up and motioned for her to come over to him.

The mood in the room collapsed. Awn stopped tossing the coin.

"Who is going to play?" Awn shouted. As Nina moved he gave no sign of seeing her, but his body twitched with the necessity to fight or compete or argue or strike out at someone.

Awn did not once look at Nina as she got up and walked toward Rodney.

"Nina, we should go," Rodney said in a very ordinary voice. "It is time to go."

Nina stood for several seconds, in front of Rodney. She moved and Awn's reaction was instant: he began to toss the coin. There was the sound of his fist smashing into someone's chest.

"Christ sake, Awn, I didn't even offer to flip with you," the Jewish Rhodes scholar said. "But if you want a real rumble I'm ready. I mean nothing barred. You get it? Awn, I'll lay you out like one of those New Zealand lambs. You dumb cricket-playing, idiot, Full Blue shmuck of a hick, with your god-damn miserable ill-fitting suits and your . . . your . . ." the boy said and stopped, convulsed with laughter. He still held a hand over his belly where Awn had hit him, but his eyes were bright with victory.

"We must go now," Rodney said quietly.

The room was very quiet.

Nina looked up at him. Her eyes were calm and for the first time her face was not provocative. She was the girl he had seen as he looked over the edge of the weapons carrier years ago on the road outside of Montauban.

Her eyes cleared. But it was confusing. She was weeping. Not hard, but a kind of welling up of tears.

"Yes, we have to go," she said. She put out her hand and her fingers were tight on his arm.

They left a room in which the atmosphere of excitement had dropped very sharply. Even before they got to the door the subtle sounds of irritation and aggression were rising.

They went out into a night which was black and warm. They walked until they had disappeared into the night.